COW

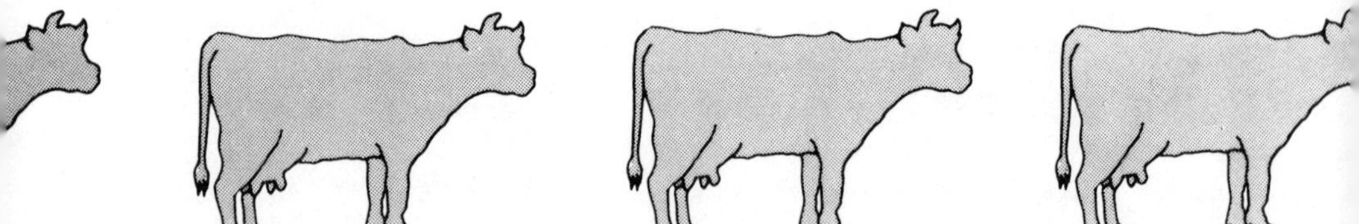

COW

A NOVEL BY BEAT STERCHI

translated from the german by michael hofmann

pantheon books ■ new york

Library of Congress Cataloging-in-Publication Data

Sterchi, Beat, 1949-
[Blösch, English]
Cow / by Beat Sterchi ; [translator, Michael Hofmann].
p.   cm.
Translation of: Blösch.
ISBN 0-394-58451-1
I. Title.
PT2681.T475B5513   1989   89-43296
833'.914—dc20

Title page design by Anne Scatto

Manufactured in the United States of America

First American Edition

. . . if ever their byres brought forth a calf of a sheer and unbrindled red, they would give it the name 'Blösch' for its straw-red hide.

COW

Many years later, when he had just got up on tiptoe for the last time to drop his card once and for all into slot No. 164 of the clocking-in machine at the entrance of the municipal abattoir, Ambrosio remembered the faraway Sunday of his arrival in the prosperous land.

After a gruelling journey from his native South across desert plains, over mountain passes and through tunnels, towards a North whose only existence had been a couple of unpronounceable names on an official form, he found himself standing like a piece of abandoned luggage, dumped in the middle of Innerwald, the village that for months he'd been trying tenaciously and vainly to imagine. At last he'd arrived! What he and his family had longed for had come to pass. Soon he would be working and earning; the first cheque home was just a matter of time; he, Ambrosio, would have succeeded where so many others had failed. But even so, scarcely arrived, he was still seized by the urge to rush after the bus while it was still in sight, to shout to the driver to stop, and to be ferried back again, through the tunnels and over the mountains, back to the light of his own village in Coruña.

But the post bus hadn't waited, it was gone, drawn aside like a yellow curtain in a theatre, leaving Ambrosio alone to face a curious audience.

A dozen or so Innerwalders, who had just been busy with cans and basins in front of the communal cheese dairy, shouting instructions to horses and dog teams, laughing and bragging, suddenly fell silent, dropped their work and stared at the new-comer standing in the middle of their village square on show like a fish on a hook, apprehensive like a prisoner outside the gates.

Nothing moved: the film had got stuck; the sound had failed, only the water in the village fountain went on splashing.

Ambrosio stood there, rooted to the spot, incapable even of

1

rolling himself a cigarette: he could only watch himself, strickenly. Everything about him had suddenly turned menacing and out of the ordinary. He felt his cropped hair round his bald spot, felt its blackness. He smelled his own sweat, his shirt was dirty and soaked, he would have liked to cover up his knobbly legs but he was wearing thin, knee-length shorts. He looked down at his little battered suitcase, looked up at the people around, looked down again: in that one second, he had become acquainted with loneliness. For the first time in his life he understood that he was small and foreign and an alien.

It wasn't until a Freiberg mare tried to jump out of her harness with a loud whinny that life returned to that Sunday night. A tractor motor started up; the Innerwalders went back to their laughing and prating; the cheeser's arms carried on grabbing pails of milk and pouring the white flow by the hundredweight into weighing pans and cooling basins; the Alpine dogs, harnessed to their carts, barked their rivalries at each other from a safe distance, and a mare struck sparks from the cobblestones with her hooves.

Ambrosio was thankful for the renewed activity in the village square, and he would have been happy just to go on standing there for quite some time, if the approach of a herd of cows hadn't forced him into a decision. They were being driven along by two boys to the fountain, which was opposite the cheese dairy and in front of the Ox Inn. At their head was a massive cow with all the self-importance of a lady mayoress, a peaceable enough creature no doubt, but not one who looked as though she would take two cowsteps out of her way for the sake of the little Spaniard.

Ambrosio picked up his suitcase and, groping with his free hand for his papers in shirt and trouser pockets, headed for the inn, where he held up to one boy's face his residence permit and a document from the immigration police. But he found himself surrounded by frowning mouths in silent faces. Eyes scrutinized him, brows were furrowed, heads were shaken then turned to the cheeser. He in turn, without interrupting his weighing, asked what the little fellow in short trousers was after.

'I reckon that must be Knuchel's Spaniard. These are his papers, see,' said one of the farmers, and passed the tatty bunch over to the cheeser.

'Well, well. It had to happen, didn't it. He doesn't look the type for spreading muck. Not very much of him is there?' The cheeser, who stood on his platform on high, puffed out his chest to bursting. 'Knuchel's nursery would be more his line than his cowshed.' He went on. 'Now listen! Knuchel's boy is always the first with the milk. Understand? He's been and gone.'

Ambrosio shook his head.

'Don't you speak German then?' he was asked, and some of the Innerwalders began laughing heartily. The cheeser cracked a few more jokes himself, but stopped when he saw that Ambrosio, realizing who was being laughed at but not seeing any malice in it, was laughing himself, and even had the nerve to start rolling the longed-for cigarette right there, in their midst.

'Mosimann! Your way takes you past Knuchel's farm. Show the little fellow where to go!'

It was night already when Ambrosio walked down the village street. He was following a hand-cart, which a stroppy boy was braking, while a red-black-and-white Alpine dog was pulling at it with all his strength, hungry for his dinner. Ambrosio was hungry too. He wouldn't have minded a couple of mouthfuls of that broth, the sweet smell of which was wafting out of a can on the cart. He had no idea that it was whey left over from cheese-making, and used for pigswill.

Ambrosio couldn't see much of Innerwald. The village street was poorly lit, and there were few lights on in the farms. But he could hear the sound of clogs, of shouting and calling to animals; he heard the clatter of milking gear being washed in the fountains, it sounded like bells; he could hear the swish of brooms, the rattle of carts, the clucking of hens and squeal of pigs, for the Innerwalders were still busy with the last of the day's tasks and the first preparations for the next morning's feed.

What he could still make out were the outlines of the farmhouses: every roof high and wide, as if it alone had to protect half the world from a savage sky; every roof a church roof. At the same time, Ambrosio wondered about the manure that was piled up everywhere by the side of the road. Veritable towers of dungheaps stood in front of the houses, perfuming the air.

Once out of the village, the boy smiled at Ambrosio and motioned to him to put his suitcase on the milk-cart.

'Another five minutes,' he said and spread his fingers at him.

As Ambrosio was only wearing sandals, he walked along the grass strip down the middle of the gravel path, which led in three loops past fenced-in pastures, past orchards running down a slope, and in a wide curve round a clump of trees into a pine wood.

The other side of the little wood, the boy pointed at a group of shadowy buildings.

'You'll find them down there, the Knuchels,' he said, waved and disappeared into the night with his dog and cart.

Before turning down a narrow track to the farmyard, which lay like another village, tucked in between two hillsides, Ambrosio rolled himself another cigarette. As he took a couple of quick drags at it, he noticed the stars had come out.

Farmer Knuchel had the habit, not uncommon in the prosperous land, of not leaving his cows waiting in milk any longer on Sundays than on weekdays. He had come home early from his walk and coffee with brandy at the Ox, and reported that while there was no actual news of the long-awaited Spaniard in the post office or anywhere else, talk in the village was mightily concerned with the truant. Not everyone spoke in his favour; least of all the cheeser. Proper cheesing had become much harder on account of the Boden farmer's insanitary Italian. The Innerwald milk wasn't what it used to be. And now some Spaniard had to turn up! They should mark his words, Farmer Knuchel's milk money would suffer and so would the standing of the whole community.

Knuchel's wife shook her head at this, muttered something inaudible and went back to the geranium plants on her veranda.

He had remained standing next to her for a moment. With his hands buried in the pockets of his Sunday trousers, he had looked out across the fields, then at the vegetable garden, and had praised his wife for the good order there, and Grandma for her hens, only then, again unable quite to conceal his impatience, to go back into the house to change, with a 'well, I'll be blowed' on his lips. Once inside, he had carefully folded his smarter trousers, and hung them on a wooden hanger inside the door, slipped into fresh clothes and

4

dry boots, and went off with his son Ruedi to clean out the shed and milk the cows.

For their part, the cows had got out of their habitual doziness, they had mooed one another awake more joyfully than usual, and soon got over the stupor of being kept shut in all winter.

Not that Knuchel's cows had a harder time of it than other Innerwald cattle. Far from it. Seeing as their farmer wouldn't allow any smooth-talking salesman of milking machines or automatic watering gear within a good three potato-shies of his farm, his cows had the twice-daily pleasure of an udder-easing milk by hand, and after each milking, a walk to the watering trough. Whereas on progressively minded farms, a cow's movements were restricted to the one step forward to the feed crib and the one step back into their dungy straw, those fortunate cowsouls of Knuchel's could regularly enjoy a modicum of unhindered physical activity when they were watered. Thanks to these visits to the trough, all the inevitable conflicts and mutual reprimands essential to maintaining the hierarchy within the herd didn't have to be either postponed until the springtime when they were put out to grass, or simply crowded into their racial subconscious. Twice a day, Blösch, the first lady of the byre, was able to give expression to her hegemony, and to discipline some insubordinate young cow with a few well-aimed butts or kicks. Motherhood in particular was conducive to overweening pride, and led to exaggerated demands, but then they were all mothers, and simply because there was one of them who had just given birth to a calf that lay bleating in the straw, it didn't mean that Blösch was about to renounce her right to be the first out of the shed, the first to dip her floppy mouth into the water trough, and draw one or two dozen litres of spittle-free water, and then be the first to lie down again in the straw. Status had to be. But the more ruthlessly Blösch ladied it daily over the procession to the trough, condescendingly, with rough country methods, and the more eager the animals lower down the cow hierarchy in Knuchel's shed were to show their respect, by smarming and sneaking their way like prima donnas from one position to the next, one privilege to another, the more productive the long hours in the byre were for all of them. While they belched up one knot after another of pre-masticated hay from their rumina,

5

and chewed around on it apathetically, in their thick skulls they could brood on revenge and make impracticable but none the less diverting plans for palace revolutions.

As Blösch happened to be heavily pregnant, and would possibly calve that very night, her domination seemed more unassailable than ever.

The farmer himself had gone straight to her after entering the shed with Ruedi. 'She's the best cow on the mountain,' said the father.

'So long as she doesn't have another bull calf,' added the son.

Blösch mooed.

The other eleven cows were also excited; they knew that on Sundays the farmer was particularly pleased with them, that on every seventh day he would be more talkative, would give them more strokes. Then, the milking and mucking out would be continually interrupted. Even before Knuchel had greased his hands with two layers of milking fat, and grasped the swollen teats with his leathery callouses, all the straight backs had to be admired, steadily increasing growth praised, lame haunches stroked, and only slowly cicatrizing grazes or pitchfork wounds dried and powdered. Dr Knuchel held his surgery on Sundays. One cow had a foot salved, another had some potato brandy from a dusty green bottle applied to a wasp sting near the eye. If there was a still-growing ox in the byre, or a bob calf or fattening vealer, then navels would be disinfected, horn clamps adjusted, and fast-growing animals would have their muzzles and harnesses loosened by a notch or two. There was time also to frot those in calf behind the ears, and Knuchel never omitted to promise those in heat the affectionate attentions of Gotthelf, the capable bull of the village's breeding syndicate.

These ministrations could not be met with equanimity by the animals. All twelve of them stretched and tautened their red-and-white patchwork hides, presented their udders, and swished about with their tails in such a way as to gladden old Knuchel's heart, so that he had to go and give each cow an extra pitchforkful of fresh straw to lie on.

After that Knuchel and son had washed the udders of their best cows with lukewarm water – behind closed doors, as they were sensitive to the draught – had prepared their teats with a few tweaks, and then milked their way right through the shed.

The yield was generous. One of the cows, young Flora, had even been in record-breaking form: counting morning and evening together, Knuchel worked out that for the first time he had pumped more than 25 litres from her milk tanks.

Flora's udder wasn't a gigantic one dangling uselessly down to the ground so that you couldn't jam a pail under it; it was small and firm, with flawless teats that Knuchel had milked first crosswise, then for a surprisingly long time at the front, rhythmically, until his finger joints were sore. The young cow had fought off the moment of drying up with every last dispensable bit of juice in her. She had arched her back, and instead of chewing at some of the feed concentrate that Knuchel had provided, illegally, but still in good faith to keep her quiet during milking, she had simply breathed deeply and stertorously.

When Knuchel was at last finished with her, he had just sat there, benumbed. Still halfway underneath her belly, and no longer quite steady on the one-legged milking stool strapped to his behind, he had stared at the brimming pail between his knees. He had pushed back his cap, wiped the mixture of sweat and dust from the cow's flanks off his brow with his forearm, and growled: 'God knows we need another milker. If only that Spaniard would come soon.'

These were worrying times for him. He had already had to have his wrists seen to on several occasions. He had sought out the healing baths on the mountain, and on the other side of it at Schwarzenburg, up the Gurnigel as far as Weißenburg. There was nothing he hated more than standing around in his cow byre, with his tendons thickly smeared with ointment, and having to listen to the milk hissing into the pails, without his participation. He had been reluctant to take his wife out of the kitchen into the byre, thinking privately that a woman had no business underneath a cow. During these grim days, his one comfort had been the fact that the spring-balance by the window bench had indicated yields far below his own averages, which were a closely guarded secret. However, he would then try to dismiss the lower figures, and when he'd been put down for rather less milk money than usual at the end of the month, he would plead excessively thirsty vealers, sickly pigs that he'd been trying to pep up with milk, and even cats, far too many and far too bold, whom he'd plied, so he said, with milk by the basinful, pouring it into their noses and ears and their greedy snouts.

All the same, the bugbear of the milking-machine salesman had come up every time. He was like a ghost, robbing him of peace of mind in the daytime, and sleep at night. His wife and son no longer dared to bring the matter up any more, but Grandma would still give him, along with the morning mail by his coffee cup, those prospectuses, true experience accounts from enthusiastic farmers, and friendly, casual invitations to exhibitions and in situ demonstrations. The very thought of this chugging, mechanically sucking machine hurt him. He distrusted the gleam of the chrome vats, the flexibility of the transparent plastic tubing; he just couldn't conceive of his cows being fed into a network of pipes and valves and pumps. He wanted to see his milk, to feel it and to hear it, not entrust it to a system that he could no longer control, and where there was no knowing where it might lead.

So Knuchel wished even more fervently for the Spaniard to arrive before his next onset of tendinitis. Because that next relapse surely wouldn't be long in coming, what with Ruedi having to go back to school, and the whole shed lactating prodigiously on account of their fresh fodder. Not just Flora, but Mirror and Tiger, Stine, Patch and Baby, they were all trying to outdo themselves. All of them had been smoothly productive, and kept still in the best cow manner: once more, in concerted unity, they had been able to prove to the defencelessly dry Blösch, unmistakably, what great-hearted Simmental flecked cattle they were. First to last, they all clocked up above-average performances. Knuchel and son had carried some 200 litres out of the byre, and their pride had even found a further object in Prince the dog, who, with lolling tongue, had hauled the milk-cart with three brimful aluminium cans up the slope to the village even more joyfully than usual.

'Wonder whether anyone'll bring in any more?' Knuchel had asked.

'That cheeser won't believe his eyes,' replied his wife, who had stepped outside.

*

Ambrosio buried the end of his cigarette in the dirt with his toe, struck gravel, and then, come what may, stars or no stars, he set a course for the Knuchel farm.

Caramba, ya estamos aquí, he thought, and stumbling a little with his suitcase as he went down the slope, he felt his senses becoming more and more acute, as a wave of impressions engulfed him. There wasn't a single detail he could avoid taking in. Here too, fermenting away, there was a towering dungheap, under siege from swarms of flies and midges. Not only the smell of it, but everything, the scale and proportions of barns and outbuildings silhouetted in the night, trees and bushes, the contours of the land and the hush up above, everything etched itself into his mind, in colours and forms he barely noticed for themselves, in melodies and shadings. Months later, he could still remember exactly how the first, the second, the third apple tree by the track had smelled, of resinous buds, and the exact blue-grey glint of the fenceposts. The grunting of pigs from one outbuilding sounded fat and overfed, they were castrates ready for slaughter, squabbling over the most comfortable sleeping places. Ambrosio smelled the broody hens, busy in their laying places behind the whitewashed walls of the henhouse. That was a smell of steamed potatoes and the cooked earth on their skins; a smell of cats, and of freshly split cedarwood. Ambrosio could also hear the snorting and groaning of some larger animal, the rattling of chains in a shed, the deep, drawn-out mooing of a heavily pregnant creature. He was just thinking, they don't seem to have a dog, when he was overrun by a rampaging bundle of fur. 'Caramba!' He had hardly set foot in the farmyard when he was lying on his back in the dirt, with an Alpine dog on top of him trying to lick the moustache off his face with its rough flannel of a tongue. 'Caramba! Un perro grande como una vaca. Caramba!' Ambrosio struggled desperately, but it was only a sharp 'Prince, hey!' that brought the dog under control. Farmer Knuchel was standing in front of the kitchen door.

Ambrosio got to his feet, brushed the dirt from his shirt and trousers, pushed his things back into the little wooden suitcase that had come open, and once more started going through his pockets for his papers.

9

There was a hearty welcome for Ambrosio in the kitchen. The three younger Knuchel children stared shyly at the Spaniard who was given a place opposite them at the already cleared table; their mother set an extra bowl of Knuchel milk under their gawping mouths. 'This is Ambrosio,' she said. 'And this is our Stini, this is Hans, and this is Thérèse.'

The great hunk of boiling beef was once again fished out of the pot, and Grandma served it to Ambrosio in slices as thick as his thumb, along with plate-sized slabs of bread. The farmer had got out the bottle with what was left of the Sunday wine, and drank to Ambrosio. At the same time, he was studying the southerner's hands as they scuttled about nervously on the kitchen table.

They were bony hands, with dry skin. Knuchel couldn't deny that they looked practical. Those pincer fingers must have often gripped and held, unsparing of themselves, done hard work, and, without shame, dirty work too. Callouses and blisters, taut sinews, scabbed wounds, strong firmly rooted nails, were what these hands had. But did they know what milking was? That was the question! Did they understand the udder and its whims? Did their rough exterior conceal the inner tenderness essential for the milking of cows? What if these hands had just been fiddling about with tight-arsed goats, and hitherto plucked a measly pint or two of nanny goat's milk for the home from between a pair of bony shanks and into some half-rusted baking dish? Knuchel's cows were no bony small fry that had to go and graze in the churchyards to weed up seven withered blades of grass from the side of a tombstone. No one on Knuchel's farm was under any illusion that milking was when some flying-fuck-born Saanen goat weed three times and thought she'd just performed a miracle. If he'd known how to, Farmer Knuchel would have loved to get Ambrosio away from the dinner table and out into the cowshed to let him have a shot at real milking.

Ambrosio himself had long had the feeling of being besieged, so he scarcely dared to help himself the way his appetite demanded. He would have preferred to take a couple of slices of bread and disappear into the night, but he had to stay where he was and parrot out: 'Sí sí! Ambrosio! Sí. Sí! España. Sí!' The searching glances, the questions, the wine in front of him, the dog under the table, and the flypaper hanging over it, it all came to oppress him more and more, it closed around him like a vice, tighter and tighter. Everything squeezed the blood against the hot skin of his face.

They were happy he'd come at last, said the farmer, only half interrupting his examination of the hands. They had almost been afraid something might have gone wrong. But now Ambrosio had got here, and that was good, because they really needed a third milker, with all the cows freely pouring out milk and on top of that, Blösch, the best cow in the byre, was about to freshen, by God, if it all went well it might be tonight, he would call him when the time came, he could be sure of that, then he could find out for himself what they were like, the cows on the highlands. And out on the fields too there was quite a bit to be done, he wasn't to think they were behindhand, by no means, they had tractors and machines more than some he could name up in the village, only, in the cowshed, they had so far been able to stave off these ultra-new developments, but then there was always work to be done on any decent farm, especially with the pasture needing to be refenced again this year, and not with pine like last time, no, in the past winter he and his son had collected some hazel staves. Also, they'd begun with soilage feeding, not that they had any need to go over the floor of the hayloft with a toothbrush to get together another cribful of hay, not at all, but a batch of clover did just go straight into the milk, you could say what you liked, but then he, Ambrosio, would see that for himself soon anyway.

In all her girded-up physicality, her body corseted till it cut into the flesh, Farmer Knuchel's wife scaled the stairs ahead of Ambrosio. The woman who was taking him along the veranda was like a tree. She was twice his weight, but neither coarse nor fat. What lay hidden beneath those skirts was well capable of work, a match for husband and farm, and, with her white apron, stately and beautiful. And she moved the way she looked, and spoke the way she moved.

'Our attic is hardly the lap of luxury, but then there's always the parlour, and our kitchen's not so uncomfortable. No, there's no need to go and hole up in there like a mouse. I wouldn't have that!'

Ambrosio hung on her movements, followed the tone and rhythm of her voice.

'There, this is the room. We got it ready nearly a month ago. We hung up the pictures specially for our Spaniard. Well now, God bless.'

When the steps of the farmer's wife had gone back along the veranda, and down the outside stairs, Ambrosio looked around his attic room.

Roughly carpentered and in clear olfactory proximity to the hayloft and feed store, it was right at the top of the farmhouse, like a dovecote. In the middle of the room was the bed, as heavy as an altar, and covered with a thick red-and-white feather bed. Next to it was a wardrobe, in another corner a chair, and in a little flower-painted cabinet a chamber pot. Hanging on the walls were several reproductions that had appeared as magazine covers.

Still holding his suitcase, Ambrosio stared at that mighty sleep altar. He dreaded the first morning of work; whoever slept on a bed like that would know all about physical exhaustion; whoever built a resting place like that for his limbs must know the joy of soft pillows after a long day's back-breaking labour.

He set his case down on the chair, got out the picture of his family, smiled at his wife and children, put the framed photograph on the cabinet and rolled himself a cigarette, which he did not smoke, however, as overwhelmed by fatigue, he climbed onto the bed and fell asleep.

In his dreams, Ambrosio continued his journey into the interior of the prosperous land, but soon there were footsteps along the veranda, the darkness creaked, the attic door opened, and a moon-illuminated Knuchel said:

'It's on account of the lead cow, Blösch. Get your trousers on and come down. She's probably pushing the hooves out by now.'

Swearing softly to himself, Ambrosio followed the farmer down into the cowshed.

All of Knuchel's cows were on their feet. They were all lined up, back alongside back, staring into their closed feed cribs, not chewing. Only Blösch, in her pride of place by the door, was lying down in the straw. The chains had been taken off her, and with great heaves she was pushing out the head of a calf. Now and then she broke off her exertions for a breath of air, but immediately she resumed them again, with still more powerful heaves that ran like waves through her whole body, from her neck to her belly, down her flanks, squeezing the milk-swollen udder so forcefully between her taut legs that it yielded to the pressure, and sent out yellowish spurts into the air. Below her tail, which went out at an angle, the slime-wet head of the calf pushed further and further into the light. Muzzle, eyes, the bumps of the horns abruptly appeared, whereupon the head and forelegs together would disappear back into the cow, only to be pushed out still further into the drop – by the next surge.

The head still showed no signs of life, the calf being born in the shed was at once limp and bulky. But suddenly it began to gurgle, clearing its respiratory tract of fluid, then, even before the rest of its body could follow, it started scrabbling about in the straw just its head and forelegs, first feeling blindly for a firm footing, turning to left and right, then suddenly there were dark eyes gleaming in the red-and-white-flecked head, squinting round in panic at the still unborn part of its body.

And then came the navel.

'Another bull calf. What the hell!' said Farmer Knuchel to himself. And to Ambrosio:

'The best cow anywhere on the highlands, but by God she's got nothing but little bull's heads packed inside her! A back as strong as a roofbeam, an udder like a bottomless barrel, so much fat in her milk you'd think we fed her on OVALTINE twice a day, and I'd like to see a prettier Blösch skin. You won't find one on the whole mountain! Same with the horns. The devil must have his eyes on her! Why else does she have to go and produce bull calves year after year?'

He emptied his pipe against the bench and went out.

Ambrosio went up to Blösch, who had turned to her now more animated half calf, and patted her on the neck. The heads of cow and calf came very close, smelling each other with flaring snot-dribbling nostrils, then, with a final mutual effort, the cord broke, and the back end of the fetus slipped out onto the straw, a bundle of calf, gurgling and groaning, swelling its breast: head and foot, rear and front halves had been joined into a single creature, a calf lying stiffly in the straw.

Blösch showed few signs of exertion. She rested a moment, took a few breaths, then she got up, which was the sign for all Knuchel's other cows to lie down, and she started drying her new-born infant. With her long-reaching tongue, she licked the blood and slime and scraps of womb off the calf's skin, and pushed it, nudging haunches and neck, until the barely ten-minute-old creature was teetering on its knees and hindlegs. The legs were thin and spindly. The calf lost its balance repeatedly, but it kept picking itself up again, like a prize-fighter, no sooner down than up again, more and more confident on its shaky legs. It was trembling all over its body, and promptly fell back into the straw.

Ambrosio sat down on the bench: the calf stood upright, still wobbling, still craning its neck out for balance, but nevertheless, inside a very few minutes one cowlife had crawled out of another, and put its 50 or 60 kilos on its own four legs.

Red and white, spick and span, it stood in Knuchel's cowshed as though it had always stood there, unlike Ambrosio it didn't seem to be at all surprised: here it was. This was its place. And now it wanted milk!

Very early on the day after Ambrosio's arrival in the prosperous land, all hell was let loose on the Knuchel farm. Clattering up and down the wooden outside staircase, and along the veranda, crashing about in the hayloft and the feed store, then back out on the veranda again, everywhere, a fiendish din!

Knuchel was cursing, he was sweating in the morning air, he stamped his wild rage onto his own soil, he punched the walls of sheds and the doors of outbuildings until his fists ached, and behind the storehouse he threw a dozen of his own pine logs over the barbed-wire fence into the pasture. Blindly, he plucked the wood from off the stack and hurled it away.

'Hell and damnation!' More kicks crashed against the kennel, against the henhouse.

Lights went on in the windows. The Knuchel household sprang from their beds in alarm. Cock and hens, dog and cows and pigs were crowing and mooing and clucking and squealing and barking; bedroom doors were flung open and slammed shut again, voices were raised in protest, hurried footsteps echoed through the house. Pushing the three little Knuchels along in front of her, the farmer's wife stepped out of the kitchen door, and stood with arms akimbo. The children clung on tightly to her apron and skirts, rubbed their eyes and stared at their father, who was only gradually coming out of his fury, still pacing up and down in front of the cowshed, as though he wanted to stamp his way right through the solid oak planks into the cistern below. 'Disappeared! He's just disappeared! Up and left us!'

'What a to-do. Goodness knows what it might have been,' said the farmer's wife.

'And in the middle of the night too,' said Grandma. 'By God, I thought there was a fire. You must have taken leave of your senses, it's not struck five in the village, and you storming through the house like a wild man.'

'What if he's gone! Pushed off home!'

'You'd have been better off buying a milking machine then, wouldn't you. But no one listens to me, do they, I'm just an old woman,' said Grandma.

'Now I can't believe he's just gone.' The farmer's wife freed herself from her children, and asked, with one hand already on the banister, 'Have you looked up in the attic? Are all of his things gone? Now say, Hans.'

'Damn it, yes,' replied the farmer, 'believe me, he's gone. His bed is empty, and he'll hardly have been sleeping underneath it.'

'His things?' said Grandma as the farmer's wife began climbing the staircase. 'That little bundle is easily tied up, there won't have been much unpacking to do, with a little cardboard suitcase like he had. No Hans, believe me, it's better this way, you should be glad he's gone, and he didn't exactly look like he was up to much either, and what are you doing scratching your neck like that, you'll have it bleeding in no time.'

Knuchel said nothing.

He had only gone up to his wife in the back bedroom very late, and then he couldn't sleep. Leaving the cowshed after the calving, he had felt abnormally irritated and galled and choked about the chest, yes, when he was thinking over the whole business again under the fruit trees in the paddock, he had even been short of breath. The affair had made his throat constrict and the tendons in

15

his milking hands tremble. Out there in the night he had picked at the trunks and branches of his apple trees, had scraped and clawed at them until it hurt. He had torn one of his strong fingernails right from its bed.

Things were going wrong with Blösch, he had long been convinced of that, and he had blamed first the cow, then his wife, and finally himself. Ridiculously spoiled that proud cow had been. Hadn't he tried to guess her every cow wish from those gloopy eyes? And now all that 'Blösch this and Blösch that' had come home to roost, that was how she paid you back for constantly patting and pandering to her, and molly-coddling her over every trifling wasp sting. He had even gone and got her a new bell in time for the last grazing season: measured and moulded and ornamented for her cowpersonally, and inscribed 'Blösch'. And now one bull calf after another came somersaulting down the drop. Knuchel had spat in the grass a few times, had tried to urinate. Why wouldn't that damn cow give him a proper cow calf? Was she too vain to accept an equal next to her in the cowshed? Was she afraid of competition from her own daughters? An aristocrat of a bloody cow, a mean-minded conceited beast, was what she was! A blue-riband animal, the pride of every agricultural show, even, according to the *Farming News*, an indispensable mainstay of high-performance breeding standards, and for all that a bellyful of no-good bull's heads. From now on, the whole of the herd, first to last, best-behaved to cussedest, was going to get a fair crack of the whip, and he would recalculate the whole feeding set-up. Milady Blösch would be forced off her high horse, and cowdemocratic principles of justice would once again rule in the Knuchel cowshed.

With these resolutions, the farmer had returned across the paddock's wet grass, and gone to bed. In spite of the short night and the bull-calving Blösch he wanted to drive out as early as posible the next morning: the grass should be harvested with the dew still on it and pitchforked into the manger but when he had gone to fetch the Spaniard from his attic to come and help, knocking several times on the door with hard Knuchel knuckles, he had found only an empty bed inside. Then the galling and choking and seething had started again, from the pit of his stomach up through his chest into his throat and finally, reached his head like a hangover.

'Now stop your scratching!' insisted Grandma.

'One thing he didn't bring with him in his suitcase was any good luck. Bloody Blösch cow squeezed out another bull calf!' Knuchel's hand rubbed over his stubbly jaw.

'There, you see! It just shows, taking on complete strangers on a farm, foreigners too, that's what you get, but then you never listen, do you.' Grandma raised her hands either side of her head beseechingly, as though to ward off an invisible swarm of midges.

'Now stop all your argy-bargy!' called the farmer's wife from up on the veranda. 'What a carry-on! All his stuff's been in the attic the whole time, and he's got a wife and children too. Here, see for yourselves! It's our Spaniard's family snap!' She held out the framed photograph over the veranda railing.

'Ooh!' Grandma turned in panic towards the farmer's wife. 'I don't believe it! You never!'

The farmer too craned his neck and stopped scratching his stubble. 'Where is he then? What's he doing? It doesn't seem right. I mean, he can't just have . . . ' Knuchel stopped. A latch clicked. The Knuchel children who had been standing by the wall, following everything with their eyes, giggled and covered their faces with the hems of their nightgowns: the upper half of the cowshed door was slowly opened.

'Well, there he is, the bugger!'

'Buenos días,' said Ambrosio, and then a second time, a little more quietly, 'buenos días', and a third time, almost inaudible, just moving his lips, 'buenos días'.

'So you've been in the byre all along. Just dropped off on the bench, eh?' The glimmer of a smile passed over Knuchel's reddened face. He took a deep breath. 'I never thought of the cowshed. It's the only place I didn't look. Well anyway, let's go. Come on. I've got it set up in front of the barn. We're feeding them soilage today. You'll see what that does for the milk.'

Without quite realizing what was happening to him, Ambrosio found himself in his knee-length shorts, sandals and vest next to Farmer Knuchel on the tractor; the motor started, and Ambrosio held on tightly to his hard dickey-seat over the high wheel, and the pair of them rattled off into the fields.

'Well, well. So he spent the night in the cowshed! That's what you get.' Again raising her arms against an invisible enemy, Grandma trotted off down to the hen-run, scooped up a fistful of corn from the depths of her apron pocket, and scattered it through the wire-mesh fence to her hens.

'Come on, Bibi. Come on!' she called. 'That's it. Come on, Bibi!'

Knuchel's fields lay under a blue-grey haze. They were burnished and breathing. Ribbons of mist passed over them towards the heights of the highlands. Pebbles were scattered by the tractor tyres, and scurried into the fields. The grass wagon was thrown this way and that by the ruts in the field track. Rakes and pitchforks clattered on the handling bridge.

'Here we are then!' Knuchel pulled on the hand-brake and jumped down off the tractor.

Ambrosio, looking for something to grip, pulled his hand back. The whole of the rear of the tractor was covered with a layer of axle grease, a greeny-yellow colour under the dirt-blackened surface.

Now at last it was under his feet, Knuchel ground, and he took his first uncertain steps on it, feeling the viscid heaviness of it, loamy and green. What a fat, sleek green. And the air was green too, and it slid coolly down into Ambrosio's lungs. Before long he would feel this ground everywhere, all over his body, feel it with every pore: it would get under his nails, into his hair, his ears! He wouldn't be able to get free of it, he would live off it, would wallow in it, plough it open and shut.

Ambrosio shifted from one foot to the other. The grass tickled.

'I'll mow now, and you take the rake. Two strips, and then we'll load it up.' Knuchel had been picking up fistfuls of grass in both hands, holding them under his eyes, flinging them up into the air with a 'Whew, damn it! Ah, they'll love this. You just watch it disappear!' Knuchel stuck a blade of grass between his teeth, unhitched the wagon, and clambered back on the tractor. The hydraulically powered mower inclined down to a horizontal, Knuchel muttered one more 'Damn it!', got in gear, accelerated, and dropped the blades into the grass.

It was very laborious raking the grass together in two long heaps. The stubble pricked Ambrosio's feet. The rake was huge. It kept snagging in the ground. Ambrosio stamped his feet and raged, pulling against it with his whole weight. He started to sweat. The four-pronged pitchfork was even heavier, and still less manageable. With its 2-metre-long shaft it was like a medieval weapon, and he just missed spiking his own foot. His hands ached. On the other side was Knuchel, effortlessly piling his heap into the wagon. Ambrosio tried to keep up, got out of breath, and when the grass was finally loaded, he dropped exhaustedly on top of it.

Back in the farmyard, the grass had to be taken off the handling bridge, had to be tossed in well-aimed forkfuls into the feed alley, and from there distributed among the mangers.

'Be sure not to give that bloody Blösch one more forkful of green than any of the others, all right!' warned the farmer.

Ambrosio didn't understand.

While his blistered hands were heaving one pitchforkful of grass after another in front of the cows' muzzles, he couldn't help noticing that Blösch hadn't pushed her head through the opened crib like the other cows; she hadn't even got up.

Blösch lay in the straw. Quite apathetically, she eyed her calf, eyed Mirror beside her stuffing herself, eyed the whitewashed wall. She, who was otherwise driven by near pathological greed, not allowing any little 2-hundredweight cow a mouthful of clover without a fight, she, who could have taken on the greatest glutton in the world for gluttony, she was simply ignoring the smell of the first new grass in Knuchel's cowshed. Everything bounced off her broad, white cow forehead. Nothing interested her: neither Knuchel nor her calf nor her fodder. Not even the cats, who propped their paws in the drop and hooked their gleaming, knife-like little teeth into the not quite detached afterbirth that dangled under her tail, plucking at it and tugging and gnawing, not even they could break Blösch's apathetic calm.

'Well, let her,' said Knuchel, 'let her hang her saw-horse steer's head. Tomorrow morning she'll be the first to shove it in the crib. I know her, by God, I know that bloody cow. She's the most gluttonous cow there ever was, greedier than Widlilismer's wife! She's been playing the prima donna now, ha, and next thing she'll be tugging like mad on her chain, butting the walls, and she won't stop until you push the crib bolt. And once it's open, she'll stuff her

face in the hay, tongue out, get underneath it, and almost choke.
The grinding and smacking when she eats! But I've had enough of
her bloody Blösch antics, and she can make a fool of someone else
for a change. We'll show that red lady. You can bet on it.'

While the preparations for milking were made, Knuchel refused
to go near the hunger-striker Blösch, he didn't have a single good
word for her calf either, and he even told Ambrosio not to spend
more time with the pair of them than was strictly necessary.

'Don't mollycoddle her, just leave her to sulk.' Knuchel didn't so
much as glance at the calf's navel, or give its skin an appraising
touch. The retina wasn't checked for possible vitamin shortage, nor
the inside of the mouth and throat for mucus congestion. All
Knuchel's attention went on the other occupants of the cowshed.
For them there was no end of patting and stroking, there were
words of encouragement on all sides, even little jokes and cow
ribbings. Ambrosio followed the farmer everywhere, nodding, and
even venturing the odd pat himself.

'There, take a look at him! He's our new milker from Spain.
Wouldn't you like to give him your hoof to shake?' said the farmer
to Baby, who was good-naturedly licking Ambrosio's arm.

It was still dark in the cowshed. A couple of electric bulbs shed a
weak light over the dozen cows. A mass of spiders' webs were
draped like a veil across the walls and ceiling. It was dark too in the
corner where Knuchel got out a shovel, dungfork, pitchfork and
broom. The farmer demonstrated the use of these implements
around one or two cows, then with a 'now you try it' expression on
his face, handed them over to Ambrosio.

Knuchel's actions were unmistakably clear. Ambrosio watched
the techniques and grips, was amazed, thought to himself:
Caramba, sabe trabajar para cinco.

The farmer worked steadily and gracefully too: he didn't so
much as crook a finger without it serving some purpose, everything was to plan, and he stood there huge and silent, and plied
shovel, dungfork, pitchfork and broom as though they were all
extensions of his arms, and not Herculean items, real monsters of
implements, the like of which could not be found in all of Coruña.

'Whoo! Whaa!' Ambrosio called out to the cows, raising and
lowering his voice the way Knuchel had done, and with those two

20

first words of a new language, he barged his way between a couple of cows. He pushed against their rumps, forced their flanks apart, and for all that he was only wearing sandals, he put his feet wherever they had to go, be it in puddles of slurry, in dirt or on sharp straw, thinking only of the three-pronged dungfork that he had to push between and beside the cows' hooves. He shovelled and hoisted the dung without grazing a single leg, spread the straw, got a few wet tail smacks in the face, but, from Blösch to Baby he performed cowpraiseworthy stallwork.

'It'll be no different in Spain,' said Knuchel. 'It's just the same, isn't it? A clean shed is half the milking! That's right, ha?' He watched as Ambrosio scraped away at the floor underneath the animals, watched the greeny-brown liquid; when the gutter clogged up, he thrust his own boot in it, and with his hands in his pockets, helped it along playfully, until it splashed richly and thickly into the manure pit. That little Spaniard, he thought, by God he'd better be this good at milking as well. He was already chuckling away to himself, and when Ambrosio had left a few twists of straw on his dungfork, Knuchel plucked the yellow strands out of the heap on the wheelbarrow and returned them to the floor. 'Just the dung, boy, just the dung!' he laughed. 'It's only the dung we put on the dungheap. And don't pile the barrow up so high. Better take one extra trip out of the shed. It's all right, there's no hurry, take your time, a wheelbarrow load like that empties in no time at all. Now come on! We want to start on priming them!'

Now Knuchel wanted to know about the Spaniard's grasp. Can he do it or not? that was the question. The knotty tendons twitched in his milker's hands. He thrust his jaw to one side, tensing the muscles in his cheeks and throat. He scratched the already sore skin. Why should the village cheeser have the right to keep poking his nose in other people's affairs? Before he'd even arrived, the way this willing Spaniard had been gossiped about, dragged like a floor-cloth across every filthy kitchen floor in the village, yes, and through all the manure pits too! That cheeser! He could find nothing good to say about the Spaniard at all. And did he know him? Hardly! And was it anything to do with him? Shouldn't the cows have any say in the matter at all? Let's see what the cows make of him.

Outside, in front of the cowshed, Ambrosio was contemplating the dungheap. It was a brownish-black hill, built up one barrow-load after another. One side was pressed against the outer wall of the cowshed, another was formed by the curve of the ascent. All 2.5 metres of the two remaining sides were covered in a meandering plait pattern. Once a week, in laborious pitchfork work, Knuchel and Ruedi had taken the loose strands and wisps of straw and woven them together, like a basketmaker with willow twigs. That gave the whole thing firmness and shape, and kept all the dung fresh and moist, inside and out.

Qué montón de mierda, thought Ambrosio. The smell dwelt in his nose, got under his skin like an ointment. Flies swarmed. The barrow was too full. A pine plank served as a ramp. It swayed underfoot. Down below, a shiny black liquid trickled into a gutter. Ambrosio could see his face distorted in a puddle. The plank was slippery. Ambrosio struggled not to fall into the manure. The pull of the wheelbarrow on his arms became stronger and stronger, he got stuck. Mosquitoes hovered round his bare legs and flew in his face. He blinked, he didn't have a free hand to defend himself with. Caramba! With one final heave, he gave the wheelbarrow enough impetus to push it up and the load began to slip downwards. Heavily and slothfully, dung slapped against dung. Caramba! If he'd had clean hands, despite flies and stench, Ambrosio would have rolled himself a cigarette on the spot. On the summit of Knuchel's dunghill, he would have stretched his limbs, and exhaled tobacco smoke from the bottom of his lungs up into the sky. Instead, he pulled the empty wheelbarrow back onto the plank and walked it back down off the dungheap.

Knuchel was waiting. He thrust a 2-pound bar of STEINFELS soap at Ambrosio, and pointed at the pump. It was a rough lump of soap that felt like a brick in Ambrosio's hands. Eso para lavar las manos? The sharp-edged block. The manure had crusted on his hands. Ambrosio rubbed them ferociously, rinsed, lathered them again, rinsed them more thoroughly. They were still dirty. He got a handful of sand together from the bottom of the trough, and rubbed that into the pores and cracks in his skin; he found a brush that was lying around, and drove the bristles under his fingernails. 'Not that!' Knuchel went up to him and took the brush. 'That's for cleaning the milking gear, the buckets and ewers and churns. Come on now.'

He laughed. 'Your mitts are clean enough anyway, they're cleaner than the midwife's. As bad as the ruddy vet, you are. He never stops splashing about under the pump either. And the amount of soap he gets through! Must be half a pound every time. Remember, you're not doing an operation, you're just milking.' Knuchel laughed and picked up a milking pail. 'Not operating, just milking, ha ha ha!'

And then Ambrosio got under one of Knuchel's cows.

It was on the mucky Bossy that the farmer had set an example, showing just exactly how it was done here on the highlands. 'There's no one in the world as precise about milking as we are here,' he said.

Bossy was a cow in her prime, with a good temperament, and if she was a bit short and low slung, she was still firm and full in all holds. But as far as patience went, she had less of that than a thirsty calf. At the first clink and clatter of the milking gear at the pump she would be unable to hold back her milk for excitement. Where the others might start mooing or shaking their heads to and fro, rattling their chains, Bossy's udder would begin to dribble at the quietest chime of metal. Sometimes just coyly, sometimes in embarrassing abundance. In the first few months of her lactation in particular she would hardly even have time to shift in her stall before yielding to the pressure between her hindlegs. The only ones to rejoice at this, though, were the cats. Summer and winter alike would find them sitting in the alley half an hour before milking time, ready to hop across the gutter and take up position under Bossy at the very first rattle. For his part, the farmer was sorry to see the white streams disappearing down the cats' throats, so he always milked Bossy first.

Ambrosio had paid close attention.

He observed how the farmer didn't catch the first few streams of milk from each quarter of the udder in the wooden milking pail, nor did he simply squirt them onto the ground, but, according to Paragraph 5 of Article 64 of the FOOD AND EQUIPMENT REGULATIONS, he collected each of the streams separately in a black dish and examined its consistency. As there had been no signs of either lumpy or flaky secretions, nor any other irregularity, the farmer had then aimed into the bucket, and begun to squeeze and tug more emphatically. Knuchel's hands had moved up and down under Bossy with surprising suppleness. Forthright, though not clumsy, they had straightaway found a steady rhythm which they kept up without interruption until Bossy was milked dry and the oval pail between Knuchel's knees was full to the brim with foamy milk.

And then it was Ambrosio's turn to show what he could do.

Having first rather awkwardly pushed his sleeves back as far as the shoulder several times, and then dipped into the can of milking fat, he cleared his throat and spat, as he did in Spain, to help the flow. He had buckled on the one-legged milking stool as tight as it would go, and then stepped out onto the floor behind the cows. The towering structures of the cows' hindquarters had risen up in front of him, like mountains that he had to move. He had to make a breach there, to get them to part, to reach the full udder of Flora, had to grab hold of the flailing tails, hold onto them and tie down their bushy ends, but the blind lunks of hide and bone didn't want to move, not an inch, and however he cow-shouted at them, however he pounded on their flanks left and right, the back legs of the animals remained knock-kneed and obdurate, their hooves were rooted in the ground, and at the front, in the thick skulls at the end of their long necks, they weren't overly concerned about this stranger who even on tiptoe couldn't see over the top of them.

Flora, who the day before had been persuaded to reach ambitious new heights in her performance, was today making common cause with her neighbour May. They were rubbing against one another with such fervour that even Knuchel was unable to get access to Flora's udder for Ambrosio. 'What a carry-on!' he exclaimed angrily. 'A right pair you are. Anyone would think they were complete novices. Now come on! Take May first this time!'

And then Ambrosio was milking.

May had mooed suspiciously as she was being primed, had stepped aside and tried to kick over the pail under her belly with her hindleg. Ambrosio had pressed his forehead against her flank, and massaged her high up on the udder just below her belly. The hormonal flow started up. May's resistance weakened, her milk had dropped, and at the first trickle, she was behaving like a model cow, standing broad and low over the milking pail.

Knuchel raised his head. His bottom lip slid up to cover his upper lip. He sucked. 'Look at you, May! First she thinks she's going to act up, and now . . . ruddy May!' he said.

May's udder was slightly rectilinear, front and rear were clearly separated, each quarter was glandular, evenly rounded and covered by healthy, protuberant blue veins; there were no scars on her teats, no cracks that might get infected, and all four were well positioned, sealed and fitted with prettily curved sphincter muscles. It was set high up between her hindlegs, and was just narrow enough to allow her an unimpeded gait. There was only a single fault with this otherwise perfect udder: there was a growth of hair on one of the quarters. It twined like thread round the pinky-yellow skin. Because of these 'devil's curls' as Knuchel called them, May had refused to suckle her calves, whose muzzles could be merciless in their insatiable thirst. They sucked and pulled at the hairs, until May could no longer bear it. Ambrosio realized her trouble immediately. He was even gentler with that teat than with the others, milking it not by tugging but by closing each finger over it in turn. It was an easy matter for him to work with care, his own hands were so cut and blistered by Knuchel's cowshed cleaning gear. He hoped the cow-warmth of the teats would help to ease the pain.

Knuchel hunkered down. His lower lip was sucking contentedly on his upper lip. He listened to the little milk bubbles popping in May's glandular tissue; it was as though it was himself milking, with his own head pressed against her belly, and he listened to the milk coming through the little valves and passages in the activated udder, listened to it collecting in the tanks above the teats, listened to the blood throbbing and pressing, and he liked the sound of the first few streams very much. There was a hard metallic drumming as they splashed against the bottom of the pail. He listened to the richer, hissing sound as the pail filled up. 'Music, isn't it?' he whispered under May to Ambrosio. 'Music.' To keep the cow from losing concentration, he rubbed the base of her tail. If only that cheeser was here, that blabbermouth, he could even learn a thing or two, he thought. Quite. And Gran too. Huh. Milking machines, milking machines. Give me that man any day. Yes, let them come now, Messrs Rep and Rep, let them roll up with their ties and their briefcases. But there you go, whenever there's something worth seeing they're never there. Not a sausage. Not even the bloke from the association. God knows I'd be surprised if they didn't produce some kind of bumf, there's always some new statistical crap from America. No more competent milkers around nowadays, well, Christ, here he is! The way they'd stare, their eyes would pop out of their heads and roll in the dung, that Spaniard's all right, you can set him to work on the finest udders and not worry, he'll not do any mischief, he's got it, his hands have got what it takes, you can see it at a glance, more than any milk vacuum, Ambrosio was much more useful! And he wouldn't run up any electricity bills either.

Still, Ambrosio's hands looked a trifle narrow on the teats, for Knuchel's liking, and at a closer look they were on the bony side too. He thought even the farmer's wife had more flesh on her fingers. But then it's what he does with them that matters. It's just clothes he's short of, he needs a decent pair of trousers, an overall, boots and some headgear; you can't go arund Knuchel's cowshed in sandals.

Ambrosio got up crookedly; the milking stool had slipped round a little. The pail was full to the brim. The farmer drew his head back in, his neck and throat shortened. May's milk weighed Ambrosio down. He staggered. Caramba, por que todo es de tamaño enorme. There was a milk churn on the dog-cart outside the door. Ambrosio held out his right arm to keep his balance. He carried the milk past the farmer and poured it through the sieve into the churn. There was a crown of foam left on it. 'What do you think, want to try your hands on another?' asked Knuchel. 'Try Flora. Just to see. What do you say?'

Ambrosio tried it.

Before he could even set foot on the floor behind her, Flora stepped aside and made room for him to sit down. She kept her tail quite still between her knees, and, at the other end, she lowered her head; the rattling of chains stopped, and the mooing was replaced by a quiet, rhythmical breathing. Ambrosio dug his feet into the straw, moved the pail up, pressed his forehead against her flank, reached out and . . . Flora was all udder for him.

'Christ!' Knuchel lost control of his lower lip. His upper lip disappeared completely. There's Flora allowing this stranger access to her, not making any fuss. He got a stool and pail for himself, pulled his cap down over his eyes, and positioned himself under Baby who was especially impatient with her milk, next to Spot at the very back of the cowshed.

The Monday morning milking was completed as a duet, in the same tempo in which it had begun. There was no slowing down. The milk flowed, the farmer laughed, one relieved cow after another went back to ruminating, Prince started to feel restless in his chains. When Ruedi stepped into the cowshed wanting to help, the last drop of white stuff had long since been pressed out of the spongy tissue of Blösch's eleven companions. They were already unchaining them.

After the watering trip, Knuchel gave the churns on the cart a stir. 'If they yield milk, you have to milk them,' he said. 'But right now we're going to eat, I can smell the rösti. Later we'll take the Spaniard round to the cooperative. He needs a decent pair of trousers, an overall, boots and something to wear on his head.'

Heavy paws scraped at the wood of Knuchel's kitchen door, one claw caught on the lintel, and the scraping was followed by yelping.

'Well, it seems it's time to deliver our milk, Prince here can hardly wait.' The farmer wiped his mouth on his sleeve and was the first to get up from the table.

Coffee can and rösti dish were empty; left next to the serrated knife on the breadboard, there were only a few crumbs. Ruedi picked them up on the tip of his finger and nibbled them one by one. Stini, Hans and Thérèse again just showed Ambrosio their large eyes, keeping the lower half of their faces well concealed behind bowls of milk. They hadn't opened their mouths to speak. It was only when Ambrosio had failed to realize straightaway that the hard crust of Knuchel bread needed to be softened in milky coffee first, that a little giggle escaped Stini. Ambrosio had made several vain attempts to bite through the crust with his teeth, and a few groaning wheezing sounds in his throat had been audible. The farmer had stopped chewing and asked, 'What's the joke?' 'Nothing,' Stini had replied.

27

Prince pulled strongly at his harness. Knuchel's hands gripped the shaft of the milk-cart as strongly as a vice. The dog panted. The farmer's boots crunched the gravel on the path. From the top of the slope, there were two curving wheel tracks that cut through the little wood between the village and the Knuchel farm. The cart jolted from one to the other. Ambrosio's short legs had to step out powerfully to keep pace. But he wanted to keep up.

He had been there at the milking, and helped. The milk that his exertions had produced was there with the rest, sloshing about, in the churns on the cart. No hay que correr. He lengthened his stride again. Behind the cart, he wanted to be just like the farmer in front, as upright and powerful striding along, not having to break into a trot.

Just before the village, on a level with the Boden farm, Prince raised his head; his gait was calm and proud. He barked, as if to say: Here, you small-time farmers, get off your mingy dungheaps, get out of your rooms and your byres and come and see how much milk we're bringing in today.

But it wasn't the dog, it was Ambrosio they turned out to see.

Frau Zaugg came to her garden fence, Frau Kiener watched from her kitchen window, Frau Stucki raised her red face from her vegetable patch, Frau Fankhauser looked down from her veranda, young Frau Eggimann stopped in front of the village shop with an empty bag, Frau Blum restrained her St Bernard, old Frau Eggimann took a grandchild by the hand, Frau Zbinden put her broom away, Frau Stalder broke off her chat with Frau Bienz, Frau Marthaler went and got her husband from the threshing room.

Ambrosio looked left and right. Knuchel walked past the farms, nodding and greeting. He listened to the clicking of the milking-machine compressors. For all their technology, Binggeli, Blum, Zbinden, Stalder, and Affolter were still in their cowsheds. Ambrosio caught all the looks, his smile twisted by a spasm under the skin. These women, he thought, todas grandes como las vacas. Let them stare. He kept up his long strides, and held onto the wood cart.

In front of the Ox Inn, cows were standing at the fountain: red and white, tanking water, slurping and snorting through their nostrils which they didn't immerse. Prince barked. The brindled cattle remained unmoved, kept formation, stayed back by back. Prince was told off by Knuchel, who led the milk-cart in a wide curve round the herd in the village square. 'You shouldn't disturb cattle when they're watering,' he said.

From behind the storehouse of the Innerwald Agricultural Cooperative the hoof-rattle of a horse team died away, and a red tractor started up, it was a HÜRLIMANN 2000. Otherwise, there was little in the way of milking traffic, Knuchel was one of the first.

The cheeser was standing on the platform at the front of the cheese dairy; he had his hands on his hips and he was waiting. He had a spotless rubber apron tied round his waist, a pair of clogs on his feet, and on top his blue-and-white-striped collarless cheeser's shirt. 'Morning!' he called out. Knuchel lifted a hand in greeting, and took Prince by the collar. 'Sit!' he said, and Prince sat. 'Quiet!' and Prince was quiet.

The cheeser hooked his hands round the handles of the churns and hoisted them up to the platform. Ambrosio waved his arms, what should he pick up? Where might he lend a hand? He hurried round the front of the two-wheeled cart, tripped over the shafts, trod on Prince's tail, an offended growl, the churns were gone, Ambrosio reached out into thin air, the Knuchel milk was already in pans being weighed. The cheeser went 'Hm' appraisingly and walked over to his high desk. Knuchel squinted over his shoulder at the receipt book.

Yesterday evening's milk had been skimmed and poured from the cooling pans into three cheese-making vats. The cream squelched in the butter churn, could be seen once every time round, white and frothy as it flowed across the glass peephole. On the press table, under three spindles that came down from the ceiling, was yesterday's cheese in its wooden moulds. It had a sweetish, soapy smell. Everything in the cheese dairy was clean, everything, the white wall tiles, the flagstones on the floor, the windowpanes, the equipment, everything was redolent of freshness and moisture, smelled washed and scrubbed and scrubbed and washed. But what Ambrosio liked was the dull copper glow of the cheese vats, where the cheeser poured the morning's milk, once it had been weighed, along with the previous night's. They were huge vats, waist high, a good 4 metres across and cladded with oak on the outside.

Whey was poured from an aluminium tank into the empty churns, and then they were loaded up again. Prince waved his tail and Knuchel was about to go when the cheeser stepped up to the front of his platform and said, 'You know your Spaniard can't go around like that, you know what the REGULATIONS say. Hygiene in the cowshed! And be sure he always washes his hands first, and with soap.'

Knuchel stopped the cart, his head was on a level with the cheeser's clogs, and he scratched himself under the chin. 'Now listen,' he replied, 'don't you bother your head about him, that man is all right. I kept an eye on him all morning, and I have to say he can milk, whether you like it or not, he can milk as well as anyone from here can. As for his clothes, there I agree with you, and we're heading over to the co-op right now, so see you round.' Knuchel took up the shafts, Prince pulled, Ambrosio pushed and the cheeser once more stood with his hands on his hips.

The manager of the INNERWALD AGRICULTURAL COOPERA-TIVE was just heaving a 2-hundredweight sack of powdered milk out of the storehouse. He stopped and said, without a greeting, 'So you've got him at last, your Spaniard?' Then he nodded at the sack on his shoulder and said significantly, 'Imported.'

He was a rough diamond, the manager of the cooperative. Big-bodied, heavy-headed, slightly flat-footed and occasionally shaven-necked and even shaven-templed. In the village he was thought of as a likeable man, but he was sizing up Ambrosio with an insolent expression, as though he were a calf on special offer. Top to bottom. He circled him twice, sidling and staring, with the load still on his shoulders. He examined him, feet, legs, hands, shoulders. From front and behind. Pero que tiene este hombre? thought Ambrosio, staring fixedly at the furthest corner of the room. The manager laughed. 'What did you say?' he turned to Knuchel. 'Needs some proper trousers, an overall, boots and a cap? You want him kitted out then. I'm not sure, Hans, I don't know if we've got anything his size in stock. There's not very much of him, is there?'

'Well, come on then, let's try something on him, show me a pair of your good trousers.' Knuchel went on ahead. In the shop part of the cooperative there was a smell of leather, hemp and feedstuff. A cow was laughing happily on a poster. PROVIMIN it said on top in big letters, Protein, Vitamins, Minerals in smaller letters below. Fertilizer, seeds, salt, machine oil, paint, chicken feed, were all heaped up in plump sacks and in buckets and cans. Equipment dangled from the walls and ceiling: spades, rakes, potato drills, baskets for stones, sickles and scythes, feed measures, hoes, axes, whips, cleavers, sledgehammers, a couple of small chainsaws, weedkiller sprayers in the finest brass, in all sizes, next to them in a corner, hand-forged crowbars, some rolls of barbed wire, and all over the place leather gear, plough-chains, halters, calf ropes, spring-hooks, straw binders, all of it dry, bright, clean and waiting, all untarnished and pristine, with red, blue or gold manufacturer's labels and trade marks on it; and all 'extra tough', 'extremely durable', 'hand-tooled', 'indestructible', 'quality', 'guaranteed for ten years'.

Knuchel pointed up at a shelf with neatly folded work clothes. 'There,' he said, 'you've got all we need.'

'Goodness,' exclaimed the cooperative manager. 'So you're proposing to get him quality stuff, and in the green too!'

'Well, yes,' said Knuchel, 'as I was saying to the cheeser, the fellow knows how to milk, he's got a feel for it. Doesn't speak a word of German, but you never have to tell him anything twice. And he's careful with it, like a glassblower, I don't mind investing in a set of good clothes for him.'

The co-op manager put his sack of milk powder down on the floor, loosened his shoulders, and took out the red pencil he kept behind his right ear. It was a CARAN D'ACHE, medium hardness, with which in the course of time he'd acquired the reputation for being a considerable ready reckoner, even beyond the boundaries of the parish. Co-op manager and pencil went together, they were inseparable. Nimbly they added, subtracted, multiplied and divided, everywhere on demand. They made their science accessible to everyone, in the Ox, in the shooting booth, at the school committee, at the fire brigade meeting, at choir practice, when milk accounts were drawn up, before the sermon, after the sermon, the co-op manager always had his well-sharpened red pencil behind his ear. Anyone who needed help with figures, percentages, rates of interest or taxation, turned to him. There were few disappointed clients, the red pencil worked fast and accurately. The figures were written down wherever: in the margin of the *Official Journal*, on a beer mat, on a wooden wall, on a cigarette packet, in the back of the hymn book, even, in the course of conversation in a field, when there was nothing else available, on the palm of his left hand. There was hardly a single calf or cow in the Innerwald area whose diet hadn't been determined by the co-op manager with his red pencil. He knew how many litres of carbolineum Farmer Hubel needed for his barn and machine shed to get rid of the woodworm without poisoning the cattle. It was he who worked out how many vitamins the old and young village bull got mixed in with their feed. It was he who was responsible for the ratio of seed and fertilizer, in short he did half the village's sums.

Only Knuchel wasn't overly impressed by the red pencil.

'What do you want that for?' he said. 'We've got nothing here that needs calculating.' He stared at the co-op manager's hand, as though it held a revolver.

'I'm not sure, Hans,' the co-op manager said falteringly, scratching his neck with the tip of his pencil. 'There's the milk powder,' he said in explanation. Then, again, struggling for words, 'It's . . . it's for . . . you know, if everyone . . . we don't go about it like that. That green-grey material is so durable, and the special cut of it, the pockets, the army buttons all double-sewed . . . what about everyone else? What would the farmers in the village say? Couldn't you . . . ? I mean, what about blue instead? Try blue. If the Spaniard stays here a year or more, then you can always still buy him the green – '

'Damn it!' Knuchel interrupted the co-op manager. 'Is he a milker or a garage mechanic? I've told you he's up to the work, so no one in the highlands need feel ashamed to have him milking our cows. No, my mind's made up, I'm having green!'

'Well, it's up to you. Whatever you say, never said a word,' the co-op manager replied.

It didn't take long to try the things on.

Even the smallest of the boots were too big, the shortest trousers too long, and the smallest milking overall had sleeves that flapped round Ambrosio's elbows. The cap covered his ears. Knuchel and the co-op manager got down on their knees. They each rolled up a trouser leg. The green-grey material was sturdy and stiff. Ambrosio hitched the waistband up to his chest. He could feel the tough seams. All double-stitching.

The red pencil totted up the prices on the sack of powdered milk. Knuchel asked for a leather strap for a belt to be thrown in too.

'Sixty-three twenty,' said the cooperative manager.

Swimming rather than walking in his great boots, Ambrosio plodded out. Qué país! Qué estoy haciendo por aquí? The dog Prince yawned. He sniffed at the green-grey farmer's cloth.

'Well, we're off then. Thanks!' Knuchel put his wallet back in his pocket. 'We've still got to call on the mayor on account of the voles. The bloody things have got it in for me. And the moles this year, they're like sand on the beach too. Well, so long, manager.'

The pencil went back behind his ear. Two arms thrust out, sleeves slid back over wrists, two hands aimed, ten fingers linked, grasped each other fleshily, massively, and squeezed one another hard. 'So long, Hans,' said the co-op manager.

Back in the village square, Knuchel shook his head. There were cowpats on the cobbles round the fountain in front of the Ox. Knuchel pointed out each one individually, and laughed sardonically. Ambrosio laughed back.

The mayor was at the back of his yard washing his milking gear. The brush in his hand pounded against pails and basins. 'How are you doing?' he asked Knuchel by way of greeting.

'Oh, can't complain,' he replied.

'What about your prize cow? Is she freshened yet?'

'Already been. Another bloody bull calf. But the Spaniard has arrived. He got here yesterday on the last bus, he's all right. I think we got lucky with him,' Knuchel replied.

'Don't take it so badly,' said the mayor, 'every time you have a bull calf in your shed it's as though you wanted it drowned in the fire pond. Really! You could get a packet of money for him as a stud animal. They're looking for bulls out of dams like yours.'

'Well, you know it's not the way I operate, they were after me the last time it happened, as though it was the Golden Calf. I'd rather fatten it up myself and let Schindler have it. We've got enough milk, and the kids will feed it until it's fit to burst. That way I'll pick up at least a thousand on it.'

The mayor dropped the brush in the water, and the last basin clattered to the ground. 'But Hans, you know, the AI Centre will give you fifty times that for a good bull. Whether you like it or not. Recently they bought a prize-winning Brown Swiss. He was just three years old. You could have built yourself a house with what they paid for him.'

'Well, that's artificial inseminaton and that, but it's not my idea of how to go about it. Do you really believe you get healthy calves that way? I'm not so sure. And you wouldn't catch me drinking the milk of an artificially inseminated cow, not me, no thank you!'

'Fair enough,' laughed the mayor. 'But on the other hand, it's artificial insemination that helps us with breeding. The best to the best. You can't do any better than that!'

'But not that way, not like that!' Knuchel replied. 'Sperm out of plastic bags. Deep-frozen if you please. Where's it all going to lead?'

'You know, Hans, I think time's up for the summering multi-purpose cow anyway. The way they're breeding them now is different. Who's interested if a cow's got a straight back nowadays or even horns. Milk is what they're after! Milk! By the bathtubful! And they're not to eat too much, leastwise not the expensive stuff. Never mind if a cow's got an udder like a flabby bagpipe, with tits like thorns with warts on and all, who cares. Main thing is she's got to give more milk than the competition. You wait! Your Ruedi's growing up. He'll be on at you one day. In agricultural college they do all their milking with pen and paper. No one's going to boast about a high milk yield before he's worked out how much he's shelling out for his PROVIMIN.'

'Oh no, Ruedi's not just bothered about making money. He minds about the land too. And the animals in the shed – '

'Yes, until it's time for him to get married,' interrupted the mayor. 'You think he'll still be living under one roof with his cows. The kind of bedroom where you can hear them in their straw, and you wake up whenever one of them is wheezing a bit. You wait! These days it's the young people who are moving out into the granny flats. It's not like it used to be. You know, in America, they don't even let cows like yours give birth. They get them multiply impregnated, and then they cut the fetuses out of their bellies and

34

implant them in the uterus of inferior animals who bear them. You know what that's called?'

'Madness,' muttered Knuchel.

'They call them receiver cows! Receiver cows, that's right!' laughed the mayor.

Knuchel scratched under his chin. 'America, America, the whole time. What kind of bloody racket is that anyway? Let them, who cares. We're all right here. Our byres were blessed before they even knew what a cow was. And the way they have them looking over there and all. Not one with a proper horn on her head, all bags of bones, and udders like a score of wasps had stung them. And what they yield is 99 per cent water, it's the thinnest milk in the world! They have to get all their decent cheese from us, that's what the Boden farmer says, and he was over there, with his brother-in-law in Oklahoma. They haven't got any farms like ours over there yet. That's for sure. But I've got to go, my Spaniard is waiting outside.'

The mayor was still laughing. 'All right, go on then.'

Knuchel stopped in front of the door of the cowshed. 'Oh, one other thing. Would you send the vole-catcher out as far as the wood some time? I'll make it worth his while. They're raising hell under the soil.'

'Right you are,' said the mayor. 'By the way, there are still a few formalities to go through with your Spaniard. I need his papers.'

'You need his papers, eh? Anyone would think I was trying to sell a steer or something. But you know the rules. At least he's not the first. It'll have been the same with the Italian.'

The mayor held out his hand to Ambrosio in front of the house. Ambrosio shook it. The mayor took his cap off and said, 'Grüß Gott.'

Ambrosio nodded, 'Buenos días.'

'So, you want to work over here?' asked the mayor.

'Sí, sí, mucho gusto.'

'That's fine then. You know we could use a bit of help, we're not short of work up here on the highlands. Touch wood.' Laughingly he tapped the milk-cart with his fingertips.

'Right, we're off then,' said Knuchel. Prince shook his way back into his harness. There was a strap that had slipped from his chest while he'd been sitting, and a rope had got between his hindlegs.

35

After a couple of steps, Knuchel stopped the cart again. 'I would have liked a cow calf of Blösch's. You know, she milks so easily and that. It's not that I've got anything against her at all. But what can you do? That's the way it is! Maybe she'll have one next spring.' Farmer Knuchel got down to pick up the shafts again.

The mayor had stopped as well. 'You could give the new bull a go. Who knows what the reason for it is?'

'That's what the wife thinks too. She's all in favour of Pestalozzi. But I still back Gotthelf. Well, I'm off . . .' Knuchel set off anew, but turned around one more time.

'No, you can't blame it on the bull. Nor the cow either. I don't know myself what it is, the devil's to blame. But it's not Gotthelf's fault. He always was good for my shed. Good stock, and he's just getting to be the right age, ha! But I've got to go, there's a lot still to do. Cheerio then, mayor.'

'Think it over, will you? I'll make you an offer for your calf myself. Say three thousand . . .'

Knuchel made a gesture of refusal, raising his right shoulder as though to protect his head, and then he grabbed both shafts of the cart. 'Now I really am going,' he said.

Blow upon blow. Iron onto wood and wood into the ground. The hammer whistled down again. The post trembled. Knuchel's earth was harder than it looked. The farmer raised his hands high above his head, ten, fifteen times before another post was rammed firmly into the ground. The sound drummed back from the wood in echoes.

It was Ambrosio who held the posts. As soon as one had bitten into the ground enough to take Knuchel's hammer blows, he went to get the next one. They were hazel posts, first-class material for fencing. The trees had been individually picked, and then dragged down the logging path. For several days in December the chainsaw had screamed, and after each load the snow between the tractor tracks had been scuffed away, leaving brown earth.

Ambrosio dropped the new post next to the old one. It felt like a tree-trunk against his back. The old fence was wobbly, the barbed wire was rusty and sagged, the posts were rotten and grey. Ambrosio was hardly any bigger than the post in his hands.

The farmer hoisted the sledgehammer onto his left shoulder. He held it down with the crook of his elbow while he spat on his hands. There was a dirty bandage round the finger where the nail had come loose. Knuchel was laughing. 'We're doing great. Not like the Boden farmer. This time last year he was doing the fencing with his Italian. Only they never seemed to make any headway. Ha! Farmer Boden was doing the hammering, and the Italian was holding the posts. Only they weren't getting anywhere. All his swearing didn't help, and he can swear, Farmer Boden, bloody hell, he can! The bloody posts were just refusing to go in the bloody ground. Then the Italian turned to the Boden farmer, and told him if he hit him on the head once more, he could hold his own bloody posts!' Knuchel laughed, Ambrosio laughed too, and the hammer came down again, and again there was an echo of drumming from the little wood.

When the last of the posts had been knocked in, and Knuchel and Ambrosio were striding back up through the paddock to the farmyard to clean the shed and milk, the children and cats were already waiting for them.

Ambrosio turned round once more to look. He was now stepping less gingerly on Knuchel's soil. Already he knew how cool the clover felt, and how soft a molehill could be when you dug around in it with the toe of your boot. He had begun to get his bearings: there was the farmyard, there was the meadow and there was the fence, behind were the arable fields, ploughed in rich furrows, and beyond them was another fence and bushes and a pasture that went from green, to greener, to greenest, and then shrubs, a whole hedgerow of them, and then another rise, a hilltop, then the treetops of a little wood, and behind that a hill, and behind that hill another hill, and behind the little wood a larger one, and behind that larger one, on the hill behind it, an afforested area with proper mountains over it, and beyond them more hills and rises with brown patches in the woods, and more woods over these woods, forests, woods to prevent avalanches, pine woods at the foot of the screes, then suddenly, white and grey, plains of ice and snow and light and rock and sheer cliffs, the contours raw and black, ascending to peaks and domed summits and needle points, and above them only a little room left for the sky, and the clouds the same as the ones here over the farmyard, and Ambrosio turned back and breathed deeply.

In the paddock, the farmer too looked back on the pasture. 'It's going well,' he said. 'Soon we'll be able to let them out. The whole lot. Before Whitsun, if everything goes well. Now let's go!' He walked past the chicken-run up to the byre door.

Inside, the cats sat down in the passage behind Bossy, and the children squeezed in beside Blösch. The calf was standing straddle-legged parallel to its mother, but facing the other way. As Blösch's tongue was rubbing and cleaning round its anus, it was sucking at a teat.

'It'll have the scours,' said Knuchel. 'Drunk too much, the bloody bull calf has! The whole passage is shat up. That's what you get when you leave them to themselves. Here, Hans, practice makes perfect, take a broom and clean up.'

'And when can I give the calf a drink?' asked Thérèse.

'No, I want to do it,' said Stini.

'Not today, maybe tomorrow,' was Knuchel's answer.

Ambrosio fetched the wheelbarrow. Stini pointed at Stine and said, 'That's my cow.' The farmer dug his fork into the straw and said, 'Yes, that's your cow,' and to Ambrosio: 'They were born on the same night. Almost within an hour of each other. What a business, I hardly dare think about it. By God, you weren't sure if you should stay in the byre or in the bedroom.' As he was speaking, he took a look behind every cow up and down the shed. 'Ay, see, we don't let our creatures shit in the village square, and they don't piss in their water either. No, we put all that back in the soil – we're not stupid!'

The loose straw was forked up to the front, the dung scraped backwards into the gutter or loaded onto the wheelbarrow. Ambrosio wanted to get out, away from the confines of the cowshed. There were children, cats, cows and calves everywhere. Spiders' webs hung down low, and he still had his blisters from using the enormous equipment. Ambrosio pushed the barrow, half empty, over the threshold, rolled across the planks over the manure pit. He took a run up the board. Qué carajo! The dungheap was humming and chirping, it was swarming with life. Sparrows exploded into the air, took up new positions on walls and branches. Swallows dived through the barn door. With his neck twitching back and forth, the Knuchel cock strutted away. His comb was a luminous red. Pflop! Ambrosio hauled the barrow back out of the dung.

After the cleaning, there was a hay feed. The cowshed was full of the murmurous sounds of cows feeding. Blösch sniffed choosily around in her feed crib. She tweaked out a few single shreds of hay. The manger was open. There were two wooden bars round her neck, locking her head into the crib. The farmer went up to her. 'Yes, you feed, that'll do you good. There's a lot of sunshine went in that.' He had fetched a tin muzzle. The calf was thrusting its head about this way and that. 'Ah, Blösch's calves, they're always as stupid as they come. But we don't leave them to nurse by themselves for more than the first two days. It's not good for them to suck too much either. They'll only get used to it and then they'll never make proper cattle, only the sort that are always waiting to bloody suck even when they are fully grown. Fingers, ears, pitchfork handles, even their own teats, hah! That's no way to be. You, Ambrosio, grab him by the head!' The hempen rope slipped over the calf's ears, the muzzle was squarely over mouth and nostrils, the eyes bulged, they squinted at what was making the sucking impossible, they rolled in their head, as though looking at everything and nothing at the same time.

'All right, kids, gangway!' Knuchel had made a bed of straw for the calf in the passage. It kicked with all four feet, resisting. Knuchel tied the rope to a ring in the wall.

'There! That's done it. What I was going to add . . . ' Knuchel hawked, cleared his throat, scratched it again. He looked from Ambrosio to Blösch, and from Blösch at Ambrosio's left hand. 'It's about . . . it's about that ring. You could milk Blösch dry in that bucket, for her calf. But you have to get rid of the ring first.'

Following Knuchel's looks, Ambrosio stared first at Blösch then at his own hand.

'The ring! Your ring!' repeated Knuchel. 'Not when you're milking. Especially when you can do it and properly.'

Ambrosio slipped it off, the children stroked the calf, Bossy was already dripping, and the cats licked their lips.

As he was washing her udder, Ambrosio noticed that Blösch was a little feverish. It was when he pressed his head against her side,

39

to milk out the colostrum, he could hear a splashing and gurgling as from the bottom of a well. He stroked her coat; skin and hair had lost their suppleness. He touched her udder, and the whole cow trembled. He cautiously milked out what the calf had left: half a pail.

Ambrosio had never seen a bigger, stronger cow than Blösch, it had never even occurred to him that such a cow might exist. But now she was sick, and he got the farmer out from under Bossy. 'Esta vaca no está bien, está enferma.'

Knuchel put his pail on the bench. Hesitatingly, with raised eyebrows, he followed the Spaniard's gestures. He stepped up to Blösch, touched her back, her throat, her muzzle. He examined her eyes. They were inflamed and inert. 'Well, if she won't eat anything!' He pushed his jaw out, and scratched. 'What shall I do? Damn it! She's probably still offended on account of her calf.'

When they were unchained to be watered, it was Gertrude, the oldest cow in Knuchel's shed, who led the way to the pump. There followed Stine, Spot and Tiger, and then Flora and Bossy. Not one of them waited for the lead cow. Blösch stayed behind in the cowshed.

Five thirty.

Morning that I can't call my own.

Give me courage to last out the day.

Yesterday.

Yesterday I overreached myself. In the end, I didn't manage a single word.

Not a squeak.

It all happened on the great screen of my imagination. That's where I can perform. The wonderful speeches I've made in the private cinema in my head! No one's more practised than I am at proposing utopian solutions in a dramatically effective way. Excuse my interrupting, Herr Bössiger, but I have an objection. Surely, in a slaughterhouse, of all places, there are one or two things that can't be defined in terms of mere facts and figures. Take for example . . .

I can't even make a fist in the privacy of my trouser pocket.

And the lump in my throat. The constriction.

It's all over long before the first 'I . . . ' Not a single word slips out. I'm struck dumb.

We slink off.

All of us.

All in different directions.

Anything not to have to face the others.

But back in the changing room, we all stood together again, in front of our open lockers. We looked at each other's stinking, bloodstained rags, and itched our scalps. We leaned over the basin, bare chested. Hügli cut his nails. Huber hogged the shower for ages; no one minded.

Ambrosio flipped the soap across the room a couple of times. It was no accident, and we were grateful to him for it.

Even the stupid joke about Fernando's garter got a laugh.

Just so long as someone said something.

We washed our faces over and over again: we filled our cupped hands under the jet of water, and buried ourselves a few seconds longer than usual in their stored-up warmth.

The door flew open, and Gilgen exploded in; he had thrown himself against it with the whole of his colossal weight.

He stood in the doorway enormously. His colour was changing the whole time: he was as white as a sheet, then all the blood shot into his head, then he turned pale again. His eyes were flickering. He kept his great fork-lift arms behind his back, like wings: his hands were open, the fingers stuck out like thorns. His jaw thrust forward, trembling. There was a BRISSAGO in his mouth. His butcher's tunic was ripped right across his chest: his gold-plated oxtooth with its tricorn root gleamed against the wire-wool hair on his chest.

No one moved.

There was quiet in the shower room.

We leaned over the basin without budging a muscle.

First Gilgen picked up Rötlisberger, and lifted him off the floor, almost up to his own glittering eyes.

Then he grabbed hold of Luigi.

One after another, he picked us up. We were like toys.

No one tried to resist.

We stood there like sacks, and let him go through us right the way round the basin.

There was calm in his fury.

It was a fury that had clarity in it, that was etched into his face, the kind of lasting fury that I'm not capable of.

Suddenly he said with a clear voice: 'Des vaches, des vaches, oui! Rien que des vaches! Des vaches! Vacas! Cows!'

His arms pointed backwards again, like clipped wings. Like an eagle.

And then he was gone.

And today Gilgen will be there again.

All of us will be there.

Every one.

Ambrosio. And Rötlisberger. Huber and Hofer and Co. Überländer too. And me.

Good boys, taking the golden hours of our mornings out into the abattoir behind the high fence at the edge of the beautiful city.

Red light! Stop!

The lights at a crossroads have gone red.

I brake.

I've been going too fast along the empty roads.

I switch off the LAMBRETTA's motor.

The traffic lights signal out into the night. A pall of fog hangs over them.

The dotted white line carries on beyond.

Dash after dash, beneath the fog.

The swaying street lamps. Silence.

No more dreaming.

No more dreams of cows.

I don't want any more stiff animal carcasses under my blankets. Is that too much to ask?

I just want a couple of hours of sleep to drown my gnawing thoughts.

A little refuge in darkness, a refuge I don't have to explain or account for to anyone. A couple of paces into the Beyond of sleep.

The monstrous bodies of calves, with eight legs and three hands, pigs with their limbs rearranged, dancing merrily on their snouts, slaughtered cows that are brought back to life.

I want to be spared the whole show.

I never asked for a fairground.

The daily nightmare is enough.

Still the red light in front of me.

And beyond the line, the clocking-in machine.

And beyond that, nothing but time, the sea of time that drowns each morning before it can begin.

And out in the abattoir behind the high fence at the edge of the beautiful city, the jostling in the changing room: Your left leg still asleep, is it? You're a clumsy git, porco Dio, stand on your own smelly feet, fuck it, I need space, and leave it out, will you, and is this my place or yours? You! Yes you! Que cosa fare? Morning Fritz, morning Hans, good morning Flödu, Gilgen not here yet, there's Buri, first as usual, asleep on the bench, he likes it here, you shut

43

your mouth, oh pardon me I thought you were asleep, it's still damned cold out, and did you see his overtrousers? Soon he won't need to hang them up any more, they'll stand in his locker all by themselves, they're that stiff with blood, you got a MARY LONG? No, mine's MARYLAND, anyone got a MARY LONG? Do you want a STELLA SUPER? Here's a PARISIENNE, you can keep it, give me a RÖSSLI or even a VILLIGER rather than that, and the place is full of smoke, a few wisps of it are blown out through the EXPELAIR into the early morning outside, what a smell in here, what, shut up? Couldn't you treat your varicose veins at home for a change? What about you and your bloody DUL-x! You forgotten where we are? He thinks we're on a football field, yeah, the *News* says so too, they're not up to much these days, lost again, where'd you get that paper from, was it the kiosk in front of the weapons factory? The station, ah the station, yes at the station, and in amongst it all, behind it, above it, beside it and mixed in with it, hardly diminished by the ventilation overnight, thick and acrid in everyone's nostrils, the smell of blood and sweat and rancid beef fat and singed bristles and soft soap and hydrochloric acid and ammonia and cowshed and gall and caked rubber and iodine and stale beer and plaster and damp and hairspray and tripes and oil and smoked meat and starch VASELINE BRYLCREEM orange peel shoe polish Gorgonzola chewing-gum cod-liver oil caraway seed sausage WINDOWLENE naphtha sage wood leatherette pig's urine aftershave sawdust vacuum coffee, never entirely to be removed by the ventilation from butchers' tunics, tripers' aprons, woollen socks, supportive braces, felt insoles, foot bandages, berets, knee pads, handkerchiefs, doubled pullovers, woolly hats, flat caps, overtrousers, workman's gloves, rubber boots, what a stink, it must smell for ever on your skin, get away from the mirror! Caramba! You're not taking my comb again! Winter's almost over, but how much would it cost, say, how much would it be, not that much surely, how much would a biker's coat like yours cost? Going cheap! Cheap! Cheap! Sí sí baratto! Niente pagare molto! That's no leather! Of course it's leather! Finest leather, skinned and tanned locally! Not holed with pitchforks, scraped with curry-combs, pulled to pieces by ropes, with some stupid Texas brand-mark on it, and not damaged by barbed wire either, and not chewed up by

44

horseflies. You understand? Leather! Real genuine leather! What? What? You call that cowhide? Try that one out on Frankenstein here! That would make a dead man laugh, that coat's made of glued-together bits of rabbit skin, but is the boy late again today? And Gilgen? Did you see him yesterday? Aschi Gilgen, Aschi Gilgen, Jesus Christ, didn't our Ernest pick you up as well? Didn't he ever! I was worried he'd suffocate, ha yes, Rötlisberger groaning away and Schnurri-Buri, did you see him, ah Aschi Gilgen, molto crazy, niente pensare, está loco sí pero qué bueno mira, and already Ambrosio's going around grabbing people in imitation of Gilgen, and shouting at the top of his voice: Des vaches, cow, you a cow, vacas, cow, capito? Jesus, Hofer's not in yet either, and he's got a car and all, but then his missus and the kids, you can't get kids out of bed these days, right, it's not like it used to be, oh come on, Ambrosio, give it a rest, move along a bit, and they immerse themselves for the last few minutes in the calm before the storm, on the bench, heads down, elbows propped on thighs, heads dangling between them like terrified animals panting, the metal doors are still clanging, and street shoes hurriedly disappearing, and rubber boots, clogs and work shoes appearing in their place, and the chinking of coins and drinks spurting into plastic cups in the slot-machine in the corner, and fanfare, there's Huber, and who's that hurrying along after him? Morning all, morning, morning, how d'you feel? Had a good night's rest? Why not go out on the piss for a change, eh? What d'you reckon, yeah why not, ha, but, yes well, that's right, eh? who says I do too much boozing? Just mind your own business, right, hey, you don't have to walk into me like that, crash, just shut up will you, how can you spend all day lying down anyway? Watch it, mind what you're saying! But it's true! He just lies down anywhere, down in the cellar on a pile of sawdust, on a salt sack, anywhere! That's bullshit, you liar! Then why does Piccolo here run off and warn him whenever Bössiger or Krummen want to see him, eh? Like yesterday, when he went off somewhere? An old man with the gout, I just want to put my feet up once in a while, yeah, fine, but when there's trouble coming, does he ever tell anyone? Ever open his stupid mouth? Ah, he doesn't like that, yes, go on looking at yourself in the mirror, your parting can't get any straighter than it is, now get up, crash! And

45

again, crash! God, my wife's a blooming cow! Crash! Huber's left his keys in his other trousers again, dice que su esposa es una vaca, why not, you've got the strength, break it open! Hit it! And again! Why don't you go ask Kilchenmann, he's got a spare set of keys, stupid ox, aren't you? Just get up on time, as if it was your wife's fault, she's no cow, it's just because you always leave your head in the locker, along with your hat! Right! Brainum shrivelledicum! Nothing upstairs, all gone, it's a pity you don't keep your own head out of sight a bit more, hang it up in the locker, it would make things a bit pleasanter all around not to have to see Rötlisberger's noddle, who's that giggling like an old woman? A little respect for the venerable head of Rötlisberger! What did he call it? A head! That? O noble bonce! Get a plastercast of it! Well, well, old Fritz the tripe, getting ideas about his head, well, well, the parboiled pig's head, pustular excrescence, mouldering calf's tripes! Yeah! But I look after it better than you do your Brylcreemed skull! One thing for sure, I'll never lock my head up somewhere, I don't keep living things in my locker, I take it with me, it likes variety and fresh air, a bit of sunshine now and again, oh come on Rötlisberger! You need it for smoking and that's that, you're worse than the VON ROLL chimney stack, one BRISSAGO after another, a real chain-smoker, cancer candidate, what his lungs must look like, you go and drink another OVALTINE, make you big and bonny and bright and beautiful and boring, that way you'll still be working here in a hundred years, and what would you get with a 1/125 exposure, focal distance 22 and 23 DIN? Grizzled abattoir worker, looking with slightly sad eyes at his unlit BRISSAGO. As if it was my head that needed it, what a bloody stupid notion, it's my heart, it does me good in there, you bet, and the clock goes on ticking, wiggling up towards the red zone, shall we get going then, or aren't you feeling like it again, do you have to punch the clock in Italy too? Luigi, Italia anche clock-punch? Ooh sí, Italia clock-punch like crazy, and you? You got red all over your card? What does he care! He can't count well enough to notice the difference come payday, but I know someone who can, he can count, and even if he's good for nothing else, the bastard, he can still bloody well count! What's keeping Gilgen? So long as he knows what he's doing, come on now, or are you going to sit around here all day in the warm, forget about Aschi Gilgen, he knows what he's doing all right, but we could use a couple more men in here, and if he's not going to turn up what are we going to do, the cows haven't got here yet, the shed was still empty a while ago, don't worry about it, we'll just take it as it comes, and if it doesn't, then why should we care . . . ?

No tinker, tailor, soldier, sailor. No rich man, poor man, beggarman, thief, but instead, a number of pork butchers and slaughtermen and hog-drivers, and tripers and trimmers and gravediggers emerged one after another from the changing room. Their constrained gestures expressed reluctance. They were still stiff from sleep, they were grumpy and they smoked, and they filed sullenly past the clock-in to work. To work, which held no attraction.

No one got red on his card, they knew the tricks of time, they knew for whom it was ticking. Half a minute late, red numbers on your card, and half an hour taken off your pay at the end of the week.

Without speaking much, they had got out of their street clothes and changed into their slaughterhouse kit. They were prepared, but the ferment in brains and bellies, the fragments of indescribable thoughts, the pointless rage at themselves and the whole world, the rage they all had in common, no one had said anything about that. Yes, one said one thing, a second said another, a third something else, a fourth the same as him, and the fifth agreed with the first, but perhaps only the sixth of them asked what was keeping their colleague Gilgen, and no one was surprised and no one grumbled, it was all the same as usual – and no one asked why.

Huber and Hofer pushed their cards into the slot of the time-clock. The machine punched them. Their fingers twitched a little. Huber and Hofer took their cards back and then both took off their wristwatches, with a sigh and plenty of palaver. They did it slowly. In order to get their watches into their trouser pockets, they had to hold in their bellies, which occasioned a further sigh. Old Rötlisberger watched them and grinned. He had long since done with timepieces, he didn't need one on his wrist or in his pocket or on the wall. Even if you've got a gold OMEGA in your pocket, your time here doesn't belong to you. Once past the clock, Rötlisberger lit himself a BRISSAGO.

– Qué frío, someone said.

47

Luigi was shivering ostentatiously. As though he was playing in an old silent film set in the North Pole. Piccolo rolled the sleeves of his butcher's shirt back down again. He swore. The GABA tablets he was trying to shake out of a little blue tin into his open palm were all stuck together.

– Here we go then. Pretty Boy Hügli went off with Ambrosio and the trainee into the cattle slaughter room. Rötlisberger trudged off towards the tripery and Buri down to the salting cellar. The rest of them tied on rubber aprons, got their cutting tools together, put up their shirt collars, and set off for the chilling-room.

Half carcasses to be sold as fresh meat hung in neat rows from wall to wall. Frayed necks hanging down, they were suspended from two hoists on the overhead rail on hooks through their Achilles tendons. On the floor, the last drops of blood, congealed and black. Everything looked pale in the dim light, there were no colours, only the cold and the smell of slightly rancid fat. And *the hanging of meat and the ripening of apples in cellars are processes that depend on controlled fermentation.* There were two dozen cows not meant for storage. They had been pushed in here the day before, still steaming, muscles still quivering, to cool down. Before the men could start on the day's slaughtering in the cattle room, these stiff forms had to be quartered and made ready for transport.

Clean hands took clean knives out of clean sheaths. Clean aprons rubbed against animal fat that had congealed into a protective layer. With horizontal incisions, the loins were cut away from the legs, the meat was peeled from the bones of less valuable parts to go into making sausages, ribs and coccyx were sawn through, and backs were split in two with well-aimed cleaver blows, those of steers at the thirteenth vertebra, cows' at the eleventh.

Bones cracked, a bent sawblade shrieked, fibres tore, meat smacked onto the floor, the chains of an old pulley rattled, and the new bleeding rail hummed smoothly. The fat and marrow and bonemeal from sawing collected on knives and aprons and hands. Work had begun. Huber pointed out to Hofer that his sawing was inaccurate. Hofer replied that he didn't give a damn. Porco Dio. Luigi shivered. He was working with Fernando, who kept looking away. Down the side walls behind the rows of half carcasses of beef, half their size and with paler flesh, was a row of slaughtered calves. Hanging on spreaders which were fashioned, according to the regulations, from *smooth, rust-free or rust-proofed material*, and were fitted with sharp hooks. The calves were slit up the front, with their loins splayed open, and were hooked up below the knee. They hung from the chilling-room wall as though crucified upside down. Fernando stared at their pierced hocks. Madonna! Ma qué fai tu!

No one liked working with Hugentobler. The tough Überländer was easygoing by nature, but even he was bothered by the man's sight: no one would trust the cut of his knife, no one was willing to hold down meat and bones for Hugentobler to saw. Überländer was worried for his fingers. He'll do an Ambrosio on me. Überländer shouted at Hugentobler. Either he should bloody well look where he was cutting, or else cut where he was looking. What the heck!

Hugentobler just grinned. He had the hearing of an artillery man, with a thick thatch of fur on his head to go with it.

The ventilation system was efficient, and cold air cut through the men's socks and trousers like iced water. Cold as a whore's shit. They responded by working still harder, by eager sawing and chopping. Let's get out of here as soon as we can, was the watchword. They worked faster and faster, with a dangerous lack of concern for their sharp knives.

Amid the growing rush, only Hugentobler kept to his own rhythm. He went on quietly, as though he was somewhere pleasant and temperate. Once again, it was a minor triumph for him. Because he was used to the cold as a refrigerator man, and was also the only one suitably dressed in several warm layers of swaddling wool. Hugentobler spent his days in the cooler department. And many hours in the still lower temperatures of the freezing-room. Look at those southerners, snivelling like wet poodles in the snow. Those Eyeties and dagos, they don't know what cold is. Instead of dressing properly for it. No wonder they shiver and shake in their little vests under their shirts. That's shut them up.

Hugentobler was an angular type. Everything about him was angular, head, nose, hands, feet, shoulders, everything. And his walk. All his various pullovers and cardigans and long johns stemmed the flow of his movements. Also, when younger, he'd been a victim of Bang's disease. The heaviness that had flowed into his limbs like molten lead during his violent fevers still affected him. His legs were never completely free from tiredness. He walked with a stoop, and for a split second his foot would hover in mid-air before coming down on the floor. It was not least on account of that that he was called Frankenstein, though he rarely heard it and never understood what was meant. He didn't talk much, ate several bars of chocolate a day, bought lottery tickets regularly, and was always pleased when the cutting up was finished and the slaughterers could begin outside. He liked being left on his own.

Überländer shouted at him again:

– Mind my thumb!

Piccolo put his knife away. Huber and Hofer piled the sausage-meat onto the trolleys. Let's get out of here. The tools were tidied away, and *meat must always have been hung for at least two days so that oxygen can penetrate the fibres and loosen them. Meat fibres thus tenderized can be ground up between finger and thumb, as is not the case with meat that is freshly slaughtered,* and only the short, thick-fleshed stumps of the loins were left hanging from the hoists. Überländer punched at the severed muscles from below. Pretty arses! *The hindquarters consist of rump, loin and round* and when Überländer was the last man to hurry out of the chilling-room, Hugentobler got a broom, and swept up all the meat scraps, bone shards and fat particles that had fallen on the floor.

Six o'clock.

We've punched the clock.

We fetch knives, bone-saws, cleaving-axes out of the storeroom.

We get the cattle room ready for slaughtering.

We smoke.

A basin under every tap, and a bucket of hot water for washing hands at every man's post.

I feel sluggish, and don't fight it.

In our trouser pockets under our aprons we've smuggled out the last of the warmth of the changing room.

Cold water goes in that canister. And powder from a packet. I give it a stir with a stick of wood. On the packet it says: 'To prevent

blood clotting with pigs and cows. Contents of one packet sufficient for 15 litres of blood. This corresponds approximately to the
blood of one cow or four pigs.'

Our faces and forearms are still unencrusted with slime, grease,
bile, shit and blood. Our boots are still clean. The dry rubber gear
is quite comfortable.

We smoke and breathe, quietly and deliberately. They'll be here
soon enough, the gases and exudations from the cows' bodies.

Pretty Boy Hügli is there.

Ambrosio is there.

The others are still in the chilling-room.

We're ready.

We could stick the first animals, start the slaughter, get the
disassembly line moving.

Supervisor Kilchenmann and Dr Wyss the vet are waiting too.

Kilchenmann is responsible for shooting, Dr Wyss for the
inspection of the meat.

No reason to be impatient.

Pretty Boy Hügli whistles the same tune once more and performs
his regular stunt: buckling and unbuckling his sheath, lightning
quick, buckling and unbuckling, on and off.

The tune he's whistling seems familiar to me.

Only the cows aren't there yet to be slaughtered.

Let's go out onto the ramp!

The stockyards and pens are empty. No bleating animal anywhere. Not a pig or calf or sheep jamming itself against the
fenceposts in the waiting enclosure. No chain rattle, no snorting,
no mooing, no screaming. On the railway tracks behind the yards,
the red rear light of a shunting locomotive disappears into the fog.

Here they come then, the cows, forced by butter mountains and
excess milk production into state-subsidized slaughtering pro-
grammes.

Cheap sausage-cows, the lot of them.

Why did they have to yield so much milk!

Their will to work is the death of them. In avalanches of milk
fat.

For days now, we've started off every morning by slaughtering
two or three dozen of these rubbish cows.

Over-production-conscious livestock experts discard them and sell them for scrap.

They get the cows' mouths open, and look at their teeth. The ground-down crowns and the gaps between the incisors in the lower jaw betray their age.

There's a goods wagon standing next to Krähenbühl's weighing hut.

The loading-apron.

It's cold.

With a bundle of papers jammed under his arm, Weighmaster Krähenbühl opens the lead seal on the sliding door of the goods wagon. He rests one ear against the wood of the door as he talks to Krummen. Krummen is impatient. He can see us standing around idly, and he starts hustling.

Come on, get on with it! Let's get them weighed and under the knife! We haven't got all day!

Krähenbühl won't be hustled.

All the papers have to be checked through first.

The morning breeze blows coolly over our forearms. It's not summer yet. The last remnants of warmth from the changing room have been used up.

In order to get warmed up, Ambrosio and I get out our knives and whet them in order, longest to shortest, on the whetting steel. With our thumbs we test the sharpness of the blades.

We put up the collars of our butcher's shirts. Ambrosio's longest knife is longer than his forearm.

He whets it clumsily.

With every scrape and drag he pulls a face.

He hates the sound of steel on steel.

Me too.

Now he tilts his head and blinks the cigarette smoke out of his eyes.

The finger-wide gap on the handle of the knife in his hand.

Only a couple of weeks have passed since the accident in which Ambrosio surrendered the middle finger of his right hand to the abattoir.

The jokes he made about it.

And the jokes the others made about him.

He's doing well. Very well. Grin and bear it.

The goods wagon opens up at last, and Krummen starts shouting at the cows.

Chains rattle. Hooves clatter on wooden planks.

Get a move on, you stupid cow! No more guzzling Alpine roses and dumping in streams! Hurry up, you fucking dog!

It's a bad sign with Foreman Krummen, language like that.

When he's that talkative!

And out in the abattoir behind the high fence on the edge of the beautiful city, the first cow appeared in the doorway of the cattle-cart. She hesitated and mooed. The skin crinkled between the black orbs of her eyes that looked dully out into the grey morning. The cow barged back towards the darkness of the goods wagon. Her forelegs were stiff, she had spent the journey tethered on a short rope, and *in today's markets trade in quality slaughter animals was good, with supply short and demand up, occasionally brisk to lively. But in quiet, rather dull markets, Bologna cattle changed hands at little over contract prices*, and Foreman Krummen pulled roughly at her halter and swore, while weigher Krähenbühl jabbed at the cow's skinny belly with his wad of papers and said, 'Yah, move, you stupid cow!'

The city was still asleep. The other side of the tracks from the abattoir was a grey wall of fog and concrete. Neon letters glowed: MATRA big and red, MACHINES TRACTORS small and blue. Over the outlines of the factories and warehouses a chimney climbed to an incredible height, through the fog and into heaven itself. At the top of it flickered the name VON ROLL. Next to it, smaller and black, was the chimney of the abattoir's own incinerator.

A train hurried by, with brightly lit compartment windows.

In front of the pens waited Pretty Boy Hügli, the trainee, and Ambrosio. The trainee shivered. Ambrosio was whetting one of his knives, suddenly stopped and let it fall to the ground.

– Caramba! Esa vaca! Blösch! Yo la conozco! Blösch! *and cattle are mammals, belonging to the order of artiodactyla, the sub-order of ruminants, and the family of cavicorni or bovidae*, and lame in one leg Blösch miserably followed Krummen out of the cattle wagon, and along the platform.

She looked like a pair of trestles, run down and emaciated, with her bones protruding, skin sagging and udder disfigured by machine milking. She smelled of disinfectant alcohol, urine and VASELINE, yards off. A pathetic skeleton that stopped one last time in front of the weighing cage and mooed long and deeply, shuddering from the base of her tail all down her spine.

Get on with it, hissed Krummen, and Krähenbühl grabbed her ear to read what it said on the metal badge pinned to it.

Blösch remained quiet.

Even during the humiliating ritual of weighing, she kept her aura of ancient creaturely warmth, *and domestic cattle belong to the species of European cattle. The original forms of other cattle species can still be found in the wild, but not that of domestic cattle. It was the aurochs which was still extant in Europe in the Middle Ages,* and immune to scorn, Blösch declined to lower her head to butt, but made no use of the strength that still dwelt in her great body. Even given the justification of self-defence, she declined to use any kind of force. She was civilized inside and out, horn to udder, and even on the abattoir platform she remained submissive and meek. These principles had worldwide currency, and Blösch stayed true to them to the last.

Five past seven.

Danger! Shooting!

A bang. The third. Then the impact, short and dull.

The cow squeezes her eyes shut, as though she's been dazzled.

Now get stuck in!

Krummen prowls round in a circle, pointing this way and that, doesn't know what to do with himself in this rage. With Krähenbühl, he's dragged twenty-one cows onto the weighing machine.

Fucking shit! We're a whole hour late starting. Just because some gentlemen in the city chose to stay in their beds.

None of us feels implicated.

Krummen stamps off, swearing. He gets the next cow out of the waiting pen. Another red-and-white flecked Simmental.

Offal-man Buri is waiting for the first entrails.

What a struggle! Fewer men every day, and more and more cattle!

54

Pretty Boy Hügli has stopped whistling. He looks down contemptuously at the three shot cows.

Another wagonload of rejects! Just like yesterday; nothing but dried sinews! Bone-hard cartilages! We'll be back sharpening our knives by lunchtime!

Just you be grateful you won't have to skin them, says Huber, and Hofer nods in agreement.

Andiamo, porco Dio, says Luigi.

Sticking time.

My privilege.

Come on Ambrosio, put your fags away, let's join the front.

Those Simmental cows are going to bleed.

Krummen's got them neatly laid out on the killing floor: they're lying on their right side, with their rumps bang underneath the electric lift. Once we've got them gutted and skinned we pull the bodies up with a steel hook on the hindlegs pushed through a slit between tendons and thighbones. Then we shove them on a hoist along the overhead rail for further processing.

When it's empty, the room has something in common with a church, big and white, with two wings and an aisle down the middle that leads up to the scales at one end. And the windows are a bit arched too, and made out of ornamented frosted glass.

Ambrosio is unhappy. His mouth keeps moving, saying that cow's name over and over again.

Blösch. Blösch.

Has he noticed that the animals are lying well? That way we won't have to move those tonne-weights of collapsed milk machines across the floor into the right position in their totally uncooperative inertia.

If a cow is to fall the right way, Krummen will have to have forced her weight onto the correct leg. If she then sticks her head out calmly in front of her, Kilchenmann will push the pin back in his gun, put in a cartridge and aim for the part of the skull that's easiest to penetrate.

That's at the intersection of two lines that Kilchenmann draws in his mind's eye across the cow's forehead. The first from the right ear to the left eye, the second from the left ear to the right eye.

The painless stunning of animals for the slaughter.

When Kilchenmann fires, the cow's head jerks upward about a horn's length, the neck arcs back, posture goes haywire and the cow collapses, first onto her horns, then her chest, then she finally comes to rest on her right flank. Suddenly she's lying there, so brutally suddenly, without any dignity, smashed down and stretched out on the ground.

I bend down over the first cow of the day.

I'm working.

The first one is the hardest. She's shifting and stretching, pawing with her back legs, stiffening her tail.

I feel for the rope down among the folds of hide behind the hump of the horns.

The coat is warm and bristly.

I touch the doomed animal just where I would stroke it.

Would I stroke it?

I look for the loop and the knot, try and undo it.

I know that, once stretched out like this, you'll never moo again. In a minute you'll be tied again by this same rope. I can feel the sweat and slobber and urine on it; it smells of milk and straw and cowshed. I re-tie it round the hoof of your left foreleg. How waxy that feels. I walk around your body, pull the rope, pull your front side back and expose your throat, then attach the loop to your left hindleg and bend down over your throat.

Then I stick you.

I plunge my medium-length knife into the rolls of hide on the cow's breast. I plunge my medium-length knife into the dying cells, cutting through skin and hair and muscle and sinew.

I open your throat, following the strands of neck muscle, cut you open as far as the gristly white of your windpipe. I sever muscle from muscle, vessel from vessel.

I cut, part, split, divide, cleave.

The trachea is free. I rest my knife on it, then push its curved point through it and into the cow. I hit the artery. The bright red blood bubbles up over my hands, washes over the blade and handle of my knife.

The last flood tide before your long ebb. I catch your life as it pours out, direct it into a basin I hold under your throat. You, mingled with the solution that keeps your blood from clotting.

Twenty seconds of quiet.

Time for me to draw two or three breaths.

In Africa, there are supposed to be tribes that bleed their cows instead of milking them. Every few days, a cow's throat is broached like a barrel, and after the bloodletting it's bunged shut again with grass and earth.

Rötlisberger said there were lots of ways of dying a slow death, and standing around in the sun on a reserved grassland in the middle of Africa stuffing yourself, and donating a bit of blood now and again wasn't the worst of them.

I protect my daydreaming by going to whet my knife.

Work may be interrupted for the purpose of sharpening one's knives.

How your blood rushes away.

It pours out of you, like an underground stream.

And me, the hangman's assistant, the slave on the red front, brandishing my sabre over your throat. It's me! Is it me? I turn you to good account, I fleece you.

Krummen stands over.

Don't dig it in so deep. I don't want the stuff to flow into the guts, I want it flowing out, into the basin, the centrifuge, and then as a binding agent in sausages.

When Krummen talks, he never knows what to do with his hands.

Oi, what about you? This isn't a fucking holiday camp. Get those cowheads out of here! Give the trainee a hand with the sticking. We're running late. Where's Hügli? Goddamn it, where's Hügli got to?

What do I care where Hügli is?

Let Krummen yell, he yelled all yesterday as well. Only not at the end, and he who yells last yells longest. As everyone knows.

I twist a short knife under the cow's scalp.

I'm picking your brains now.

Your ideas exposed to ridicule.

I turn you onto your horns.

The skin is tight over the lower jaw and larynx, it's easy to slit through it as far as the bloodbath of your throat.

You leer at me nakedly.

Your skull is riddled with little red-and-white veins. I cut through all the neck fibres, to the bottom vertebra.

It's easy for the blade to slip on the lubricated bones here, or else to get trapped in an articulated joint and snap off.

Done.

Off with your head.

I stand up and stretch.

You've been put to the sword.

My back aches.

Now get the tongue out of the pharynx. I wash it under the tap. It's difficult to get a firm grip on the eyes, so that I can sever optic nerve and sinew. The orbs keep slipping from my grasp. I dig deep into the sockets for a better grip.

You've seen enough.

Hungry, the shimmering nerve and the oiled membranes in the empty craters.

Who'll play?

What?

Blinde Kuh!*

As if it was all over.

Before I move on to the next throat, I slash open your udder, right through the warm tanks. The dam of calf and steer and ox must be drained. The milk must be emptied away. I stab four times. I turn away. My eyes are burning.

I can't bear to see the white streams at the back, and the red ones at the front any more.

Get away from the fringe of skin round the throat on the floor.

You're still bleeding.

*Literally 'blind cow'; blind man's bluff.

:3:

Puffing and panting. The path was steep as far as the wood. Ruedi and Prince were pulling the milk-cart while Ambrosio pushed. The rope secured four churns, each of them full to the brim. And Knuchel hadn't stinted his calves either, or reduced his supply to the household. In fact, the farmer's wife had even had to fight him off. 'What am I going to do with all that milk?' she had asked.

The fresh feeding was coming through. Knuchel clover grew on richly fertilized soil, and when it was forked into the cribs, fat and juicy and with dewy dandelion leaves in amongst it, the cows didn't need a second invitation. They ate with relish, squirting and squelching and smacking. Every last blade was tongued up, and while there was any left in front of them, none of them would chew cud. They were good working cattle, converting it all into milk and meat.

Then there was the fact that Blösch was completely restored. She had at last got over the loss of her calf, and seemed also to have forgotten the farmer's coolness towards her. For a few more days she had stood, pining and withdrawn in her corner. Slime had dribbled from her nostrils, and the splashing in her insides had continued. The farmer had guessed a lung infection. However, the vet was unable to confirm that in his diagnosis. He wasn't sure what was ailing the cow, he had said. Some internal infection? No, that was out of the question. A shot of penicillin wouldn't hurt in any case, he had added, with the syringe already in his hand. The next morning, at watering time, Blösch was once again the first one out, and with all the usual carry-on too. She stopped in the doorway, half in the cowshed, half out. She controlled the narrow pass to the watering trough. The rest of the herd mooed at her, making no secret of their impatience, but none of the bevy of possible successors would try a butt. Blösch was their lead cow, as she always had been.

59

But Check was another one who had played a part in the further rise in Knuchel's production. She had finally freshened, ten days late by the calendar. The farmer had gone and stood in the passage behind her every couple of hours. Her udder had become so swollen that she could no longer stand without treading on her own teats, and it hurt her to lie down in the straw. Knuchel had had to make up a corset for her, out of canvas and a couple of leather straps that he fastened across her back. Thereupon the chequered cow – her hide was covered with five patches the shape of fried eggs – had not only dropped her overdue calf, as white as snow, she had also begun her lactation, setting immediate new records of her own.

And what had flowed from the milk-mad Knuchel cows now stood on the milk-cart: heavy and plentiful. Ambrosio dug his toes into the gravel to push.

The path levelled out near the end of the little wood. Nettles and thorn bushes fringed a little patch of grass. Ruedi stopped and sat down. The silence was broken by the cry of a child floating up from Knuchel's farm, by an isolated outburst of pig squealing and rattling milking gear. The farm itself could not be seen from there.

'Why he won't take his tractor up to the cheese dairy!' said Ruedi. He was out of breath. 'Even Kneubühler takes his piddling 50 litres in his LANDROVER. We must be off our heads.' He rested his back against a root and gazed up at the sky.

Ambrosio took out a cigarette. Virginia tobacco, a PARISIENNE. 'Es de aquí,' he said, broke it in two, and passed one half of it to Ruedi. He put the pack back in his trouser pocket and looked for his lighter. It consisted of some tinder rope rolled into a ball and a simple flint. He flicked the tiny iron wheel with his thumb. The wheel rubbed against the flint, a spark caught on the tinder, Ambrosio blew on the little ember, and lit his half cigarette.

Prince stood panting by the cart, ready to go.

'Wonder if there'll be more of that stupid talk there again today?' asked Ruedi, coughing.

'Tranquilo, tranquilo. No te gusta fumar?' asked Ambrosio.

'If they could hear themselves . . . look, here comes the field-mouser, Fritz Mäder.' Ruedi raised one arm, and pointed up at a ridge.

Like a deer, the field-mouser pushed his way through the bushes at the edge of the wood. He leaned forward and passed through them, untroubled by the undergrowth. The foliage bowed, branches and twigs slid along his body, brushing his grey cape and his face. The field-mouser made no effort to avoid them. The branches closed up again in his wake. He had a stick which he didn't use. On his back he carried a wooden box. He stopped and straightened up. He was a tall man.

'Come on, let's go,' said Ruedi.

'Vamos,' said Ambrosio.

Ambrosio could already call all Knuchel's cows by name, and he knew their moods and preferences. He could steam the potatoes for the pigs by himself. He knew how the farmer's wife wanted her vegetable patch watered: the lettuces more than the beans, and the tomato plants no more than three times a week. However, he hadn't yet been able to discover the cause of the rhythmic banging that sometimes made the wooden walls of his attic shake in the evening, when he was lying on his bed smoking, but gradually, he was getting accustomed to life on the farm. On the other hand, he got little change out of the village. He would never be able to read those faces. All that loose flesh and muscle round those thick lips when they gawped at him from their farms. The probing of the eyes, uncertain behind a veneer of pride. And would he ever manage to scratch his head with the same hand with which he raised his milker's cap? Never. Nor would he ever be able to give emphasis to something he'd said by thumping his right fist against his right hip in the local manner. He might practise for a hundred years, and still not be able to roll his sleeves up over his biceps with the exquisite precision he could observe on the village square. He would never learn how to keep one arm calmly concealed behind his back while making expansive gestures with the other in illustration of some evidently momentous words. No, he would never master the art of being an Innerwalder. The language was another barrier. For a long time he had suspected that the greater part of communication there was silent anyway. The words would follow after, but so incredibly slowly, it was as though they'd first had to be invented. Ambrosio was able to tell them apart, and already he tried to arrange syllables, or sometimes just to count them. But the words rarely seemed able to achieve much on their own. There were some faces that would look embarrassed as soon as the lips began moving. On others, the brow would furrow straightaway. It was only later, always later, that something might happen. The words would be spoken, then there would be a silence, and then, only then, would there be an answer or a reaction. How could he ever learn that silence?

A lot of things would remain inaccessible, forever beyond him. He could feel it and see it. He saw it in expressions and gestures, he saw it in the farms, the fields and pastures. All the houses in the village had broad, powerfully framed doors that creaked and groaned on their hinges, and they had heavy granite treads like boundary stones in front of the worn oak thresholds. The fields covered every inch of available land, they had been ploughed and harrowed and rolled to the edge of the path and beyond. Small-checked, spread out according to some unfathomable design, they surrounded the village. Every day would bring something to astonish Ambrosio, and every day he would discover fresh instances of ornately executed fieldwork: how the tracks of machines and wheels would go meandering along, zigzagging, fitting the contours of the hills, tracks elegantly following the natural curves, tracks that graced the landscape like lacework. And he saw it in the pastures as they greened for the cattle waiting in their cowsheds. These pastures were on steep slopes that were less easy to cultivate. And yet, not only were they fenced in for the cows, they were reinforced, barricaded, protected to a height of 2 metres, with liberal use of barbed wire.

Ambrosio would never understand it.

They unloaded in front of the cheese dairy in the square.

Securing ropes were untied. Long threads of spittle hung from the panting tongues of dogs. Horseshoes, gumboots and wooden clogs scraped the asphalt. Up on his platform, the cheeser puffed out his chest. Whey steamed. It smelt of cowsheds and salt and Friday night. Hands in trouser pockets, hands scratching, hands resting on steering wheels, hands raised in greeting, hands clasped round churns heavy with milk, hands pointing, hands talking. Sinews tautened and muscles bulged under green farmer's cloth. Hey up! Milk was hoisted from carts, was carried off, weighed, admired, written down, milk flowed and hands wrote, cigarettes

62

slipped out of yellow packs, tongues clicked, there was laughter, and in between pauses, talk: it was no longer news that Knuchel had his cows milked by a foreigner, but had they heard what this Spaniard was doing on the dungheap of an evening? Scratches, and some premature laughter. He was practising the pole-vault with a dungfork. And why was it that he no longer took his baths in the pigs' feeding trough? It was too deep for him, and anyone who didn't believe it could ask the man himself, because there he was, just arriving with the Knuchel milk.

Hands laughed, hands stroked thick necks, hands pointed at Ambrosio. Ruedi grew red.

And did they know why the Knuchels' dog Prince had such an offended expression nowadays? It was because he was having to share his kennel with the foreigner. And why did the carpenter and the blacksmith go to Knuchel's farm? The smith was putting an extra wheel on the dungbarrow, and the carpenter was building a bridge across the gutter. Glances dropped contentedly. Jaws wobbled and heads twisted with laughter. Ruedi and Ambrosio lugged four churns to be weighed. Yes, by God, he was a right little runt, someone said, but the farmer was singing his praises all the same. But then what else could he do, seeing as he'd got him, came the reply. Now how much would a fellow like that cost, came another question. Oh, they were cheap, dirt cheap, you couldn't get a proper milker for wages like they got. Yes, cheap, said another, a real milker would cost you a lot more, and they weren't easy to find either, but then at least you knew where you were. A foreigner in your cowshed! Next thing, you'd have the swallows flying under your cows. In fact, they weren't all that cheap, came the objection, where they came from they hardly had enough to eat, and they were earning good money over here. Yes, exactly, otherwise they'd just have stayed at home, it was argued. And hands dug deeper in trouser pockets, and fingers poked in ears and noses.

Ruedi shook his head. 'Blatherers!' he said. Ambrosio was unperturbed. He joined in the laughter, grinning up at the sarcastic faces.

'Ruedi, hombre! Vamonos!'

Ambrosio lay on his bed, smoking. He had the lid of a tin of milking fat for an ashtray. He played with his lighter. He had taken off his socks and draped them over the shafts of his boots. An open airmail letter had fallen onto the floor. Ambrosio felt the air on his toes. He drew on his cigarette. The lid lifted on his belly. He blew a smoke ring. It climbed towards the ceiling, and slowly dissolved. He blew another one, and a third.

The sound of chains rattling came up through the wooden walls. Vacas no fuman, thought Ambrosio. What do cows do in the evening? What goes on in their heads? Those great heads on the end of those great bodies! Vacas grandes como elefantes. Yes, he would tell them that at home, how big, how unbelievably huge the cows were. And how greedy.

During the feed before the evening milking, Ambrosio had noticed how Blösch wouldn't even touch her own pile to begin with. She would ignore the portion in front of her, and go for her neighbour Mirror's instead. Greedily she pushed herself against the bars of the manger, and stuck her neck across into her crib. With cowtypical gulps, Blösch plucked hay from Mirror's ration. She collared one tuft after another. It was only when there was nothing left within reach to steal that Blösch started in on her own hay.

Ambrosio listened to the cows shift from one foot to another, and then one after the other they lay down. He imagined the way their dewlaps would dangle into the straw as they ruminated.

Caramba! De nuevo! The banging began again. Dull and rhythmic. Boom. Boom. Boom. The wood panelling shook. Ambrosio stubbed out his cigarette. It sounded as though heavy objects were being smashed against the wall downstairs. Ambrosio threw his lighter in the corner. He sat up on his bed. One of the pictures on the wall showed an old man sitting on a bench in front of a farmhouse smoking a pipe. The farmhouse resembled Knuchel's: wooden, with an overhanging roof. The old man had on a black woolly hat, and was surrounded by children who were listening to him, as quiet and attentive as Knuchel's children at table.

The banging would not stop. Boom. Boom. Boom. Ambrosio went over to the window. The floor felt cold to his bare feet.

Ambrosio looked at the window. His fingers had passed over the

64

glossy frame and the joins many times already. It was a window with two casements that fitted trimly and tightly into their frame. Ambrosio held the iron bolt by its brass knob. He rested his forehead on the back of his right hand. He loosened the catch, then pushed the bolt back. The window shut itself, wood pressing against wood. Ambrosio opened the small upper casement, shut it, opened it again, shut it again. He pressed his nose against the lower pane. Outside, the night was grey over the hills on the highlands. Car headlights flashed and disappeared. On the left, a lantern flickered in the pasture. Its yellow light moved this way and that, as though there was someone moving around down there. The old man with the stick and the box on his back? The wild mouse-trapper? Ambrosio lay down on his bed again. The banging had stopped. Still he could find no peace.

'Come on, Thérèse, don't sleep at table! Give me your plate. Not that one, the other! You too, Ambrosio, there's enough there, have some more, for God's sake!' Farmer Knuchel plied the serving fork to such effect that the gravy splashed right across the table. 'Meat and sausages are the best vegetables,' he said, and then the farmer's wife remarked, with her mouth full, 'That's you all over isn't it? A platter of tongue and pork, you've always gone for, but what's the matter with your fingernail? Why's it not getting any better? You sure you don't want the doctor to see it?' She looked at the bandage on the farmer's hand.

'I expect he's applied some cow dung on it,' said Grandma.

'What are you talking about!' Knuchel took up his fork in his left hand, and kept his right under the table. 'Pour me some more wine instead, would you.'

'You know you should be more careful, otherwise you'll get blood poisoning. Ugh, watch yourself,' warned the farmer's wife.

'Bah, stuff! Have another piece. We won't want to be heating these pigs' ears up again. What about that tail, no one want it?' Knuchel pointed at the meat platter. His neck muscles moved as he chewed, and fat dribbled from the corners of his mouth. He swallowed and nodded, 'You know what? We could keep one of the piglets in the third pen for ourselves, fatten it up for the autumn. Pork and beans, lovely.'

'So you want to have the butcher come round again after all?' asked the farmer's wife.

'Why not? They're a fine litter, and you'll know what they've been eating. And you can keep an eye on the butcher, so you know what goes into the sausages. I'll go and mark one of them with a blue riband. Then you can see that he gets the best stuff to eat, and roots around in the fresh air a bit.'

'But once Überländer actually shows up, you'll hardly be able to wait till he packs his knives and goes again. You just about chased him off the farm the last time he came.'

'He got through half the wine in the house! Everything, even the sausages, had to have wine mixed in, and he was always having to try a bit first. Come off it. He was off his head last autumn,' Knuchel protested, then stood up to go.

'What are you doing about the cows? Are you going to leave them out on the pasture?' asked the farmer's wife.

Knuchel stopped and scratched his throat. 'Let's wait and see for another day or two.'

'But you've got the new fence up, the wind has dropped, it would save you a bit of work in the cowshed.'

'It's not the work I'm bothered about. It's more the hay. The grass won't run away. It's not as mild as all that either. In the cowshed they're flailing their tails like anything. There's a good chance of more rain.'

'But you used not to stand waiting, you said the air and exercise was good for them. The earlier the better you always said. Nothing's the matter, is it? Are they not all healthy, or something? It's more than that half bushel of hay, is it?'

Ruedi slid about on the corner bench. 'It's Bossy, Mother. She's gone and kicked over the bucket.'

'So that's it. Bossy's spilt her milk. Why didn't you tell me right away? You can be pretty tight-lipped sometimes. Well, it'll have to be tomorrow or the day after.' Knuchel's wife pushed her chair back, and started collecting the plates. 'So that nervous cow has gone and upset her milk again,' whispered the grandmother.

'What's done is done.' The farmer shrugged his shoulders. 'Shouldn't cry over spilt milk. Here, who's that coming?'

Prince barked, and the children rushed out through the kitchen door, followed by Ambrosio.

A black MERCEDES 190 diesel stopped in front of Knuchel's cowshed.

'It's the mayor in his MERC!' Ruedi called into the kitchen.

Ambrosio threw Prince a bone. He sniffed at it, then went on barking. 'Our Prince doesn't eat pork bones,' said Thérèse.

The mayor asked the children where their father was, gave Stini a pinch on the cheek, and surveyed the yard. He took his hat off in front of the door, scraped his feet on the threshold as on a doormat, and said good evening. Still scraping his soles, he said: 'If I'd known you were eating dinner, I'd have driven on. I didn't want to trouble you, I had some business in town, and I was coming home the back way, so I thought, why don't you just stop by?'

With a look at the scraping town shoes, Knuchel asked the mayor inside, and the farmer's wife said, 'Oh, we've been finished some time.' And Grandmother said why didn't he, and if he liked, there was still one pig's ear left, and the beans were soon warmed up.

'Or would you prefer a coffee?' asked the farmer, 'or a tot of schnapps?'

'No trouble, please for goodness sake. I was just popping by. But a cup of coffee would be nice, if you happened to have – '

'Now come on,' protested the farmer's wife. 'A coffee's no trouble at all.'

The mayor set his hat down on the table, and perched on the edge of a chair. 'Well, you got them on the pasture yet?' he asked Knuchel.

'He's not in any kind of rush this year,' Grandma replied, while Knuchel was getting back to the table.

'I see you've got your new fence up. They're good posts, aren't they? A fine fence,' the mayor continued.

'Well, you do what you can. I put it up with the Spaniard.'

'A useful man is he, your Spaniard?'

'Yes, so he is. And we need to get the milking done and all, here in the country.'

'Good milkers are thin on the ground, aren't they?' said the mayor.

'Yes,' said Knuchel.

'Anything on that calf of the prize cow's? You remember what I said? Did you give it another thought?'

'Blösch's calf? He's nursing well, putting on weight fast. We've got enough milk, after all.'

'So you'll fatten him up and give him to Schindler? But I told you – '

'Even last week Schindler was telling me that AI calves are fetching more now. The prices are going up like crazy. 100 kilos dead weight – '

'But Hans, summer's on the way, they can't be worth that much now.'

'If only you knew,' Knuchel laughed. 'The people in the towns only want the very best quality. Schindler's having to go as far as the French cantons to get all the veal he needs. He buys every one he can lay his hands on. He told me if I had ten calves ready fattened, he'd take the lot. The heavier, the better.'

'Yes, but when he starts doing his accounts, then it will all sound different. Then he'll be telling you how he can't make anything, how he's always having to put in money of his own, and how the butchers are getting out of having to pay him his full whack. If one's not an out-and-out fox all over then at the very least the liver will have been no good, and you'll be the one to pay. Come on Hans, we know Schindler.'

'That's what I keep telling him, but he never listens to me,' lamented the farmer's wife.

'That's not true,' protested Knuchel. 'Don't make our calf-dealer sound any worse than he is. It's all down to the calves, how well we look after them, what we feed them on, real milk or just imported powder. And us with our pure well water. No, Schindler's never deducted anything off what he pays me.'

'Well, God knows what you feed them on! Everyone says there's no calf as fat and well grown as a Knuchel calf.'

Knuchel blushed. 'Bah, don't believe it. You'd think we whipped a dozen eggs in with their milk each time. You, Thérèse,' he said after a while, 'go and get me my pipe from the parlour.'

'Here, have one of these!' The mayor pulled a packet of RÖSSLI STUMPEN from his breast pocket.

Knuchel hesitated.

'Go on!'

'Thanks,' said Knuchel.

'And the Spaniard, is he around? I could pick up his papers and take them with me, seeing as I happen to be here.'

'He'll be around. Probably in the paddock, playing with the children. Thérèse, go and call Ambrosio,' said the farmer's wife.

'What papers are you referring to, and what are they for?' asked Knuchel.

'Oh, passport, residence permit, work permit, so we can have him properly entered in our records. Then people will know who he is.'

'A man ought to be allowed to work without having to get special permission. All this writing things down that goes on.'

'Everything has to be kept in order, though, because of taxes and so on. You've got to keep an eye on foreigners, Hans. They can't be allowed to just do what they want. They've already got them in town, unregistered foreign workers.'

'Yes, in factories or on building sites, where they take on anyone who turns up. But it's different here in the country. We know what work means here. You can't compare our Ambrosio to some illegal migrant worker!'

'But he is a foreigner, and so he has to be registered.'

Ambrosio had been playing 'gallina ciega' with Stini and little Hans in the paddock. To the children, the game was known as 'blinde kuh'. They tied a red handkerchief over Ambrosio's eyes and he had to try and catch them. To their amusement, he had crowed exuberantly like a cock, while the children had mooed. When he heard Thérèse calling him, Ambrosio took the handkerchief off. Straightaway little Stini called out, 'Now give me back my hanky!'

In the kitchen Ambrosio was told to get his papers.

He looked in puzzlement at the Knuchel faces, shrugging his shoulders and shaking his head.

'Residence permit, identification papers,' said the mayor.

'No entiendo,' Ambrosio shrugged his shoulders again.

'Birth certificate, driving licence, work permit, family book, vaccination certificates, anything you've got in writing.' The mayor spoke in a loud voice.

69

'By God, he hasn't got a clue what you're talking about,' said Knuchel, and held out his left hand in order to mime writing on it with his right. He drew exaggeratedly large circles on the air.

Still louder than before, the mayor resumed: 'Marriage certificate, pension card, visa, entry from the police register, health certificate, employers' references, passport, immigration police!'

The farmer's wife and Grandmother gasped. 'Po . . . Po . . . Po . . . Police?!' The farmer was just as surprised.

'The immigration police,' said the mayor. 'Just the papers from the immigration police.'

'Quieren ver a los documentos?' Ambrosio had understood.

He returned with his passport and several official forms in his hands.

'There, that's that,' said the mayor, 'our clerk does everything by the letter. Everything has to be just right.'

'Ah, he's worse than the co-op manager he is,' said Knuchel.

The mayor unfolded Ambrosio's papers, and flicked through them with an inquisitive eye.

'A passport,' said Thérèse, who was standing by.

'A blue one,' said Ruedi.

Ambrosio watched his papers disappear into the mayor's pockets. He left the kitchen without saying anything.

The mayor was satisfied. He sipped the last of his coffee, got to his feet, picked up his hat and asked: 'Could I take a quick peek at your cowshed and see how the calf's doing?'

'Yes, all right.'

The twelve Knuchel cows were lying in the straw in front of the closed manger. They turned their heads towards the door, radiating boredom. The three calves scrambled to their feet.

'God bless,' said the mayor as he stepped inside.

'That's him, Blösch's calf,' said Knuchel, pointing at one of them.

'This one?' The major touched his skin, pressed and pinched him fore and aft, stepped back a pace to consider size and proportions, stepped forward again, and looked under the tail and belly. He loosened the rope on the muzzle, peered into the calf's mouth, thumbed back an eyelid and inspected the white membrane. 'Ah, that's a fine sight,' he said. 'He would have made a fine bull, and there you go, fattening him up just like any ordinary calf. A pity.'

Knuchel gave the mayor a cloth. He wiped his hands on it, the fingers locked, sought out a clean bit, then went on kneading each other. Without taking his eyes off the calf, he stopped and cleared his throat. 'You know, Hans, er, it's not that I want to make trouble or anything, but I had a visit from the cheeser. He's got a point, you know. I noticed it myself earlier. There isn't a doctor's certificate among the papers he showed me.'

'Now, goddamn it!' Knuchel exclaimed.

'The cheeser was saying he was entitled to insist, it's in the regulations.'

'What a bloody idiot! Ruedi told me there was trouble brewing. Even the manager was making a fuss over a pair of trousers. And now the cheeser too! Jesus! Why are they all out to fix our Spaniard? He's a decent fellow, hasn't done anyone any harm, and he's dependable. And all done in that hole-and-corner way!'

'Don't you get so wrought up over it. You shouldn't pay any attention to the gossip either. I mean, they had it in for the Italian before. The cheeser just thinks something's wrong with the milk again.'

'An idiot he is, that big mouth!'

'Well, you know him, he always has to grumble a bit, otherwise you might start to overlook him. But then you can't call a cow brindled unless there's a bit of white on her.'

'So what's supposed to be the matter with my milk? See for yourself! They lie properly, they eat properly, they drink properly. No, mayor, my cowshed is a damn sight tidier than that cheeser's front room!'

'He thinks there might be germs.'

Knuchel looked beyond the line of cows lying in the straw, took the RÖSSLI STUMPEN out of his mouth, and said quietly: 'So it's the milking machines again, right? Hygiene, right. Hygiene! That's what they say. But you tell me, what's cleaner about a machine? The main thing is, you look after the animals, that you wash and wipe the gear twice a day, and that you give them enough straw. What's going to go wrong there? It's hardly Ambrosio's fault if the cheeser can't make cheese, and the milk goes sour in his hands.'

'I was just telling you, Hans. Maybe you should send him to see a doctor here, then he'd have a certificate. Rules are rules and you have to keep a clean cowshed, the cheeser's right enough there.'

'We're bringing too much milk for his liking, I know. And it's got more fat in it too. More than he knows what to do with, the idiot!'

The mayor made to leave.

'It's stupid, complaining the whole time, but if ever *you* want something done, you've got a hell of a job persuading them,' muttered Knuchel as he shut the cowshed door. He hasn't sent the field-mouser round either. I've already told him twice that would be more useful than driving round the highlands spouting nonsense. He could feel eyes drilling holes in his back.

He dropped the RÖSSLI STUMPEN in the gutter, where it hissed quietly.

'Well, I'll be going then,' said the mayor.

'What, are you off already?' The farmer's wife came up, watering can in hand. All sorts of goodbyes were exchanged, profuse thanks expressed, and apologies. With every backward step he took, hat in hand, towards his car, the mayor mumbled another 'thank you' or 'goodbye', and 'thanks again for the coffee', he said twice.

In the kitchen, Grandmother had also gone up to the kitchen window to watch the MERCEDES leave. 'At least Schindler always has some sweets for the children when he comes,' she said.

It hadn't escaped Ambrosio that Sundays on the Knuchel farm were also a celebration of work. The feeding of the animals was conducted in freshly washed clothes, cleaning and milking were done with new creases in the trousers of farmers' green. Knuchel took his time, he teased his animals affectionately, there were smiles and laughter, many interruptions. The grass for the feed was cut a little later in the day, and the children came along too. Little Hans was allowed up on the tractor, and he even held the steering wheel. Stini brought her straw doll along.

In the Knuchel kitchen, Grandmother was in Sunday mood. She drank an extra cup of coffee, and the farmer's wife had her white apron on.

There was even more chiming than usual with the milking gear at the water trough. The milking pails were plunged deep into the water. Everything had to look neat and new, everything was picked up twice, held in the hand, and looked at from above and below, from in front and behind.

If the farmer had been slow and deliberate with the cows after breakfast, so was Ambrosio now with the sweeping. He swept with a birch broom. He swept the hayloft, he swept the path, he swept the threshing floor, he swept the feed passage, he swept leisurely, always from left to right, he swept each little straw from the planks over the manure pit, he swept the concrete terrace in front of the house and the gravel area behind it, he swept the kennel, he swept the ashes from the place where the potatoes were steamed, he swept underneath the wooden trough where the pig feed was stored, he swept from the moment the milking had been finished, he swept as he had never swept before, he swept as he had never guessed it might be possible to sweep, he swept the way Knuchel liked it done.

A shot cracked in the silence.

It exploded like thunder on a clear sky, from the wood over the farm. And then a second and a third. Ambrosio stiffened, and the birch broom slid from his grasp. 'Qué pasa? Maldita sea!' Nothing happened. Stini and Hans went on playing in the yard without looking up, Ruedi pored over his moped engine that he'd taken to pieces over by the granary, Prince snoozed in his kennel. Not a trace of excitement anywhere. No windows were flung open in the house. No one came running out from behind the dungheap with arms aloft, nor did anything tumble out of the sky onto the broad farmhouse road, no Knuchel hen stopped pecking in the chicken-run, no Knuchel cock thought it worth his while to crow.

Heavy gunshots now followed in quick succession. Ambrosio looked inside the cowshed. Not one cow had climbed to her feet in the straw, only the calves on their wobbly legs were upright, staring as ever.

'Hijo de puta!' Ambrosio grabbed at his bald patch. Farmer Knuchel was leaving the kitchen with a gun over his shoulder. He had changed his clothes, and wasn't paying any attention to the shooting. Ambrosio started feeling for his cigarettes and lighter. His fingers fumbled along the seams and rivets of his trousers without finding the entrance to a pocket.

'What are you standing there for, looking like a stuck calf? Have I grown horns suddenly?' The farmer laughed. 'This is my carbine, and we're shooting today.' Prince emerged from the kennel and crept round the farmer's legs. Knuchel bent down and wiped his toecaps with a rag, then, satisfied with the result, marched off.

Farmer Knuchel marched steadily up the track from the farm, and off into the countryside. He looked neither to left nor right, he marched away as though he could hear a drum in the distance, or perhaps a tune played by the village musicians. He had a brown felt hat on his head, he swung his left arm and gripped his rifle sling in his right. He held it in his fist, just below his left shoulder, and so tightly that the veins and sinews appeared on the back of his hand. Knuchel walked purposefully. He listened to his boots creaking and crunching on the gravel. The sound corresponded to the way he felt, it even gave him inspiration. He felt good. Here I am, Hans Knuchel from the Knuchel farm, I have twelve fine cows in my cowshed, and pigs and hens, and I grow good food for them on my own ground. Don't let anyone try and pull my green carpet away from under me. No one's going to knock me off my stride, or block my path, or else! Stomach in, shoulders back, chin out, I can walk tall here, I've grown up on this soil, and so has my bread. With every step, he enjoyed the sense of his own weight, with every pace he caressed his own earth underfoot. Already he had reached the edge of the wood.

Ambrosio watched him stepping out, watched the brass on his gun barrel glinting in the sun. He stopped patting along his seams and rivets, picked up his birch broom and hurried off after the farmer. The shooting was going on without interruption now.

Ambrosio flapped and fluttered up the path, he tripped and tramped and trotted along the edge of the road, for a couple of paces he tried to break into a run, then he swore: 'Hijo de puta! Qué país!' and he went back to his reeling progress of before, wrestling the while with his broom, which he first carried over his shoulder, then trailed behind him like a tail, and then used like a stick, rowing through the air. Quite out of breath, he reached the edge of the wood, he hurried through it, leaning forward like a hen in too much of a hurry, and in constant danger of falling flat on her beak.

Knuchel had left the village road that led up to Innerwald, and

74

was making for a little rise. It was pasture land, fenced in the Innerwald manner with barbed wire stretched from post to post. Ambrosio had passed this little hill four times every day, it was a hump, a hillock, like many others in the highlands, but now there were three red flags stuck in the ground here, red cloth on 2-metre-high poles dotted on the pasture. And it was behind there that the shots were going off.

The farmer disappeared behind the hill, Ambrosio could just see his brown felt hat. He took the broomstick in both hands and slowed his pace. Creeping along, ducking his head, he approached one of the flags. The shots were so close now, he could hear them whistling, feel them ripping the air. No longer did they boom and echo, they went off smartly: crack! crack! crack! They pained him, almost as if they were exploding in his head.

Ambrosio left the path behind the red flag, went into the grass, took a few more steps, and suddenly flung himself onto the ground. The shooting was coming from a barn very close to him, and he'd almost strayed into the line of fire. The scene imprinted itself onto his mind in a flash: there were gun barrels levelled, behind them men lying on their bellies on brown mats with contorted faces, jaws pressed to gun butts, eyes clenched shut, and limbs shaken from the recoil after firing. A picture of pain and fury – here in this gently undulating landscape? In the middle of these carefully tended pastures?

Ambrosio lay down flat and buried his face in the grass. He heard the empty cartridges tinkle onto the stone floor of the barn, and how the locks of the gun snapped shut between shots. Dragging the broomstick along by his side, he crawled back, not yet daring to stand up. He was scrabbling through the grass on his belly when a hand gripped him by the ankle. He kicked himself free, turned and leapt to his feet, brandishing the broomstick.

'Ma che cosa, che cosa fai tu? Piano, piano!'

Ambrosio looked into a pair of dark eyes that were no Knuchel eyes, and into a half-laughing, half-scared face where there was no fleshy pink blob, but a proud nose, narrow and slightly hooked, far finer altogether than a Knuchel nose. Ambrosio swore in his surprise: 'Qué cabrón! Hijo de puta! Un italiano! Eres italiano. Un italiano en este pueblo!'

'Che vuoi! italiano, italiano! Mi chiamo Luigi, eh sí, Luigi!' said the other.

'Tu eres Luigi?' asked Ambrosio.

'Sí, sí, Luigi!'

'Me llamo Ambrosio yo.'

'Fa piacere,' said Luigi and pointed to the broom that Ambrosio was still holding threateningly aloft.

Ambrosio stood helplessly in the middle of this pasture, pointed his broom in every direction, and listened to the cracking and whistling of gunfire and listened also to the vowel-rich words Luigi was addressing to him. Luigi spoke joyfully and exuberantly, but Ambrosio wasn't listening to what he was saying, only to the sound of it, the melody, and it calmed him down. When Luigi held out his hand to him a second time, he shook it and followed him, still talking and gesticulating wildly, back down the hill. Luigi stopped behind another hump on the slope. 'Ecco,' he said. From this position, they could see the whole shooting range. The marksmen's barn was on the left, and up on the right, towards the village, what they were aiming at. Black-and-white targets disappeared into the ground, only to resurface again, accompanied by red pointers.

'Hijo de puta!' Ambrosio wanted to turn away. Away from this banging. What kind of secrets would the other hills be concealing? What was behind the one over there? What was behind that wood, and what did the brown patch of earth over there signify? A bottomless abyss in the midst of treacherous green? And why was everything around him stacked up on itself? One fence on another, hill behind hill, mountain after mountain, right up to the cloudless blue sky? Never again would he take a chance like that.

Even before the church bell started tolling and drove the men of Innerwald out of their shooting barn, singly or in groups, but all of them with their fists round their rifle slings, Luigi was opening the door of the cowshed on the Boden farm. He did so with dramatic gestures, fiddled around for an unnecessarily long time with the bolts, gabbling away wildly all the while. It was only when he switched the lights on that he became hushed and almost reverent.

At the click of a switch, the twenty cows lying in the straw stopped their ruminating. Luigi waved to Ambrosio, and then in long Sunday strides he paced about like a sergeant in a barracks yard, clapped his hands and shouted: 'Hey, ufe! ufe! ufe there!'

Ambrosio watched as one cow after another jerked her head backwards and got to her knees, how folded hindlegs searched for solid footing in the straw, how they already lifted their cruppers slightly, how they stretched their hip joints and at the same time moved out their right forelegs and set down their right feet. Ambrosio saw that bits of straw were shaken from skin and udder no less energetically than on the Knuchel farm, that evidently all Simmental cows were equally orderly, and that the Boden farm cows needed only half a minute to carry out the order to get up out of the straw and stand to attention in two tidy rows. 'Muy bonito,' he said, nodding to Luigi. 'Muy bonito.' Yet it hadn't escaped him: there was no bull in the cowshed here either.

Encouraged by this demonstration of obedience on the part of his cows, Luigi demanded of one last restless animal that she stop twirling her tail. He gave her a smack on the crupper, and punched her. When a kick on the left hindleg met with no more success, Luigi laughed to cover his disappointment, and turned back to Ambrosio, gabbling about the peculiar character of the cows in the prosperous land.

Ever since their meeting at the firing range Luigi had been laughing and talking and swearing without stopping. He had also plucked at Ambrosio's overlarge clothes. He himself was wearing a brown suit, yellow shirt and black shoes. On the meadow overlooking the Innerwald firing range, he had produced a white pocket handkerchief and spread it out on the grass before sitting down. Thereupon, without interrupting the spate of his conversation, he had pulled down his cuff-links from inside his jacket sleeves. Ambrosio had stood and watched, propped up on his broom. And then it had been the turn of his necktie. As Luigi had plucked away at it, he had come to talk about the shooting range. He had explained the significance of the various pointers that were hoisted up after every shot. Luigi knew when one of the Innerwalders had scored a bullseye. The shooting was quite good today, he'd said, and when everything about his suit had been set to rights, he had pointed down to the Boden farm, and the scattered fields and pastures that belonged to it. Over there was the barn, the building next to it was the bakehouse, and behind it were the property of the retired farmer and the new cowshed. The new cowshed over which he had his own 'camera', his own room with running water, 'acqua calda e fredda'. Ambrosio had got out his cigarettes and offered Luigi one, whereupon he had been invited to come and take a closer look at the Boden farm.

As they had left the cowshed, Luigi carried on with his explanations. He knew the sky over Innerwald, he had discovered which way the wind blew on the highlands, and talking the while, he conducted Ambrosio to 'camera mia'. He had a bottle of GRAPPA there, and some NESCAFÉ as well.

The room was in a newly constructed farm building, which housed a tractor garage and machine shed as well as open accommodation for fattening animals. The new boards creaked under the lino as they went in, and they could hear animals breathing, and, at regular intervals, a humming noise that was caused by the automatic watering gear which hadn't been given a separate supply source. In the middle of the room was the bed, with a table next to it, and on the ceiling, a piece of flypaper on which insects, mostly caught only by one foot or wingtip on the honey-yellow surface, had frozen in extraordinary positions.

Luigi put the GRAPPA on the table, tipped some coffee powder into two glasses, held them under the hot tap of the wash basin, got out of the raffia suitcase on the floor a couple of boxes of lump sugar stamped REMN. OX INNERWALD, and offered Ambrosio one of the glasses, while he stirred the other with his finger. Meanwhile, he was explaining, pronouncing the 'k's and 'ch's as 'g's, all about the Gnuggel farm and the 'chisser', punctuating his melodious Italian with the occasional proudly rendered bit of local dialect, even the odd oath, calling several men 'fugging greeples'. However, the field-mouser, whom he had praised and whom he had much to be thankful for, was his 'golleague'.

Luigi warned Ambrosio 'in nome di Gesù Cristo' not to go too near the shooting hut again, he would be taking his life in his hands, because no one here could take a joke anyway, least of all during their target practice. He himself had once poked his nose in there when he was still new in the village. He had really just wanted to see what was going on. And 'mamma mia', two of them had dropped him in the nettles. 'Wops' had no business in the shooting hut, it wasn't a fairground booth, they had said. And suspected him of being a spy. 'Attenzione! Molto attenzione!' said Luigi, with his finger wagging.

After a few swallows from the bottle of GRAPPA, Ambrosio began to thaw out too. First, he just said that he had a bottle of COÑAC in his own room, but then he became more expansive, until he too became quite carried away by the sound of his own voice, and bubbled and talked away quite as eagerly as Luigi. Soon they were both talking at once, and filled the little room with their languages. They talked and talked, with shining eyes, amusing themselves so much that they frequently burst out laughing, toasted each other, and pointing at the broom which Ambrosio had left in the corner, ironically aped a few rifle drills. The bottle on the table was empty before they'd even begun to ask themselves how much the other could understand of his talk.

When the bells rang out to signal the end of the service, Luigi accompanied his guest out to the Boden farm pastures. Slapping a fencepost with his palm, he repeated his suggestion that Ambrosio should come along to the 'Ogs' in the afternoon, to meet his 'golleague' the field-mouser. Ambrosio accepted, shook hands with Luigi, hoisted the broom onto his shoulder, and started on the walk home, past the hill with the red flags. So long as the bells were ringing, the shooting wouldn't start again, Luigi had shouted after him.

In the little wood above the Knuchel farm, a woman came towards him on a bicycle. She climbed the slope effortlessly, and pedalled silently past Ambrosio. He had stepped down into the ditch, and marvelled at the woman's enormous thighs and equally massive calves.

As he turned into the farm road, he saw Knuchel. He was standing in a pasture and prodding about in a molehill with the toe of his boot, before bending down to continue with his hands. Shaking his head, he got up again, and, seeing Ambrosio, showed him a couple of earthworms wriggling away. 'They're good for the soil,' he said, 'this here isn't!' and kicked at the molehill.

'Let's go in and eat,' he said. 'There's boiled beef today.'

*

79

In the quiet evening hours, and on Sundays, when there was no work to keep him from his broodings, and the longing for his wife and family made him particularly melancholy, it had become a necessity for Ambrosio to go and sit in the byre among the cows. Here he was able to think and dream, it was here that he felt sheltered and understood, ever since that night he'd spent there, when he'd first arrived in the prosperous land. It smelled just like the cowsheds of Coruña: of straw and whitewash, of timber and tar, of milk and manure.

When Ambrosio shut the door behind him, he was feeling stirred up. He smoked several cigarettes, kept the dungflies away from him with his only newspaper, which he'd read long before, and stared at the cows dozing in the straw.

He found the cows as doughty as Knuchel and ever so buttoned up. They too preferred gestures. Before they ever mooed, they would clash horns a couple of times, kick out, piss and shit on each other and flick their tails. But then their discretion didn't seem unnatural to Ambrosio, the cows were certainly less taciturn than all the silent types he met both in the farm and the village.

'Qué país!' He scratched his bald spot, spat into the gutter and nodded at Blösch's calf, which was standing beside his bench and staring at him sorrowfully over the top of its tin muzzle, as though full of understanding and sympathy.

A snort came from Baby at the back end of the cowshed. In her boredom the stupid cow was feeling sorry for herself. Baby was so clumsy that she often caught her front foot in her rope and chain, or found herself trapped in the bars of the manger by one of her long horns. Ambrosio had already had many occasions to be angry with her. She was slow-witted, and no milk pail could be safe when she was around.

'Qué país de vacas tontas,' he sneered. Next door to Baby, Spot shook her head and rattled the chains. She was bothered by a fly in her eye. When Ambrosio turned away again, his attention was caught by something on Check's hide. Those large red patches on her had never struck him in quite this way before. He tilted his head one way, then another, he blinked, stood up, was it the poor light in the cowshed playing tricks on him? He went nearer no, there was no doubt about the shape, peculiar, the outline was one he knew well, the area between the patches on her back, that was the top of the Iberian peninsula, there, below Check's hipbone was Barcelona, there was the Costa Brava, and down on the belly was Gibraltar, precisely, it was the outline of Spain, there, up by the shoulder was Coruña, and the edge of the patch on the cow's skin flickered before Ambrosio's eyes, and his thoughts started to wander: those Knuchel cows! It was worth it, watching them in their meekness, closely and often. Ambrosio studied the expression on their faces, he examined the peaceable architecture of their bodies, whose jagged clumsiness seemed made for putting down roots and standing still. Who could imagine one of those imposing but coarsely joinered lumps doing a gallop, never mind participating in natural animal combat?

He couldn't conceive a real liking for these animals. As a short little southerner he had cause enough to be wary and mistrustful of anything outsize and overgrown, and this particular breed had just been poured too stiffly into its cumbersome form. He would have liked the animals to have had a little more gaiety, he doubted whether they felt properly happy in their lethargic bulk. It was an imposition on them. And the eyes! They were far too honest, the way they peered out of those vast and hollow skulls! Domestic animals! he thought contemptuously. No, he had already wasted too much time looking for some trace of fury in their expressions for him to feel able to admire these Simmental cows. He hadn't found even a grain of wit about them, only morbid forbearance and dignified passivity. In their lofty fussiness, and their exaggerated sense of their own worth, there was nothing to compare with the pride and the nimble rage of a young bull from Coruña.

But for all their bloody-mindedness over unimportant details, Ambrosio was prepared to allow them a civilized readiness to compromise on serious matters. A bloody fight, a fight to the death, that didn't exist for them. And he couldn't deny that these overbred bodies had something reassuringly decent about them, it might well be dull, but the warmth they radiated, their incessant inner activity, their endless ruminating, digesting, multiplying, lactating, producing-even-while-they-slept, all that impressed Ambrosio in spite of himself. Sometimes their uninterrupted productivity seemed positively godlike to him, and he learned to respect it. It all made it still more unfathomable to him that, as yet invisible but menacing enough, the butcher's knife should be hanging over them, Blösch and Baby, Flora and Check and Spot. Every cow in Knuchel's shed had a vertebra that one day would be split. All of them would one day climb unwept and unsung the shit-smeared ramp of a cattle-truck and disappear in the direction of the slaughterhouse.

With one last look at Check's flecked skin, Ambrosio left the cowshed to go up to the village, to the Ox.

The flags were no longer out above the little wood, and the shooting had stopped. With his beret on his head, Ambrosio walked along the verge of the road, beside the fences. He passed three children playing, a dog, and, once again, the woman on the bicycle going downhill this time, swooping past him at a terrifying speed. And through a lath fence he saw beside the fire pond the cheeser's wife bending down over a flowerbed. Her dress had sweat stains under the arms, and was stretched tight and blue across her back. On a dungheap was a cockerel resting on one leg.

The Golden Ox inn had a tiled roof like the farmhouses, and on the side facing the village square it had a round arch that reached almost up to the gables. There were blossoming lime trees in front of it, and some garden chairs and tables under a dark oak, in a little area bordered by laurels. The gravel crunched under Ambrosio's sandals. At the top of the stairs leading to the door, he saw a mighty threshold: in this village one had to be careful when entering unfamiliar territory. In the frontage above him window stood by window, all of them brilliantly polished, and all of them adorned with geraniums, green shutters and white curtains. On the wall above the entrance was a gilded wrought-iron ox the size of a small calf. Its silhouette was squat, with a neck bowed as under a yoke, and head hanging low. On one side of the passage it said DINING ROOM above the door, and there were various official announcements on the wall. Over another door was an enamel sign GUESTS. Here Ambrosio heard people talking, and he went in.

A few Innerwalders who had been sitting on corner benches, backs to the wall, immediately fell silent and turned towards the door. 'Buenos días,' said Ambrosio. He took his cap off. The room was as low and dark as the furthest corner of Knuchel's cowshed, but still Ambrosio recognized all the faces, the co-op manager, the cheeser, the farmers. They were the same faces that stared at him in the village, they were the same men who pointed at him, who made jokes he couldn't understand, who plucked at his clothes when he came into their midst in front of the cheese dairy, morning and evening, with Farmer Knuchel's milk.

A chair was pushed back, and the waitress came up to the bar. Luigi stood up somewhere at the back. Ambrosio made his way to him between the tables. On a green velvet cloth were four pink scrubbed hands, making a star. At first they were immobile, but now they were moving again, fumbling for the cards while the four players were still busy looking at the little Spaniard. Then a murmur of greeting, undirected and unenthusiastic. The necks lengthened again, brows unfurrowed themselves, mouths snapped shut, a match flared up and lips closed round a spittle-wet stub of tobacco.

Opposite Luigi was the field-mouser, old Field-mouser Fritz, suspected by the whole village of sectarian machinations and worse. He was the binoculars, the ratman, the eargrubber, the mumper and the nightwalker of the highlands. It was: Mind you don't touch his rags! Out of his way, boys! and the farmers' wives would send their children into the house when they saw him coming up the farm road with his long stick.

Ambrosio said some more 'buenos días', Luigi was happy, and called the waitress over, and the field-mouser, seeing Ambrosio was looking, slowly opened up his left hand, which was lying on the table like a clay prosthesis. Luigi laughed and said, 'You muser, always you blaying!' But Ambrosio stared at the black fingers spreading out and disclosing a palm that was ploughed with scars, cracks, callouses and gashes. Bits of sand and earth had become embedded in the brown-black crust of skin. The face of the field-mouser was as the hand: the nose a shapeless swelling the size of a potato, the skin seemed to breathe through the enlarged pores, and it put forth stubble and brows, and knotty blisters, warts and carbuncles, as fallow land grows weeds. Steel-blue eyes, dimmed by alcohol, studied Ambrosio, and while the hand slowly closed again and turned onto its palm, the field-mouser said:

'Upon your belly you shall go, and dust you shall eat all the days of your life!'

Ambrosio turned round. The voices behind him were growing louder once more. 'Have you seen Knuchel's Spaniard? He's wearing those Holy Land sandals of his again,' said one Innerwalder. 'Yes, Knuchel's cut-price milker,' said another. Luigi waved his hand, indicating to Ambrosio not to pay any attention to the talk behind him, and that he should order something to drink, the waitress was already asking a second time. Ambrosio was still astonished by the breadth of that earthy hand, when the smell of a young woman reached his nostrils. She stood very close to him, so that he could feel the warmth from her body. He gestured cluelessly at the cups and glasses all around, and shrugged his shoulders.

'Kaffee fertig,' said the field-mouser. 'Yes, a kaffee fertig! A spoon in a glass, then coffee till you can't see the spoon no more, and then schnapps till you see the spoon again!'

Ambrosio nodded, and the waitress said, 'One kaffee fertig, thank you,' and was gone.

'You, muser, show him what you got in your pogget,' Luigi nudged the field-mouser, but he pretended not to understand. At Luigi's second prompting, he still managed to ignore the attention being paid to him with an unconvincing show of modesty, thrusting his chin out and looking round the bar, but the third time he stretched out as far as he could, wedged in between his bench and the edge of the table, and dug around in his clothes with a dirt-encrusted paw until finally he produced a bundle of something resembling rubber bands tied together. The field-mouser waved it about, giggled, and trailed it through the air under the noses of Luigi and Ambrosio. They were grey-yellow mouse tails that had been chopped off, and they disappeared again immediately. 'Water voles. Just caught them on the Boden farm. Terrible this year.'

To Ambrosio's surprise the waitress returned to the table with her tray full of crockery. He had just ordered a coffee. Luigi smiled knowingly and said, 'Eh! Che cosa vuoi!'

A wide-brimmed coffee glass stood in a saucer on some tissue paper. In one little dish, brown outside, white inside, were two sachets of the same sugar that Luigi had produced from his

84

suitcase. Another little dish bore a miniature silver jug full of cream, with a miniature spoon next to it, ornamented, and marked with a stamp to show it had been produced in the prosperous land, and underneath it all a napkin embroidered with trotting oxen.

'Two twenty-five please, if I can take it now please,' said the waitress, and Ambrosio was captivated by her hand underneath her frilly white apron, scrabbling about in a leather bag full of jingling coins over her belly. That was where they kept their money!

In the meantime, the field-mouser had cleared his throat, and with his tuberous nose sniffed the air like a dog. He slithered about this way and that on the bench, pushed against the table, and got to his feet without standing fully upright. 'Upon your belly you shall go, and dust you shall eat all the days of your life,' he said loudly, and after teetering between bench and table edge, let himself drop back again. As he fell back, his head slumped so far that his face disappeared from view beneath the brim of his hat.

There was derision from the other tables, comments, to the general effect that he'd had too much to drink, but still none of the other guests were concentrating fully on the field-mouser. What interested them, indirectly and covertly, were the two foreigners.

After their conversation of the morning, Luigi would have liked to intoxicate himself with talk, and he was eager to get going again in their Mediterranean mixture. Ambrosio would have been only too happy to oblige him, parrticularly as he had some new questions of his own, such as who the woman was with the powerful thighs who was such a gifted cyclist that she caused havoc on the field roads of Innerwald, and uphill at that, and where this rocky man came from, and what he used those hands for, and what the waitress's name was, and why the mouse tails, only his own speech sounded foreign to him here, and he felt he couldn't talk properly in this room. Fleshy-faced farmers were looking at them, swollen necks stretched out, the laughter grew louder. The sound of foreign syllables, Luigi's exuberance and Ambrosio's reticence, everything incurred the displeasure of the other customers.

'Well, well, so the Spaniard will be left in charge of Knuchel's farm when the farmer himself is off doing his military service,' someone said. But was Hans down for this year, came the question back. 'Yes,' came the reply, his unit was with the 18th regiment, light infantry, and they were off exercising in a fortnight. 'Hans Knuchel's unit's been called up?' queried the co-op manager. The first he'd heard, he said, and forgetting that for once it wasn't his pencil in his hand, he whitened the back of his neck with the piece of chalk he was using to keep the score. 'You can see for yourself,' said the cheeser. 'All the schedules are up on the board outside, the refresher courses and inspection days.' And when the co-op manager put his cards down, pushed his chair back, went outside and started reading one of the small-printed official communications, the cheeser called to him through the open door: 'Here, you're looking at the calendar of market days!' and the other two players could hardly suppress their mirth.

There was more laughter and grinning when the field-mouser tried once more to get up. Several times he flopped back onto his seat, then he raised his arm threateningly and hissed, 'Upon your belly you shall eat and go dust all the days of your life.'

'Yes, you're right,' said the co-op manager, returning to the table. 'There'll be all kinds of goings on on Knuchel's farm while Hans is away.'

'And I'm supposed to be cheesing, and I've yet to see a doctor's report, when it says so in the regulations,' said the cheeser.

Teetering half upright, the field-mouser began cursing to get the attention of the room, at first incoherently, then audibly enough to obtain silence, and when the last pink face was turned towards him, he leaned on Ambrosio's shoulder and said he was the field-mouser, the field-mouser of the highlands, and he carried his money around in a moleskin, there was room for it, and if there was anyone present he owed money to, and wasn't it the case that if you came down too hard on rats they'd start producing a nestful of little ones every month? With these words, he appeared to lose his balance completely, but he caught himself again on Luigi's shoulder.

Because he understood poison, he continued, yes he was a field-mouser, and a trap once set he'd never forgotten it, not in thirty-five years, and if someone brought him a handful of earth, he'd tell him the field it came from, never mind what had been growing on it, but then those Innerwald thickheads, what did they ever see? By St Ulrich he'd show them, and when a young farmer got up and made tracks towards the field-mouser, but then sat down again, he said: 'For thou shalt not be ashamed of the dirt under thy fingernails!' And after he'd asserted that while everyone knew which farmer produced the biggest calves, only he, the field-mouser could say where the mice did best for a living, he took his paws off the shoulders of Luigi and Ambrosio and roared: 'You should all sacrifice a golden mouse for every farm in the village, because there's a plague of them on you all!' And collapsing back onto his bench, he whispered, rolling his eyes, 'I'm the field-mouser, the field-mouser I am.'

Thereupon he slumped forward across the table, knocking over a coffee glass in the process. A rough, snoring sigh was heard. The battered hat fell from the old man's head, rolled across the table onto the floor. The young farmer who had just sat down again, now moved his chair, picked the hat up off the floor and said: 'Right, that's enough of that.' A fist crashed down, a beer bottle burst open.

'Damn it now!' said the cheeser.

A pink hand grabbed the field-mouser by the collar. 'Leggo,' said Luigi. The hand jerked the field-mouser to his feet, and Luigi lashed out. When another hand gripped Luigi, Ambrosio's elbow swung into an Innerwald beer belly. A dozen hands grasped struggling limbs like steel tongs. Only the field-mouser didn't put up a fight.

'Seems you can't even play a quiet game of cards on a Sunday any more,' sighed the co-op manager.

Luigi, Ambrosio and the field-mouser were thrown down the steps of the Ox. The young farmer knocked his hands together as though to remove clinging particles of dirt, and said: 'That Spaniard struts about on our land as though it belonged to him, just like the field-mouser does.' 'And in green clothes and all,' chipped in another Innerwalder. 'They've come all the way here to open their flies and piss on our roads!' said a third.

87

In the cattle room of the slaughterhouse at the edge of the beautiful city, the rush was on. The swearing had become audible, the men spat, waved their knives about, spat again. Fucking shit! Those stupid asshole cow-handlers! And the wops! Three men short already, and now Gilgen's stayed away too.

Krummen's face was brick red. There was no rhythm to the work. They were already an hour behind.

The first half dozen cows were slaughtered by all the men together. Only after that could each one settle to his task and go from one animal to the next concentrating on the same actions routinely and repetitively. For the moment, though, everyone was doing everything, and even more ponderously than usual.

The most ponderous of them all was Ambrosio. He was standing there shaking. He was weak in the knees, pale-faced, and staring at the knife in his four-fingered fist, then at the cow's shin in his left hand. He had skinned it, and sawn it off at the knee. The hoof wobbled about on the end of the slithery white bone; the tendon had been cut. *Our slaughtermen have the material before their eyes, and are themselves in the best position to assess the value and size of a correctly cut hide, and the wastage and loss in one poorly cut.* Ambrosio stepped away from the carcass, which now had only three legs pointing up in the air.

– No work? Fast asleep? Or is he looking for his middle finger again? Huber and Hofer hissed with twisted faces. Ambrosio didn't hear them. He froze. Krummen pulled the fourth cow into the hall on a rope. Ambrosio dropped his knife a second time. The cow being pulled in was Blösch. Blösch, the lead cow from Knuchel's shed. Ambrosio stepped back. It was seven years since he'd last seen that cow, but he recognized her at once, out on the ramp in front of the cattle-truck. She loomed out of the morning mist like a ghost, limped into the weighing cage, and weigher

88

Krähenbühl, frowning sarcastically, noted down a pathetic animal live weight in his notebook. The onetime pride of the highlands, the mainstay of Innerwald breeding, was being led to the scaffold uncelebrated and unheralded. Nowhere a ceremonial bell, an organ intoning, a fanfare calling to attention. Where was Blösch's cow bell? Where was the embroidered ribbon? Where was the village band?

Blösch still showed no sign of resistance. Cowpeaceably, as though she had juicy Knuchel grass under her hooves, she stood beside Krummen and waited.

She was worn to the bone, her straight back had turned into a jagged range of protruding vertebrae, the horns were spindle-thin and decalcified, on her left hindleg a poorly healed wound from a pitchfork was still suppurating, her hocks were swollen, and her skull drooped from an emaciated neck.

Animals of the classes cattle, sheep, goats, swine and horses are – with exceptions in an emergency – to be stunned by a bolt or bullet to the brain. Krummen didn't even look at the cow in his grasp. Kilchenmann! Shoot! Blösch lay long and lean on the floor.

Ambrosio had already got as far as the first cow in the centre aisle of the abattoir. He was making his exit with equanimity. Abattoir-Marshal Bössiger showed up, but he didn't get involved, he kept away from the front. The more livid were his lieutenants. And the full blood-basins! And the shanks! Can't you ever be left to yourselves? Do you need someone to wipe your botties too? What about these heads? Get to it! Goddamn it! Ambrosio! Ambrosio! Where the hell are you off to?

Ambrosio stared into space.

Krummen hissed first at Piccolo, then at the trainee. He barked out orders, made one man stop the work he'd just embarked on, didn't tell him what to do instead, trod on someone else's toes, wanted to inspect the knives, got in the way of everyone. Huber and Hofer followed suit, scattered pointless commands, splashed Ambrosio with water, then with blood. When Krummen's back was turned, they swore at each other, said it wasn't the first time they'd been in a slaughterhouse, and that they knew quite well what to do. Several times they stole a glance at Bössiger, but he just kept quiet in his white overall, and pretended to check some entries in his black notebook, as if nothing was amiss.

89

Ambrosio backed out of the hall. He was splashed with blood. His boots squelched with every step as though he were wading through a swamp. Where his trousers weren't covered by his rubber apron, they stuck to his legs. *For Thou hast made him Lord of all Thy creation: setting all beneath his feet: sheep and oxen, and the beasts of the field.*

Without touching it with his hands, Ambrosio opened the door of the washroom. Pretty Boy Hügli was standing in front of the mirror, combing his hair.

Ambrosio didn't go in.

He carried on down the long central corridor of the slaughterhouse. His sheath and whetting steel clinked together on his hip, and bumped against his legs. The corridor was like an empty and endless tunnel, and Ambrosio trotted along down its length, on and on, with every step the clinking sheath tapped his thigh, and Ambrosio swung his head in time to his steps. Soon the slaughtering would break through the double door of the room and overflow into this passage, with machine noise, battle cries and gunshots preceding it. The victims would follow, by way of the weighing machines and control books of the handlers and weighers, past the meat-inspecting vets, judged and stamped, weighed and numbered, Blösch too would be pushed along here on a hoist, those parts that didn't go straight on to offal or tripes, or the hide and lard stores, would come creeping out here, her head would be piled up in a mound on a trolley with the other eyeless and hornless cowheads. In wheeled basins, in steel containers, in a jumble of lungs, hearts, kidneys, spleens and livers, would be Blösch's insides, gleaming wetly in luminescent colours, taking on new forms like those of the headless shapes at the bottom of the sea, but the corridor was as yet still untouched by the products of the slaughtering process.

Only the chest stood there. The chest that for weeks had been shunted about from one side of the corridor to the other. The chest that was always in the way, and which now and again would be furiously kicked by someone.

A chest of fir, some 2 metres high.

Ambrosio didn't notice it.

*

Seven fifteen.

They're shouting again.

Orders.

Everyone wants to give orders.

Go on then.

Cows two and three have been stuck and headed. We grab their legs and turn them onto their backs.

As we turn them over, Überländer pushes an iron support underneath their bodies to help balance them.

Heavy bitch, says Luigi.

Huber and Hofer are whirling about, bickering. Just to show Bössiger how indispensable they are. It's always the same.

Bössiger doesn't pay any attention.

Piccolo slits the cows' bellies open, pulls out the guts and makes a bit of room inside. Then he saws through aitchbone and sternum.

Io niente pressiere.

Piccolo smiles.

With powerful cuts, Huber and Hofer take off the hooves, the ankles and the shins.

And there's Buri too, bending over a carcass, fumbling with his gutting knife. Enormous Buri, wobbly and stiff on his pins. He protests. He's always made to do other people's work as well as his own. His gutting knife looks tiny. No one ever helps me when I get behind. Buri's waiting for the intestines of the first cow to be ready.

Now the fourth is lying on the ground, twitching. I recognize her. She's the one that had Ambrosio yelling out on the ramp.

Where's Ambrosio?

I bend down.

What a thin animal. Skin and bone. A sagging back. Long, pointed bones poking out all over the place. As though they were trying to puncture the skin. Bones. Bones. No fat, no padding. Nerves, sinews and bones.

The cow moves, arches her back.

But she was quite tame before the shot, quite calm.

She slides about on the floor.

Straw-red all over.

A blushing Blösch hide.

Just on her withers, the base of her tail and her head, a few splashes of white.

She picks her head up off the floor.

The horns are long and even. Marked by many births. You can't make out the individual rings any more.

I press my knee down on the scrawny throat.

The red hairs are grey at the root. The hide quivers nervously, uselessly. A shudder, up and down.

I can only just get through the skin. So tough she might have been tanned alive.

The cow thrashes around. She's still obstinate, still fighting, in spite of the hole in her head. The cow rolls over.

I fight for my balance.

For the Lord is the shadow over your right hand.

My confirmation text.

I feel the strength underneath me.

The neck tries to beat up and down, like the tailfin of a dying fish.

I put my rubber boot down.

Concentrate!

I stick.

I miss the throat artery the first two times, and hit it at the third attempt. The red blood jets up, the heart pumps it out into the light in violent spurts. She can't have that much . . . it's not possible.

The throat underneath me trembles harder.

A groan, a rattle trembling through the windpipe, a quiver, a shudder: I get up.

Go.

The cow lifts her head. All wobbles and trembles: she pulls her weight onto her front feet. She's trying to get up.

With nostrils dripping red, she trumpets through the slaughterhouse. She sits there and rolls her head round to the right, the left, the right again.

I retreat.

The cow bleeds from the wound in her throat.

The proud horns. Cow's antlers.

I'm glued to the wall, the knife in my outstretched hand.

There! The cow collapses, gone, her nervous strength exhausted, she lies in her blood.

Piccolo stares at me.

All right. The ghosts have been exorcized.

No one has stopped working.

Kilchenmann just forgot to push the arm's length of wire through the bullet hole down into the spinal marrow.

Too much had remained undestroyed.

A bloodless feeling in my head.

I close my eyes, with my back to the wall, I slip down into a crouch, and try not to think any more.

and Ambrosio in the corridor of the slaughterhouse, past the chest, never saw it, knives dangling, the little Spaniard bloodboltered all over and the centrifuge in the machine room still neat and new, still quite unblöschbloodbespattered, but already it will be flowing together from jugular and carotid, citrate added to it as an anti-coagulant, until Luigi arrives with the big funnel, sets it up on the centrifuge, and the blöschblood will run, separated out into blood sediment and oily plasma, and away with it in an aluminium canister, the blöschbloodplasma will finish up as protein supplement for sausage filling, first it will splash about on walls, on ceilings, blöschstains everywhere, the last traces of a cow on Luigi's arms and legs and on the stone floor it will drip, oily, it will creep under Luigi's bootsoles, he struggles to keep his balance, stretches his hands out in front of him as he carries the plasma-canister away, the chance of slipping dead certain and didn't Ambrosio wind up on the floor once already, the seat of his pants drenched in blood and Ambrosio sees nothing, hears nothing, just out of this corridor, how alive I must be among so much liquid death, and he trots across the forecourt of the slaughterhouse, blindly onto the approach road, walking down the middle of the road, hey! Ambrosio! towards the horizon, sheath dangling, sheath bumping, get off the road, the porter's shout, and beer in bottles and in others none not bock not stout not special brew in crates steadfast green soldiers by twelves by twenty-fours, secured with chains, each under other, above beside between, five layers high on the factory beer-transporter which changes down a gear,

Ambrosio hears no emptybottlerattle only walks along down the centre line and a SAURUS comes hooting hotbrakeblocking, and Ambrosio carries on and the SAURUS following the FBT slaughterhousewards, through the gate in the fence, upskip thousand bottles fit to leap out of their crates and a humchoke round the entryway curve cowbodythudding against the animaltransporter-dinoSAURUSplanking, four hooves gripless on the dungboards and a blow the rope halter tight to the ring, hornless the skull smashes and in the body greenferment comes up, squeezes flatulence unruminable as the gums press the beerbottles clatter foam under the patent tops down into the canteen cellar right at the back of the yard and on the ramp the SAURUS drops its tailbridge, rattle rattle fresh air nostrilbreaths latticegates shut weighed in the cage with nudgefinger pushing weights threehundredandeightyseven kilos of youngcow marked down for SAURUS-owner and animal-dealer Schindler with canteen landlady empty bottles hydraulically rearloaded on the factory beer-transporter shakerattleandroll and in the waiting pen, up the green from bellies all bole by bole waitingchews the youngcow.

Seven thirty.

Krummen's getting going.

They're all doing the same, pushing themselves.

Nothing but ugh ugh ugh.

In the hurry you forget the time – sometimes.

Just don't loosen your grip on the knife.

My hand is clammy. I don't feel well. That cow earlier did something to me. My nose is bleeding. It was as though she was on invisible puppet strings, the way she got up. The gurgling. The trembling.

I chisel away wildly. The scraps of skin I pull at keep slipping from my grasp.

And today of all days.

When I wanted to be so strong.

Krummen wants to catch up.

In a mad rush he drags the cows in and turns them over.

Kilchenmann puts the brake on: not too much haste! Easy, he says, easy does it.

I can keep up. I'm not falling behind. You don't leave me standing.

Like Piccolo with the flies on the canteen walls, we flatten the cows on the slaughterhouse floor.

Goddamn it, you fucking bastard!

Krummen never used to swear at the animals.

He even gets violent with them. Don't you . . . ?

One arrives with red streaks across her nostrils, another limps up with an open wound on one leg. She can't grip the wet granite properly.

The cows never used to bellow like this.

Krummen drives them along at the double to a vacant slaughtering bay.

One cow has no horns: disturbed, she crawls before Krummen on her knees.

He's got himself a whip.

Kilchenmann says his firearm has to be cleaned. And he needs different shells. The amount of gunpowder used for each animal has to be calculated afresh according to the thickness of the skull and the density of hair. These ancient sausage-cows here were too thick-skinned and hard-nosed, bull-headed they were. And if one of them had marrow already shrivelled away or dried up, you could rattle the wire around in her spine for ever and not achieve anything, you just had to shoot more slowly and meticulously. He disappears into the weighing office.

Krummen protests. Puffed up, he stands next to the cow.

The cow tries to free her head. Krummen holds her tight in an armlock, squeezing the cowhead to himself. It takes more than cows to bother him. He looks at the carcasses on the ground. The first of them headless, without recognizable animal shape; the others still mooing for the last time, still full of warmth, life and blood.

He's perfect, the way he drops them.

Ten points every time.

The victor.

And who tends the vanquished?

I brush the sawdust off their bodies.

My nose is dripping too. My grimy face!

I go from rope to rope, udder to udder, throat to throat, cowhead to cowhead.

Just be careful with the knife.

He's standing over me, looking at my nose.

I turn away.

Have you got a nosebleed?

What me? Where? Of course not.

Even when bending down, I try to get my body weight behind the blade.

You're pale!

I hear the cow snort and scrape against his apron. Knock him over, why don't you. But he'll break your neck first. He clasps her goggle-eyed head hard against his belly.

I want to find that rhythm again, that feeling of concentration, absorption in work and forgetting everything else.

Luigi pulled a full uterus out of the ghost cow's body.

Just don't think about that damned cow.

Don't tighten up.

My head isn't muzzy.

I don't feel numb.

Nothing hurts.

My hand is steady.

My nose isn't bleeding.

I have no abrasions on my hands, not a single cut the other blood can eat into.

And the fourth vertebra in my back, that's just the centre of the universe.

Don't pay any attention to the splashing blood! Just drive your blade under the scalp, don't slow down, don't think of anything. Don't think. Don't think. Don't think. Don't . . .

I approach the next cow from behind. This one doesn't try to stand up afterwards. Not all of them are possessed. I tie, I open, I stick, I bleed, I skin, I scalp, behead . . . I dig through skin, sinew, flesh, pain, crawl along, lash out with my knives, look for cover behind the pressure of work.

Well hurried is well survived.

As I empty the basin where the blood collects, I straighten up.

I stretch my back, and feel my wrenched vertebrae with my

hand. Gilgen can talk. Gilgen's got a broad back. A healthy back. You need a strong back.

The cow that wouldn't die is spreadeagled and hoisted into the air.

She'll never walk again.

Her uterus lies grey-blue on the green granite floor.

Piccolo pushes a trolley for the intestines. He isn't allowed to carry on into the inner chambers of the cow by himself. He just transports the stuff out to the tripery. He's waiting for Hügli, who's probably posing in front of his dressing-room mirror, rubbing VASELINE into his face.

I'm already cutting my seventh throat.

The loneliness of the headless bodies behind me, the hopeless gurgles ahead.

The guts, still digesting, bloat the stomachs round as cannon-balls. A thin whoosh of air, and I smell the pressure released through the relaxed sphincter.

Bony beside every body, the appropriate peeled skull, with empty eye sockets.

Each of them is hung from a spike that is stuck through the nostrils. All the parts of a cow have to be kept together until the vet has checked them.

Meat-inspection rules!

By the side of each spiked skull, the tongue of each. The rope halter.

Behind it, the slowly filling blood-tank.

All my work.

My handiwork.

Jesus fucking Christ!

Krummen's getting impatient.

Kilchenmann! Damn it! Shoot!

Easy, boss, replies the voice from the weighing office.

The cow's getting nervous, she flares her nostrils, whisks her tail. No one is better than Krummen at inspiring a cow to stoical-aristocratic behaviour just before the end. But no cow will stand quietly in a slaughterhall for more than five minutes.

Just keep her away from me.

I nick the artery in the throat under my knee.

Nothing!

Has my knife lost its point?

I stab it in, hard. The blood spurts, bubbles out, pumped by the still-beating heart.

In the slaughtering bay behind me, Kilchenmann finally applies his gun, pulls the trigger and the cow drops from Krummen's arms like a stone. He doesn't look, doesn't watch her fall, crash and die.

Just as long as he can play the boss.

He goes from one carcass to the next, checking our work: once they've been skinned, there isn't to be the merest trace of dirt from the hide; no blood in the meat; no gall in the fat; no slime on the tongue; no puncture in the guts.

The slaughterer's art.

Krummen sees the fourth cow already hanging, and no one disembowelling her. He walks up and down a couple of times, his left hand sweeps in a wide arc round his whole bulk, he buries his fingers in the cloth across his bum, and he yells.

Where's Hügli got to this time?

Jesus Christ Almighty!

And Ambrosio!

Piccolo smiles quietly.

I try to smile back, feel the crust on my face, haven't got a hand free to scratch my chin.

I peel the scalp right off.

Change of knife.

I slowly pass the medium blade across the whetting steel. The short knife needs sharpening too.

With all the bloody hurry I slipped.

I must have blunted the point on one of the iron rings concreted into the floor.

In the middle of each killing bay is a heavy iron ring in the floor. Once they used to tether the animals to them before knocking them down with a poleaxe or a butcher's hammer. Later on, they were still used for heavy steers. A rod with spring-hooks at either end was clicked in through the ring in the floor and the nose ring.

Here's Hügli.

Like a guilty dog, he slinks in at the side entrance. He looks sharp. He doesn't buckle on his sheath, he takes it down off the rack, and with practised elegance, rolls himself into his belt, moving his hips like a woman and tossing his head back.

That's good, Hügli. Your gun belt. Hear the music, can you? Film music.

Now I know what tune he was whistling before.

And my hands! I nearly broke off the tip of my knife.

There must be a tendon somewhere in this neck cartilage.

Wonder if that fourth cow carried a portent in her belly?

Perhaps one day something amazing will come out of one of those bellies.

Hügli gets ready to start disembowelling.

There are still a few fibres holding the carcass together.

Hügli severs them.

As always: You hope for a sign, an answer, but nothing comes. Only the slobbery guts hanging down the front of the broken-open cow.

It looks as though she's puked them up.

She doesn't have any more secrets, she's made a clean breast of things – there's nothing out of the ordinary about her.

The usual octopus of stomachs and intestines.

No word from the cow oracle.

Her insides are outermost. The workshop of her belly is empty. If she had an incubus it wasn't incubating in there.

Hügli waves his longest sword around in the air. Couldn't Piccolo have waited for fuck's sake? What if everyone just started tweaking at bits if they felt like it! This membrane here had to come out first of the lot. Preferably without getting the whole thing covered in shit.

Hügli yells. It's always him that gets the blame.

Yell all you like. You can't compete with the machine noise.

Io? Non ho fatto niente io! Piccolo thrusts his hands in the air, as though Hügli had pulled a gun on him.

Another victorious duel. And now he works exaggeratedly slowly. If the slaughterhouse was a Western. You do what you do.

Piccolo wants to know what that membrane is for.

Pot roast! Pot roast! shouts Hügli. So the juice doesn't run out. Capito?

You know what you know.
Molto bene, for make a de roas!
I nod to Piccolo.
He smiles.

Ernest Gilgen was livid.

Ernest Gilgen, the master-butcher of the abattoir, Ernest Gilgen, the Tyrolean giant, Ernest 'Aschi' Gilgen, Ambrosio's friend, Ernest Gilgen, who didn't slaughter cows so much as chop their roots, and fell them like trees, Ernest Gilgen, whose prodigious strength was famed far beyond the walls of the slaughterhouse, this Ernest Gilgen now clenched his pincer fingers into fists. His jaw twitched and jutted forward, and a thick vein swelled up in his throat from the collar of his shirt, to just below the stubble on his unshaven chin. He could have run away, like before, over fields and meadows, through a gorge, through a whole mountain valley up a scree to a glacier.

He paced back and forth in front of the kiosk on the approach road to the slaughterhouse.

In tin cans and gherkin jars were bluebells and irises stood in water. Gilgen drew his left foot back, and turned away, took aim again, pulled his foot back further – and at the last moment kicked the rubbish bin instead. Pieces of scrap paper and newspaper fluttered through the air; bottles rolled across the pavement onto the road.

– Here, you! What's up with you, Gilgen! As though she couldn't breathe, Frau Kramer, the kiosk woman, banged her hands against her chest. Herr Gilgen! And so early in the morning!

– Nom de Dieu! Sacré tonnerre! All right. Give me a beer. Gilgen reached an arm into the kiosk, and laughed across to the munitions-factory workers as they came nearer.

Several engineers, turners, precision-tool makers, fitters and gunsmiths were hanging around the factory gate. They wore navy work clothes, and had their hands in their pockets and grinned at Gilgen and looked at newspapers over each other's shoulders. Ten minutes to go till the siren for the eight o'clock shift. They grouped themselves round the swearing butcher, and kept an eye on their colleagues as they arrived.

Upright bodies in long coats, stooped bodies in short coats, on bicycles, motorbikes and mopeds, bodies sitting well back in cars, smoking and non-smoking, drove up to the red-and-white crash barrier at the entrance to the weapons factory. It went up and came down, the porter looked at the faces and let them pass in the morning fog. Hands were raised in greeting from handlebars, gloves were pulled off and Engineer Müller wished Porter Hirt a good morning, and Precision-turner Schuhmacher greeted Tool-maker Käser, Mechanic Küfer spotted his colleagues Waldmann, Holzer and Zimmermann in the crowd turning up for work and Fitter Meier nodded to well-wrapped Equipment-fitter Schäfer. The gunsmiths Maurer, Gerber, Kohler, Wagner, Amman and Eisenschmied all wished one another a good morning. Colleague Beck slowed down on his VESPA, and nodded in the direction of the kiosk. Electrician Jäger beamed in his new OPEL, while Apprentice Ackermann started undoing his coat and loosening the strap of his crash-helmet while still on his bike. Many faces remained hidden behind scarves and hat rims, behind spectacles and windshields.

Grey figures on wheels on asphalt against foggy background.

Only Ernest Gilgen was colourful.

His fury was colourful, his laughter, his swearing, his shirt. His scalp was reddened by the cold, by rage and by beer. Ernest Gilgen was there, completely there, in every vein, awake and wrathful, and the engineers, turners, precision-tool makers, fitters and gunsmiths warmed their spirits at his fire. They dug their hands into their trouser pockets, egged each other on and started teasing him.

– Here, Gilgen, are you drunk already?

– You drunk again?

– Still drunk!

– Still living on Meat Street?

– Taking the day off?

Their lungs blew out smoke. They stood among clouds of it, like fire-eaters by their flames. They had paper bags jammed under their arms. Ham sandwiches. Sausage sandwiches. For their morning break.

– Anyone want the paper?

– You really taking the day off?

– Well, what if I am? Hey? Today Ernest Gilgen's going to give blood. Yes, give blood. No rubber boots and rubber apron for him today. You know what they can do with them? There was scorn in his rage, contempt for the brick buildings behind the slaughter-house wall in the direction of which he spat. Here! This is where they can put it! Voilà. He grabbed his trousers, grabbed hold of everything his shovel-sized paw could hold between his legs. He bent his knees, held his belly and grabbed, shaking the bulge in his trousers, as though he was trying to squeeze the juice from his testicles. Let them kill their own sausage-cows if they like. Moi, je suis vachement bien ici!

– Haven't you got enough blood in your alcohol?

– Have to have a few more pints!

– Especially if you're going to give blood at the Red Cross.

Engineers, turners, precision-tool makers, fitters and gunsmiths grinned. Crazy butcher!

– Hey, Gilgen, do you know the one about the boy who leaves school and doesn't know what to do?

– Huh, tell me then.

– Well, the teacher went round to talk to his parents. Your Hans is nearly finished school, he'll be leaving in spring. What plans did you have in mind, hey, what's he going to do? Engineers, turners, precision-tool makers, fitters, gunsmiths all took a step nearer the speaker. Some of them were laughing in anticipation. Gilgen, a couple of heads taller than any of them, leaned down like a giraffe. A suppressed snigger, an elbow dug into ribs.

– Well, what did his mother say?

– Well, she says, they'd been thinking about it, her and her husband, and had talked it over a few times, and they'd thought that as their Hansli was so good with animals, and liked being with animals more than anything, well, they thought, why not let him be a butcher?

Laughter erupted from the faces of engineers, turners, precision-tool makers, fitters and gunsmiths. They jabbed each other in the side, peeked at Gilgen, patted the joker on the back. They went on drinking, Gilgen bought a few bottles. He stood in the circle and drank to them all. A karate chop with the side of his hand took the cap off a new bottle. The white foam ran down the green glass. Gilgen licked his lips.

He had learned long ago to be tolerant of mockery, even when he was drunk. Let them laugh. He'd known teasing all his life. But teasing had cost him a bit too.

Gilgen had taken his first few steps in one of the frontier valleys that were particularly noted for their breed of cattle – Eringer Shorthorns – but which were also talked about for the way the fir trees were dying there. Gilgen came from a high mountain valley, a village that clung to the slopes, protected from avalanches by forests planted above it. The wooden houses were scorched by the sun. They were built with larchwood planks. Sometimes spruce was used. Fir, for the very newest. They were simple but lofty constructions. If a growing family found itself short of space, they could add another storey to their house without any difficulty.

The lanes between the houses were named after animals. 'Le Chemin du Mouton blanc', 'Le Chemin du Loup'. The main street was called 'La Rue des Vaches noires'. Outside the village, there were no lanes worth the naming. Nor roads either. Stony tracks led up the slopes. The mule was regarded for its firm stride, and for cattle the ability to climb was an important aspect in breeding. All the men wore stout shoes.

The women wore black skirts with black bodices, white lace blouses, and they tied red kerchiefs round their necks. They wore black bonnets, even on weekdays. The children they bore were healthy, children no sooner born than they had lines of stubbornness in their rosy faces. The priest was the most greeted man in the village. An aura of duress, punishment and hard work clung to him.

The life of the people was closely tied to the life of their animals. Like nomads, the men climbed the tracks after their herds in the summer. After a couple of weeks, when a slope had been well grazed, they moved higher. Always with measured tread. Always with the loud sound of cow bells. In the huts they made cheeses which they strapped onto wooden frames and carried down to the village on their backs.

Livestock breeding was on an ambitious scale. Herds of three or four hundred came together on the communally managed upland meadows. In fierce battles, the lead cows fought for ascendancy. The cattle contested the few grazing places, and in order to maintain the sizeable herds, mowers climbed the mountains as far as the tree line and beyond. The mowers were proud men with faces that were carved like masks. Their skin was weather-stained. They had carbuncles the size of cherry stones. On their quests for winter fodder for their animals, no climb was too dangerous or too steep. Before a mower laid into the juicy, wild grass with his scythe, he would announce his taking possession of the place by loud yodelling. The echo would magnify the yodelling. That way, no one would scale a dangerous face to no purpose. The hay was collected in rips, tied in bales, and again, carried down to the nearest hayshed on the mower's back. The men wore hooded shirts, to protect the backs of their necks.

If there was any time left to spare, the men worked on barriers against avalanches. Or, on summits visible from the village, they would erect new crosses of larchwood.

Gilgen was born on 10 May 1925. Both parents unknown. The community handed the child over to an already numerous family. Next, hire boy on the slopes. A strong Alpine hand leads him out of the village. It's Sunday. Women in red kerchiefs and black bonnets watch the lad go, stand by their garden fences, and wring their hands.

Four hours' walk above the village, in the middle of a pasture, the Alpine hut. Stacked gneiss, weathered fir beams. The slate roof weighted by great boulders. Below, interconnecting stalls and rooms for animals, cowherds and helpers. Men and animals breathe the same air, drink from the same well. Further down the slope, the second hut. For smaller animals. Free grazing for heifers and cows in calf. Salt is stored there. Very close at hand, the ring of mountain tops. A tight horizon, an entire world.

Ernest Gilgen is seven years old, but he looks more like ten. Excessive secretion of growth hormones. It's his job to mind the goats and gather kindling for the cooking and cheese-making. A little farmhand. Known as 'le boûbe'.*

*From German, 'Bube', boy. Not real French.

There's not much talk on the mountain. Least of all with the boy. In general it's better to eat too much than talk too much. Nevertheless, stories. There are stories told about dwarfs and goblins, of rushing torrents and mountains tumbling down. When the moon is full, a strange fear often takes hold of the people on the mountain. As though a dragon lived nearby. Nightmares for the hormonally imbalanced boy.

Over the winters, back down in the valley. Attends the village school. He is administered the alphabet and a little knowledge like a beating. Age eleven, he's more than a head taller than the teacher, who rules over the village youth in one overcrowded room.

'Le boûbe' is teased and laughed at more and more.

One time he writes down his real name. He stamps out the letters with his boots on a snowy field. In enormous writing it says: ERNEST GILGEN.

Rescuing a lost kid on a rock face, in impassable screes, first consciously aware of his feelings. What is inside. What is outside. This world of hardness doesn't end at his body, at the tips of his fingers. Boulders everywhere. He is convinced there is jagged rock in his own breast.

Learns the trade: animal husbandry. Milking. Carrying. The sacks of salt he has to carry from the lower hut to the upper are too heavy. He is often asked to do too much, because of his size. A sack of salt falls from his shoulder. Bursts open. The white salt pours into the green grass. 'Le boûbe' is told off. People wonder if his existence is worth it. For whom. A no-good beanpole of a farmboy. Let him cut hay. The mowers have already been everywhere. He hunts dormice. No green in this stony world.

The heaviest load of all: the stones in his breast. Dogs bark at him. Girls are afraid of him. The women giggle in their red kerchiefs and black bonnets. They rest their bare forearms on their garden fences. At thirteen he has a moustache and is so rawboned, people say that he's got a sizeable shot of steer's blood in his veins. That he drinks sour cream straight out of the biggest churn. That he eats grass. Catches foxes and kills them with his bare hands. They say: Where he goes to cut hay no man has ever been. The wildest mower in the whole wild valley.

A giant figure in a condition of advanced brutalization. And still a child. Curiosity now compounds his fear when he hears stories at night. The story of the three rich sisters, for example. All three were virgins. The fourth, now dead, had been married. The three sisters torment the widower. They work him harder than an animal. The man telling the story describes absolving death as a world without compulsion, without punishment, without work. In the snow, the persecuted man at last found blessed peace. Ernest Gilgen crouches in a corner and listens.

In the autumn there is a surprisingly heavy snowfall. A descent with the animals is impossible. They are snowed in. The teacher gives Ernest Gilgen permission to miss school. Fodder is needed up on the mountain, milk and cheese have to be carried down into the village. And firewood. In the hours under a crushing load, he counts the stones in his breast.

The hut for him comes to resemble what the men describe as hell in their stories. The fire under the enormous cheese vat. The heads of the animals. Hooves. Horns. The equipment. Tongs. Pitchforks. The boy is hunted in the dark. Grasping, clutching hands.

One full moon he leaves the hut. Trudges through the snow. He doesn't turn round. The three rich sisters are wallowing after him. On his trail. The tormented man had found a world without compulsion, without punishment, without work. Ernest Gilgen spreads out the stones in his chest, and lays them in front of him in the snow. Everything grey shall become white and clean. His fatigue at the end of the day is great, and he falls asleep immediately.

A crunching sound. Where is he? Is he made of snow? Something bumps his face. A puffing, the other side of the crust. Is there a mountain moving? He's cold. He's so stiff, he can hardly move. There's a cow standing over him. Her tongue is rough and warm. Steam comes out of her nostrils, her horns can touch the stars. Everything glitters. The world is made of glass.

Fir trees, domes, peaks, all awake.

Ernest Gilgen is awake.

He is in the pen belonging to the lower hut. Three cows stare at him. Like sickles, the horns against the deep blue sky. The cow licks her mouth. He had laid out his stones in the place where he'd dropped the salt. He gets up stiffly. His breast is light. He lies down in the straw with the animals.

106

He saves rye bread for the cow that wouldn't let him sleep. He takes the best hay into the lower shed. This cow must become stronger. He takes her by the horns, and wrestles with her. Doesn't let her get up, forces her to lie down. The path through the wood down to the village is always snowed up and icy on the steep inclines. As he walks, he looks at his toecaps. He makes plans. His head burns. When he looks up, he sees the mountains the way he saw them behind the cow on the night of the full moon: awake. He has plans for his cow. His footfall is now unfaltering.

The climbing cows of the Eringer breed are squat, dark brown to black. A reddish tinge on the flanks. Short-head cattle. Poor in the characteristics of domestic cattle. The brain still relatively large in proportion to the rest of the body. The eyes lively. The number of vertebrae in the tail not diminished. Few infantile characteristics. Eringer cattle grow, but they rarely weigh more than 500 kilos. In difficult terrain no cow is found at higher altitudes than the Eringer. History: they served the Romans. Guest cattle. Native Roman breeds had coarse manners. Humpbacked, no dewlap, ugly, but strong and hard working. Indispensable in the fields. To still their calves, the Romans used the modest Eringers as nurses. Foster-mothers who came down from the slopes.

And Ernest Gilgen's plan for his cow: the crown of the lead cow. She has to win at the spring contests for supremacy on the pastures. Cow in command of the whole mountain. He spoils her with feed, talks to her, walks her over ice, drives her up and down steep slopes. She has strong legs. A stately cow. A strong cow. And every day he takes her by the horns to wrestle with her.

At the rough wooden table, an argument over a piece of cheese. For the first time in front of the men, 'le boûbe' uses his strength for his own purposes. He is immediately left alone. His crooked spine begins to straighten. Now when Ernest Gilgen is on the road at night between the valley and the Alpine huts, he looks up at the stars. He's erect, even on thin ice he walks upright. His tread has become so sure. As alert as a mountain goat's, as calm as a mule's.

The Alpine meadows are green now. Calving time. His cow drops hers early. Then the big day comes. He gives her wine to drink, stuffs her with rye bread one last time. With every step, she plants a pair of hooves in the earth, as though she wanted to put down roots. He takes a stone, and sharpens the black tips of her horns. The judge from down in the valley files them down again with his penknife. At the end of a bell harness, Ernest Gilgen leads his hope to the place of battle, where the animals measure up against one another. Instinct. First, a bored moo. He holds salt under her nostrils. A collision, a butt. Suddenly, two pairs of horns interlock. As though by accident, a coming together with another cow, forehead to forehead. For several combats she is victorious, beats all the animals near her. Inferior cows give up straightaway, depart the field as though nothing had happened. None fights a lost action. The men of the Alps notice the outsider. Who's that? She never took anyone's eye. It's tougher against the favourites. The odds are stacked. She has to attack uphill. 'Le Boûbe' is told to shut up and save his protests. Once, she buries a horn in the ground. Clods fly. Straightaway she levels her nostrils at her rival anew, aims with one eye, and takes off, her head below her shoulders. She changes the angle of attack with her butt. She stays undefeated. The Alpine herdsman is amazed. He has no idea she has been in training, and kept on a special diet. She is garlanded, but they are stingy with the flowers. Even so, Ernest Gilgen swells with hidden pride. Yes, you can. It's proven. You can plan, decide, prepare, execute. You can want. Ernest Gilgen laughs. He won't be pushed around any more. The men's orders to him, their taunts, are a thing of the past. His crooked back grows as straight as an ox's. Too straight. Walking upright, the boy is too big for the men.

The War begins. A butcher is needed. The hired hand becomes an apprentice boy. What was the mountain community going to do in the long run with a giant in their midst? He was a threat to order. A foundling, at that. A 2-metre-tall goat-minder goes down to the valley with the next load of cheese.

On the whole, not much homesickness for village, Alp, mountains.

His teacher prays before slaughtering an animal. For steers, he gets the priest to give his blessing. Gilgen, standing by, tools ready, knives sharpened, hears an echo of the 'Ranz de vache' prayer that the herdsman used to call out in his powerful voice from the entrance of the hut in the evening.

With the soldiers in the village, the first chitchat, the first argy-bargy in another language. Le boeuf, the ox, la vache, the cow, fermez la porte, shut the door. Ha ha ha. La maîtresse, the mattress, le comestible, the gumboot.* Now how strong is the gigantic mooncalf really? The soldiers challenge Ernest Gilgen to wrestle. Didn't he have neck muscles like a steer? He learns fast, has them out on their backs, and laughs. He's had enough occasion while working in the mountains to learn the national traits of working hard, and botching, showing defiance and pulling faces.

There's talk of his good-natured strength.

The first time he slaughters a cow himself, he cups his hands and drinks the blood from her veins so that she'll live on in me, he breaks a molar out of her jaw, and has a hole made in it so that he can wear it round his neck.

After his apprenticeship, his years as a journeyman. He orders a set of knives for himself. Boning, skinning, sticking, scalding, shaving, scraping, paring and drawing. The handles big enough for his hands. Every blade with his monogram. Real swords he has made for himself.

In addition to the knives, he still needs the clothes of the guild. Ernest Gilgen rolls up his sleeves of his butcher's shirt at a horse butcher's. Two days later, he rolls them down again. He crosses the mountains, slaughters in German-speaking parts. He's met with mistrust and ridicule. Pub brawls. The pride is still stiffening along his spine. Not a trace of any deformity now. Just big, incredibly big. A man built like a tank. Girls blush in his presence. He's someone I'd rather not meet in a dark place. Masters' wives and landladies look at his hands and say nothing. A butcher. If he ever. You can imagine them dripping blood, those gigantic paws. When they're at rest, the fingers are like curling snakes full of strength and cunning – and yet, silent and confused. Without knives, Gilgen's hands are helpless and huge, hurrying ahead of the rest of him, always handling, always hungry for the wood of a knife shaft, hungry for meat.

Gilgen wrestles. At numerous fairs, he spoils the fun of the local heroes. He hasn't many moves in his repertoire. They are enough. He wins often and easily. And yet judges begrudge him maximum points. He never buttons on the wrestler's ticking trousers without

*cf. Gummistiefel (Germ.).

thinking of his Alp. When he steps onto the sawdust, for one moment he sees the whole arena as full of cows. He sees them lock horns and drive against each other. Several times, Gilgen was disqualified for laughing excessively. We want wrestling here, not that stupid bloody laughter.

Then the episode with the prize bull. Between bouts at the fair, Gilgen plays around with the crowned animal. Then, to the delight of the crowd, he lays out the twelve-month-old steer. The Marignano faces of the wrestling set turn away from him. Just pretend we never saw it. Ernest Gilgen is banned. The joker gets the red card. We won't miss a chance like that. He might make champion otherwise. We'll have him banned till the end of the season. Relief in the wrestling community.

Thereafter, malice and glee. Punch-ups. Trouble with the military authorities. Misses his refresher course. A canton policeman's dog is found drowned in the fire pond.

New job as a sausage-maker in a medium-sized business. His seventh in ten years. In the storeroom he happens upon three dozen sacks of fine flour. Stacked between tubs of guts and salt barrels. Ernest Gilgen asks the boss if he's in the bakery business as well. Oh, that flour? That was mislaid during the war, and just turned up on some shunting tracks. A whole wagon load. It was going cheap. But what did he want it for? Well, he'd been meaning to talk to him about just that. It concerned the sausage filling. Gilgen might just mix in a bit of flour, not too much, just a little, the way it used to be. They'd used potato flour then. Mais, la guerre, c'est fini. Non? Yes, of course, but they still had the flour. Then Ernest Gilgen showed him some black specks near the top of one open sack. The mice have got in here already. Oh, a bit of mouse dirt. Just give it a good stir. Gilgen had misgivings, but he stayed. It wasn't easy finding a job then.

The boss gives him some powder to mix in as well as the flour. The sausages were pale. Despite paprika, despite pickling salt. The reddening that occurred during the smoking process wasn't enough. Gilgen sniffed at the unmarked plastic bag that the boss left next to the spice scales. Was it colouring? That was illegal. The short answer: he understood about as much about business and the law as a cow on Sunday. He should bloody well do as he was told. If that didn't suit him, he could just.

A few months later, there's a constable leaning against the swing door of the sausage kitchen. Thumbs hooked into the belt of his uniform. If Gilgen would accompany him back to the station, in the castle. There was something wanted sorting out. The old canton vet had died, and his successor had had samples taken from the local butchers. Lab tests on meat products. Why is this mince so red? Why these cervelat sausages? When there's next to no meat in them? The boss denies all knowledge. Gilgen here, big Gilgen, had been making the sausages. And Gilgen gets it in the neck. Ah, they had the measure of him. People came from miles around to testify to his character. So big, Your Worship, so proud. This tree needs its branches pruning every now and again. Ernest Gilgen gets three months without the option.

Shortly after his arrival in the Penal Institution Sitzwil, a letter from the Society of Butchers, another from the Wrestlers' Union: In view of the circumstances, membership withdrawn. And Gilgen laughs. What a joke. The bed-wetters.

Allocated to the prison farm, Gilgen learns more about working with Simmental steers and Simmental cows. The biggest in the land. Mightier than tractors. Gilgen shows great sensitivity in dealing with them. Released early for good conduct, despite his appeals.

Can't find work. That big, and a criminal record. The scruffy Tyrolean giant. Casual work. Shovelling snow. Part time at the slaughterhouse. Boozing. Well known at the Meat Street drinking places. Nights sobering up in police cells.

Acquaintance with Louise Frölicher, forty-two, onetime barmaid at The Golden Bell. Now waitress at The Sword. She discovers the child in the big fellow. Later, before the court, is found partly responsible for Gilgen's recidivism.

It was the time of rising meat prices. Landlords were greatly interested in getting quality cuts of beef on the cheap, e.g. entrecôte, fillet, rump. Ernest Gilgen acquires a delivery van, calls himself a door-to-door butcher. Drives out to remote pastures, keeps an eye out for cattle, young cows. At night he strikes. He rustles cattle. The farmers scratch their necks raw as they count their herds. Now goddamn it. Gilgen cuts up the small animals on the spot. Buries the skin and the innards. Sells the meat unstamped, on the black market. He enjoys working in the open air alone with his victims. The run blood, the smell of the organs in the dewy grass. The opened earth. Louise Frölicher recruits customers. One night he's dazzled by several converging beams of light. He stands there in his bloodied apron, knife in hand, arms and shoulders bare. He's surrounded. Arrested. He struck once too often. Fury among the farmers. Send Gilgen to the gallows! Two years Sitzwil without the option.

Back to the steers and the oxen. More good behaviour. An inclination to exuberance. No respect for authority. According to the Director of the Court of Chancery. A live steer does not belong in the prison kitchens. Oxen should only be driven from the shed once the door is open. It was irresponsible to give milk-cows fodder that has been badly stored, and has become alcoholically fermented. Cows should be able to stand on their own feet during milking. And, later on in the text: when such disturbances and others similar have occurred, Prisoner Ernest Gilgen regularly admits his culpability by loud guffawing. Therefore, after due consideration of the circumstances applying, etc., etc.

After his release, an enterprising guardian gets him a job at the slaughterhouse. You can express yourself there. Only the manager has been informed. And the foreman was a champion wrestler. Maybe you could. Why don't you try? Fräulein Frölicher would certainly not be averse to the idea, should you be thinking in terms of regularizing. Have you ever been in a slaughterhouse before? Have you ever been with Fräulein Frölicher before? But Ernest Gilgen did as he was counselled.

His last promotion: From guardhouse to slaughterhouse.

After Ernest Gilgen had shown such good humour while listening to the butcher joke, the engineers, turners, precision-tool makers, fitters and gunsmiths had nothing against accepting the bottles of beer offered them by the powerful hand of the slaughterman. Here: cheers. Here: bottoms up. Here: your very good health. First Gilgen drank to them, then they to him. He knew how to take it at least, that big Gilgen, he didn't cut up rough when they had a bit of a laugh.

Let's have a bottle of beer before the shift starts. And the group moves closer to Ernest Gilgen.

– When I get back from the Red Cross, I'll tell that joke to Krummen, that bastard. You can bet on it. Cheers!

– Krummen?

– Krummen? Is that the champion wrestler?

– Does he work in the slaughterhouse?

– Sure, he's the foreman.

– He's your boss, eh Gilgen?

– Boss? Ha! He can find someone else to boss! The arselicker. Oh what I'd do to the bastard! Ram him into the ground unpointed. He won't be giving me any more orders. Not me. When he's near me, I feel irritation. Here, in my arms. And Ernest Gilgen stepped back, he needed room for a swing, to show what was coming the way of Krummen. Gilgen ground his teeth, the blood surged to his head. Let me get my hands on him! I've fancied wrestling with him for a long time now. What I'd do to him!

– Here, Aschi, watch yourself. He was in the regional finals again this time. He came runner-up. He's a strong guy, someone ventured.

– Strong! You ever seen him on sawdust? Little white ballet shoes he wears, a little white singlet for the judges. A Sunday wrestler! Lifting weights and swilling OVALTINE is OK, but there's no power in here, in his belly, no juice. He's a tactician. A sportsman. He doesn't scare me. Gilgen had gone into his wrestler's crouch, he grunted and pretended to be pulling up a foe by the ticking trousers used in 'Schwingen' wrestling. In front of the kiosk he put on a demonstration bout against an invisible opponent. The tip of his tongue thrust out in familiar fashion, *and the earliest documentary evidence of clothes-wrestling occurs in the year 1235*, and the veins in Gilgen's neck were almost bursting. He mimed an overarm throw, knelt down, and pretended he had someone wriggling under him in the gutter. I'll do that bastard Krummen!

Engineers, turners, precision-tool makers, fitters and gunsmiths laughed and made room for Gilgen, and then suddenly a rival attraction appeared on the scene. Hands felt for matches and cigarettes, hands began to scratch at skin, hands in the pockets of work trousers suddenly played even harder with cocks and balls through the cloth, hands that had just now been calmly fingering the newspaper, now crumpled it, hands tightened round beer bottles. What in God's name was that?

Going down the middle of the slaughterhouse approach road, on the white line itself, was Ambrosio. He was wearing full slaughterhouse gear, he had his knives at his hips, his rubber boots and his rubber apron on. He approached with wild, staring eyes, not looking to left or right, only shaking his head in time with his steps.

– Ambrosio! Hey, Ambrosio, mind out!

The brewery lorry drove past him, hooting. He didn't notice it. Livestock-dealer Schindler, at the wheel of his SAURUS cattle-transporter, roared down the approach road towards the slaughterhouse gates. Ambrosio didn't get out of the way, he just went on walking, his eyes fixed on the horizon, like a sleepwalker's.

– Sacré tonnerre! Gilgen jumped up, straightaway he was on the street, pulling Ambrosio off it. You could have been dead! Nom de Dieu! Mind where you're going! Now take a look at this clown!

The engineers, turners, precision-tool makers, fitters and gunsmiths saw something that Ernest Gilgen had long since stopped noticing: they saw blood. It was animal blood, and it was out of place. Half excited, half disgusted, they stared, made faces, spat in the gutter. No one paid any attention to the siren sounding in the factory yard for the beginning of their eight o'clock shift. Hands rubbed tips of noses, dug around in ears, scratched here and there, flicked the ash off cigarettes. The grey routine had been broken, here was a day that didn't begin like all the others. An index finger tapped a temple, a head inclined to one side, a jaw worked, moved questioningly aside, the sinews that appeared showed that the open mouths were about to form words.

– Hm.

– Well.

– I don't believe it.

– The bastard.

– All that blood!

– Is that the way they work?

– Bastards.

– Look, it's even on his bald patch.

– Well, where there's meat there's blood.

– Hey, Gilgen, I thought you stuck cows to make sausages from the blood. Do you all take a bath in it first?

– Here, Ambrosio. Gilgen had been to get more beer. The rubbish those gents from the weapons factory were talking again.

– But it's true. No decent man would look like that. You can see him. And anyway . . .

– Decent man, eh? Wait till what happened to the student yesterday happens to you. He was talking rubbish too. We dipped him in the blood-tank.

Gilgen went up to the speaker with clenched fists: Just leave my friend Ambrosio in peace!

And the engineers, turners, precision-tool makers, fitters and gunsmiths all took a step back. Keep a bit of distance from that blood-dripping Gastarbeiter! And from Gilgen too. Maybe he'll flip his lid. Who can tell with someone like that? A butcher. Just as well he's nothing to do with us. And that whole slaughterhouse anyway. There was something dubious about it.

Every day they saw the brick buildings, the smoking chimney, they saw aproned figures behind the abattoir fence, and they were familiar with the livestock-transporters, and the delivery vans of the butchers in town, and they knew some of the slaughtermen, who, like Gilgen, sometimes came to their kiosk to get a newspaper or a beer. The lowing of the cows in the railway wagons on the sidings they had heard as well, and they ate meat every day and liked it, but what exactly happened to the animals under the angled glass roofs, behind the high fence, what happened? What had to be done before a cow became a joint of meat lying in the delivery van? What kind of process was it that spat out blood-rinsed foreigners as a kind of by-product, and allowed them to wander out through the gates?

In the heads of the engineers, turners, precision-tool makers, fitters and gunsmiths were a few childhood memories, painted over with a big brush, and mixed up with nasty scenes from war movies. The way the cat had screamed when Grandpa drowned it in a well. Or how the fish bled when you smashed their heads against the pier. And the grey horse that pulled the milk-cart, that stumbled, and unluckily ran itself through on the shaft of the cart. Was that not the schnitzel that showed through where the skin had been torn away? It must be something to do with living and dying. Someone had to shoot. With a carbine. With a pistol. Some kind of firearm. There was a smell of gunpowder anyway. You knew that. That was enough. You didn't want any blood-soaked Ambrosio in front of your kiosk. Let him push off. He smells. Tell him to wash. The bastard!

And Frau Kramer too came out of her kiosk, looked at Ambrosio, and stood in front of her bunches of flowers.

– That horrible blood.

– Come on, let's go, I feel sick.

– My stomach's turning.

– There you are, foreigners.

– And Aschi Gilgen.

– I don't want to know what they do to those animals.

– Cows will take anything.

– Yes, they even take orders from Italians.

– Come on, let's go.

They pushed each other a little indecisively, no one wanted to go on the shift alone. Backs of hands wiped beer-moist lips after the last mouthful.

– Right, let's go. I'm coming.

– Well, go then! Push off! Clock on! Gilgen laughed derisively at the disappearing group of engineers, turners, precision-tool makers, fitters and gunsmiths. He was still shouting when they were already at the barrier gate at the entrance to the factory yard. Think you're something special! Because they call you Herr, and you've got pencils behind your ears. Mais vous aussi, vous êtes des vaches! You're pale! Pale! Gilgen crowed at them with throat stretched out, and body leaning forward. You're all of you yellow, you conceited weapon factory yellow bastards. Mind you don't prick your fingers on your pencils, you could bleed to death! Ha, ha, ha. Ernest Gilgen doubled over with laughter.

Ambrosio didn't laugh.

Ambrosio was smoking. He scraped the blood crusts off his face. Off with the mask. How indifferent he suddenly felt to these people. He hadn't looked at any of them. Why should he? And those stupid jokes. When he lost his middle finger they laughed. He had only watched their mouths as they spoke. Little caves opening and shutting above him, and in each hole, he had seen the shimmering pink mucous membranes, and hidden behind those, he guessed, was where the little word-sacs were, those bags in numberless heads that were reserved especially for him, that opened only for him, and that were still always empty. Everywhere, they poured emptiness over him, why me? Those dark throats spitting out grunt and crash sounds that coiled towards him like worms. He had never been able to understand any of it. Never. And how remote now was the desire to understand.

Ambrosio only wanted to smoke now, to smoke his cigarette in peace. Nothing else. No, he didn't feel like going and giving blood with Gilgen.

And in the cattle room, Pretty Boy Hügli had slit open the belly of Blösch as she hung by her hindlegs, and started an avalanche of entrails. Slimy and knotted and green they dangled from the cow, *and the stomachs of the ruminants may be classed as rumen or paunch, honeycomb, omasum and abomasum*, and the paunch was still jammed inside Blösch's carcass like a swollen sac.

Piccolo went for it. He dug his fingers into the spongy tissue and began tugging.

But only the ball of honeycomb, omasum and abomasum slipped out of the slit-open belly. And the intestines were in Piccolo's way. They resembled a labyrinth of containers, tubes, locks and jets: a power station inside a cow, a protein factory full of industry and profit, and *the nourishment first reaches the rumen in a barely masticated condition, and is then tossed back and forth between it and the honeycomb for mixing and reducing. It is then returned to the mouth in portions for further intensive (ruminative) chewing where, worked to a pulp, and chemically treated, it is conducted directly into the omasum and the abomasum*, and, however hard Piccolo tried, the sac of the paunch would not leave the cow.

Then Pretty Boy Hügli intervened. He removed the net membrane – a transparent coating of greasy linings resembling a spider's web – hung it on the rack over the slaughtering bay, put his knife away, and helped Piccolo pull out the paunch. When all the entrails were lying on the handcart, Hügli tore the duodenum in two to free the intestines from the stomachs, and take them across to one of the tables by the wall.

– Here! So you have something to work on, and don't fall asleep again, he said to intestine specialist Hans-Peter Buri, who prodded the splattered mass with his fingertips and made a face expressive of disgust.

– All shat out. And inflamed with it. It's ancient stuff, don't even bother giving it to me.

– Buri, don't talk crap! Are you an intestine expert, or aren't you? Any Italian can strip a nice juicy beef intestine. Show what you're made of! Hügli had soiled himself with dribbled stomach juices. He wiped his hands on his apron.

– Bunch of crap, growled Buri. He plucked at the guts, and *the intestines of a diseased animal, one suffering from an inflammation of the intestines, will often be red, swollen and sticky*, and finally Buri just shook his head. No, Hügli, with one of these, you're rarely left with anything usable. You can put on kid gloves, strip them in warm water, and still be left with a few rags at the end of it.

And while Blösch's intestines were flying in a high arc into the container for condemned material, her stomachs were sliding about on Piccolo's two-wheeled hand-cart. The surface of it was greasy with blood and slime, and the heavy paunch threatened to slip in front of the axle. Piccolo swore. This could be dangerous. It had happened before, one of those vast fodder bags had tipped the handles upward, and lifted him off his feet. Once a rumen weighing 150 kilos had fallen out and flopped onto the floor in front of a cow that Krummen was bringing in. First the cow, then Krummen, had slipped on it. There'd been blue murder afterwards.

Piccolo gripped the handles still tighter and manoeuvred the cart out of the back door of the hall, and into the abattoir yard.

He made for the entrance to the tripery, and *in the trade ruminants' stomachs are termed: tripes.* A blast of hot air sent swathes of steam his way. There was the loud hum of electric lifting gear. In every corner there was boiling, gurgling and hissing. Drops of condensation fell from the ceiling, here everything was either red hot or ice cold, and all of it was wringing wet. In two rows by the wall were vast boilers the size of camp kitchens, only visible in outline, because of the steam. This was Fritz Rötlisberger's territory. He was the master of the tripery, and he was just now hauling some of yesterday's batch from one of the boilers. They'd had the smell and the toughness boiled out of them for fourteen hours. Like the catch in an enormous eel-net, Rötlisberger held them suspended in a metal basket in mid-air. With an iron hook, he grappled at the hot metal, and towed his prize along an overhead rail to a water trough, where he let the whole lot go. The cooling water overflowed and splashed through the entire shambles.

– Porco Dio! Fridu! Que cosa fai tu? Piccolo jumped back.

Rötlisberger giggled. Here, hold this, he said and gave Piccolo his lit BRISSAGO. I'm going to wash my face. He dipped his hands like a ladle into the rinsing water and washed the sweat off his face. Not only did Rötlisberger eschew rubber boots in favour of real wooden clogs of cow leather and young oak, he also declined to tie a rubber apron round his waist. Instead, what he preferred were burlap aprons, of which he wore five at a time. The inner one of these was the driest, and it was this he used to wipe his face on.

– You molto crazy, said Piccolo, and glancing at the paunch in the cart, Rötlisberger asked:

– You expect me to make tripes out of that? Those old shitbags? Let Krummen clean them himself. Or, you know what? You can take the whole lot across to the office. Dump it on Frau Spreussiger's desk.

– You molto crazy, said Piccolo.

– That's right, porco Dio. Niente comprendere, eh? Rötlisberger giggled again and set to work: he slung Blösch's stomachs out of the cart onto the tripe table, and snip-snap, all the containers were slit open and flip-flop, they were all tossed inside out, and Rötlisberger scraped the fodder and the stinking debris out of the honeycomb, out of the villi of the stomach walls, and *the contents of the rumen of slaughtered animals may be used as fertilizer*, and the air was filled with never-belched gases.

Piccolo turned up his nose. He had stayed standing next to Rötlisberger to admire his nifty handiwork. Rötlisberger had hands that had cleaned the tripes of generations of cows and bullocks, and they had mutated accordingly. By dint of working on the spongy green membranes of innards, by dint of the permanent moisture and the continual alternation of hot and cold, they had grown larger and larger. They had evolved into starfish

119

paws, and when Rötlisberger kept them idly at his side it some-times looked as if he had three faces, and sometimes three fists.

When Blösch's stomachs had been scraped clean, and splashed into the boiler for sub-standard tripes, Piccolo took up his cart again. As he left, he turned round once more:

– Hey, Fridu! No si fuma gui! he yelled, and so doing, backed into Krummen who, on the way from the pens to the slaughtering room, cow in tow, had just stepped into the tripery. Foreman Krummen swore mercilessly and went on. The cow followed him tamely, as on leading strings.

– Rötlisberger! Where are you? Bössiger wants to see you! You hear? Thick steam enveloped Krummen and his cow.

Rötlisberger moved another metal basket full of tripes from the boiler to the rinsing trough. Chains rattled, the lifting gear hum-med, Rötlisberger could hear nothing.

Then the outline of a cow loomed up in front of him. A pair of horns were coming towards him.

– Christ! Now they're bringing the tripes in on the hoof! But no dice! He grabbed a ladle, and doused the cow with tripe-water.

Jesus fucking Christ, damned idiot!

Krummen flipped.

– So you have to take the fellow a personal invitation, and he goes and flings boiling water all over you! Goddamn it, that does it! You're just clowning around in here! And you hold up the Italian. For Jesus Christ's sake! One of them walks out, another one comes in here and hides, the dealers don't deliver the goods, and the boneheads from town can't even be bothered to fucking shoot the beasts!

– Now give it a rest, will you! And what are you doing with a cow in here anyway? I mean to say. And shouting at me. I never saw you!

– Yeah, sure. I believe you. Cunning old bastard. You were there yesterday, though, weren't you? Whipping them up, that's right. But enough is enough, you wait. As if there wasn't enough aggro with the foreigners anyway. Now you go and see Bössiger in his office! Read me? Krummen had to yell again. Rötlisberger had opened up the pressure valves on a boiler and turned on the lifting gear again. When the hook had come down far enough to pick up the wire basket in the boiling water, Rötlisberger stopped the loud buzzing with the push of a button, and asked:

– What's that?

– Go to Bössiger! You'll know what it's about.

– Oh yeah? And why doesn't he come in here then? It's the same distance. Or is he worried about getting his nice shoes wet?

– Ask him yourself, you old buzzard! Krummen turned away. He yanked the rope. The cow bucked. Krummen tugged harder. It was a narrow space between the boilers and the troughs and carts, and the floor was slippery. The cow was nervous. She couldn't move, she felt trapped. She refused to go forwards or back. Krummen swore and smashed his fist in her muzzle. Rötlisberger grabbed some tongs, nipped her tail, and let go. The cow leaped up in the air, landed with one hoof in a bucket, tore the rope from Krummen's grasp, and set off at a gallop out of the tripery. The bucket clattered against the floor. Krummen set off in pursuit. Rötlisberger laughed and went up to the door.

Immediately above him on the wall hung a barely recognizable cow skull. Moth-eaten and spider-webbed, a hideous yellow-grey colour. Only the horns were still intact.

Rötlisberger took a puff at his BRISSAGO.

Seven forty-five.

Huber and Hofer have got that devil's cow under their hydraulic knives. They pull at the hide, stretch the inside of it, and get their knives in. Skinning is hard going. Hofer sticks the tip of his tongue out of the left corner of his mouth. When he does another cut with the knife, it goes back into his mouth.

The cutting-tool hum.

The meat on the flanks parts reluctantly from the inner fell, which is scarred, tick-drilled, diseased.

Like a pair of trousers, the skin hanging down round her ankles.

But fuck it! I can't get into it. Not the rhythm, not the forgetting, not the losing yourself in the work. I have to see everything, hear it, smell it. Today I don't dissolve in the bustle of it.

I try to keep up, get ahead: ambitiously. With blunt knives. With a shaking hand.

I whet and sweat.

What are you staring at?

Surely you're allowed to sharpen your knife once in a while.

Überländer comes and stands over my cow.

Give me the knife! Sharpen it, don't brush it. You could sit on that with your bare arse.

I splutter vainly.

The rings. The iron rings.

It's on account of . . .

You can't see them, for all the scraps of skin on the floor. Or you slip. The edge is gone.

Grind it?

Now?

As if I was allowed simply to go off and sharpen my knives while working.

Mishaps come about with bad tools.

Überländer is insistent. Working with blunt knives! No thanks. Now off you go and sharpen it. Before you cut yourself.

How can I rage? Hate? Punch?

I press harder on the handle. Flesh and hide resist me.

Go. Click. Like a slaughterman. Butcher's pride.

I gulp.

My lips flap against one another. Every muscle in my face is loose. I can feel my pallor. The lump in my throat.

It should go.

Up and out.

I should stand up.

Stand up, roar and clear off.

I toss my head the way Hügli does, and don't feel any bigger.

I press my lips together the way Huber does, and don't feel any more secure.

I thrust out my jaw the way Hofer does, and don't feel any stronger.

I narrow my eyes the way Krummen does, furrow my brow, turn my chin aside, tense the sinews in my throat, clench my teeth, and don't feel any more aggressive.

Luigi gapes at me and shakes his head.

Porco Dio.

Bloodied nostrils drip. I hear the bellowing of cattle. One ring

122

fixed in the floor, the other in the nose. Harnesses buckled tight. The ring cuts into the mucous membrane. The rattle of chains, spring-hooks, blinkers, slaughtering masks, beatings. Muzzles foam, spittle flows, eyes roll white. The nose-ring cuts harder. The horns. The neck, curved and upright like the comb of a cock. Two tonnes and more of tamed steer's flesh. And the axe splinters the obtuse head, the brains squirt out, and every second animal refuses to lie down. Another blow. Same again. You wait . . . a snuffle: The mighty head shakes. Shears! The whorl of tight curls on the wide brow. Hair to a thickness of five fingers dampened the blow. The curls fall. The axe bites, and the broad back goes under like a proud ship at sea.

For crying out loud! What's the matter with you?

That grovelling Überländer has gone and fetched Krummen.

His hand.

It sweeps in a wide arc round his whole bulk, digs in, burrows in the seat of his pants.

Bit pale, aren't you? Don't you ever go to bed? Get a decent night's sleep!

He checks my knife. Passes it over the hairs on his left forearm. Jesus. A kitchen knife! Are we butchers or aren't we? Use a reed like that and you'll only get hurt.

I get to my feet.

The throat below me stretches. The cow trembles.

Get your tools in order! Right away! Got it?

He turned round once again. And be sure you sharpen it properly the way you were told. Don't fuck around with it like a scythe. Or else, Jesus.

Not many cows had nose-rings. The lighter ones were held in a slaughterman's grip. The bigger ones were tied down. The rope passed round the horns three times, a loop flicked through the floor-ring, and the hammer was raised.

The lockable peace of the toilet beckons.

Door's shut. Bolted: occupied.

If you have to go, you have to go.

I've got no more toilet tokens any more.

The urinal doesn't tempt me.

With my index finger I press the wart on my right thumb. A

feeble electrical pulse through my hand. A trained wart pain with every heartbeat.

I like the tiled walls of the abattoir passages. Just walk on. Thirty seconds of bare wall.

The noise, the sticky dampness of the hall, left behind.

Sleeping as I walk; sleepwalking through the slaughterhouse.

At the canteen, they're unloading beer.

A chilling-room is open.

I go in between the hanging half carcasses. Hundreds of them, rank and file, arse by arse. All of them weighed and stamped, the backbone sawn in two. And now you're waiting for the muscles to stiffen. The lactic acid is going to demolish your cell walls. Tenderize you.

Young cows should have a layer of fat on them. Fat keeps out air and unwanted bacteria, makes for a juicier roast.

A pulley chain rattles.

An iron hook between two ribs, the knife down along the flat bone, the handsaw through the backbone, and you've got a quartered cow hanging up there.

A forequarter rides up into the airy heights of the chilling-room.

I hide behind one of the carcasses.

Don't let it be Bössiger.

The buzzing of the refrigerator plant would drown any cries.

I don't cry.

I carry on on my roundabout route, I'm yelping inside, I'm amazed my back doesn't give way. The vertebrae all stacked up on top of each other, like a column of toy wooden blocks. They hold. I walk. I'm falling over myself, but I'm walking. My legs carry me, the column of vertebrae in my back doesn't collapse.

On, on, along the wall.

Misery.

Like a dog that's disgusted by its own warty paws.

Oi, you! What a face you're making.

Rötlisberger.

What's up? Where are you shuffling off to?

He stops. A stiff-hipped old man, bowed and tired the moment he leaves the tripery. Only wearing one of his burlap aprons.

Must have left his strength behind with the other four, on the nail behind the first of his boilers.

What do I say?

My knives are blunt. I've got to sharpen them.

Ah? You slipped again? Well, if you don't concentrate.

He's bound to be off to pick up more BRISSAGOS from the locker room. They get damp in the tripery. He smokes nine of them every day, nine of those smelly coffin nails. They'd make me puke. They've turned him green anyway. Grey-green and ancient he looks.

I'm having to go to the office. Something's up. So long as it's nothing to do with that bloody chest.

I think Bössiger's watching the sticking, in the chilling-room.

That's all right then, he says.

I'll go up and wait in the office. Frau Spreussiger's there anyway. I don't mind looking at her udder for a bit. Not a bad rump either. And the legs, Christ!

He shuffles off in his wooden clogs, as though on a set of invisible rails.

I should go and whet. Better get toilet tokens in the break. If Krummen allows me my break, that is.

Rötlisberger bends down.

You can see it hurts him like sparks shooting through his back and hips. He puts his BRISSAGO down on the threshold and goes into the office.

The farmer's wife stood at the basin in the Knuchel kitchen. She fished plates and cups out of the dishwater, wiped them with a cloth, now and then scraped off a bit of hardened rösti lard with her thumbnail, dipped them one at a time into the basin full of clear rinsing water, and left them all to drain in a wire rack to her right. At the same time, she kept looking through the open kitchen window to check what was going on in the yard outside.

On the grass under the fruit trees in the orchard, her three little children were playing with wooden animals and tin cars, the Knuchel doves were assembling on the ridge of the barn roof, the sparrows twittered on the telephone wire, there was an expectant hush in the chicken-run, and the dog and the cats were toing and froing in the yard. Prince, panting and wagging his tail, would only sit for a few seconds at a time, and the cats had for once not disappeared into the fields at the end of the morning milking, but were still loitering by the door of the shed. For the Knuchel farmer had decided on this mild almost summery day to let his cows out onto the pasture for the first time, and that in spite of the hoarfrost, which was not without its dangers for limitlessly greedy ruminants' stomachs.

Muffled bell tones were heard from the byre. The first cow was about to be unchained. The farmer's wife hurried. She worked fast. So fast that Grandma, who had taken a cloth from the clothesline and had started drying up, first shook her grey head, and then, as she trotted back and forth from the draining board to the kitchen dresser, wiping vigorously at each individual piece, moved her lips in silent disapproval. But when the clanging in the cowshed became more animated, and the bursts of it were heard in rather quicker succession in the Knuchel kitchen, then she did manage to ask the question that preoccupied her, namely whether the farmer's wife would really keep a close watch on those cows. For she, Grandma, would hate to see some petulant young cow running down into her vegetable patch, and trampling on all the seedlings.

'Don't worry, Mother, I've got my hazel switch to hand. The moment Blösch leaves the stall, I'll go and see that they keep well away.' But Grandma's mind would not be set at rest, and she went on to complain piteously about this unnecessary releasing of the cows, which had always been an unpleasant business, and especially when Hans was going about geeing up the nervous creatures to the extent that, my goodness, no sooner will they have taken a dozen steps outside the shed than they'll all be jumping the garden fence. Yes, it was true, she said to the farmer's wife, she could look disbelieving all she liked, but she knew how it was, and how it would probably be this time too; it would take some misfortune, a child trampled, a broken leg, before they saw sense. And that Spaniard, he simply frightened the wits out of her.

In fact, though, the red-and-white hides of the Knuchel cows were already curry-combed to top shine, and for some days now, the farmer, Ruedi and Ambrosio had been preparing the animals for their move out on the pastures. The hooves were all trimmed, the horns rubbed down with oily rags. 'We're not having our cows leave the shed in the filthy condition of the Boden farmer's animals. We'd be ashamed of ourselves,' the farmer had said.

The cow bells were ready too. Ambrosio, who was continually astonished at the habits and customs in the prosperous land, had been polishing them according to Knuchel's instructions. In the loft over the cowshed, now swept empty of the last shred of hay, Ambrosio had taken rags, shoe polish and SIGOLIN, and had polished away for hours at the cast bronze bells, and the tin chimes, and the neck-straps that went with them. Their weight had amazed him, the way the cows' names were already cast into them, the way they were ornamented with little crucifixes and laurel wreaths.

And now the heavy instruments were to be distributed among the cows. Who would get which bell to wear? The farmer and Ruedi were not agreed in every case, so there were discussions and trials. Which young cow should have her newly burgeoning ambition reinforced by a somewhat larger bell, and which old lady should have her now rather overweening notions dispelled by a smaller one? Since the last pasturing the previous autumn, the pecking order in the Knuchel shed had changed, that was a fact, and the whole twelve-tone Knuchelglockenspiel would have to be retuned accordingly.

The farmer well knew that a judicious allocation of bells could avert a possible argument, because the cows should make good use of the valuable pasture time, and not waste their energy in unnecessary bickering, still less in bitter in-fighting. 'No, let them bite into the grass and eat, that puts fat on their bones and milk in their udders,' he said.

Ruedi was in favour of once again giving the second biggest bell to Gertrude. After all, she was the oldest cow in the shed, and she'd been rather unenthusiastic lately, he argued. His father replied, the bigger the bell, the more upright the walk, that was so, Ruedi was perfectly right, but Gertrude, that blasted cow, she'd already been sick once, and that hadn't left her unaffected, and her milk was getting less, if anything, even though she'd just freshened, no, she just wasn't what she once was, she could scarcely justify it, you could give her a big bell and all the patience in the world, and get nothing in return.

Several decisions were taken in a provisional way, and tomorrow, when they'd seen the whole herd on the pasture, then they would have a better idea of where things stood, said the farmer, and when the last neck-strap had been buckled, and Ruedi went over to Blösch's stall to start unchaining her, then Knuchel opened the lower half of the shed door, and picked up the whip he'd left to hand.

Blösch took her time. As though to try out the bell first, she tossed her head, then raised it so high that her horns almost touched the ceiling. She mooed quickly, bent her back in order to be able to turn round more easily, and slowly emerged from her corner. The manoeuvre was a demanding one for an enormous cow, and she had little room in which to execute it, so little that she couldn't avoid brushing against her neighbour Mirror with her own dewlap all the way down her back. After that unintended caress, her bell finally and fully sounded, and the lead cow of the Knuchel herd promptly stopped and bulked widely and mightily in the doorway. Only her head and neck were over the threshold, in the open.

Before Blösch took her next step forward, she mooed three times in succession, at first deeply, like an alpenhorn, but then more piercingly, in challenge. The sound that emerged from deep inside the cow through her outstretched throat was a cantankerous bellow, and at the same time an authoritarian trumpeting that scattered all the doves and sparrows, made Prince start barking, caused the farmer's wife to hurry out of her kitchen, hazel switch in hand, and served as a signal of departure to the entire Knuchel herd.

Now the unchained cows grew animated, no more bored glooping at locked feed cribs. All turned at once, barged into each other, tinkled and clanged with their chimes and cow bells, whisked their tails, and mooed impatiently back.

'Whoah, whoah!' said the farmer. 'Don't overdo it, the grass isn't going to run away from you.' But no sooner had Blösch vacated the doorway than Mirror and Stine wedged themselves into it with their great bellies and for a moment were stuck, unable to go forwards or back. Once in such a situation, though, no other cow had Mirror's ability to cowpush and wrangle in the national style. The more junior Stine had no alternative but to take a step back into the shed. That in turn earned her a jab from Gertrude's horns, to which she directly replied with a kick.

More massive cowbodies were barged aside by others, more rear hooves slipped into the drop where they sought vainly for footing, and in their flailing and panic they splashed slurry everywhere, and worsened the scramble. There was a grazed knee for Bossy when she stumbled over the threshold, before the whole herd had finally crossed the planks over the cesspool and was driven out of the yard.

Unlike Farmer Knuchel, Ambrosio had stayed behind in a corner of the shed. He hadn't been able to see where he might usefully intervene with his stick. It had all been too quick for him. A little bemused, he followed the exuberant herd, but then the sight of them soon delighted him. The red-and-white cows formed a horizon of flesh and blood, contrasting prettily with the blueish morning sky. The heads and horns and silhouetted bodies looked not unlike the mountain chain that they obscured from Ambrosio's sight. Vacas como montañas, he thought.

The farmer's wife had hurried down to the orchard ahead of the herd. 'Hurry, children, out of the way!' she called. 'The cows are coming!' She picked up little Hans in her arms, and shooed Stini and Thérèse behind the protection of an apple tree. Their toys had been left lying in the grass, and Blösch once more brought about an interruption in the progress of the Knuchel herd to the pasture. The brightly painted wooden animals and toy cars on the ground caught her eye, and drew her away from the path. She thrust out her neck, dipped her muzzle into the thick grass and sniffed and licked the toys. She moved her jaw and larynx as though swallowing something that had caught in her throat and choked her.

A crack of the whip to the base of her tail got her moving again. But no cow had dared overtake her, she was the lead cow, and had to be the first out onto the pasture. Nevertheless, there had been some disturbances towards the rear of the herd. Bossy and Flora had galloped off together, bells clanging wildly, and stupid Baby had managed to slip down to the vegetable patch after all, where, while not expressing herself among the cabbages in the way anticipated by Grandma, she had still managed to do considerable damage simply by lying down on the soft ground.

Once they were on the near pasture, the usual jockeying for position started, with all the cows wanting to graze in the middle of the herd. The animals used all sorts of tricks to try and outwit each other. None of them actually butted, but they were all squinting to left and right, all watching how the others responded to their bells, and voicing claims and threats by changes of direction and little menacing movements of the head. A step to the left, half a step to the right, a quick tongue flick to a conqueror's shoulder or udder on the part of the loser, in such subtle and civilized ways were the positional quarrels of Knuchel's cows fought out.

The farmer watched all of this from the paddock. He listened to the chimes and bells. After a while, he pointed at the herd with his whip, and observed to Ruedi: 'The clover looks so fine, you wouldn't mind being a steer yourself for a while, and biting into that, but what do those cows do? Nothing but squabble! You'd hardly notice it, but that's what they're up to, each is out to score off the others.'

For his part Ambrosio was more interested in the newly erected Knuchel fence. He'd worked on it for days, sweating and swearing at the enormous piles and the hard ground, and now nothing had happened, the barrier had not even been tested, none of the cows had so much as brushed one hair against the barbed wire. Ambrosio wondered why the whole thing had had to be so deeply anchored in the earth, and so solidly put together, when the Knuchel cows were only going to stay in the middle of the pasture anyway?

When they returned to the farmyard to see the calves, which had stayed behind, little Hans began crying loudly in the paddock. He sat in the grass among the toys, sobbing. On his way past, the farmer asked what the trouble was. He wasn't going to stop for him. Ambrosio, though, bent down to the little boy, picked up one of the carved wooden animals, and mooed a few times, to cheer him up. But that made little Hans cry even more bitterly. He didn't want to play with a cow. 'I want my car. My car's gone. Give me back my car,' he screamed.

As the cows were only allowed to graze in the daytime, because it was still cold at night, it took all of two weeks before the Knuchelglockenspiel started to sound harmonious to the farmer's ears. But to the farmer's wife, going about her business in the yard, there still seemed to be too much wild pealing from young cows gadding about, or even jumping for joy, which didn't consort with her standards of decorum for the Knuchel herd. There was still a little too much discord in it for her liking.

Where Gertrude was concerned, Ruedi had been proved right. With the second biggest bell round her neck, the old cow started to perk up, and gave more milk too.

It was Flora who created near-insoluble difficulties. Here was a cow so ambitious and so immoderate that she simply couldn't find her place in the herd. By pressing for a rank at least two places too high, she drew the anger of all the other cows. She even went so far as to challenge Spot, who was four years older than herself, and much heavier. She was injured, and while the farmer nursed her, the farmer's wife was incensed. A blinking cow like that needed to be brought down a peg. She should be locked up and given starvation rations. That meant no more PROVIMIN for starters, no more lavishing that on greedy Flora.

'Young blood,' said Knuchel, who, after his wife's vehement words, was once again trying to master the situation by means of a subtle exchange of bells. But he could only put an end to Flora's escapades by sending her out to pasture with no ornamentation at all, no bell, no chime, not so much as a goat bell round her neck.

Flora apart, the herd calmed down quickly after the first two days' grazing. The older cows in particular were happy to concentrate on assuaging their limitless appetites. In the morning they came out and then looked and ate their way down the slope, neatly fanned out, until their plumped udders reminded them of milking, and they reassembled at the top of the slope, to be led back down to the cowshed.

But as yet, Blösch wasn't on heat again.

Until one fine Tuesday morning, Ambrosio – sitting under Knuchel's lead cow, bucket between his knees, forehead pressed to flank – stopped. Was that all the milk Blösch was giving?

Ambrosio stroked the cow's fore-udder, stroked her red hair, clicked his tongue alluringly, but however hard he tried, he could get no more milk worth the mention to squirt from the teats.

Knuchel saw the bucket, barely one-third full. He sat down under his lead cow, scratched his throat, and said: 'Well, well, so she won't give any more? That would figure, with all the mooing and tailflicking. She's been nervous all morning.'

And later: when the Knuchel cows, after milking, were unchained for watering and grazing, Blösch straightaway shifted her weight onto her hindlegs, mooed, and in the tight confines of the shed, tried to rear up, her forelegs kicking, and mount Mirror. Her horns smashed into the ceiling, and her tail brought down cobwebs. Dust was everywhere. Mirror jumped aside, and banged into Gertrude. Bells and chimes clanged, there were loud moos of protest. The farmer weighed in with his whip until the whole herd had followed Blösch outside.

No sooner were the cows standing peacefully once more by the well to drink, than the farmer's wife, just stepping out of the kitchen for a moment, cried out: 'Hans, Hans! Quick! Look at Blösch!' Without resisting at all, Knuchel's lead cow had permitted herself to be mounted by Flora, no, she even arched her back as though receiving a bull, and thereby gave further evidence of her heat.

'Well, well. First a milk strike, well, we've seen that before. And there I was thinking the bloody cow was playing up again. It seems you have to watch her like a hawk twenty-four hours a day.' Knuchel took Blösch by the bell-rope. 'All right, finish drinking now, but then we're taking you back to the shed,' he said. And, again to his wife: 'It's unbelievable with this cow. Do you remember she was bulling once, and wanted to get on top of me? Luckily, there was a post in the way, otherwise – I don't know what. If you left her to herself, she'd probably jump the highest part of the new fence in her impatience. Then she'd trot up through the wood, and take some puny village bull on board in the middle of a potato field.'

'Well, maybe not quite that bad. No need to exaggerate,' said the farmer's wife, across the backs of the cows as they drank.

'What do you mean, exaggerate? I know her!' Knuchel defended himself. 'Last year I had to secure her with the two heavy chains. And even then she tried to smash half the feed crib. But we'll take her up there today, and I'll see that she's coupled with Gotthelf himself.'

The farmer's wife opened her mouth to draw breath. To say that there were other bulls worth looking at, that Gotthelf wasn't the only one by any means. But as the cows lifted their heads just then and stepped back from the well with muzzles dripping, she contented herself with just shaking her head.

Calling 'Ho!' and 'Hup!', Ambrosio drove the Knuchel herd minus Blösch down the paddock onto the meadow. Gertrude took over the lead. Only Mirror was unhappy about this new disposition. But in an attempted breakout, she was so greatly handicapped by her chime, which hung round her neck like a tin sack, that she thought better of it after a couple of bounds.

Before going into the kitchen, Knuchel held onto the doorpost to kick off his dung-covered gumboots, and also remove the upper part of his farmer's green work clothes. 'As soon as supper's over, I'm taking Blösch along to Gotthelf,' he said. 'She has to be covered today. Ambrosio can drive her for me.'

'Are you going to get changed just for that?' asked the farmer's wife, who was peeling potatoes at table with Grandma.

'Oh, it doesn't have to be Sunday best, no, but a fresh overall wouldn't come amiss. This one's already quite, you know, and people might think we had to economize on the laundry. I wouldn't go into anyone's house wearing that, and once you're in the village, there's always one thing and another. And I should look in on the post office too.' Knuchel hooked his thumbs under his braces and opened the parlour door. Before he had quite disappeared, the farmer's wife asked what he had to go to the post office for, whether the milk was already on the way up to the village, and where the children had got to.

'The children went along to the cheese dairy with Ambrosio,' said Knuchel without turning round and with his thumbs still tugging at his elasticated braces. 'And to the post office because it's something Ambrosio asked about. I think he's wanting to send money home to Spain. The first time. It's best if I go with him to the postmaster!'

Grandma looked up from her work.

The farmer's wife began turning the potatoes round faster in her hands. She dropped them in the earthenware bowl only half-peeled. Suddenly she stood up, plunged her hands into her apron, and entwined her fingers as though trying to graft them together. 'You know, I don't like seeing the way the children seem to follow Ambrosio round the whole time, and I don't know, Hans, I haven't said anything, and you must continue to do what you think best, I don't mean to butt in at all, of course not, but really, I think you know what I'm getting at, don't you? It's none of my business, you know what you're about, but does it really always have to be Gotthelf?'

Farmer Knuchel, who had stopped in the doorway and looked over his shoulder at his wife, snapped his braces and went back into the kitchen.

She wasn't about to get mixed up in his business, no, the farmer's wife continued. But he could see for himself what the upshot had been for the last three years. Not a great deal. And at the same time, it must have been particularly hurtful to him, and what with the tendinitis, one had to bear that in mind too.

Sometimes it was too much for her, to see the terrible way he clawed at his throat. 'Well, what do you say?'

'Well, what? I'm not happy with the way things turned out either. But you can hardly give Gotthelf the blame for it, and you won't find a finer bull in a hurry.'

'Oh, but Hans, take Pestalozzi, now he's got just as much flesh on his neck if not more. And he's agile, you know, round the flanks. Last week, when they were taking him up through the village past the shop, I saw him. He's so healthy-looking and strong. And Frau Gfeller said he's the best bull the community ever bought. I can't remember a finer-looking bull, anyway. Hans, if only for a try, just once,' the farmer's wife said beseechingly. 'Just once. And he's agreeable, too, Pestalozzi, everyone says so, and when he's covering a cow he's better than Gotthelf, not so choosy anyway, I mean the way *he* behaves is sometimes not good to watch, from what I hear. Sometimes he thinks no cow's good enough for him.'

'Well, if you think so, we could try him out, but on her account, too, you know, I wouldn't mind giving Gotthelf another chance, who can say, maybe just one more, and then suddenly we'd have the loveliest heifer in the highlands in our shed. They make a good pair, they go well together, and he always came on as excited as Dung-Hannes on his wedding day when it was Blösch, but if you say so, and Pestalozzi's one they've brought from the outside, I don't know, he's not one of ours. But let's hope for the best.' Knuchel held onto a doorpost, pushed himself off it, and disappeared into the parlour. His socks left sweat prints on the kitchen floor.

The farmer's wife stared at the two stains. She had expected much sterner resistance. For days she had been preparing herself. She had drawn up a long list of reasons to persuade her husband to change his mind on the choice of bulls. And now she was disappointed by the ease with which it had been accomplished. How she would have liked to build up her imposing case for Pestalozzi. There was his Breeders' Syndicate points' score, which was only just below Gotthelf's on the latest league table. And then his far more attractive and less fearsome horns, the evenly patterned hide, the short but droll forelegs, and then, particularly dear to her heart, those tranquil and beautiful eyes. Never before had she seen such eyes on a bull. Pestalozzi had exactly the kind of expression whose absence she so regretted in the younger Knuchel cows, Flora particularly. These seemed to her to be becoming ever more pert, insubordinate, even insolent. Surely things used to be different on the pasture. She hankered after some calmer blood in the byre. But why had the farmer given in to her so quickly? 'Hans, Hans, what's the matter?' she said quietly to herself.

Grandma sat there and said nothing.

After supper, Knuchel got Blösch out of the shed, put the long halter on her and set off ahead. Ambrosio followed, cowherd's stick in hand. But he had no need to drive her. Blösch trotted obediently along behind the farmer. Now and again she mooed, but she was never difficult. She seemed to know where they were headed.

The mayor, who ran the biggest of the Innerwald farms, and kept the two Breeders' Syndicate bulls in his shed, had been notified over the telephone by Frau Knuchel. 'Well, bring your cow over, if it has to be today,' he had said.

With his hands in his trouser pockets, he stood in front of his cowsheds, drew at a RÖSSLI STUMPEN and looked himself up and down carefully to check that his clothes really were as clean as his wife had assured him they were. And, to be quite sure there was no untidiness anywhere, he looked round the equipment and the cowshed implements.

A twig broom lay on the edge of the well. The mayor picked it up and put it away. He rolled up the milking-machine tube more neatly. And there were marks left by the dung-cart outside the byre.

As he was putting the broom back behind the barn door, Knuchel and Ambrosio were coming up through the village with Blösch. After the greeting, Ambrosio took over the halter. Approaching the shed, the mayor said to Knuchel: 'Well, I hear you fancy a change,' and, as he leaned over the lower half of the shed door to open it from inside, 'and might one inquire why?'

'It's not that I've got anything against Gotthelf, quite the contrary, maybe it's nothing to do with him, but it's all those bull calves. For years now. And my wife was of the opinion it might be time,' said Knuchel, not forgetting to murmur a 'good luck' as he crossed the threshold into the cowshed.

The mayor took his RÖSSLI STUMPEN between his fingers and shook his head. 'Well Hans, if you fatten all those calves and give them to Schindler! You've only yourself to blame. If only you'd sold me the one for breeding. He would have made some bull! I've got a real eye for them. He would have made such a fine bull. One for the national show. But what's done is done.' He put the RÖSSLI STUMPEN back in his mouth, and started talking more casually about an open byre that he'd had built for his fattened oxen. They might go across afterwards and have a look at it. Through some rather convoluted talk, the mayor also managed to suggest that they hadn't just finished with milking, far from it. A milking machine like that really paid its way, and it must have been almost half an hour ago that they'd washed and tidied everything away.

Knuchel said nothing. He scratched his throat, and looked round the cowshed. The animals had been liberally provided for, with the cows up to their knees in straw. Their hindquarters were clean and dry. The feed crib was shut. Walls and ceiling were newly whitewashed. Now and again, a cow would lower her head and activate the automatic waterer with her muzzle. The shed was spacious and light, except right at the back, where the two village bulls stood, where it was darker and also warmer. Knuchel sniffed the hot, slightly acrid smell of the bulls, and patted Gotthelf on crupper and back.

The mayor took an iron bar with a spring-hook welded on at one end. 'Right, let's see what Pestalozzi thinks then, eh? Tell your Spaniard to bring the cow into the paddock, it's always the quietest there. I'll bring the bull along.'

'I'd rather take Blösch myself, you never know.' Knuchel left the cowshed, and the mayor wedged himself between the two bulls, using the iron bar to make a passage. Then he got working on chains and straps. 'Right now, put that tongue away!' he called to Pestalozzi, who had a brass ring in his nose and red-and-white leather round his brow.

The mayor tightened the bull's frontlet, clicked the spring-hook into the nose-ring and said, 'Right, let's go,' and led him out of the shed on the iron rod.

Pestalozzi was one of the biggest bulls in the prosperous land. He was so broad that he scraped the doorposts of the cowshed on

137

either side with his belly. Barely four years old, he had visible qualities that no adjudicator could ignore. His chest measured 281 centimetres and he had come to Innerwald with an officially certificated weight of 1227 kilos, a weight that he'd since been able to increase to 1246 kilos in the good highland air. Everyone in the village was agreed that he was a mighty bull. The women in particular found Pestalozzi as big and beautiful as the last wagonload of hay before the rain. A glorious future was predicted for him.

Only Farmer Knuchel was a little sceptical.

Pestalozzi had a slightly untidy, off-white dewlap that dangled down between his legs from his neck. Thick folds of hide also concealed the base of his throat and his jowls. At the slightest pretext, they would wrinkle up, forming curmudgeonly pouches at the corners of his muzzle. His regard was veiled, and sometimes without expression, not least because of the little curls tumbling over his eyes. In fact, Pestalozzi's hair was curly and shaggy even below the shoulders, which some found attractive, and others unworthy of a bull. 'What do our animals want with ringlets like that?' Knuchel had asked once.

This shagginess on his forequarters was one of the features that Pestalozzi had inherited from his maternal grandfather Jean-Jacques, and it was enough to turn him into his spitting image. Jean-Jacques was not a real Simmental bull, he was a Pie Rouge, and thus belonged to a breed of red-and-white cattle that, while originating from the prosperous land, had changed somewhat for the better under the more liberal breeding conditions and improved climate abroad.

For Pie Rouge not only dropped curly bull calves, they also produced heifers that were quite exceptional milkers, all with considerable udder measurements, and they also passed on to their heirs a very high fertility. So high, in fact, that Jean-Jacques, along with a few other model Pie Rouge bulls, were reintroduced to their native cowsheds to breed back into the domestic stock, and reinvigorate the blood. Of course, the foreign blood was straightaway diluted, but nevertheless Pestalozzi so exactly resembled his grandfather that even the odd farmer who knew his bulls was surprised at the resemblance. 'A chip off the old block,' several had said.

Ambrosio was another one to be surprised. 'Qué país,' he muttered, as the mayor led Pestalozzi so effortlessly by the nose. It was alarming. In this country the dogs are as big as the calves in Coruña, the calves are as big as cows, and the cows are bigger than elephants. This mountain of muscle! A back like a roof. A chopping block of a head. So much power, and so tame. Pestalozzi moved along in a leisurely way. Only his half-covered eyes were rolling, as flashes of white sometimes showed. His breath came in fits and starts.

Blösch was nervous. She swung her rear this way and that on skipping feet, and she kept moving her tail. Pestalozzi gurgled faintly, lowered his head and sniffed at a blade of grass. 'Now for Christ's sake!' said Knuchel, who had Blösch by the halter. As though his oaken legs had put down roots, Pestalozzi stood motionless behind the cow. 'Now why do you think we paid a king's ransom for you? Get on with it, you bugger! Or I'll teach you! She is bulling, isn't she?' said the mayor, with a glance at the slime that hung down in great threads from Blösch's cleft, and he tugged harder at the bull's head with the iron rod. Forced up against her, Pestalozzi smelled at Blösch's crupper. 'You're not there to stand and contemplate her arse, you're to mount her!' The mayor's brow furrowed with worry. He beckoned to Ambrosio: 'Here, give me your goad!' he said.

While Pestalozzi was getting a dozen blows on the ridge of his horns, Knuchel was inspecting his undercarriage: 'Is he tired?'

'Can't be bloody tired! For that money, and the way he eats! Come on, take the cow, we'll try them out in the the box if the bugger can't be bothered to jump her.'

The box was a cage where the cow was enclosed on three sides, and the bull, approaching her from the open side behind her, had a couple of boards on either side of the cow's belly where he could rest his feet for support during copulation.

Blösch allowed herself to be put into the box willingly enough, it was Pestalozzi who jibbed. The mayor tugged at the bull's nose-ring until, snuffling loudly with pain, he scaled the boards, and lay on Blösch's back. When nothing further happened, Knuchel said: 'Now, mayor, seeing as we're here, why don't we give Gotthelf a try? I'm sure *she's* willing. What do you say? Here, Ambrosio, hold her while I go and get the right bull. Pestalozzi's not up to it.' He led Blösch out of the box and passed the halter to Ambrosio.

'No te preocupes, ya viene el toro,' said Ambrosio softly to Blösch. She was hard to hold, throwing her head to the side, plucking at the rope, taking Ambrosio with her, and mooing. The rope burned his hands. Blösch twisted and turned, kept trying to break loose, and whisked her tail as though she had to keep off a whole swarm of horseflies.

Gotthelf was a few kilos lighter than Pestalozzi. Nor did he have the curls on his body, only on his forehead. His head was white, so were his back, his flanks and his feet. All the rest was red. Gotthelf was more muscular than his neighbour, and he was four years older. He too was well known in the area. He was of good parentage. You could read his pure-bred ancestry in his face. He had the head of his father, who had been hired out as a stud bull in foreign service, and had thus developed a particularly wide forehead. In size and bone structure, though, he was more like his uncle Ferdinand, who, as a draught ox, had also led a life of service.

It was his maternal ancestors who had given Gotthelf the external marks of the breed. They came from the Oberland, and on that account not only had fine sets of horns, they were also good climbers, and had broad udders. Now and again one of the cows in the family would manage to attract attention at a fair or exhibition, whether as an honourable mention, or even as points victor at the herdbook prizegiving.

When Knuchel led Gotthelf out of the shed, the two bulls met and stared at each other. Pestalozzi snorted loudly. Breath steamed out of his nostrils. But Gotthelf wasn't interested in his rival, he wanted to go on, and trotted purposefully out to the paddock. Knuchel had to hold him back somewhat with the iron rod.

As night was falling, Blösch was at first not visible at all, and then only as a dark shape between still darker trees. But Gotthelf's nose twitched. His nostrils flared, he stopped and lifted his head, his throat rattled, and his pizzle shot out of the tuft under his belly. He pawed the earth with his forehooves, swung his scrotum about between his hindlegs, as though to say: 'Right, where is she? Bring her to me! What are you waiting for?'

Blösch too pushed nearer, sideways, with head bent away. Only by forcing her to circle round the trees in the paddock could Ambrosio keep control of her.

Blösch mooed.

Farmer Knuchel nudged Gotthelf's neck with his elbow: 'See, that's her coming! She's burning, it's killing her, her udder's hurting, she wants it so!' And calling from the shed, the mayor asked how Gotthelf was doing, whether he wanted to, whether he could, whether the cow would let him.

Gotthelf could, and Blösch let him.

As soon as the cow's hindquarters were in front of him, the bull reared up and his pawing forehooves found the branches of an apple tree. Everything happened very quickly. The muscles tensed and flexed, first on his hindlegs then all over his body, showing through the hide as though chiselled. Swaying to the side, he plunged his pizzle into Blösch's vagina, gave another thrust, grunted, his great chest shook, he foamed and panted for breath, through the black flames at his nostrils, and Blösch trembled, she drove her forelegs into the ground, her hindlegs seemed about to give way under the colossal weight, her dugs were like thorns, she threw her head back, caught her horns in the apple twigs, the whole tree was swaying, and no sooner had Gotthelf slipped back into a fancy crouch, and then got his forehooves back on the ground, than Blösch turned her head towards the village street, mooed, and pulled so hard on the rope that once more Ambrosio had difficulty holding her.

'So it seems you did want to. Come on, bull, you can put it away now,' said Knuchel.

Scratching the crown of his head, the mayor came up and said: 'What a wretched creature that Pestalozzi is! What's the matter with him? Say what you like, there's a lot to be said for artificial insemination. There you know where you are. And so does the cow. What a time all this takes. I've had enough. You have to wait for the BOSS-BOYS to play a cow yodel on the radio before Mr Bull will condescend to mount a cow. It's the truth. But now, Hans, I'll show you the new shed, hah, seeing as you're here.'

Knuchel took Gotthelf back, and followed the mayor behind the tractor garage, to a farm building not properly finished.

The mayor switched a light on, and said: 'This is it.'

In an area walled in by bare bricks, Knuchel saw a half-dozen fattening oxen. He got his pipe out and filled it. After the first puff, he asked: 'And do they just shit where they feel like? Anywhere in the shed?'

'Oh yes, but only until they've been trained. Then they'll shit like pigs, all in one heap.'

'All of them?'

'Sure. Then all you need to do is go in once a week with a big shovel and a hosepipe, and your livestock's clean again.'

'But what about the dung?'

'Now Hans, where's the sense in chasing after every pound of cowshit, and every squirt of piss? I'd rather pick up an extra sack of fertilizer at the co-op instead.'

'You mean chemical fertilizer.'

'Yes.'

'You know, mayor, we've always done well enough our way, using our own dung. Our animals like eating, and they eat a lot. They're healthy beasts too,' Knuchel added, and turned away.

'You and your dung,' said the mayor, turned the light off, and followed Knuchel, who went on ahead in silence, cleared his throat, stopped and said in a worried voice:

'You know, it's a right bugger with the mice this year. They're everywhere. There must be many more of them than in years past. But what I wanted to ask you was where the field-mouser's got to? He's only been down once. Any idea where I might catch up with him?'

'Well, there's voles up in the villages too, you know, awful. The field-mouser's no need to go down as far as you, he can clean up right here. But if you want a word, he'll be down in the Ox most of the night. He gets so many tails together as it is, he's never short of money for a drink.'

'Well, if that's the way it is. I've still got the postmaster to see, on account of my Spaniard. I'll look in at the Ox later on,' said Knuchel, and put out his hand, which wasn't shaken.

The Innerwald post office had been closed for several hours.

Farmer Knuchel took his pipe out of his mouth, pressed his nose against the glass door, while the newly coupled Blösch, on the end of the long halter, arched her back to urinate. 'Now, by Christ!' said Knuchel. The window was frosted glass with a steel lattice behind it. Without looking at the opening hours posted on it, Knuchel knocked on the doorpost. Nothing stirred. He knocked against the letter-box in the wall of the house. A dog barked on one of the farmyards that the night had turned into a single black shadow. Blösch tugged at her rope.

Knuchel pointed at a garden fence next to the door, gave Ambrosio the cow, and saying, 'Tie her up,' trampled a whole row of flower seedlings and shouldered through a thorn hedge. He had spotted a light on in the window of the postmaster's flat, behind the office rooms in the same building.

Stretching to get past a window box of geraniums, he tapped on the pane.

The postmaster opened up in his shirtsleeves, leaned on the sill, greeted him and said, 'What's wrong, Hans? What's the trouble?' Knuchel passed his hand over face and forehead, lifted the cap off his head with a couple of fingers, scratched his hair with the others, and said, trying to squint past the geraniums into the parlour, where the postmaster's wife was just turning down the television: 'We want to send some money down to Spain.'

'The post office is closed, Hans,' said the postmaster.

'Well, and why's that, if I might ask? Am I supposed to leave off milking, just so as to come here and bring you money? Go on, open up!' said Knuchel, and was already shouldering back through the thorn hedge.

The postmaster swallowed, sighed, shot a guilty glance at his wife, and shortly afterwards appeared behind the glass door, jangling his keys. 'Well, so that's him, your little Spaniard, I've already had one or two letters from him come through. Oh, and I see you brought a cow along too,' he said as he unlocked. He had pulled on his grey office coat, and was doing up the buttons from top to bottom.

'You're not putting that on specially, are you?' asked Farmer Knuchel.

'You wouldn't go into your cowshed without your overall trousers either, would you?'

'Yes, but I work with dung,' said Knuchel, whereupon the

postmaster observed that what mattered wasn't so much whether it was money or mail or dung you worked with, but that you had the right attitude. 'Yes, that's the main thing,' he added, and, doing up the last button on his coat, disappeared behind the counter.

Ambrosio hesitated by the door. This house was only made up of rooms, each with four walls and a floor and ceiling, the most unexceptional thing in the world, and yet he continued to feel oppressed by these Innerwald interiors. This post office gave him a sense of danger. Was it the dimensions? The building materials? The cleanliness? The cow waiting outside? Was it the two men, who needed so much space for their sweeping gestures, and so much air for their sluggish speech? And the things on the walls! Enlargements of postage stamps gleamed behind glass. One series of flowers, another of rocks, a third of various cattle breeds. The depicted animals were red-and-white, brown, black-and-white, and brownish-black. Not a bull among them. On the promotional posters there were yellow post office vans on steep mountain roads, swerving round grazing livestock. All cows. And ALWAYS USE THE POSTCODE over the letter-box.

'How do you want to send this money, then? Cash on delivery?' asked the postmaster, who was laying out cheque book, forms, stamp, ink pad and sponge on the counter in front of him.

'Yes, I suppose so,' said Knuchel.

'And how much?' The postmaster's hand hovered over a form.

'One thousand,' said Knuchel.

'One thousand?' The postmaster's raised eyebrows appeared over the top of his horn-rimmed glasses. 'He's doing well out of you, your Spaniard.'

'We're not doing badly by him either,' replied Knuchel.

'And what about the spicka da language, how's he doing there?'

'The language? Not much there. But he usually understands what you tell him to do. No more than that.'

'Well, let's try him out, shall we? Can you spell me the address?' said the postmaster turning to Ambrosio, who vainly did as asked. After he'd been forced to tear up three forms on account of various misunderstandings, the postmaster gave up his pretence of understanding Spanish. He held out the biro to Ambrosio, and said: 'Here, write it yourself, don't know who taught you your spelling.'

Then Ambrosio put down ten one-hundred notes. Slowly, one on top of the other, he laid them on the marble counter. Knuchel's lips moved as he kept count, and as soon as the last note had been paid, he said: 'He has been saving, our Spaniard. He's sending almost his entire wages off to Spain.' And for his part, Ambrosio reflected that in three months he'd had barely half a dozen opportunities to spend any of it, but soon he would treat himself to something, first, he would go to the village shop, where he bought cigarettes, and choose one of those sports bags that you could tie at the top, and then he would ride into town, to the station where he had first arrived in the prosperous land and from where he had caught the yellow bus to Innerwald, and at this station he would buy himself a newspaper with the Spanish football results in it, and he would buy some wine, proper wine, and then he would look for a watch, a handsome wristwatch, and he would have them take it out of the shop window and tell him about it, and then he would wear it on Sundays, and maybe in the evenings as well, wear it far down on his wrist, outside the cuff, the way Luigi did. When Ambrosio signed the receipt at the place indicated for him, his signature seemed to flow more smoothly than it had ever done before.

'Ho, yes, your wife will be pleased down in Spain, when she gets this! And the children! If you want, you can tell them there's more to be earned where that came from,' said Knuchel. 'Our cattle have a good appetite, here in the highlands, they give streams of milk, and the weather's promising for later this year too, only the new bull's a bit of a disaster and there's a terrible plague of voles in the soil, but apart from that there's not much we can complain about, what do you say, postmaster?'

'I think you're right there, Hans,' replied the postmaster, separating the stamped receipt carefully from the form in order not to damage either of them, and keeping three fingers crooked in the air. 'They say the mice are awful, so I've heard,' he continued, without looking up, 'but that apart, everyone's got a couple of flitches of bacon hanging by the fireside at home, and I don't know what's supposed to be wrong with the new bull.'

'The new bull's lame, that's what's wrong! Can't get it up!' said Knuchel laughing, thinking the while that a man like the postmaster who only worked with two fingers at a time would hardly have much idea about livestock breeding. And he got ready to go.

The postmaster put forms, stamp, sponge and cheque book back in a drawer, turned the key, and emerged from behind the counter to show Knuchel and Ambrosio out. With his hands buried in his trouser pockets, he stood in front of the door and looked at the restless Blösch, who appeared incredibly big to him in the dim light of the street lamp and dangerously horned. Then he looked at the area she had defiled in front of his house, at the broken hedge and the trampled flowers, and said: 'I suppose you've got to go now. She seems in a hurry to get back!' But while he shook Knuchel's hand, wished him a good night several times, said three 'Adieu's', and for some reason, or maybe merely out of habit, thanked him for something unspecified, the postmaster thought to himself: Yes, go before your damned cow starts shitting or uproots my fence, get out of here, go! And when he locked the door again, and heard only the sound of hooves clopping into the distance, he growled to himself: 'That cow wouldn't lick another cow's calf. Someone from here could have used that money. What are we playing at, sending it down to Spain?'

And before the postmaster unbuttoned his grey work tunic, he fetched a damp cloth out of the broom cupboard, got down on his knees on the flagstones of the post office, and removed the marks left there by the boots of Knuchel and Ambrosio. He swore as his arm moved rhythmically to and fro.

Having reached the village square, Knuchel set his left foot on the staircase up to the Ox, brushed the dust from his overtrousers, and said: 'Well, let's see if we can still catch the field-mouser, Fritz.'

Ambrosio, who was leading Blösch to the well, shook his head. 'Yo no,' he said.

'What? Aren't you thirsty?' Knuchel straightened up, and when he saw Ambrosio's index finger waving to and fro like a windscreen wiper, he rested both hands on his knee and pushed himself up. 'Well then, leave it.'

On the threshold to the bar, Knuchel wiped the dirt off his soles, took off his cap, and the pipe out of his mouth. 'Good evening, one and all,' he said in greeting. The customers in the Ox fell silent, turned their heads and two dozen hands stopped raising beer glasses, playing cards, smoking, and worrying and scratching through shirts and trousers. As though they had ears, the hands lay beside glasses and cards, for a few seconds nothing stirred, then work boots and shoes slid over the floor, swollen veins rubbed against chair legs round which footwear had entwined itself.

Well, by God, it's another full house, but I don't feel like playing cards, and my time's too precious for nattering with the cheeser. Knuchel rubbed his neck. Where would he sit? He pointed at the field-mouser, who was sitting at a table by himself at the very back of the room, with his head on his folded arms, and appeared to be asleep. 'What's the matter with Fritz?' he asked as he took a place on the bench that ran along the wall.

'Ah, Field-mouser Fritz is sleeping it off,' said Stucki, an old farmer from the village, and another Innerwalder, Eggimann, shouted across three tables, 'Why, look, it's Hans Knuchel!'

'I just happened to be up in the village at the end of a day's work.' Knuchel asked for a beer, puffed at his pipe, and before he'd realized it, the net of conversation at the Ox, a loose weave that extended through the whole room, had settled over him as well.

The talk was of the Obermoos farmer who was about to sell his small, but heavily indebted property and move with his family to the city, where he had found a job in a factory as a porter or a forecourt gardener it was thought. It was Stucki who saw the story as another tragic example of flight from the land. Knuchel disagreed. That was *Farmers' Weekly* talk. If someone was really going to flee the land, he'd have to go a lot further than just some factory in the city. 'Yes, that's right,' Farmer Eggimann backed him up. 'Some have come back with their arses in far finer trousers than Overmossy's got on, you can be sure of that.'

What Knuchel then had to report about his visit to the village bulls was not only listened to with keen interest, it also had the effect of splitting the customers of the Ox into two rival camps, each accusing the other of exaggerating and of complete inability to face facts.

Knuchel praised Gotthelf, made mention of his own Blösch, whose fame had spread way beyond the highlands, and reckoned he'd never quite trusted Pestalozzi, how could you trust a bull with ringlets, and, scratching his throat, he added that he wouldn't be at all surprised if the Bull Committee of the Breeders' Syndicate should feel compelled to sell their expensive bull this selfsame year, and at a loss.

But that would be slaughtering the goose that laid the golden eggs, that was irresponsible talk, and Knuchel must be blind in one eye, came the reply from the supporters of Pestalozzi. What about the tests on Gotthelf's latest offspring? Wasn't it time the gentlemen learned how to read a statistic! Just touching and looking closely at horns and scrotum wasn't enough for the modern-day assessment of a bull! The AAI had shown that often enough!

Knuchel merely laughed, looked round in amusement, and asked: 'What about pedigree breeding? Eh? And leave your Association for Artificial Insemination out of it! Are they the reason we've got healthy cows? Yes, by Christ, are we farmers still or are we gold-digging cross-breeders?'

A murmur arose at this, and the customers at the Ox reached for their glasses, and while they drank looked to see what reactions were being registered, however cautiously, on faces to their left and right. All wrinkled their brows – but only as much as their neighbour did. All raised their eyebrows – but not too high.

Farmer Blum, with his diploma, was the first to speak clearly amid the murmuring: 'But it's mad, experts everywhere are researching and finding new methods and procedures, only we here in Innerwald, we act as though we knew it all ourselves, and were incapable of taking on board one or two improvements. It's true!' And he blushed and fell silent. 'That's right,' large-scale Farmer Strahm took up the theme. He had recently been in the veterinary hospital and one of the doctors there had wanted to show him something, for which he had had to put on a rubber apron and other boots, Strahm said. The vet had led him to an experimental cowshed. There he had seen a young cow with a regular window fitted into the side of her belly, so you could look through it and see the ruminant's stomachs, and even the grass, ever so clearly.

'For Christ's sake now,' laughed Knuchel, 'were our learned professors unaware that what a cow eats goes into her belly?'

There were various responses to this remark – some giggled,

others shook their heads and tut-tutted at Knuchel's narrow-mindedness, and spoke of great beams of fir trees suddenly having disappeared from the sawmill and turning up in the eyes of some people they could mention – then the village farmers on Knuchel's left began to speak of the latest state-of-the-art milking technology. Knuchel listened for a while, and then said: 'Look. I'm glad you've got your clickety-click gear if you're happy with it, but please leave me out. What do you have to keep on praising your milk suckers for?'

That made the cheeser take the cigar out of his mouth, swing his card hand behind the back of his chair, turn to Knuchel and say: 'There are some that have milking machines, and some that have foreigners in their cowsheds!' The co-op manager added in the same tone that, as far as noise went, one of those foreigners made quite as much noise as a milking machine, particularly on a Sunday.

And when large-scale Farmer Strahm also started in on him, then, for the first time in weeks, Knuchel felt the choking in his throat again.

Strahm had just been praising his own milking system with especial fervour, and had even volunteered the opinion that these milking machines were God's gift to the milk producer, and that he was proud to be involved in the industry now, in the age of the milking machine. Strahm asked Knuchel how many large cattle units he actually had in production, because these latest technologies weren't beyond the means of the small or medium concern, on the contrary, this machinery should interest even the very smallest farmer.

Knuchel banged his beer glass down on the table, put his pipe in the ashtray, and, as though to prove that he wasn't a small farmer, he stood up, cleared his throat and spoke: 'I have no large cattle units in my shed! I have cows, and all of them are prize-winning Simmental cows! Blösch, outside by the well, is the best of them, Baby's the stupidest, Spot is the youngest, and they are all more than good enough for me. As long as I have hands to milk with, I won't have any milk sucker on my farm!'

He had spoken loudly, loudly enough for some of the Innerwalders to exchange glances, as though to say: Who's that bellowing in our Ox? Not content to stay at home and work or clean or play the wild man there? But when Knuchel sat back down on his bench, at the very back of the room, the field-mouser raised his head, his rutted features stared off into space, and he croaked: 'Dust art thou, and to dust thou shalt return! For thou art as the dirt under thine own nails!'

Here, too, there were murmurs round the tables, jaws were scratched, eyes squinted left and right, anything rather than take up a position too speedily and be exposed, but one head after another turned back, heavy Innerwald bodies shifted their low centres of gravity on chairs and benches. It was apparent that to a man the customers of the Ox were turning away from Knuchel to level their full contempt on the field-mouser at the back of the room.

The old man rubbed his eyes with his earthy hands, crushed his hat firmly onto his head, and complained to himself, half aloud, that night had fallen, and he should be gone, but once again no one had woken him, he wasn't even able to trust the waitress. Slowly he stood up, and emerged from behind the table. In his grey-black outer garment, he looked like a gigantic bird of prey, testing his wings.

'Yeah, you!' jeered old Stucki. 'It's long dark. You and your devotions!'

'Why don't you go to church instead for a change?' said the cheeser, and talking all at once, the other customers at the Ox opined that no one should be surprised that the damned root-gnawing of the moles had got to be so bad when the village's own field-mouser drank every sundown, or any rate slept through it, and still speechified afterwards, and they nodded up at the old man as though aiming to butt him with their thrust-out chins. Soon one wouldn't be able to go for a walk in the churchyard without continually tripping over some cursed molehill, said the cheeser, and old Stucki shouted that they had counted more moles this year than in any year since 1933, and he went on to say that his boy Samuel already had three of the cows in his byre suffering from leg strains, on account of missing their footing on molehills while out grazing! Even Blum, the agriculture graduate, threw angry looks at the field-mouser, and said that the community couldn't go on entrusting its pest-control policy to that knife-grinder, and it was high time to take the bull by the horns, because only yesterday his wife had discovered another damned tunnel right under her rhubarb bed, the whole thing was undermined, it was so bad it gave you sleepless nights. True, true, the Ox customers chorused, if someone just drank and slept and acted pious, what did that add up to, of course given such conditions the voles would multiply undisturbed, and that as quickly as a northwesterly gale, and who could be sure what this homeopath of a strolling tramp was doing with the 50-kilo sack of poison that the community had so blithely handed over to him.

But the field-mouser straightened his wrap, stooped to pick up his box of tools, got his lantern out from under the table, took up his staff, and confidently crossed the room. The steel caps on his earth-encrusted boots were clearly audible. His eye hastened ahead of him, clear and unclouded, as if it were gliding over a field in the moonlight. From the beginning, his staff pounded rhythmically on the floor-boards; it was the slow, economical rhythm of a man used to covering long distances. The coat, draped round him like a cloak, his hand on his staff, all gave him a look of great inner peace. The field-mouser offered no insult, no hint, however tiny, of self-defence, he simply left, with such intangible sublimity that the customers at the Ox were left staring in perplexity at the door after it had closed behind him, before realizing that they had wasted their words.

When bodies and limbs once again shuffled into more comfortable positions on benches and chairs, when Innerwalder hands again picked up glasses and cigars and playing cards, then Knuchel remembered he had wanted a word with the field-mouser.

'Damn it! You shut the byre door, but the cow's bolted. I've missed him. That's how it is with talking.' Then he called the waitress to pay for his beer.

But even before Knuchel could get to his purse in the trousers he had on under his overclothes, Armin Gfeller, a farmer with a smallholding behind the Galgenhubel hill, came over to him and sat down. Gfeller had a beer bottle under his arm and a glass in his hand. 'Not off already are you, Hans?' he asked.

Knuchel went on rummaging in his back pocket, halfway between bench and table. When he had at last extricated his purse, he replied that his cow was still outside, and the Spaniard, Ambrosio, was waiting for him as well.

'Aha. Your Spaniard is waiting,' said Gfeller.

'Yes, he didn't want to come in. Must be our beer he doesn't care for.'

Armin Gfeller sidled nearer and smiled. 'You know, Hans, before you go, there was something . . . well, I wanted to ask, how about, well, what do you say, look, the mayor, he said to me yesterday, and seeing as you're here in the Ox, it's about, say what you think . . . would you have any hay left?'

'Hay? Me? What for?'

'Hah, what for? I miscalculated. It happens.' Gfeller's mouth was a thin slit stretching from one ear to the other. 'I took on too much livestock for fattening. The two cattle from the Boden farmer, that ox of yours, they make a difference. In fact they're eating the roof off my head at the moment. I can't just shovel PROVIMIN into their cribs, and my grass, well, it's coming on, but slowly, and so I thought, instead of mowing too much early on, I thought, well, it's only a couple of bales I need, and if the mayor says . . . well, what's your answer?'

Knuchel went red. As though his hayloft hadn't been swept bare for at least two weeks now, but was still full to the rafters of last season's hay, he thought, appalled: Am I going to let his sorry cows eat my hay?

Gfeller, raising the glass to his mouth, but then straightaway putting it down on the table again, and scratching his ear, continued: 'With that ox last autumn, you know, we came to an agreement pretty quickly, and I remember saying to my wife at the time, that Hans Knuchel's a nice fellow to do business with, that's what I said. So how about it? I could come and pick it up.'

'Hay for sale! Dear me, no, Armin!' said Knuchel, and thought: That Galgenhubel farmer can finger his ears and tug at his earlobes as long as he likes, but here he is now, trying to play the trader. What a stupid notion, everyone wanting to flog things off to everyone else, and preferably without lifting a finger, make such a heavy profit they should be ashamed of themselves, but work, actual work, no one was interested in that. 'No, Armin. I'm not a travelling hay salesman,' said Knuchel. 'I plough my land, I sow, I mow grass and I harvest for our farm and our cowshed, not for trade, not for switching things round hundreds of times this way and that, that isn't my line. All I have to sell is my milk, livestock now and again, a pen full of pigs, or a calf, and in the autumn what we can bring in by way of barley, rye, hops and potatoes. Not hay.'

'But why, Hans?' Gfeller's voice quavered. 'You've got your animals out grazing already, and you've got more than enough land, but I never said anything, I only asked, and there's no law against that.' However, he thought, he wasn't going to take a lecture from someone who practically dislocated his shoulder in getting his purse out because he was so worried about spending the odd fiver too much that he kept it buried in his back pocket under three pairs of trousers.

That was all right, said Knuchel, he wasn't going to take it amiss, and it was true, he had to admit that his cows had been out in the pasture for a while now, but that was the fault of the weather, it seemed to be smiling on him just at the moment, and it was good for the animals, they were doing themselves proud out there, and, he added after a pause, the sound of the bells on the meadow below the farm, that didn't bother him at all, no, not in the slightest, his wife would occasionally complain when one or other of the cows acted up, but otherwise, no, and he was looking forward to the warmer weather coming, when he could leave them out all night, and perhaps it wasn't too far off, what with all the cowtail clouds in the sky. They were a sure sign, he finished emphatically.

When the waitress came, Farmer Knuchel exchanged a few friendly words with her, he inquired what had kept the landlord away that evening, and, banteringly, whether he would have to pay for Blösch's use of the parking space outside, and, getting to his feet to return his purse to his back pocket, under the over-trousers, he said, looking down to Gfeller: 'Oh, I'm looking forward to it. You sleep sound at night when you hear them grazing. I don't think there's anything better than having your animals outside in the meadow at night! Now then, I've got to go, my Spaniard's waiting, and I think my cow prefers standing in the straw at home to standing in front of the Ox.'

'Yes, of course, you've got your Spaniard,' said Gfeller, no longer making any effort to smile. His cheeks sagged loose and pink, but he was grinding his teeth, and when Knuchel started to take his leave, to nod, and to shake hands, he asked him aloud, 'How's it all working out, then? You pleased?'

'What with?' asked Knuchel.

'Oh, with your Spaniard. You don't regret having him come here?' Gfeller sipped at his beer, twitched his left shoulder, and scratched his left knee under the table with his left hand. He was eyeing Knuchel, who smiled complacently before answering: 'Oh, it's going well, I'm very pleased with him indeed, he's willing, and he can milk as well as anyone from round here. As for complaining, you never hear a word, he does what he's told, and he does it the way you show him. And he's just as good with the animals, and with the children too, so I've really nothing but good to say of him.'

'Yeah, we've noticed he's settled in here,' the cheeser joined in, whereupon the co-op manager forgot to deal the cards. 'The little bugger feels quite at home here in the Ox too,' said Armin Gfeller. Most of the clients were now squinting in the direction of Knuchel, who scratched his throat, and backed towards the door. He seemed to be swaying, so emphatically did he move his weight from one foot to the other. When young Eggimann piped up, loudly and stammeringly, that b-b-bugger Sp-p-paniard already felt s-so at home, it's as though he thought he'd b-b-been b-born here, then Knuchel put on his cap, scratched the hair under it, and said: 'But look, he's working here in the highlands with us, I'm only saying, but anyway, I've got to go, I've got the cow waiting.'

'Never mind how long he stays and works here, he's still a stranger,' said the co-op manager who was now dealing the cards, and rapped the table with his knuckle for each one. 'Just because no one's saying anything, that doesn't mean anything.'

That was right, the cheeser backed him up, because if someone came to the cheese dairy wearing the green, then maybe it wasn't too much to ask that he should at least learn the language. 'That's the least of it,' cried Armin Gfeller.

'Now damn it all!' Knuchel took another pace back, and cursed the tightening that had begun in his chest, and now so constricted his throat that he could hardly speak. 'The language isn't easy for him, and he's small, that's right, but he's wiry. Yes, he's a wiry little fellow! And whether you believe it or not, he's never one to hold back at work, he's not worried about breaking sweat every now and again, and I know one or two who could learn something from him in that regard! But it's time to go, all right, I'm off now. So, good night! See you around, all of you, adieu Fräulein!'

No sooner had Knuchel clicked the door in the catch than the noise swelled behind him, and the laughing and swearing could be heard out on the staircase.

Yeah, roared someone, that little Spanish bugger was wiry all right, they'd seen that when he'd picked a fight. Everyone talked at once, trying to outdo one another with abuse and denigration. Yes, but the boys had salted his bacon for him, had shown him who was in charge here, and they had to when foreigners didn't understand how to behave themselves here, and were they just expected to stand and watch, and what else were they expected to put up with from them, no, you could say what you liked, but the next time his sort tried anything at the Ox, he would be flung into the nettles, or dunked in the well till he saw stars! That wasn't enough, came another loud voice, they would smash a hole in his head, big enough for Knuchel's prize cow to drink out of. Another calmer voice pointed out that while the field-mouser had tended to drink too much before, still, he had become much worse, and a year ago he hadn't been nearly so talkative, and if that wasn't the fault of the foreigners.

But Knuchel strode through the village, behind Blösch, whom Ambrosio was leading. He could hear only the clopping of hooves on the asphalt. Yes, the best cow in the village, and they couldn't produce one like her from their sheds, no, they only had large cattle units! Knuchel would have loved to swear loudly into the night, but all his endeavours were in vain, for a long time he couldn't make a sound, his throat was choked tight. And he'd left his pipe behind, left it lying in the ashtray. Once more he couldn't swear.

When they had passed through the village, and could see to the left below them the silvery-black buildings of the Boden farm and above them on the right, the dark heights with five bright gunshot holes where the targets for the shooting range were placed, then Knuchel stepped up his pace, first caught up with Blösch and patted her neck, and then with Ambrosio, to whom he remarked: 'Those village farmers! The blockheads!' Ambrosio didn't understand the farmer. Nor did he understand it when he suddenly stopped in the middle of the lane, stood with feet apart, and shouted up at the village, through cupped hands: 'For Chrissake! Jesus! Large cattle units and milking processes! Have none of you got a brain left in your heads?'

Just before the little wood, the farmer stopped again. He pointed to the roadside, where, in spite of the darkness, several dandelions could be seen, and said, 'Pretty aren't they? the cowflowers.'

Once back in the farmyard, Ambrosio led Blösch to the well, then took her into the cowshed and tied her up for the night. The farmer, scraping his soles clean by the kitchen door, wished Ambrosio a good night.

The railing of the external staircase was trembling slightly when Ambrosio touched it. He could feel through the wood that the farmhouse beams were once again being shaken by the mysterious banging. When he got up to his room, he could hear it very clearly. Boom, boom, boom! it went, coming from downstairs.

:6:

Did I forget to knock?

Frau Spreussiger jumped, her swivelling chair squeaked, a mirror flashed under her desk. Herr Rötlisberger! Oh, you gave me quite a turn!

– So I see. Rötlisberger stood with his thumbs hooked behind the bib of his burlap apron in front of Bössiger's secretary in the abattoir offices. Making use of her boss's absence, Frau Spreussiger had just rubbed some ATRIX into her hands, and quickly, mirror, mirror in my hand, who's the loveliest in all the land, inspected lips, complexion and hair.

– Do you want a word with Bössiger? Or not? I'll give him a bell. He'll hear a cheep on his bleeper, she said as she reached for the telephone and dialled a number. But what about you, Herr Rötlisberger, how are you? You don't look well.

– What's wrong with me?

– Well, you don't look very healthy to me.

– Old, don't you mean?

– Now, Herr Rötlisberger! I didn't mean it like that! A man like you in his best years. Please sit down! Rötlisberger remained standing. Behind the desk he could see a pair of knees pressed together, and nylon-stockinged, only half-covered thighs.

– I always said I should have worked in an office, sighed Rötlisberger.

– Did you now? said Frau Spreussiger coquettishly, and without lowering her bosom, and keeping her pelvis forward and her skirt tight, she swivelled round on her own axis. She knew how to move with elegance among the shiny dust-free surfaces of office machinery and office furniture.

– Yes, by God, an office, that would have been something else! Rötlisberger took off his cap and scratched his hair. But what

157

can you do? Then again, I'm sure you have some pretty rough times in here too. Am I right?

– Herr Rötlisberger, if only you knew! That business yesterday, ooh! And I'm the one that gets yelled at. If he catches that student, that Lukas, she said, half whispering, then there'll be trouble. That's for sure.

– That's good, because Lukas will be coming round today again. That's good.

– Ah, there you are. Come into my office! The door had burst open, and Bössiger was suddenly in the room. A flood of excess energy preceded him. His open office coat flapped round his legs, making him look bigger and broader than he really was. The bleeper in his breast pocket was still going. In three strides, Bössiger was behind his desk in the next-door room, he dropped his big black book down on it, and pointed a forefinger at Rötlisberger, who had followed him only as far as the doorway.

– You're to start acquainting Fernando with all aspects of tripery work right away. We need you elsewhere, Rötlisberger! Bössiger was speaking loudly. We've got a responsible job for you!

Rötlisberger took a step backwards.

Frau Spreussiger's fluent movements came to a stop. Her red skirt suddenly seemed even tighter round her bum.

The bleeper was still sounding.

– What do you say? How long will it take you to get Fernando familiarized with the work? It won't have to be done as scrupulously as it was in your time. The tripes that we sell fresh on the day, they don't take long to scrub. Make it a bit easier for him than you made it for yourself. Show him a few short cuts. Can we say three days? Will that be sufficient? Of course it will. Fernando's been with us for years.

– He can't do it, said Rötlisberger, scratching his hair again.

– Bah! Of course he can!

– And what if the tripes stink? Or if they're completely green? How is someone going to learn that in three days? My God, Herr Bössiger, you need to develop a feel for it. You don't do that in three days.

– A feel! You just need to show him very clearly how it's done.

158

Write down the temperatures and boiling times. After all, Fernando's the best of our Italians.

– Fernando's Spanish.

– Rötlisberger! No snail-dances! Spanish, Italian, Yugoslav, Portuguese, Turk, who cares? He's reliable, and he's got the hang of it faster than a few of the trained butchers. I'll give you the rest of the week if you like. But we need you in the intestine-washing department. And as soon as possible. We're reorganizing. You'll be taking over in a supervisory capacity.

– Aha? A supervisory capacity? Rötlisberger took a step nearer the desk. Is that meant to be a promotion?

– That's right. Lighter duties, less exhausting. Bössiger sat down and switched off the search device.

– It's that chest! muttered Rötlisberger but Abattoir-Marshal Bössiger said:

– At the moment we are losing too much in the intestine-washing department, we need someone there with a sense of responsibility.

– Load of rubbish. You're not promoting me onto the dungheap. No thanks. Whenever there's one of those crates standing round in the corridor, it means you want to try and turn me out of the tripery. I'm not playing! Rötlisberger turned and left the office.

– Will you stay here, ordered Bössiger, so decisively that the triper stopped in his tracks.

– Today's Tuesday. I want you in the intestine washery on Friday. Understood? Straight after the nine o'clock break, you'll be taking Fernando into the tripery.

– Like that, is it? I see. If someone does a job well all his life, that's nothing. He's shunted around like a potato. Just like that. All at once, a stooge is good enough to do his job. Yeah. Just move on, old fellow.

– Rötlisberger! Listen. And shut the door. Bössiger spoke quietly. No one doubts you. You're a first-class triper. You do the work of two men. When we wanted to put someone in under you, you weren't having it. You wanted to do it all by yourself. And you do it well. Right. We've never had any complaints about the tripes. But you're getting older too, Rötlisberger. You too. You need to move on to some lighter task, before we lose you altogether. The intestine-washing department today is rational and mechanized and we're going to be expanding it. You won't be under the same strain there, you won't be made to lift and carry any more.

– Don't kid me. In that box out there, you've got one of those robots, and you want to put me on him. You want to turn me into a machine-minder if it's the last thing you do. Why else call it a supervisory capacity? But, Herr Bössiger, I've learned a trade, I'm a butcher and sausage-maker, OK, and I've worked with tripes for over thirty years! And as far as the machine goes, no, let me finish, if you didn't know already, I'll tell you now; machines don't get on well with me! Not at all. On the contrary, when I touch one, it's apt to break. It gets stuck, my God, machines have caught fire under my hands, one machine even blew up, like this! Rötlisberger raised his arms, clenched his fists, and flung them asunder. Just like that! Bang! Blown to Buggery!

– End of discussion, said Bössiger. On grounds of organization and hygiene, Fernando is taking over your job, and you're moving to casings.

– What? Hygiene as well?

– Isn't that your BRISSAGO out on the doorstep? Be sensible! Have you any idea how many complaints we've received about your smoking? You don't even bother to conceal your BRISSAGO any more. The chief inspector wanted you thrown out ages ago. It's only because the director had a word with him personally that you're still here. But this is it. You won't be hiding out in the tripery any more. And while we're on the subject, do you know that people have been saying you're inciting the Italians, and that it was you who brought in that student Lukas? And what about yesterday? What happened yesterday? Where were you yesterday? Where, Herr Rötlisberger? Can't you see that we have only your best interests at heart?

– I don't need anyone to have my best interests at heart, or anywhere else. I do my job, and now you want to stick me on a machine, but I'm not a push-button butcher, I'm sixty-three, for Christ's sake, leave me alone. God, why not fix the pot where it leaks, as if there weren't more important things needed doing than chasing me out of the tripery.

– Please, calm down! What have you got to object to? Firstly, a machine like that is quite idiot-proof, it won't jump at you, and secondly in the intestinery you will still be doing important, respected and well-paid work.

– That's just it. Rötlisberger leaned across the desk. Bössiger shrank back. Put an idiot on your idiot-proof machines, not me! And important, respected, well-paid work. Herr Bössiger? Who respects it? Who pays it? Have those men in the office got any idea of the kind of stuff that's come my way in the tripery? I'm not that cow-stupid. Don't imagine you can pay us for the things that swill around our feet, and get hosed down the drain. You think you can stuff all that in the pathetic pay envelopes you give us? Ha! Right!

Rötlisberger stomped off. Bössiger reached for the telephone, and Frau Spreussiger once more for her mirror: she was snow-white.

Eight fifteen.

Whetting.

The turning stone rips sharpness into the blades.

The emptiness inside me. How quickly it returned. Suddenly the wheels grip, the drive belt hums, and I feel my guts being crushed, sliced, corroded.

The stone turns unevenly, and water splashes out from under the shield.

Eight hours to go.

I could put my medium blade away, lift my right arm, my hand could open and turn, and I could stop the electricity, cut out the motor, dead.

The stone would go on turning for a while, slower and slower. Then it would stop.

I test the blade with the tip of my thumb. I slice it across my thumbnail. The tiny fibres of metal tickle.

Can silence kill?

The way that cow got up on its forelegs to bellow.

When sand clogs the drain under the stone, the water used in the whetting collects and dissolves the soft stone.

At this hour, men in grey coats are going to offices.

We're back in the arena.

We're always there, and always surprised to find ourselves there.

The heavy side of the lopsided stone comes up, and as it falls away, the rotation speeds up, and a splash of water lands on my forearms and apron.

The men in grey coats are standing in bus queues and raising their hats in greeting. Each time they bow almost imperceptibly from the waist. Many carry umbrellas over their arms.

Remember that you're a slave in Egypt.

Something should have bellowed and raged in me. Of its own accord. Independent of me. I would have liked to watch. A spectator of my own self.

And satchels are flying through heated classrooms. I hear them clattering onto desks.

What is it drives us out into the cold rainy morning three hours before sunrise? What lures them away from their warm wives? They tiptoe into the kitchen, down the stairs on hushed soles, out into the night.

I press the point of the blade against the fine-grained whetstone.

And the gentlemen in hats and coats say goodbye on doorsteps to wives in brightly coloured dressing gowns.

I watched with Ambrosio as Gilgen whetted an axe during the lunch break. At the end of work, he shaved himself with it in the locker room. He didn't say what he wanted it for.

Will he come back?

Will Ambrosio?

I just have to make sure that Kilchenmann pushes the iron wire down into the marrow of every cow.

The men walk through the streets very uprightly. They carry briefcases and most of them are acquainted.

It is the oil between stone and steel that makes the sound of whetting bearable.

In a story there was a boy who stood all alone in front of a house at night, sharpening his slate pencil against the soft stone surround of a pump.

Only a single thread off the blade is ground on the whetstone: a barely visible wisp of steel. The individual fibres are picked off the stone by hand. Bössiger said: If anyone forgets to drain off all the water, he'll be paying for the next stone!

He had been held up on the way there, said Überländer. By the time he rattled up on his JAVA, the farmer had lost patience and done the shooting himself. At point-blank range, with a double-barrelled gun, he had aimed first at one eye, then the other. Why the eyes? The devil only knew. At any rate, the shots had ripped away half the cow's cranium like a hat, but she hadn't lost consciousness. Wasn't even lamed. While the farmer reloaded and the farmer's wife chased the children away, the cow had pulled herself up again. Without turning off his JAVA engine, and still in his coat, he had stuck the cow right away.

And Krummen: seventeen times the two apprentices had hit the calf on the head, back in the days when a wooden hammer was still used to stun lightweight sausage-calves.

But then he had told those two guys the kind of butchers they were.

Without interrupting his chewing, Überländer said he had kept on telling the farmers he butchered for, for God's sake not to shoot until he got there, you needed a proper gun and the necessary expertise. After all, it wasn't a wild boar hunt.

First through the chilling-rooms, then down a side passage. Perhaps steal a look outside. A bit of sky. Anything but the direct way back.

It's true too, Überländer had added after a while.

In his own way, that is, with the greatest reluctance, Buri had joined in. You might say that everything at SWIFT & CO. in Chicago went off at a hellish lick; sometimes an ox would still be waving his tail at one end, while at the other his tongue was already being pickled in vinegar.

Ice-cold air greets me outside the deep-freezing room. Ventilators like aircraft engines.

Hugentobler territory.

You know, Überländer had told the farmer, you could have killed an elephant at three hundred paces with one of those cannonballs you used.

Before the meat goes into the freezing-room, it is stacked here by Hugentobler, and instantly deep-frozen, amid fiendish din. Minus thirty-seven.

Outside the cattle slaughteringhall, the wooden chest and the smell of cattle fat at body temperature.

The warmth that rises from those opened cow bodies.
Back to work.
With sharpened knives.

Buri's hands felt the intestines. Sensitive as a blind man's, they plucked here, pinched a little there, stopped tentatively, and moved with a serpentine grace over the ruffle spread out over the wooden table. It was the sixth of the day, and by no means a bad one. Small and large intestines felt tough, thick enough for cervelat and tongue sausages. Buri swore. So far he had only been able to throw away Blösch's lean and inflamed intestines. There was still more work for him to do here.

The final 75 centimetres of the large intestine go with the tripes. Buri measured and cut. Rectum and anus flopped into a basin, and then Buri got into position: one boot pushed forward, head and neck bent, and he began to reel off 40 metres of chitterling into a plastic bucket. Pulling evenly, he parted the long tube from the ruffle with his knife. After every finished move, he nodded his head. His eyebrows frowned. He concentrated on his knife. A moment's inattention, and the whole intestine is ruined. Buri was sweating. He wiped his forearm across his brow. He finished. He put his gutter's knife away, and went in with bare hands, into the fat-padded remnants of the insides of the sixth cow.

Buri no longer had the strength of a butcher. He wasn't even properly healthy. His colour had taken on something of the gall-gut green that his hands had to burrow in every day. He could no longer keep his back straight either: his walk was stooped and broken, as though his bones had rubbed one another down as he dragged himself from one side to another in the halls and passages of the abattoir. Buri had a wooden leg.

But Buri was still a giant. A tired giant, but a giant all the same. However ponderous his movements might be, his chest was still as big as a barrel, his shoulders were broad, and his proportions massive. The more striking was the gentleness that flowed, smoothly, almost womanishly, but alive as quicksilver from his wrists and out through his fingertips as he worked. It was with positive tenderness that he treated each apparently indissoluble knot of delicate intestine, and quickly and effortlessly sorted it into a little pile of fat, a little pile of veins and tendons, and a few tubes, which he knotted at both ends, and, according to colour and calibre, dropped into one of his various buckets for further processing.

Cleanliness was Buri's first commandment, his pride and his joy. There was never dirt on his apron, and it was rare for him to get besmirched. Buri had a low opinion of butchers who, after five minutes at the gutter's table, looked as though they'd fallen into a cesspit. He himself wouldn't touch an intestine, unless there was a bucket of hot water standing by, and if, for all his delicacy and expertise, an over-porous gut did happen to tear, he wouldn't stop until the tiniest greenish stain, the least taint of stomach juices had been removed.

But intestine-man Buri wasn't the only one who had gone back to his proper post once the slaughtering had got underway. As the cow-demolition process had advanced, all the others too had gone to their individual places, like grenadiers leaving the vanguard. Together, as a team, they had got things moving, and now the wagon was rolling, it was that that was setting the pace. Each man had to fight alone, on his sector of the red front.

Krummen brought in the cows.

Kilchenmann shot.

The apprentice got the cows ready for sticking, he bled and headed them.

Fernando and Eusebio carved off the horns and shins. Together with Luigi, they turned the cows over onto their backs.

Hacking and sawing, Luigi opened up the bodies, took off the udders and tails, and attached the hindlegs to a lifting-hook.

Hügli sent the carcasses up into the air and eviscerated them, removing heart, lungs, kidneys and liver.

Piccolo took the stomachs into the tripery, and came back with the empty barrow.

Huber and Hofer worked the skinning gear, cutting and tugging the red-and-white hides off the cow skeletons.

Between trips to the pens, Krummen split the carcasses in two.

Überländer tidied and wiped and washed what was left to be weighed.

Swiftly and eerily the animals had their familiar form stripped away from them. No sooner were they dead, than they were hanging upside down on the overhead rail, naked and steaming, passing the keen gaze of the meat inspector. And the whole thing accelerated further, the din grew still more intense: the hydraulic knives whirred, the chain-lifts rattled, the electric saw chewed and shrieked and chattered its way down the spine of a slaughtered animal, the guillotine precision-crunched hooves and bones, and Kilchenmann's shots flew, bang, bang, bang, through the hall. The noise accumulated and washed back over the men in a hundred-fold echo, as the blue veins bulged on temples, on blood-smeared forearms, swelling under the mounting pressure of the slaughter as the pulse stopped in the breast of one cow after another. Red flowed from the throat wounds of the animals, red slopped from blood-catching basins into tanks, red dropped from the walls, from hooks and from aprons, from the faces of the men, from their knives, from their meat-chewing swords.

Blood dripped onto the scraps of skin and tendon on the floor, turning them into one slippery pudding. In a puddle of everything that dripped and dropped from sagging organs and limbs, Krummen's rubber boots sought a foothold. Blösch had to be split.

Krummen took one more look round. Even with Gilgen and Ambrosio absent, he had kept forcing the pace. The resentful glances hadn't escaped him. Didn't escape him now.

– Are you proposing to milk those cripple cows, and put them up for the night? I want them out of here! Before the calves come, he shouted, while he held the electric bone-saw against Blösch's croup.

Blösch's hide lay spread out like a carpet on the floor behind Krummen in the middle passage of the slaughterhall. Meat side up. Huber and Hofer were standing over it, pointing out scrapes and scars, bruises on the flanks, a purulent eczema on the neck, and no fewer than seventeen places where bot-fly larvae had got through. Huber said: Sieve! Fucking rubbish!

– Wouldn't even make shoelaces, said Hofer.

– What are you waiting for, then? Salt it and get rid of it! Krummen shouted at them.

Like a wet canvas tent, they folded Blösch's hide into a parcel the size of a suitcase, tied a rope round it, and left it on the floor behind the slaughtering bay, next to the grey-blue uterus.

The bone-saw started up with a whine: the teeth wouldn't bite, they only howled imploringly, protesting, idling at high velocity, and *bones consist of 1. The compact substance (hard as a tube of concrete)*, and Krummen spat on the sawblade. The spittle hissed.

– Fuck! All right then. Krummen picked up the cleaver. He took it back over his head, and slammed it down. Nothing. He raised the metre-long blade higher, and swung it down even harder.

Suddenly there was silence in the hall. Pretty Boy Hügli gaped as he sidled closer. The apprentice raised his head, and sharpened his knife. Huber and Hofer switched off their skinning gear. At the intestine table by the wall, even Buri stopped work.

Krummen's jaw trembled. He circled Blösch's body like a dog circling a tree.

– Where's the other cleaver? Did you hear me? I want the big cleaver! He shouted, without taking his eyes off the carcass. The big cleaver! That fucking fossil cow! I'll show her! Jesus! She's got it coming! And *the bones form the body structure: the 'backbone' supports the trunk*, and Fernando handed Krummen a monstrous cleaver. It was so outsized, so unmanageable, that no one used it any more, and it even had rust stains on it.

Krummen seized the wooden handle, pulled the heavy implement to him, and tested the sharpness of the blade. He spat on his hands. All eyes were on the bone that would not break.

Krummen wound himself up.

– Now, you bastard! he screamed, and dealt the Blösch cadaver a masterly blow on the rump-bone, but nothing split. No crack, nothing. He hit it again and again, raising the steel ever more furiously above his fire-red face, shouted and groaned and stamped and swore. All his blows were deflected like water off glass. Blösch's rump-bone defied Krummen's strength, as though it had turned to stone. Krummen rained down blows, but this backbone was indivisible.

His blows splashed on the glass bone with less and less precision. Buri turned away, shaking his head. Huber and Hofer shrugged their shoulders in bemusement, and switched on their skinning gear once more.

– Now, by God! I don't believe it, said Überländer, and once

167

more Krummen rolled his eyes, ripped the steel high above his head, and with the last of his strength sent it crashing down next to the rump-bone: the right pelvic bone broke and splintered. Überländer twitched, as though the blow had been meant for him. Hügli winced. Krummen was chopping his way through the loin. The vertebrae cracked. Smashing the right sirloin, he went on chopping parallel to the backbone, hacking through the hoops of the ribs, through the lateral bones of the thick neck vertebrae, making an ugly pulp of the steaming dark red flesh, blindly he smote at the last vertebra, the balancing atlas, until the two halves of Blösch's carcass, more shredded than split, fell asunder, and the iron in Krummen's hands, suddenly unresisted, bit into the granite floor.

Eight forty-five.
    I try to hide my glee.
    Wrestler-king forced to his knees by cow.
    She gave me a fright, but she threw him.
    Can cows really not hate?
    That's what comes to him for his condescension and maltreatment. He shouldn't have dished out so many blows.
    Usually words are enough for him.
    Yes, he, most silent of word-misers, only nodding, pointing, indicating, at most growling or shouting, he, who with his professional pride and wrestler's honour, doesn't dare throw out more than three or four syllables at a time, words are usually enough for him.
    But that old ghost cow avenged herself.
    You've got all the blood running back into her guts!
    Watch it! You're through the other side!
    Hügli can go and stew himself. Back to the locker-room mirror. Whistle your Ennio Morricone!
    There's just a thin trickle from the throat under my knee.
    When Krummen gets to them, they all start going crazy.
    Because she's not dead. I defend myself.
    Ha! Not dead! Hügli laughs.
    Just pay attention and don't wander. That's right.
    Because she's still trembling.

Still glowing with warmth.

If that collapsed heap is still alive!

Once more I push my skinning knife up behind the tough skin of the forehead of a feebly bleeding cow.

Stop cutting her hair!

Shout all you like.

On the horns, that I've got the skull resting on, the rings are close together. Each one a calf, each ring the ring of a year. The fetus, splashing about in the uterus, indicates his pilfering of his mother's calcium store with a ring-shaped stunting of his mother's horns.

Dr Wyss is standing by the cow that frightened me, and that Krummen couldn't split.

In his hand he holds a knife as sharp as a scalpel. A delicate, light metal sheath for it hangs from his doctor's coat.

He points at the botched half carcasses.

He's after something, and Überländer shrugs his shoulders.

The meat inspector nudges the uterus on the floor with his shoe.

The veins in Krummen's forehead were that shade of blue.

If something doesn't go according to plan, he can only shout and swear. He lost his rag. He, too, in an invisible cage.

I am not alone, with my own will supplanted by my will not to will.

Deep down, Krummen knows neither peace nor aloofness from his work. His wrestler's gait: show! His laconic manner: show! The casual way he wields the tools: show! When something touches him, like that glass cow did just now, he suddenly changes colour, explodes, can only rant and hop and swear.

Would he take a step to freedom?

We could all get up, turn round and go.

Just go.

Like hens.

Given the choice: undernourishment and cold out of doors, or plentiful grub in a cage, hens would choose freedom.

I keep still.

Someone has to do it.

We all do what must be done.

Only in Utopia, said one of Lukas's friends, only there was the slaughtering done by serfs, and outside the cities. These were medieval ideas, though.

169

Another swallow of blood squeezed out of the throat. The basin that catches the blood puts pressure on my spine. Enormous thing.

Then there's blue murder: Dr Wyss wants to know where the blood of the fourth cow has got to.

His vet's knife disappears into the delicate sheath.

Hasn't anyone here read through the meat-inspection rules properly!

Dr Wyss is speaking loudly. Back in his office, it would have been called shouting.

How often do I have to remind you, gentlemen, that before the meat inspection is completed and the carcass duly stamped according to regulation, no cow's blood may be poured into the tank with the other blood? Is that so hard to understand? Now be so good as to pour away all the blood so far collected today before my eyes. Gentlemen. The fourth cow goes to the cheap-meat department, her blood is not to be allowed into general circulation.

Kilchenmann unrolls the thick hosepipe.

Hügli and Überländer say nothing.

Together they tip out the contents of the blood-tank.

A red flood covers the floor, and meets the jet of water directed by Kilchenmann.

Huber and Hofer sharpen their skinning gear. They cast sidelong glances at me.

And then the quiet of the morgue: chewing, munching, biting into the smacking pork sausages out of the hot water in the pail at break time in the dark eating hall, and beer bottles pop open, air is let in under sweat-drenched cloth, belts loosened, the belches rise from way down, ah, the first swallow of beer, and greedy guzzling in rows at long tables, only Krummen, rage-red, the grimly chewing face, sits alone, sees nothing, hears nothing, says nothing but at the back of his neck, the muscles play, twitch, twitch, and Buri glances at him, you get cows like that sometimes, and it's not possible to split them, not often but sometimes, and it's a disease, everything goes into those animals' bones, they get hard as iron, I know, I've seen it a couple of times before, at SWIFT & CO., and Buri goes over to the pail, and fishes another sausage out of the water, bites into it, fat squirts out, and Rötlisberger is in there too, and he bites, and Hügli wipes his face with a big handkerchief and protests with mouth full, don't need to spit at me, eat your sausage by yourself, and Piccolo sets off on his fly hunt, smack, one more mark on the dining-room wall, and Krummen opens the newspaper, his hands are shaking, and he sees nothing, hears nothing, says nothing, and Rötlisberger stares venomously at Hügli, goes on chewing, Hügli moves back, stop spewing all over me, you bastard! And Rötlisberger gets up and sits next to Krummen, who moves his forearm protectively over the sports page, a Krummenrumbling: What are you coming here for, eh? Spitting at me now? Can't you even eat your banger in peace without bothering me, and smack! Piccolo laughs, that was the second stroke, bloody hell I get dem, and in comes Master-Baker Frutiger with two baskets, baking smells: here's the cake! What about you? Try a sausage? Click-clacking, Überländer's tongue emerges, I've got something caught in my back teeth, three fingers digging around in his mouth, traces of blood still on the hairy back of his hand, and then, examining the recovered meat fibre: Nut kipfels? Hey? Got any nut kipfels? Give me a couple, here's the money, and Luigi grabs the curved biscuits, holds them against his temples like horns, moo, moo, moo, he goes, and won't pass them on, laughs and moos and smack! Piccolo another triumph, and another, smack! Give them here, Luigi! Hey! Luigi! And he laughs and laughs, and now stop it you fool! You meathead! Yes, you're a meathead! Come on, you berk, you silly bugger! What a stupid joke! And still Luigi moos and laughs, and Christ, watch it! You must have got an itchy hide! Why do those foreigners behave like pigs at a carnival the whole time? Fucking hell! And where's Gilgen? Where's Ambrosio? And I'm going to the canteen, you off to get a drink? Then bring me back a bottle, or make it two, and yeah, yeah, drink, drink in the name of the Lord and chop your paws off afterwards! You watch what you're saying! And a MARY LONG lights up, and the coins jingle in Master-Baker Frutiger's hand, yes, he's seen Gilgen, he knows where he is, out by the kiosk in front of the weapons factory, that's where he is, and Ambrosio with him, and you should have seen them, they were keeping half that bloody shift away from work, and Krummen sees and Krummen hears, and Ambrosio was still in his apron, yes, of course, that blood-covered apron he had on, and still got his knives buckled on, and Krummen shoots his jaw, puts his left hand on the chair under his bum, and who wants another custard slice? Fresh today, yes all right, I'll have one says Hofer, give me one, of those pus-strips, and Huber gets up, yes, I'll have one too, and Krummen explodes, Krummen speaks: God damn the fuckingshitheadbastards! Hanging round the kiosk the great arsehole, while we're killing ourselves here! And right at the back, out of deep eye sockets, goggles the apprentice, says nothing, chews and stares and pale isn't he, Gilgen was going to donate blood, today, yes, at the Red Cross, and he wanted to take Ambrosio with him, the loon, what are they doing giving blood? Not working is what they're doing, lazy sods. Work-shy layabouts, gypsies, vagrants, and we're supposed to get through our work with the likes of them, don't get so worked up about it, I've had just about enough, same here, and those fucking Eyeties, and Fernando gesticulates, eh watsheet, yeah, yeah, you can laugh and you can wave your hands around like a combine harvester, that's about all you're good for, but you should all be rammed into the ground, yeah right, unsharpened, ma che cosa vuoi, mamma mia yourself, now you're laughing again, laughing, yes, they can laugh, and they can make holes in the guts and fuck up all the intestines, they can do that, says Buri, and they can cut holes in the hide you can put your fist through and we get the blame for it, they're good at that, says Hofer, and pissing off to the bog every ten minutes for a smoke, they can do, or a wank, says Hügli, and Buri says it's all a matter of scale, you see, you must think on a bigger scale, at SWIFT & CO. in Chicago, it wasn't the end of the world just because there were one or two more animals out in the pens! You tell that to Hugentobler, this isn't Chicago here, and Krummen folds his newspaper together neatly, gets up, the chair crashes against the wall behind him, corners of his mouth pulled down, stands there like a Neanderthal with his receding forehead, invisible club at his feet, his eyes as though he was about to launch another blow with his cleaver, and the order comes: There's another little cow out in the shed, and I want the apprentice to bring her in, you hear, and you're to go with him, yes, you, and Krummen points with his newspaper at Überländer, show him the holds, he's to estimate the weight, it's about time he learned how to bring in a cow on a halter! Now? Today? Überländer stops, you see the half-chewed biscuit in his throat, why now? Don't you

172

think? Why today? He's never yet taken in a cow, and what are you mouthing off about, Bössiger says so, and smack! another fly sticks to the wall, and time's passing, and Krummen puts his watch back in his trouser pocket, looks around, shaking his head, Überländer goes on chewing, the apprentice stretches his back, you'd better watch out, because a cow can smell it if you're not quite sure what you're doing, you've got to show them who's in charge, yes, they can smell it, and what are you trying to put the wind up him for? For Chrissake! And the same with Huber and Hofer, nothing but choking down cake, and empty bottles disappear under the table, you shouldn't drink so much, and you can't talk, you and your BRISSAGO, shut up, and the door crashes shut behind Krummen, and what's eating him? What's the matter with him? And you're asking? Did you see the hole in the floor he made with the cleaver? Fucking terrifying! And you go and chuck tripe water all over him! That wasn't my fault, ah, give it a rest! It was that cow, he wrecked a whole sirloin, it just finished him off, she was rock hard, and what would you have done in his place? God, that cow's a sight! It hurts your eyes, and now Ambrosio's run off, just like that, gone! Yes, those cow halves are pretty fucked up, they're going on the cheap-meat stand, and Gilgen is going to have a hard time when they stick him in jail again, but if you never, ever complain even a tiny bit, then they'll never take us seriously, and what are you talking about now? And they want to promote me, he said, put me in charge of the machine in that chest out there, and the student? Yes, that fool, he probably takes you seriously now! Take the little weed, the milksop, grab him by the tail, give him a bit of stick, dip his head in the blood-barrel so he knows what he's got his long hair for, let him spit blood for a day or so, that's doing something, that's better than sounding off, and Buri says he's not sure but a couple of clips round the earhole never hurt anyone, big mouth, chewing bread, but meat, meat, by God there wasn't much of that, you saw that yesterday and he wouldn't be coming back, you could bet on that, and he could go and take his snapshots elsewhere, and Rötlisberger should stop pretending, should be pleased, they won't be promoting me to any intestine washery, of course they will, and you're a fool because you'd have a cushier time there, my God a cushy time at my age, learning how to feed a machine like that, I can't do that, oh crap, any old monkey can mind one of those slime-machines, there's nothing to it, yes, it's dead easy, well if it's so easy why don't they stick a monkey up there, and not old Rötlisberger, I'm a triper, you at your age, and what's my age got to do with it, eh? If they stuck a proper monkey in there, they'd have the animal welfare people breathing down their necks in no time, but everything's got an end, only a sausage has got two, but don't worry, an old ox like me kicks hard, I'd chuck the lot in, oh stop that, why don't you go join them at the armaments factory kiosk, the three of you go well together, and take that student with you, and he can take pictures of you all, and Luigi's listening, and Fernando's listening, and Pasquale's listening, and José's listening, and Piccolo's listening, and not one of them says anything, and the apprentice is stretching, and Piccolo goes smack! on the wall, but he's not laughing any more, and if everyone was like you! Oh, go and lick Krummen's paws, if you want, but I've got a head, here, knock! But what's eating you, we've got a few things going for us here, we're not short of work, and parking's no problem, yes parking's worth something, here in the yard, you've always got a space, exactly, that's what my brother-in-law said, and when the beefing programme is finished, then things will cool down a bit, and other people's cows always have bigger udders, but we're here, and cows should be milked, not sent to the knacker's, and go crawl up Krummen's arse, but mind out because he's got his head up Bössiger's, who's got his head up, and now give it a rest will you? It's not easy for them either, and this morning at six there wasn't a single tail in the shed, well, and if the goods arrive late, is that my fault? Surely it's right to try and get things the way you want them? Well, but all that running and cursing and hustling and criticizing, you'd think, and it's getting worse and worse, and you really should have been a preacher not a triper, if your mouth could ride a bicycle you'd have to put the brakes on going uphill, and with both hands, oh, let him talk, no, as late as that? Oh shit! We're late, we've got to go, fine words never slaughtered a cow yet, and benches are shifted, trousers done up, one more sip, a STELLA SUPER dies next to a PARISIENNE in the ashtray, come on then, andiamo, and Rötlisberger's BRISSAGO is still going, and . . .

*

174

Nine-fifteen.

Cigarette away.

Why not stay for lunch too, while you're about it?

Let's go.

Who cares?

That gut would have to burst.

Haven't I had it coming for weeks now, like a gigantic wheel that sooner or later will roll over me?

I gulp.

Well, come on, if we have to, they'll have their reasons even if we can't understand them.

Überländer ties his rubber apron round his waist as he walks. It's less a walk than a fidget, and he waves to me to follow without turning round. I tramp off after him. My stride isn't characterful, but it's long and heavy.

Courage.

My toes feel the empty space in my boots, but their shafts squeeze my calves.

Überländer stops at the door of the cattle hall.

Hey, Kilchenmann! he shouts, the apprentice will be bringing in another cow to be shot, so don't put your gun away just yet.

We'll manage that one too.

You can if you want to. You want to if you can.

I don't want to.

Not even if I have to.

You would sooner not.

I don't even dare to demand the toilet tokens owing to me. Stand up, go up to Krummen, and say I want . . . I didn't have anything to eat either.

Nothing but bearing up, enduring, surviving, getting through. Getting through is their favourite. Get through this or that, you have to get through it. He got through it. It was terribly hard, grim, inhumanly difficult, but he got through it. Everyone has at least got through cadet school.

Get through.

You can if you must. You will if you must.

If only I could swear properly.

Heaven . . . God . . . Devil . . . I can't swear.

175

For days now, I've had no peace in my lunch breaks. I couldn't lie down on the wooden slats on the floor. Or on the bench in the locker room. No more catnaps.

I had to get out in the lunch breaks.

From the loading-apron by the railway tracks to the sliding doors of the killing bays, to the animals' entrance to the slaughterhall, I wandered all over the slaughterhouse terrain. I passed from one grille to another, along the bars, through the maze of squeeze gates, driving passages and waiting pens. Absent mindedly I opened the bolts on the doors, drove away a calf that was following me, climbed over pigs that had been hurt in transit, pulled muscles or a broken leg, and lay grunting at me from the furthest recesses of cages. I hardly saw them. The pain of those pigs, lying around in passages, separated from their herds, was not my own pain. And the thin-shanked sheep, thrusting their woolly heads between the bars of their folds, and bleating at me, didn't interest me either.

I drifted.

Apparently aimlessly, only to find myself sooner or later standing by a snorting cow in the cattle stall. There was no getting away from it. Every day I wound up among these animals.

And in my thoughts, I untied them.

Whole herds of them.

As though I had to rescue them from a fire, I unchained them and drove Simmentalers, Freiburgers and Eringers through the gates and out into the open.

I kept going up to them.

I touched their backs, their necks, their heads.

Don't be afraid. Don't be afraid, I whispered to them. It's all right, don't be afraid.

I tried to take away their fear, when it was they who had me with my back up against the wall.

Now I can feel the pallor in my face.

Überländer opens the door of the first pen. It's empty. A smell of dung, urine, hay, sawdust.

I choked. Now it's got me by the throat.

The second pen is empty. In the third is a single cow.

There, says Überländer. The cow is standing right at the back.

She tugs at her chain, snorts out air through dripping nostrils. She's restless. Her ears are circling and pointing.

There now, what kind of live weight would you say?

Eh? What do you think? An estimate. Look at her. Imagine you were wanting to buy her.

I don't want to buy a cow.

Eight hundred kilos! I burst out with.

Eight hundred kilos? That frail little thing? What are you looking at? Is there another cow in there? Or haven't you got any eyes in your head?

Six hundred kilos!

Little under-age Miss Simmental here? Now watch it, you. One of these days you'll be doing your qualifying exams, and you've got no idea of livestock. You'll have to get it right to within 20 or 30 kilos, or else!

Else what?

Weighing-master Krähenbühl looks in. Broom in hand. Another one of Schindler's. Nervous little thing. And in late.

Krähenbühl vanishes.

But what I was going to say, there are dealers who are rarely out by more than 5 kilos. You need practice. Look at one or two animals every day. Properly, mind. Remember how the quarters are put together, watch the proportions.

Live weight. Dead weight. Meat yield. Degree of fat. State of health.

The cow bends her neck, lifts her hindlegs by turns.

She wants out. She's used to straw and hay and long ropes. She wants to get out of this gloomy pen, away from the thin layer of sawdust, and the empty feed trough.

Are you scared? Überländer laughs. I'll bet you she's not more than 400 kilos. Just on 400. Nicely filled out round the pelvis, but not yet broad. Shoulders barely winged. Bones only sticking out slightly. Not like some old nanny. No, she won't have had more than one calf. And her height. Small, small. A good little cow!

Überländer perks up. I notice how he likes being near the animal. He responds to it. Talks to it. Touches its back, its neck, its head.

A fine head, a light head. Now see this. They've amputated the horns. A crime if you ask me. A head always seems lighter without horns. You have to bear that in mind.

It should be outlawed.

Taking a cow's horns away.

I made an effort.

And what's she here for? She's not a feeder cow.

Maybe she refused the bull. None good enough for her.

If she doesn't want to. Oh well.

Now he scratches his own neck.

Doesn't look to be ill. Would have made a fine cow once. Oh yes. Look what a straight back she has. Like a broom handle. A straight neck like a duchess.

His eye follows his hand, as it strokes withers, back and loins. With his other hand, he fondles the full flank.

Nice and plump.

And then? What do you do next? After you've made your estimate? Seeing as we're here.

His hand still lying on the back of the cow.

I . . .

Did you not talk about it at trade school?

I know the cross-hatched places in the drawing in the book: ear hold, middle hold, rib hold, loin hold, breast hold, udder or scrotum hold.

Then I . . . I determine the condition of the meat.

Touch all over, finger, feel, palp, grope, pinch, squeeze. With my fingers I am supposed to feel through her dusty hide for deposits of fat between her muscles. My fingers are to tell me whether her flesh will be marbled or not, my fingers are to knead various parts of her body, and tell me what they are like inside

Dig in, then.

And now she's even licking me.

This cow isn't ready to be slaughtered: her flesh is still over-heated from her journey here, and her muscle tissue is full of unwanted hormones.

Quiet! Keep still!

Instead of quietening down, she's rubbed her neck raw.

She scrapes and moos.

The shoulder hold is well developed, with a good layer of fat.

She's fat here too.

Here, you've got to go about this differently! Überländer brushes me aside. You've got to grab her properly, like this! There! If you can't even get a good fistful, God knows you won't get far in life. Look at this breast grip, there, get the whole dewlap in your grip. Not half-hearted like a schoolgirl.

Überländer bends down underneath the cow. Without being bothered by her fretting, he puts his arm round her neck. His hands grip the holds on her hide.

You won't feel anything otherwise.

My throat tightens.

And the whole thing rolls forward irresistibly.

Over my voice, over my own lack of will, crushes everything, and still I go on turning with it.

I cling to the cow, trying at the same time to keep my chin off her back. I grab, I grab her flesh.

That's right, says Überländer.

The udder hold shows whether the intestines will be well coated with fat.

The skin on the udders is soft, warm and greasy. The hair almost downy.

Jesus Christ allfuckingmighty!

Did I tell you to come in here and grope her for half an hour? That's it. A cripple cow like that is easily sized up.

Krummen!

He taps his goad against his apron.

Überländer scratches his neck again.

Right now, bring the goods into the hall. We're almost finished in there, and you're fast asleep.

No, leave it! The apprentice is taking the cow in.

Überländer lets the chain drop.

Krummen goes on tapping his stick against his apron.

And forever talking to the animals, he says.

You master-wrestler, you. I touch the cow's back, neck and head. It's all right. No noise.

Avoiding the tongue, I first untie the rope from the ring under the feed crib.

At least she's got no horns.

She follows my movements with curious eyes.

Right now! If you go in front of an animal, it will take you for the lead cow and follow you.

I don't feel like a tussle. Please let there be no test of strength this first time.

Head down! Keep still!

I'd rather a slow and reluctant cow than this one.

Preferably one of the clumsy sort that has to be pushed under the axe like a block of wood, or even carried there.

No joyous skipping about, please.

I don't want to wind up under your four-footed trampling body.

Right! Get her in the correct grip from the outset.

Überländer's vanished.

As soon as she's untethered and unchained, the cow shoots her head up, barges me aside, and aims for the light at the opening of the pen.

Once in the stallway, she flares up, jumps forward and back, moos, and swings her tail around.

Krummen has to take evasive action.

Hey, whoah there! he shouts.

I shorten the rope, and hold on to the halter. So close to her neck, I start to get an idea of the power in that body. I lean against her front flank, without the slightest effect.

The cow pushes out of the stall sideways. I am simply dragged along. A loud jangle, pressure against my stomach. My sheath clatters against the doorpost.

Hell's teeth! Watch out for your knives! Krummen flings his arms up.

I have disregarded the one and only commandment of the last walk.

He didn't notice.

For thou shalt not go unto the waiting beast without divesting thyself of the sharpness of the knives at thy side.

Outside, among the poles and rails of the barriers and driving passages, between stock pens and slaughterhall, I pull the cow's head towards me.

Quiet! Be quiet! Calm down, will you! You'll trample me, knock my knives out of the sheath into the air, crush me against a barrier.

By jerking at her mouth, I manage to break her forward momentum.

Don't let go.

I push against her belly, jerk at her head.

You damned . . .

She turns, she turns a whole circle. She's trying to brush me off. Tied together, we can't get off the merry-go-round. We turn, once, twice, three times. A staged first walk for me, a staged last for her.

I'm stuck to her again.

Helpless.

Everywhere on my skin I can feel the dust from her red-and-white hide. It bites into my face, my chin, my throat. I curse the pain in my hands, and the spittle running down from her muzzle.

The hemp rope softens and starts to get slippery.

I begin to sweat.

And my knives!

We go on turning.

Don't let go!

Krummenroaring.

Don't let go! Get a hold of her! I told you to take a stick. Krummen gives the cow a whack on the base of the tail.

She leaps up, rips rope and halter from my grasp. I lose my balance. A kick on the upper arm sends me onto the floor. Another kick. I am hurled against the slaughterhall wall. My knives fly jingling from their sheath.

I feel warm wetness in my left boot.

Fucking hell, you bitch!

Krummen hits her. He will catch her. The gun in Kilchenmann's hand will click. Then the shot, the impact, the thud on the abattoir floor.

I will collect my knives, go and whet the damaged blades again. I will lie down on the bench in the locker room. Today I will go and lie down in the locker room in my lunch break. I will go to Krummen and say: I want my toilet tokens.

A knife has pierced my boot. In order to take it off I lean against the wall of the slaughterhall. It says NO BICYCLES in red letters on the crumbly plaster.

The wetness in my sock.

Sweat.

A little red stain.

A little pain in the ball of my foot.

The butcher's little dispensary should contain 1 pr. scissors, 1 pr. tweezers, 1 small bottle of iodine or styptic powder, cotton wool, gauze and bandages, and it should be within easy reach of potential danger sites, preferably clearly marked with a red cross; and it is further recommended not to gesticulate while holding a knife, nor to walk about knife in hand. It should be put away in the knife-holder (sheath). Protection against highly dangerous knife wounds in the stomach and groin areas is afforded by a protective apron of light metal mesh. Knives should have shaped handles to make them comfortable to hold. They should not be left lying around on tables, still less at the bottom of containers; and since, generally speaking, a butcher works on his feet, he should have solid footwear, which will help prevent flatfootedness, varicose veins and tendinitis. Be on guard against erysipelas, psoriasis, Bang's disease, swine fever, tetanus, and all occupational illnesses. First aid prevents a condition from deteriorating: with heavy bleeding, press the wound together firmly with sterile gauze, and bring the injured man to a doctor. In cases of bruising from falls on slippery ground (wet, greasy), on hides or waste matter, or in incidents involving animals (kicks, horn wounds), injuries on meat-hooks and the like, give the accident victim neither food nor drink! Internal injuries! Take him on a stretcher to a doctor.

The skin of a fetus has its value too. Tanners are eager for the soft hides, and *delicate calfskins are dyed naturally in standard or fashionable colours, shorn and printed, worked into summer or winter furs,* but they must be intact, and Krummen lashed out with his boot at Blösch's uterus. He pushed the kidney-shaped sack ahead of him on the floor. Scraps of fat and bits of sinew everywhere. Yah, fuck it! I always have to do everything by myself.

The arched windows of the cattle slaughter room were clearing. Condensation poured down the panes. Kilchenmann put the last of the cows, which had had to be slaughtered separately onto the scales. Two hundred and thirty-seven kilos slaughter weight. Überländer collected the ropes. They had to be taken away and washed. Here, give me one of those halters, said Krummen. Piccolo took the gall bladder off the rack, and slit it open over a basin, *and gall stimulates bowel movements. It digests fats. In industry it is used in the production of cleansing materials (soaps), and in the printing trade,* and the gall of cattle is viscid and glistening like gloss paint.

Krummen opened up Blösch's uterus. Amniotic fluid splashed back over the blade and his hands. The fetus was light brown, with a white mark on its forehead. It was lean, with a back like a greyhound's, and its damp hair gleamed cleanly. Krummen detached the skin at the head, and pulled it back a couple of hand-breadths. He slung the halter round the exposed neck and attached the end of it to the nearest ring in the floor. He attached the loosened flap of hide with a meat-hook to a lift pulley. He pushed a button. The motor hummed, and Piccolo raised his head. His face was covered with spots of gall. Gall dribbled down his arms and apron. Between floor-ring and lift, halter, fetus and skin tautened. The lean, blue body slipped soundlessly from its sheath: first the front half of it, then the loins, the back legs flipped up, the hips clicking as they were dislocated. Last of all the tail slipped out of the inverted hide.

Krummen bent down and untied the rope. The fetus would have become a female calf, and *at nine months, the length of the fetus is 90 centimetres. Well haired. Testicles in scrotum. Milk teeth present, incisors and molars,* and the halter, removed from the neck, dropped at Piccolo's feet. Get rid of it! Krummen left the skinned body lying beside the bin for waste material.

– When you're finito, subito lavare gall, e poi hang up calves! Got it? Piccolo nodded his green head. Always the same orders, and always the same emphasis.

There was more shouting at the entrance to the slaughterhall. Bössiger had come upon the split carcass of Blösch in the long corridor.

– Get Krummen here! Fast! Did you hear me? Bössiger had thrust his arms out, he circled round the disfigured cloven carcass that was suspended from the overhead rail. For the moment Blösch was only conditionally edible, and *edible meat (defined in article 52 ¶ 1 of the Meat Inspection Regulations), is stamped with an oval stamp, conditionally edible meat with a triangular stamp according to the design shown (Fig. 1). Meat from animals of the type: horse is further to be stamped with the word 'Horse'*, and all Blösch's lymph nodes were swollen; the flesh was dark, almost black, and heated. It felt dry and sticky. It drooped from the protruding bones. 'Gelatinous and feverish!' had been the verdict in the meat-inspection report. And Dr Wyss had ordered a laboratory inspection.

But Bössiger was remonstrating.

– What kind of massacre is this? Fine butchers you are! He pointed to the hacked sirloin. Krummen drew his head in and clutched his trousers. As he'd done a moment ago with the carcass of the cow, Slaughterhouse-Marshal Bössiger now circled Foreman Krummen. The dogs got that one, I suppose?

– If we're short-handed . . . if you have to do everything yourself! If you . . .

– Then you just hack through the sirloin! At 30 francs the kilo! That's the limit!

– But it's headed for the cheap-meat stall anyway, Krummen defended himself, and *all customers are urgently advised to boil meat purchased from the cheap-meat stall until it is quite grey in the middle*, and Krummen was in despair. That cow destroyed my tools. I blunted two cleavers on that great bitch.

– Now listen to me, Krummen! Bössiger said roughly. The purchasing department want to see a higher throughput of meat. If this carcass was in slightly better shape, it wouldn't have got a triangular stamp on it. We need sausage-meat. A cow is no good to us as cheap meat. We want to produce frankfurters, cervelats, and bologna.

– Well, what am I supposed to do? Gilgen's gone, Ambrosio took off like a crazy chicken with his head in the air, the apprentice gets himself knocked over by a little slip of a cow, and the stooges bungle more than you'd think was possible. Whenever they happen not to be on the crapper!

– Now don't give me that. You've got better people here than at the main plant. Have you got any idea how hard it is to find trained butchers? They don't snow down from the sky, you know! Give your people a good grounding! We just have to make proper use of them. Show them how! What you teach them today, they'll be able to do by themselves tomorrow.

– Yes, but a stooge is a stooge. I've said I need six butchers in order to manage the extra workload, and what do I get? An apprentice, a Spaniard, and half an Italian who doesn't know one end of a knife from the other!

– Do you think we're keeping good butchers in the deep-freeze?

– Well, if Gilgen didn't keep inciting them the whole time! And Rötlisberger puts in his tuppenceworth too.

– But Krummen, they're cutting their noses to spite their faces. Don't you worry about them. Bössiger hurried off, stopped again. And I don't want any more blood lost! We need every drop we can get, he said, and disappeared into the office.

Krummen went back to burrowing in his trousers. His jaw was working. Train the stooges! First the wops have to learn to cut the feet off a cow! Then wash, stir blood and scrub guts. We'll manage the difficult things. As if anyone could do our work for half the wages, just because he's got a big mouth on him! What do these white-collar types think goes on here? Let them come out in their white coats. They can push pencils around all day, a cow's still got four legs on her, and before you can make her into sausages, she still wants sticking and skinning.

Nine forty-five.

Air!

Light!

A few breaths of fresh air. I have to fetch the calves in. Willingly. Anything to get out of the steam and the stink.

Beyond the abattoir walls, other brick walls and chimneys. Factories, warehouses, plumes of smoke over the foundry stacks. A passenger train. The main line is very near. It thunders past the ramp. So close to the station, many of the passengers are still standing up in their compartments, taking coats off, stowing luggage away.

The one bit of green anywhere is around the administration building behind me, which is where the meat inspectors come and go.

There's a smell of singed bristles.

I cut myself in the heel.

It doesn't hurt, but . . .

The way Huber and Hofer stared at me! As though I had horns. They were cleaning their skinning gear with water and compressed air, and looking at me.

In the pen next to the main driving passage lies a solitary pig. It's gurgling and there's froth coming out of its snout.

I should care what Huber and Hofer think of me!

I'm not a coward. Am I a coward? A foreign worker in my own country is what I am. But I did ask for toilet tokens.

I surprised myself. Krummen plonked himself in front of me, grabbed at his arse, but before he could get a word out, I told him I needed some tokens. He didn't hear. Go to the calf ramp! See if the goods have arrived!

I don't feel very well. I have to go . . .

God Almighty! They all want their tokens. Do you have to shit five times a day? Or have you all got the runs?

Then I went and almost apologized for it.

I'm so conciliatory.

Never push for anything – always yes, sir, amen, sir, three bags full, sir.

As if I had a voice built into my chest like a car radio, forever promoting peace.

Be crushed in peace.

We're under pressure, he said, I couldn't go now. But he gave me a token, one with another number on it.

My number is 272. It says it on my tokens, and my card, my locker, my clothes and my envelope on payday.

If I make a mess in the toilet, they can check up in the lock of the WC, and find out it was No. 272 that did it.

Watch it! Or you'll have another accident. You look pale. Don't come back without the calves, mind.

There was a worried tone in Krummen's voice. Was it me or the calves he was worried about?

I walk upright and breathe deeply. My rubber boots scrape against my rubber apron.

How frail I am. How thin my skin is.

What is a human body, here on this asphalt, surrounded by steel and concrete?

I feel the hardness of the ground under my boots.

In the cage, half a dozen calves gawp at me. Five straightaway push through the wire gate into the driving corridor.

The more mobile, the better.

Hup, hup, hup.

The sixth calf stiffens, digs in. It stretches its neck and shrills its head off.

I push it, tug at it, shout at it, punch it.

Hup, hup, hup.

You bastard.

That wasn't even half a step.

You blockhead!

He keeps up the horrible squealing. A continuous monotone, like a car alarm.

I can't carry you into the calf hall.

The tail is sticking out. There's a yellow discharge all over its behind.

Now it starts to show: my fall did take something out of me. I only make about an inch at a time with the calf.

I stick a finger in its mouth for it to suck.

It bites. It won't let go. It follows my hand.

Bad accidents happen during calf slaughtering. Since beer doesn't exactly improve accuracy, one man hanging up a calf got hit by the knocking hammer. The blow, just enough to stun a calf, shattered his skull like a china vase.

In front of the sliding door to the calf slaughterhall, I lock the six calves in a pen again. They stand huddled together in a corner.

My own mishaps at work are never spectacular: a graze, a fall.

Six calves ready to be hung up.

I'll tell Krummen.

Clunk. Shut the gate. I'm just another one of those door-bolters.

The calves start to shrill again. The slaughter alarm continues.

Slime-shitters!

What can they do about it?

They've got swollen knees and crippled feet.

Because, for reasons of hygiene, they're kept on latticed floors, where they can't put their feet down properly.

Stop standing around!

You're not at the zoo.

I grind my teeth together till it hurts.

Always howling, the God damned . . .

I kick out at the sliding door.

I run off.

The calves go on shrilling.

Out of the hall, out into the passage.

I look neither left nor right.

The toilet door crashes shut.

Token in, shake, it falls: VACANT.

I tear the cabin door open and crash it shut.

ENGAGED.

I breathe.

My skull hasn't grown any harder, but I've got fists hard as hooves.

The better to bang on the wall with.

Insensitive to pain, hard as rock.

But what am I taking it out on?

A shithouse wall!

And only because I'm positive that no one can hear me.

I sit here in the draught, with a cold bum, drumming on the shithouse wall, there isn't even any graffiti, no cunts, no cocks, no scribbles. Nothing, nothing whatsoever on these surfaces: no phone numbers, no cry for help, no horror, no dribbles of sperm, no snot.

Not here!

All piccobello.

No drop of blood.

Only me.

Small and helpless, untrousered, banging and knocking and yelling in bewilderment.

You can lick my arse the lot of you!

I'm alone.

A lonely drummer in the night, alone in 2 cubic metres of lockable shitting freedom.

And don't be afraid of the foreign workers, Bössiger had said to her right on the first day. Just don't be provocative. Be decent and friendly. Apart from the canteen lady, you're the only woman on the premises.

Frau Spreussiger was walking down the main connecting corridor towards the weighing office. There was a weight on Bössiger's overall checklist that didn't accord with the official weight. That would mean a meat yield of less than 35 per cent. Frau Spreussiger, would you go and see Kilchenmann right away, I want to know what the story is behind this dead weight, he had said.

Frau Spreussiger stepped around a stain on the floor. The corridor between the cattle slaughterhall and the chilling-room was full of cow carcasses sawn in half and hanging on the rails. On the frayed necks, the muscles were blue, and the sparse fat yellow. Don't step in anything wet! And the way it all hangs down up there, and drips and steams and smells. The bodies dangled slackly 4 or 5 metres above her head, it was as though the sky was full of meat, but nowadays it took more than a cow carcass to bother her.

– Grüß Gott, Herr Sperandio. Luigi was navigating the blood-tank round some trolleys filled with innards, and past the wooden chest that waited outside the door of the cattle halls. The cows were finished and had all been stuck. Right! Bang the stuff in the centrifuge, Krummen had hissed. There's only a little tank full because of your cock-up earlier, so let's not sit and stare till it evaporates. Get it out of here, Subito!

– Whoops! Frau Spreussiger got out of Luigi's way. Some blood slopped over the rim of the tank. Don't step in anything wet. Luigi's hands were as knotty as roots on the trolley with the blood-tank. She liked that, and the dark skin under the crusts of blood.

– Attenzione! Mamma mia! Luigi was too late. Frau Spreussiger tripped on the pallet with the wooden chest on it, which had been getting in everyone's way for days now. She stumbled. There was another pool on the floor. Frau Spreussiger brushed against a carcass. Ee, that sticky, bloody substance! She shrank back. She put out her arms for balance, and as she did so, her skirt slipped another hand's breadth over her knee. There was a snigger from the door of the chilling-room, where Hugentobler had posted himself as look-out. Thin knees she had, and bluish veins under her nylon stockings. In the cattle slaughterhall, Piccolo craned his neck to see. Porco Dio. To get the benefit of her for a moment longer, he took a couple of steps to the side, knife and gall-bladder in his hands. Pretty Boy Hügli appeared in the doorway of the toilet. He saw Frau Spreussiger and stopped. Huber and Hofer were approaching. They carried their compressed-air knives. They were walking so slowly, they were hardly moving at all.

– Look at those thighs, said Hofer.

– And calves, said Huber.

– Bit on the skinny side, mind.

– Yes.

– She'd never make a farmer's wife, that one, said Hofer.

– But that's some udder! said Huber admiringly.

– Yes, she's like a Holsteiner. They're all skin and bones and udder. No meat on them anywhere.

– Now don't tell me you wouldn't . . .

– Oh, it's all claptrap anyway. Hofer turned into the calf hall. There's only one of us who's screwing her, and we know who that is.

– The bastard. Huber stopped. That rump is a bit of all right. A straight back like a young cow, and she must be all of forty.

Huber himself was fat. It spilled in folds round his vest into his shirt and trousers. He had a beer gut as well. He laughed at Pretty Boy Hügli, the charmer, who had slid out into Frau Spreussiger's path, as smooth as vaseline. He'll have to do a lot more combing before he ever gets in there. Huber finally took his eyes off the red skirt, and followed Hofer into the calf slaughterhall.

Frau Spreussiger had previously worked as a typist in the main plant, and it had been quite a shock to find herself suddenly as Bössiger's secretary at the abattoir. No one had asked her what she thought of it. She'd been the oldest person on the factory admin staff. According to the head of personnel, it seemed she was also the most self-reliant. She was the only one for the job, he had said when she'd been transferred.

At the beginning, she had been disgusted by the smell that crept out of the slaughterhalls, and squatted, fresh and damp, in every corner. She had sought to wrap herself in protective shrouds to abolish the contact between her skin and the blood-soaked air. Within a week, she had doubled her consumption of cigarettes. She was now getting through three packets of MURATTI a day. She smoked and smoked, wore only polo necks, or high necked-dresses, and dug out some old headscarves she had from the back of a drawer. She had gone into several department stores in order to get hold of large quantities of cheap cologne without attracting too much attention. Now twice a day during office hours, morning and afternoon, she rubbed herself with it from head to toe, and she carried perfume around with her everywhere, and there were sticks of deodorant in her handbag.

No sooner would she get home in the evening than she would scrub herself raw with hard soap and pumice stone in a hot bath. As though she'd actually been working side by side with the butchers all day under a shower of blood, she rinsed her hair again and again, and after her bath, she treated her face to a steam bath of camomile. Anything to get rid of the smell of the slaughterhouse world.

She cut her fingernails and toenails short, used only clear varnish on them, and left her wedding ring at home in the drawer of her bedside cupboard. Then, by chance, she'd come upon an article on skin problems in a women's magazine. *Whereas only 7 to 10 per cent of the general population suffer from warts, research has shown that 28.5 per cent of slaughterhouse employees are afflicted by them.*

Frau Spreussiger had been panic-stricken.

However, after a month had passed, and she still hadn't experienced all the distressing effects she'd been afraid of, she began to relax a little.

She continued to buy only cold meats, particularly corned beef, and now and again a veal-bratwurst or a little brawn, but never anything that was recognizably meat by shape or colour. Herr Spreussiger would have to wait a long time for her to cook him a Sunday roast. If you want something to sink your teeth into, as you say, you'll have to cook it yourself, she'd told him.

But she was starting to enjoy her new job at the slaughterhouse.

The squealing of pigs, when it happened to penetrate the double door to her office, no longer caused her to make typing errors. She had settled down. She no longer avoided Bössiger's searching glances when a bull bellowed loudly in its despair, and, after a first fluffed shot, more loudly still. It happens, she would say.

And she liked being around all the men. The foreign workers were always cheerful, forever laughing and casting lustful glances in her direction. Oh, how they talk! The way they gesticulate with their hands and feet. And the sight of the armed and aproned forms of the laconic butchers would often send a shiver down her spine. All those looks, so many pairs of eyes behind every corner. She felt young and desired by all the men as they stood in her way, their arms and hands dangling and dangerous. But she was still smoking her three packets of MURATTI a day, and her wedding ring was still at home in the drawer.

In the passage outside the calf slaughterhall, Pretty Boy Hügli stroked Frau Spreussiger's elbow. Well? Won't you come and join us? he asked.

– Oh, there's so much to do in the office. And Bössiger's in one of his moods again. If only you knew.

– Don't be like that. We're about to start on the calves. Come and keep us company.

– But, Herr Hügli, I have to go.

– Come in and see the way it spurts out.

– But that's not fit for a woman. She wanted to loosen Hügli's grip on her arm.

Hügli tightened it. What? Then what is fit?

– Let go of me! What's the matter with you all? There, that's done it, now I've got something splashed on my stocking and it's your fault. Frau Spreussiger had stepped into something wet. It's blood! Blood! she hissed, and stared down at the stain on her fingertips.

– But don't you like it if I hold your arm a bit? Hügli no longer knew what to do with his hand.

– Who's going to get me a fresh pair of stockings now? She hurried off, Hügli staring after her as she stalked off angrily towards the weighing office. The silly bitch! She's only after Gilgen anyway.

Pretty Boy Hügli had seen Frau Spreussiger with Ernest Gilgen by the railway tracks at the back. She'd trotted along in front of him like a little calf. Then Gilgen had grabbed her from behind and spun her round. He'd said something to her, but she'd only shaken her head virtuously. Not with you, you gorilla, Hügli had crowed. But when Frau Spreussiger had walked on and noticed that Gilgen wasn't following her any more, she'd turned round and laughed, and at the end of the driving passage, at the lattice gate before the outer door to her office and Bössiger's, she had looked round and, seeing no one but Gilgen nearby, she had pretended she couldn't draw the bolt back. And then Gilgen had sprung to her assistance. He had poked and prodded at her hips with his fingers. He had driven her in front of him, back to the first cowshed. They were hardly inside it when she was already reaching under her skirt. Hügli had gulped when he saw her knickers. That Spreussiger, such a smart piece, and with that Tyrolean ram of a Gilgen, who shaves twice a week, and stinks like a load of pigshit? And for five-minute sessions in the nine o'clock break, up against the hay bales in the first cattle pen! When Hügli had been paying court to her for weeks in vain.

He had been deeply offended.

Still, better that than a wop, he'd thought.

In the weighing office, Frau Spreussiger had wiped her stockings clean with a cloth and stepped up to Weigher Kilchenmann, who was standing at his desk, entering figures in a book.

– Herr Bössiger would like to know why the seventeenth sausage-cow this morning had a live weight of 620 kilos, and only 180 dead?

Weighing-master Kilchenmann flicked back in his control book, put his finger down at the top of a column marked 'Comments of the Meat Inspection' and *the determination of the slaughter weight of butchered animals is subject to legal conditions that are contained in the Meat Inspection Regulations,* and Kilchenmann slid his finger down the column.

– Here! he said. Abcesses!

– What do you mean? Frau Spreussiger raised her shoulders. Why so much loss of weight?

– Infections, growths, septic sores, plum-sized purulent boils in the flesh. Do you understand, Frau Spreussiger? Sites of past infections, stinking discharges. The surrounding areas all have to be cut away.

Frau Spreussiger turned pale. Fine. That's all right, she said and ran out of the weighing office. In the long passage, she looked neither at the drops of blood on the floor, nor at the staring eyes. Infections! Plum-sized boils! Septic sores! Stinking discharges! echoed through her head.

'Look we plaited it left here, see? Now we plait it to the right, to make a pretty zigzag. You stick your pitchfork in – you'll have to reach up a bit – and twist the handle until you've got a whole strand together, and then hold onto it, or else you'll lose it all again! And then you push it back in at the bottom, again at an angle, you see?' The farmer was plying the four-pronged pitchfork at head height, showing Ambrosio how to weave the pattern into the Knuchel dung. The dunghill was man-sized. It was exhausting work, and there was no shade. Sweat poured down both men's faces, from under their milking caps.

Ambrosio thought he could feel the smell of cowdung settling right at the back of his nasal cavity, and continuing to ferment there. 'Qué mierda!' Decorating dung! He hardly knew what to think. 'Carajo! Hijo de puta! Caramba!' And promptly Knuchel nodded in agreement: 'These horseflies are a plague! Drat them! But you know,' he went on, 'it matters what raw material you have. There's no point in braiding any old stuff. No, no. You need to have proper straw, wheat straw is the best, and the longer it is, the better for the dung.'

Ambrosio lit himself a cigarette. As he stuffed the bundle of his tinder back into his pocket, he saw that, as ever, the cows on the Knuchel pasture were all grazing in the same direction. Blösch and Gertrude were in the middle of the herd, Baby and Stine on the outside. And up by the little wood, he saw a moving cloud of dust. It was the woman on the bicycle who emerged between the bushes, racing down the little road, head in, upper body leaning forward like a pro's. Already he saw the knot of her hair. She gripped the handlebar with one hand, the other was holding her skirt. The brown cloth was tight around her thighs. Those legs! Qué mujer! And the way she flew past the apple trees!

'She's some cyclist, isn't she? She'd be good on the Tour de

Spania!' laughed Knuchel, standing cock-a-hoop on top of the dunghill. Ambrosio laughed too, and they went back to driving their pitchforks into the heavy muck, muscles tightening, lifting, pushing, plucking, and pulling it from place to place, as they puffed and sweated and swatted at flies and the piled dung lay smooth and even.

'There, that'll be Schindler now.' Farmer Knuchel leaned on his pitchfork. A LANDROVER surged up the hill, braked and turned into the farm track. Its trailer wobbled and jounced from side to side on the deep ruts made by the tractor tyres. A wooden cage clattered on top of the trailer. Hens fled cackling for their lives. Prince barked, and, out on the meadow, the cows lifted their heads momentarily from the grass.

Calf-dealer Schindler swerved round the cobbled yard, put another hen to flight, and came to a stop in front of the dunghill. 'Did you see the midwife just now?' he asked as he got out.

'Yes, and I reckon she'll wrap herself round a fir tree one of these days.' Knuchel climbed down off the dunghill, and wiped his right hand on his overtrousers before offering it to Schindler. 'You've come about the Blösch calf, I expect?'

'To look at him, yes. He's fattened up nicely, your wife was saying on the telephone.' Schindler took out his blue cowherd's smock and pulled it over his head, but then got stuck in it. Knuchel came to his help, but the calf-dealer got into even more of a twist, and started wheezing under the thick cloth, saying that he would buy himself one that buttoned in future. 'A right stupid shirt that one is too!' observed Knuchel.

When his head finally appeared, the calf-dealer whistled through his teeth: 'Whew! That's quite a pile! Some dung you have here!'

'Yes, our dung is high all right, and I was thinking of taking out a couple of loads and spreading it, but then it's also near the time when we can leave the cattle out to graze overnight.'

'Quite right. Less of a job cleaning out the cowshed that way.'

'On the other hand, you don't get the full benefit of the dung either. That has to be said too. Now what about the calf, Fritz? Do you want to have a look at it?'

'Right, yes! Let's see it!'

'All right? Seeing as you're here!'

Some calves were bleating at the back of the otherwise empty cowshed. Knuchel untied the biggest of them, took off its muzzle and asked: 'Well, what do you think?'

The calf held its forelegs wide apart, lowered its head, shuffled and looked up at the calf-dealer, who approached it and touched its neck with a pink, fleshy hand.

'Can you use him or not? We didn't give him any eggs, but fat milk more than enough.' Knuchel stepped back and kneaded at the cloth of his left oxter with his right hand.

'It's like he's almost got a bit of a dog's back, you know, not really that fleshy towards the tail.' Schindler touched the calf all over, and stroked its loins.

'A dog's back! I don't believe it!' Knuchel went to touch the calf himself. 'Look at the way the breast has plumped out, how broad it all is, that's an A1 stew.'

'Now, Hans, breast is all well and good, but it's not so much in demand as once it was. Who buys breast of veal nowadays? The butchers want nice kidneys, calves' kidneys are where the trade is. And a couple of fillets, preferably weighing 6 pounds apiece, and an enormous liver.'

While Schindler looked inside the calf's mouth, and thumbed the eyebrows up to see how white it was behind the dull blue pupils, Knuchel ground his boot in the straw on the cowshed floor. He smashed his fist against a beam of the feed crib, kicked at a chain that dropped from it, and, reaching the front of the stall, he punched the blackboard on which he'd chalked up Blösch's name, the date of her last heat, and her expected calving date. There you had it, he growled to himself, you stuffed those bloody Blösch calves with milk from both ends practically, to get the breast to grow, and then the calf-dealer suddenly decided he wanted more meat in the tail hold. That kind of thing wasn't to be borne.

'You know, Hans, maybe you even overdo the milk.' Schindler wiped his hands on his blue blouse. 'You've got a lot of iron in your soil, your water's too good. It's healthy, of course, but you get red veal, don't you! This one here will probably turn out to be another fox. And if they deduct something for that? Maybe you should, you know, ask at the cooperative, or you could – '

'That takes the biscuit! Milk powder and calf supplement! We've

196

got milk of our own!' Knuchel felt the choking about to reach his throat. Hurriedly he added: 'And if our milk's not good enough to feed a calf, I'd like to know what is!'

'You've got a fine product, I've never said anything else, it's just that nowadays they are finding out new things about how to feed and water and stock-up scientifically.'

'Well, it wouldn't hurt you to try some of that yourself! You've become pretty heavy lately. You can't deny it. But tell me! What's your decision? Do you want to load it up or not?'

Schindler peered down at his own belly: 'You know, Hans, you should eat for as long as you're allowed to. Who knows what things'll be like in Heaven? They won't be over-generous. Spirits only in tiny glasses. Anyway, sooner a belly from overeating than a humpback from overwork. Heh, heh, heh, heh!'

'But the Blösch calf, do you want it?'

Schindler stopped snickering. 'Did you ever know me not to take a calf off you?'

'Take it off me! That's exactly as if you were doing me a favour! Take it off me! You've certainly never overpaid me. Don't say you lost out on the deals you've done with me!'

'No, not that, but they haven't made me a wealthy man either, and all in all, Hans, the calf-trade doesn't look too clever at the moment. You do what you can, but even so, I'm having to start dealing in cattle too, and I wanted to ask you if you happened to have a cow I could take.'

'What, now in June? With the hay harvest almost upon us? Not likely.'

'Nor a bullock?'

'Can't do it, Fritz. But if you're going into bigger animals, up in the village, you can pick up Pestalozzi.' Knuchel grinned and pointed back over his shoulder with his thumb in the direction of Innerwald. 'There's a shagged-out bull over there.'

'You're not serious?'

'Well, yes, our mountain air doesn't seem to agree with the gentleman. Some do well on it, but others sicken. But then no one listened to my advice. They're still trying to bring him round with injections, but you'll see, it won't go on much longer, and they'll have to sell him.'

'I'm glad you told me, not that cattle are hard to come by, mind you. Some farmers are having to sell two or three head, because the mice have wrecked their pasture land.'

'Bad, isn't it? You know, there are meadows that look as though a drunkard has been out ploughing on them. One heap of earth after another. We haven't had to harrow whole fields here yet, but they're a plague, and you know, up in the village, there's a campaign against the field-mouser. Oh, the way they moan, and you know what, the devil's in it, they're still playing up over my Spaniard. I'm going to have to let him go, if I only knew how and where to.'

'What's that?' asked Schindler, and sat down on the bench in the cowshed.

'The cheeser, the mayor, they're all playing up. Half the village is playing up, trying to needle him the whole time. Same with the Boden farmer's Italian. It's very bad. And he's a fine fellow for all that, bit on the small side, but willing.'

'Not exactly a giant, is he? But what can he do, your Spaniard?' asked Schindler.

Knuchel thrust his hands into his pockets, pulled them out again straightaway, flung them wide, and said loudly: 'Work! He can work! Isn't that something? And he's a quick learner too. He's much more than a cow-minder, Fritz. He's someone you can really use. I've kitted him out too. He came in sandals, but now he's got a proper outfit: boots, good trousers, the things a man needs to work in.'

'Well, I could try, it's just a thought, but maybe a butcher would . . . they're always saying there's no one in the whole country who's willing to work.'

'Well, Fritz, why not? I'd be grateful to you. I have to do my military service now, bang in the middle of the hay harvest, what about that, but after it's over, well, if someone could use him. I was always of the opinion that a cow with bigger horns would get through the village all right, but no, it's gotten worse, you can hardly send him up to the cheese dairy by himself any more.'

Schindler got up, stepped out of the shed, and said: 'Don't worry, Hans. Something will turn up, it won't be for want of trying on my part. Can't promise anything, mind. And where is he now, your Spaniard? He could help load up.'

When the Blösch calf, without its muzzle, was standing in the cage on the trailer, it sniffed at the straw spread out underfoot, gawped through the wooden slats, shivered as though it felt cold, and blinked its eyes: it was the first time it had been out in the sun.

Knuchel went to get its registration from the parlour, and Schindler checked that the number tallied with the one on the calf's eartag. He folded the paper, and said: 'Well, let's see what happens. If it's over 120 kilos, and the legs are meaty and white, then we'll settle it on the basis of today's A1 calf price. I'll be round again in a week or so.' And then, after several handshakes and repeated farewells, the LANDROVER and trailer rumbled back up the farm track. The wooden chest rattled on the trailer. Between the slats, Ambrosio could see the calf as stripes of red and white.

Knuchel shut the lower half of the byre door from the inside. He propped himself on it, resting on his elbows. With one hand he scratched his forearm, the other he just dangled. Against the bleached wood, the spread fingers resembled the prongs of a fork-like implement.

Ambrosio looked down at the nearside pasture. This time, none of the cows had interrupted their grazing.

Milk and morning coffee shone in the corners of mouths. It was Sunday. The three little Knuchel children sat on the bench in the corner behind the kitchen table. Today they chewed leisurely, filling their cheeks alternately. When they came to swallow, they lifted their almost invisibly blond eyebrows, opened their goggle-eyes still further, and craned their necks like choking swans.

Opposite the children sat Grandma and the farmer's wife. Ambrosio's place was on a low stool next to Ruedi at the bottom end of the table. The place at the top was empty. For the past week Knuchel had been at his military refresher course.

Before he had walked up the road to the village in his uniform on the previous Monday immediately after the morning milking, and disappeared into the little wood, the atmosphere on the farm had been poor for some days past. There had been differences among men and beasts alike, with kicks in the cowshed and cross words in the parlour. In the evening, the inexplicable knocking that shook the beams of the house had regaled Ambrosio's ears for longer than usual.

Farmer Knuchel had worked incessantly ahead, like a man driven. He had bought several months' supplies at the co-op. 'For when I'm doing my service,' he had said time and again. All at once, it seemed he felt he had to settle all kinds of trivial details. He had tried to anticipate all eventualities in the period of his absence, for instance, going out to mow a hay meadow, in spite of the unfavourable weather forecast. Ruedi had been offended. 'Anyone would think none of us had ever seen a hayfork before! Why doesn't he let us do it?' he had said, and Ambrosio, who had noticed tears in his eyes, and who felt particularly useless himself, had patted him on the back. When the hay was duly spoilt by the rain, the farmer's wife had managed to hold her peace for three days, before finally losing her temper on the afternoon of the fourth, a Saturday.

Although there was neither a shortage of space in the cesspit, nor any other urgent cause, Knuchel had set off, quite out of the blue, with a load of slurry in the direction of the meadow. Alarmed by the noise of the tractor, the farmer's wife had first shaken her head in incredulity before leaving the flower garden on the sunny side of the yard, where she had been working, and crossing a beet field with giant strides to intercept Knuchel before he reached his destination.

In her indignation, she had taken her trowel with her, waving it menacingly in the air, and then, having leapt out into the path of the rumbling tractor, levelled it like a pistol at the farmer, who had immediately changed down and asked her: 'What are you doing here?' She had replied that he should turn the motor right off, and then she had said what she had to say.

It just wasn't to be borne any more, for days her head had been like a hive full of bees, she'd felt worse than a dumb hen, and purely on account of him, and no other cause, she had complained. It was true, and the others felt the same way, Ruedi was depressed, Grandma wasn't opening her mouth, and even the Spaniard was slinking round the farm like a beaten dog. And so now he had to go out manuring, on a Saturday of all days, so that it would stink the whole of Sunday, when they finally had a bit of time to sit out in front of the house. She felt quite ashamed, she had said. For as long as she could remember, no one had ever been to get the manure barrel from the back of the barn on a Saturday! It was no way to carry on, and she would be pleased when the time came for him to go away and do his service, he'd had to be away from the farm for a few days before, and they'd certainly not been at a loss without him then. But the way he was acting, it was as though the whole family was about to go off to some remote place for the holidays, and there would be no one left at all on the farm, to clean the cowshed or to milk, and it just wasn't to be borne! And if the weather should happen to turn, then God knew that together with the remaining menfolk she would be perfectly capable of loading the odd cart with hay and not upsetting it in the first ditch they came to! 'But then you don't even trust us to do this much,' she had said, pressing her right thumb and forefinger together and holding them up in front of her right eye.

Then, taken by a fit of sobbing, the farmer's wife had hurried back across the beet field, caught her foot among the tops but steadied herself before she fell, and had turned round to say it would be far more sensible if the farmer were to start to get his army things together, because there would certainly be a to-do before he had them all safely in his kitbag.

In the meantime, Knuchel had climbed down off his tractor, scratched the crown of his head under his cap, and then, with his fists buried in the pockets of his overtrousers, walked round the tractor, dug at a molehill with the toes of his boots and said: 'Gah! If a man can't cut hay because of the wet weather why shouldn't he go and manure instead? It would be a kindness to the meadow.' Back on the tractor, he had called after his wife not to worry about his army gear, he could pack a kitbag in no time at all, and once she'd checked that there were no buttons missing on his coat, it wouldn't take him more than a couple of hours to get ready.

Then he had turned tractor and manure barrel round once more, but had taken care not to push the release until he'd reached a piece of grassland a long way from the farm.

The following day, as he was packing, there had indeed been further commotion. First, Knuchel had been unable to find his army knife, then further deficiencies in his equipment had become apparent. The mug for his water bottle was missing, and the blacking brush from his shoe-cleaning kit. And his coat wouldn't fit into his knapsack properly. Late on Sunday evening, the farmer had still been on his hands and knees on the parlour floor, making further vain efforts to roll up the thick green material in the approved manner. His swearing on the subject of the equipment regulations had been plainly audible up in Ambrosio's room.

But now all was peaceful in the kitchen.

The farmer's wife set another jar of newly made redcurrant jelly on the table, and cut thick slices from a loaf that she held against her bosom. The thickest slice was given to Ambrosio. Then she too went back to chewing. Red rings formed round the mouths of the Knuchel children. No one spoke.

When the first shots rang out from the firing range, Grandma said: 'There we are. They're shooting again today.' The farmer's wife nodded and said after a little while, still chewing: 'Hans can hardly wait to get the carbine out from under the bed each time.'

Thereupon Grandma laid her hands, which were almost like a man's hands, used and wrinkled, but soft too, and very alive with their brown spots, laid them like a peel around her coffee cup and held it up to her mouth, not to drink but to drink warmth, and she said: 'At least we won't have him around in the kitchen. He's always getting under our feet on a Sunday. Oh, I'm pleased every time he has to go shooting or go out in the fields or something. At least then you can put the soup on in peace and quiet.'

The farmer's wife stared at one of the blue dots on the milk jug and said: 'Yes, when Hans can't work, you hardly know what to do with him.' And when Ruedi got up and announced that he wouldn't be back for lunch, she only replied with an absent-minded, 'Never mind'.

Ambrosio left the table together with Ruedi. The Knuchel herd was already out on the pasture, but the calves were still in the shed and there was one whose navel string was discharging pus, and only slowly drying out. Ambrosio wanted to see to it first. Then the mousetraps had to be checked, emptied and reset, and the farmer had also given instructions for the pig that was being fattened for domestic consumption to be let out after breakfast for half an hour.

It was to get a chance to run about and roll in the dirt in a totally routed-up area behind the henhouse that was kept specifically for the purpose.

Only after these tasks were finished, did Ambrosio get the big twig broom from the feed passage to start sweeping. He even swept outside the kitchen. The farmer's wife went over to the doorway, with her dish-cloth and cutlery in her hands, and said: 'There will be good haymaking weather after all next week if everything is so neat and tidy.' But while she spoke, she dropped the bread knife which landed point down in the doorway. The farmer's wife was frightened and shrank back, behind her Grandma looked at the knife quivering in the wood. 'What will you do now?' she asked.

The farmer's wife laughed, took the handle and said: 'You'll see, we'll have visitors.'

'Won't be that!' said Grandma.

'But if a knife sticks in the ground like that, it means there's something in the air,' insisted the farmer's wife. 'Doesn't it?' she asked Ambrosio, who nodded as he carried on sweeping the Knuchel dust with his willow twigs in a semi-circular pattern.

Ambrosio was feeling good.

After lunch he had gone and sat with the calves in the otherwise empty byre but he had soon got bored, and didn't even stay long enough to hear a cigarette end hiss into the gutter: a little ritual Sunday sound that he had begun to take pleasure in.

Instead he went for a walk up in the Galgenhubel.

The Galgenhubel was a hill just outside the village where he and Luigi and the field-mouser had met a couple of times on fine afternoons for a drink from a bottle one of them brought along.

As he set off down the farm track, Ambrosio thought of Knuchel's commands to him, all the points of instruction that the farmer had demonstrated to him. He thought of the work that he would do in the week ahead. The potatoes had to be sprayed before Knuchel's return. He mustn't forget that. Knuchel had shown him how to use the portable spray-tank that you strapped on your back, and had also told him that the two rows on the left edge of the field didn't need poison. Not a drop was to fall on those plants. Those potatoes were for their own use, and the pigs in the sty and the women in the kitchen had no preference for especially large specimens. 'The main thing is that they taste good, and they keep well in the cellar,' he had said.

Above the wood, Ambrosio heard panting. It was a suppressed groaning, suggestive of physical effort. And then a bell. Ambrosio leapt aside. The woman on the bicycle! Her arms stiff against the handlebars, her head down between her shoulders, she was toiling up the hill to the village. She panted for oxygen, the air in her wake smelled of sweat. She had to be the most strapping woman Ambrosio had ever set eyes on. Her thighs were cranks, her calves pistons. Not for one instant did she take her eyes off her front wheel on the gravel road. She was a pedalling machine where metal and flesh were as one! And how evenly she conquered the climb up to the village!

Ambrosio passed the locked-up marksmen's hut, crossed the Innerwald shooting range, and then he spotted the field-mouser in his floppy felt hat and earth-stained cloak, standing on the Galgen-hubel like a personification of the landscape. The old man's boots were rooted in the grass, he leaned on his stick, and he aimed his incomprehensible words at the highlands. He was oblivious of Ambrosio's aproach.

Luigi was sitting on his handkerchief on the grass, with his back to the grey shape of the field-mouser. Ambrosio shook his out-stretched hand, put a blade of grass between his lips, and spread out his own handkerchief to sit down likewise.

Both Luigi and Ambrosio wore brown suits and ties, and had contrived a way of resting their arms against their knees that gave prominence to the dazzling display of wristwatch. Ambrosio was laughing, and Luigi was pointing at the rock masses of the Lower Alps with a sweeping gesture. The Galgenhubel was the only common part of Innerwald that offered a panorama, here they could sit and gaze southwards, staring at the jagged mountains, without attending to the field-mouser, not troubling to listen to words they wouldn't have understood in any case.

And the old man was content with their mere, mute presence.

From all around came the sound of heavy cow bells and the ringing of the tin chimes.

On the pastures of the village, including that of the Boden farm in front of Luigi and Ambrosio, between the shooting range and the village road, the grass had grown back strongly. This sunny day had been preceded by a couple of days of wet weather.

For some of the Innerwald cattle, though, this growth was too little too late. The grass on some of the hay meadows adjacent to their own grazing pastures was considerably thicker and higher. To make matters worse, the cows had been robbed of many square metres of grazing by the plague of mice. Within each impatient herd, there had been more recourse to horns, the fight for grass had become fiercer, and the bit of fresh green now sprouting back on ground that had been cropped down several times wasn't enough to keep the animals from throwing the odd glance at what lay beyond the barbed wire. Every calf was aware that on the other side of the impressive fences flowered the red cow-clover.

And this in spite of the rain which, by flooding and washing away the underground network of passages, had put an end to the unhindered spread of the mouse plague. Strong variations in temperature, also disliked by the rodents, had done their bit as well.

In many places there was still one mound of earth by another; there were still spoiled fields, which in their churned-up and furrowed condition bore less resemblance to Innerwald fields than to unearthly crater landscapes. In fact, every other one of these brown tumps was nothing but an abandoned nest. But even on the Boden farm pasture, that was not enough to make the cows forget their reduced rations: and clover, lucerne and dandelion still spiced the air.

'Caramba! Mira las vacas!' Ambrosio jabbed Luigi in the side. Never on the highlands had Ambrosio seen a herd grazing so close to a fence as these cows down there. The cowbells! They were sounding notes of protest.

'Eh! Che cosa vuoi?' asked Luigi, and shrugged his shoulders languidly.

The cows were eating their way towards the fence that ran alongside the village road, but they were uncommonly close together. Every cow had just enough space to be able to whisk her tail freely against flies and horseflies. But evacuating and scratching were problematical. If a cow was a little exuberant in the way she pumped out the contents of her bladder, her high arc would force the animals behind her to take evasive action. In addition, the centre of the herd had already moved in such an unwonted quarter that the three young cows grazing on its right flank now found themselves hard pressed by the fence.

One of them moved her forelegs apart, circled with her ears and lowered her head like a bull at bay. She had come into contact with the barbed wire.

Another went down on her knees, pushed one leg out in front of her, and laid her throat and forequarters down on the ground. Her bell was silenced. Greedily, she shoved her head under the fencing, and her tongue set about the dandelions that grew on the verge of the village road.

A third scraped at the wild moss on a fencepost like one possessed.

Ambrosio was astonished. Luigi appeared unmoved.

And the field-mouser carried on speaking in his unmelodious way, spitting out his words in rhythmic bursts, with his eyes gazing beyond the hills towards the horizon: 'And forever with our toes in the dirt and the dung, our feet like leather, yes, like leather when I was a boy, in the summer we were always barefoot, yes, until far into the winter, and often the grass was cold, like ice it was in the mornings, and when we went to fetch the cows from the pasture, they almost froze, sometimes we saw a place where the grass was flattened, there a cow had lain, and we ran to it, and there the earth would be warm, and we would stand on that spot for as long as we could, and afterwards we ran after that cow, and sometimes our feet grew so cold – '

'Caramba!' Ambrosio leaped to his feet.

A brindled cow of medium height trotted out of the middle of the herd straight towards the fence. Tossing her head to and fro, she walked alongside the barbed wire. Her chimes rang with resolve. She stopped in front of a post that rose out of a piece of ground studded with molehills, then she mooed, slid her horns underneath the top line of barbed wire, craned her neck and uprooted the post. It still hung by its barbed wire and quivered. But when the brindled cow got her horns free again, she put her hoof on it, pushed it over and trampled the fence to the ground.

'Hijo de puta!' said Ambrosio. 'Porco Dio!' said Luigi. The Boden farm cows put their heads together, mooed in a variety of different keys, stretched, turned and trotted over the demolished fence down the escarpment and onto the village road.

No time was wasted. The cows made straight for the fodder. Soon the dandelions were missing from the roadside, and while the most adventurous of them tweaked at the red clover in crisp bunches from the hay meadow on the Galgenhubel slope, some others set off down the road, and turned into a cabbage field.

The field-mouser ground his teeth, came out of his reverie, broke off his droning monologue, and sat down in the grass next to Luigi. 'Holy St Ulrich! The Boden farmer's beasts are on the village road!' he giggled, and slapped first himself and then Luigi on the knee, rootled in the ground with his stick, gestured up at the village and said: 'The midwife's about due. She's probably just been having coffee with the minister. There, there she is, see her with her head down, she's just in time!'

Luigi also noticed the woman on the bicycle. 'La levatrice! La levatrice!' he shouted exultantly, leaped up and cried, 'Qué donna! Qué donna!' He clenched his fists against his chest. He would give his right arm to spend a night with the left leg of that woman. A thigh and he would be happy! That woman had divine legs! he exclaimed, leaping and prancing about, and opening his arms as though to embrace a tree-trunk. What he'd never been able to do on his own, those cows would manage for him. No speeding past this time!

The midwife turned a corner and headed straight for the runaway herd. She rang her bell. She did not brake. She rang and rang uninterruptedly, although she had already taken one hand off the handlebars to gesticulate. 'Shoo! Shoo!' she called out. Only at the last minute did she put her brakes on. Dust rose from the gravel as she skidded with locked wheels up to a cow, and before even taking her feet off the pedals, she began lashing out at the animal. 'What do you think you're up to! And on a Sunday too!'

None of the cows took a blind bit of notice of the woman, who put her bicycle down on the roadside, and then spotted the three figures on the Galgenhubel.

'I don't believe it! It's just not possible!' She climbed the slope and shouted: 'Oi, you up there watching! Why don't you come down and help get those animals off the road!' She stopped, stood still, shaded her eyes with her hand, and craned her neck to study the three figures closely: 'Are those the foreigners there?' she asked. 'Ha! As I thought! Now will you come down and drive that bull off the road! Right away! Do you hear?' She stamped angrily along the slope, supporting herself with one hand, but she still slipped, and, in falling, rucked her skirt up. Like two naked bodies, her mighty thighs lay in the grass. They were white as milk. Luigi gulped and forgot to shut his mouth. Ambrosio sat down again. He scratched his bald patch. So much meat on one leg! The field-mouser laughed and shouted, 'Catch a mouse, did you?' And then, triumphantly: 'Those cows, eh!'

The midwife gestured back with her arms, got up, one hand holding her skirt, the other supporting herself on the slope. 'Now will you come and get that bull off the road!'

'If that's a bull, then I'm another! And you know what that makes you!'

The midwife turned round, climbed back down the slope, picked up her bicycle where she'd left it at the roadside, lifted it over the flattened fence, pushed it between the molehills around the cows and back on the road, then she mounted the saddle again and pedalled off down towards the little Knuchel wood.

'Qué mujer!' said Ambrosio. 'Mamma mia!' said Luigi. The field-mouser giggled.

When Ambrosio and Luigi had driven the Boden farm cows back into their field, and done some quick repairs to the wrecked fence, Ambrosio took his leave. It was still rather too early for the evening milking. His guess was that the Knuchel cows wouldn't yet have climbed back up to the paddock from the furthest corners of the pasture, to assemble at the gate. Usually they liked to spend the hour before they were collected for watering and milking standing on each other's toes, or maybe, if the sun was shining, affording shade for one another. Today would be the same . . . Then the Boden farm cows reminded him: hadn't a similar liking for dandelions that

208

flowered under barbed-wire fencing lately become apparent in the Knuchel herd? Hadn't he seen Baby and Bossy standing suspiciously near to the fence on some occasions? Hadn't Blösch once set about a molehill with her horns?

And hardly had Ambrosio gone a couple of hundred yards down the road when he saw first a couple of horns, and then the whole of a cow's head. 'Hijo de puta!' From behind the shooting-range heights came the sound of familiar cow bells. The entire Knuchel herd was grazing there.

Ambrosio ran straight across the meadow to the edge of the hill. There was Baby, chewing and gawping, there were Check and Flora grazing, further down were Stine and Spot in knee-high clover, and there, in the juiciest, most luscious green of all, immediately in front of the closed shutters of the marksmen's hut, there was Blösch tucking into the very finest of the grass.

The tongues of the Knuchel cows, still green from ruminating, snaked out of their muzzles, licking up the PROVIMIN they were given before evening milking. Their lower molars ground against the toothless gums of their upper jaws.

The air in the cowshed trembled, shaken by animal greed.

Ambrosio had hesitated briefly in the feed passage. Was it right to go on giving those cows such highly concentrated nourishment? Would the extra energy derived from it really go to their lactating glands, or might it not lead to a further free-for-all? He didn't think he could manage a second pasture revolution! One breakout through the Knuchel wood, the shrubbery, and onto the virgin pasture of the shooting range, that was enough.

And yet Ambrosio did not find it difficult to decide against reducing their intake of concentrate. Like yesterday, like the day before, he had picked up one of the sacks from the pile and hoisted it onto his shoulders, to tip it straight into the manger.

He had even given them half a sack over the stipulated amount. He wanted to make absolutely certain that the milk-production figures would be up to scratch. During his period as caretaker ruler of the Knuchel cowshed, the milk quantity was not to go down so much as by a single litre. Ambrosio would move heaven and earth to see that it didn't. Even if it meant using the hosepipe . . .

But it was more than simple ambition that kept Ambrosio from punishing the Knuchel herd where it hurt them. Since last Sunday, when he'd seen them standing in the luscious green, he had felt more drawn to the character of these Simmental cows. Hadn't they been bred specifically for limitless greed? Altogether, Ambrosio felt that he'd wronged them in his previous estimation. They weren't nearly as demure as they looked, and they knew quite well that they had horns on their heads and power in their necks.

The gentle hiss of a cigarette end rose from the gutter.

Ambrosio sat down on the cowshed bench, his elbows on his thighs, the tops of his rubber boots pressing against the back of his knees. He was just about to start milking. He played with his lighter. The ball had become much smaller. Ambrosio had already burned up a considerable part of the tinder in Innerwald. His ear itched. He picked a bit of dried clover out of the hair at the back of his neck. He itched all over. At last, the weather had turned, and, under the command of the farmer's wife, they had started to get the hay in.

For three days Ruedi had been driving all over the Knuchel meadows on the tractor, towing all manner of appliances and machines. He had mowed and raked and turned. The smell of hay was everywhere. One forkful after another was heaved onto the wagons. Huge loads were built up with bulging overhanging sides, and a haypole – a heavy round beam – had been laid lengthwise on top of the hay and pulled down at the back by means of a rope pulley, to press the hay down and make it secure for the drive over the rough Knuchel tracks.

The sweat flowed. The upper arms of the farmer's wife burned red. Grandma brought their meals out to them by the wicker basketful. Cheese, sausage and bread, wrapped in red-and-white-striped cloth, and litres and litres of mint tea and apple juice that were somehow never quite enough.

And now, while the slightly damp hay on one meadow was being raked together and hung on racks overnight for fear of hoar-frost and the threat of rain, Ambrosio had gone in ahead of the others to clean the cowshed and milk. The cows had had to do without their pasture out of doors. During the day, they were better off inside, away from the attacks of insects. When Ambrosio appeared, they had climbed up out of their straw, and, tempted by the concentrate, shoved their heads into their mangers. That way the back of the stalls was easier to clean. There was already room under every udder for bucket and milking stool. Ambrosio had pushed the clean straw to the back, and carted the dung out of the shed, and now, in a minute, he would dip into the milking fat. Half a minute. Ambrosio felt the heaviness in his limbs. A day in the Knuchel hay. With those gigantic tools, in that heat! In Knuchel fashion he rolled up the sleeves of his milking blouse.

Blösch mooed. She had licked up her own portion of formula and a fair bit of Mirror's as well. She moved her hindlegs wider apart. Her milk-plumped udder was jammed in between her lower thighs. She wanted to pull her head back out of the feed crib. Her horns smashed against the wood.

Bossy was restless too. Half a dozen cats lay in the alley behind her, impatient for milk. But Ambrosio had avoided all chiming and tinkling, and so her leaky udder wasn't dribbling yet. Like Blösch, Bossy tried to extricate her head, but her hindquarters went alternately too far to the left and too far to the right.

Ambrosio stuffed his lighter into his pocket, and suppressed a desire to land a kick in the middle of the rabble of cats.

Those cheeky beasts. 'Carajo!' Why don't you chase mice?

The calves were hitched up between the bench and the door. They tugged at their ropes. One of them bleated. Tienen hambre. Ambrosio stretched. He took the bar of STEINFELS soap off the shelf. He would probably have to water the calves himself today, the Knuchel children were still out playing on the mown meadows. They were making hiding places for themselves under the hay racks and whooping and squealing with laughter. Today they wouldn't be there to creep up on Ambrosio and laugh at him under the bellies of the cows, and run away when he pointed a teat in their direction, and sent a stream of milk after them. Ambrosio looked at the head of one of the calves. They all looked the same. Those pronounced but blunt forms with their childish roundness, their mass, the concavity between muzzle and skull, the thick lips and the taut skin round the eyes. These characteristics of the calves kept putting him in mind of the human faces of Innerwald. Didn't all of them in the village and on the farm have those same very weak cheekbones? Loose flesh under their chins? Just like that roll of skin on the throat of this calf?

And the strong curve of the skull, with so little musculature below it! And that wide forehead with the rounded edges, suggesting bumps and bruises that often looked as if they might put forth horns! And those highly developed nodding muscles in the neck, and that look from under the mostly hairless eyebrows! Calf-like they were!

And what about himself? Had he already . . . ?

He touched his chin and mouth. He felt relieved to feel the skin still taut across his throat.

He finished his preparations and sat, hands greased and the bucket between his knees, under Bossy's udder, which, to the delight of the cats, had now started to dribble.

Every now and again, Ambrosio leaned aside while milking to glance down the feed passage at the door. Maybe a little blond head would show up after all.

Ambrosio racked his brain over it, but in vain, he couldn't understand it! No sooner had Knuchel returned from the refresher course for reserve troops, than the banging at night had become louder again. Every day for two weeks it had grown quieter, and now it was once more echoing through the beams of the house, boom, boom, boom.

And the cats became cheekier. Ambrosio had chased them out of the cowshed into the fields several times. Unavailingly. Now, with the farmer back, they settled in the freshest of the straw with hours to go before milking.

The behaviour of the farmer's wife changed as well. She was proud; half the hay harvest had been brought in in her husband's absence without any probems. But now the thickest slices from the loaf were once again to be found beside his plate at the top of the table, and the blue, red and yellow aprons were rarely seen outside the kitchen and garden.

The farmer himself was quiet and calm. 'When he was called up, he was fidgety and as wound-up as a calf's tail, but now he's hardly scratching any more, just now and then on his throat. His service has done him the world of good,' said the farmer's wife to Grandma.

When the farmer himself was asked how his military service had gone, he replied: 'Fine. It was fine. The weather was kind to us, and we were never without a bird to put in the soup, my, that was some refresher camp!' So saying, he pressed his lips together and nodded his head, like a cow scraping her horns against the bars of her crib. 'We were able to get hold of some wonderful horses this year. That was a sight, us gallivanting about the mountains on board! No, it was fine in the army, as fine as a holiday by the seaside.'

But soon, he was scratching skin and scalp rather more often.

The mayor had telephoned. He'd begun by asking nicely after wife and children, then he'd wanted to know who'd been present at the refresher course, and had even pleased Knuchel with the news that for days now that damned Pestalozzi couldn't be induced to cover a cow, and so what Knuchel had predicted would probably come to pass, and they'd have to cut their losses and sell off the expensive bull. But would anyone still want him? the mayor wondered. One should at least be careful to talk about it as little as possible, because Pestalozzi still had a name far beyond the highlands, and it might be possible for the Breeding Syndicate to come out of it all without suffering too much of a loss.

The mayor had spoken about the bull for a while, and gone on to other village topics, before suddenly announcing in sharp tones that in Knuchel's absence there had been a further deplorable episode which he had probably heard about already, as it involved the Spaniard. Together with the Boden farm Italian and Field-mouser Fritz, the old prattler, Ambrosio had been boozing on the Galgenhubel, and quite immoderately at that. The midwife had caught them turning the Boden farmer's beasts loose.

When the mayor went on to say that the cheeser had now had it up to here and finally wanted to see a health certificate for Ambrosio, and that he himself was hardly best pleased by the whole matter, and would rather that the whole of the highlands weren't abuzz with talk of the foreigners in Innerwald, Knuchel had already stopped pressing the telephone to his ear, and was instead holding it in front of him and staring at the receiver. It seemed to him as though hordes of invisible beasts, whining, humming vermin were coming out of it. It's as if that large-scale farmer, that tiresome know-all of a mayor, had shrivelled up and were sitting in the black bakelite tub of the earpiece. And at this point he had hung up.

He would have liked to hear from Ambrosio what had happened on that Sunday afternoon on the Galgenhubel. He tried to talk to him, gesturing and miming and asking and indicating, even mixing in a few scraps of French with his Knuchel German, something he had never tried before his military service, but all his efforts at clarification failed. Knuchel and Ambrosio confronted one another helplessly. But it wasn't possible! He's looked after my animals so well. Ambrosio drinking! On the Galgenhubel! What lying dog thought up that one? And something with the cows too. It's as if one had gone missing from the cowshed, or wasn't giving milk. He'd never do anything to a cow up in the village! They can try that one out on someone else. I won't believe a word that midwife says any more. Maybe they should look to their fences. They'll just have to make them stronger if their pastures are so meagre and grazed down, hardly surprising if a cow can't stand it a moment longer in there!

The story of how his own herd had taken flight had not reached the farmer's ears. His wife, apart from Ambrosio the only other person to know about it, had not told her husband. She knew her Hans. How he would have crowed! The Knuchel fence had been repaired. Ambrosio had dug up a few square metres of mouse-loosened ground, and pitched the posts in it freshly. And he had removed all traces of trampling and dung from the little wood.

But there was another piece of news to cause itching in the Knuchel scalp and choking in the Knuchel throat. The Innerwald village council had decided unanimously to halve the reward money for mice, which it had previously put up to combat the rodent plague. The field-mouser was only profiting from their own misfortune, and adding insult to injury, he was making fun of the worst-afflicted farmers with all manner of oaths and devilment. It was a scandal. And he drank like a hole. No, Fritz Mäder, that useless windbag, would have to be kept on shorter commons, and a shorter rein, they had said.

Knuchel was of a different opinion.

'They're treating the old fellow like a naughty boy. Who's it going to help, I'm asking. Now, when he can at last earn himself a bit of money, now the old fools turn round and behave as though he's just been cutting felt hats in strips the whole time, and claiming mouse-tail money for them,' he said to his wife, who replied that the wretched rodents had indeed been burrowing wickedly, that in many places in the highlands, and in Innerwald, they had eaten quite a hole in the money bags of many a proud farmer. 'I can quite understand them being wrought up about it,' she said, whereupon the farmer had retorted that that couldn't possibly be laid at Field-mouser Fritz's door. That was sheer bullying. The mice had wrought destruction up and down the land, and some of it worse, far worse, than in the highlands, as he had seen for himself on his refresher course. 'No, those idiots! They're just out to save themselves a few pence of mouse money!' said Knuchel. 'As if it was a doddle trudging about the fields at night when it's as black and wet as the inside of a cow's belly. And Fritz was telling me himself how they begrudged him the water in their wells, everyone was doing him down, and they laughed at him when he wouldn't strew poison because it would kill the martens and the weasels and the owls and everything else that eats the mice. No, woman! Say what you like, up in the village there are some who have more dirt on their hands than Fritz has on the soles of his boots!'

The farmer's wife nodded in full agreement, but she also thought that since Hans had come back from the army, he'd done a lot of talking about things that bothered him. And she looked at Knuchel's fingernails with some apprehension.

When there was a telephone call the following day from Livestock-dealer Schindler, the farmer finally scratched a bloody wound in the skin of his throat.

Like the mayor, Schindler began by asking politely after Knuchel's wife and children, before going straight on to the health of Pestalozzi. How was the tired bull doing now, what would the bull committee of the Breeders' Syndicate decide, had Knuchel already heard details of this or that?, Schindler inquired. Knuchel told him what he knew, and his answers so delighted Schindler that he sniggered a few times and said: 'I'll offer them the price for sausage-bulls, they'll make eyes like saucers,' but then all of a sudden he was talking about Knuchel's Blösch calf: 'Oh, Hans, I'm sorry I wasn't able to tell you earlier, but you were away with the army. Well, it had the weight all right, it had better, and it was nicely plumped up, but by Christ, it was a shade too red for their liking. There wasn't a thing I could do about it, and I had to take a deduction.'

Knuchel took the news in silence, which alarmed the dealer and even made him mention, somewhat incautiously, as he tried to overcome the silence at the other end, how he had been looking round for a job for Ambrosio in the city, as Knuchel had asked him, but was having no success. He'd mentioned the case to various master-butchers and to the head of personnel at the meat factory, but they'd told him that a foreigner couldn't change his job just like that, much less his whole line of work. No, it wasn't possible to just go ahead, because then the immigration police would get involved. You see, there were quotas for foreigners in every branch of industry. When one had been allocated to agriculture, he would have to stay on a farm. Those were the rules, explained Schindler.

Knuchel, who by the mere fact of having been called away to the telephone while milking, had been put in a bad mood, did not return to the cowshed immediately. He went to hide among the pigs, to give the blood on his throat a chance to dry. But the creatures, who hadn't yet been fed, began to squeal. After the clicking of the bolt, they expected their swill right away, that was what they were used to, and they buried their snouts in empty troughs. 'Are you going to start whining and all!' Knuchel bruised his knuckles against the wall of the pen, tried again to urinate, and, leaning against a partition as he did so, he caught sight of the pig that had been set aside for domestic consumption. Without taking his eyes off him, he said: 'Ha, you there! You've been eating my best potatoes for long enough now! You're fat enough as it is! I'll see to it that you go under the knife this very week!'

In the kitchen, they were appalled by Knuchel's intention. 'Slaughter?' Ruedi asked, and the farmer's wife had to sit down, at first she simply wouldn't believe it was true, and then she tried to make the farmer see reason. 'Do we have to slaughter a pig now in the middle of a hay harvest? Whatever for, Hans? Think of the flies! Where will you get the butcher from? Where would we do the smoking? And didn't you say the last time that you'd never have any butchering done at home ever again, and certainly not by Überländer?' she protested. And Grandma added: 'She's really just a little sow still. Very, very lean she is.' The old woman spoke quietly under her breath, and in her agitation, she carried the dried crockery piece by piece from the dresser back to the draining board.

'Überländer will do fine, we'll just have to see that he doesn't drink too much.' Knuchel was implacable. 'That sow will be scalded and slaughtered! And by Sunday, what's more! If I have to scrape the bristles myself!'

That very evening Knuchel asked his wife for the telephone number of travelling butcher Überländer. He had to ask for it several times. When the farmer's wife finally gave him a piece of paper and said: 'Here it is, 22 59 67,' then Knuchel scratched off the plaster that his wife had made him put on his throat, and said: 'Won't you do it? Just tell him we want him to do a bit of butchering. And I'll pay him well!'

Fritz Überländer's first reaction was to think it was a joke. 'Is Hans pulling my leg?' he asked the farmer's wife, and the farmer himself had to come and speak, saying that no one was playing a prank or anything stupid like that, and that they'd be pleased if he could make it this week. He would see to it that it was worth his while, said Knuchel.

Fritz Überländer didn't hesitate for long. He had a part-time job at the slaughterhouse, and he could get the day off, though he would have to work something out, and there was also the consideration that in high summer, the ham and the bacon needed double quantities of salt, Knuchel should bear that in mind. He would also require more water, and it would be pleasanter if they could do the scalding and butchering in the barn or the hayloft, somewhere with a bit of shade anyway. He was worried abut the flies, and well, it was funny, normally Knuchel would only think of butchering round about the middle of November. It had worked out well enough too, by the calendar!

'Never mind that, Fritz. You can butcher and make sausages wherever you please, just come. At least this week the moon is still crescent,' replied Knuchel.

Luigi and Überländer pulled the first calf under the rack. Krummen held it tightly round the neck. The rope went round the left hindleg immediately above the knee. They had taken their knives off, all except for Pretty Boy Hügli, who was standing there, wondering whether to lend a hand or not.

– Shoot! yelled Krummen through the hall. Shoot! For God's sake! We haven't got all day! This isn't charity work! Chrrrrchuarrrchoootuh! As though he was getting rid of his mucous membranes once and for all so as never to be troubled ever again by irritation or congestion of the throat, Krummen hawked up a mouth-filling snot projectile, and looped it into the waste container.

– Just coming! Kilchenmann fitted a cartridge into his firearm as he walked. Does there always have to be this mad rush the whole time, he protested under his breath, without looking at anyone.

Suspended from the rack hung a gleaming hook, and under the calf six hands grabbed six cold, dank forearms, the three men locked themselves round the wriggling limbs of the shaggy-coated Simmental. They squatted down like weightlifters, straightened their backs, the veins stood out on their necks, they held their breath, and Hup! the calf lost the ground under its feet, it squirmed, its neck shook, its tongue frothed, it kicked and screamed. Luigi grimaced, his face was pressed against its flank, Krummen's jaw trembled, he couldn't keep it up much longer, the looped rope passed over the hook, and Kilchenmann, as always, as he did a hundred times a day, took aim with his bolt-gun, fired, and paff! Six arms let go of the calf. Roast, stew, soup bones, 160 kilos or so, hung on the end of the rope, swung back and forth, tongue on the floor. Three drops of blood trickled from the hole in the skull, and rolled down over the white blaze. A whole world had turned upside down.

Überländer spat. Luigi cleaned his face, burying it in a dry patch on the right upper arm of his butcher's blouse.

– Next! Krummen opened the sliding door of the waiting pen. If a certain gentleman would agree to participate, we might find it a little easier next time!

Luigi took the second calf by the tail, Überländer held the horns. It was an overfed animal with deformed legs and imbecilic eyes. It allowed itself to be towed into the hall without resisting, it was lifted and shot, and *the smaller the animal, the faster is heartbeat. A high temperature, movement, and fear are factors that will raise the heart rate.*

– That one! Krummen pointed to the third calf. It was smaller, and still had some of its navel cord, brown and half dry, hanging like a little rod under its belly. It had a curly hide. As the men in their rubber aprons came up to it, it dug its front feet in, and made a show of defiance, as though it was a game. It wanted to butt, to horn, to fight. Luigi laughed. Überländer gave it a tap on the back. It leaped up like a goat, and skipped into the calf slaughterhall. As it kept hopping up, it was easily coaxed under the hook on the rack, and was soon swinging on its rope.

– Right, I want the apprentice to stick! ordered Krummen. And what about him there? What's he want now? Behind the hanged and shot calves, the man from the veterinary hospital had appeared. He stood with outstretched arms, rowing and balancing on the slightly sloping floor, on which the blood was only starting to flow. He had on a grey orderly's coat, and had a way of walking that was like a tiptoe.

– I'd like a heart, please, one that's still beating! He had a container like a thermos flask, with a liquid in it that would keep a freshly taken heart beating for several hours.

– Experiment! he said.

– What are you lot experimenting on? asked Überländer.

– Well, if only we knew, replied the man from the veterinary hospital.

– All right then, you stick, said Krummen to Überländer. We'll get another crippled dog of a calf. You can take its heart then. The apprentice can stir blood.

Überländer strapped on his knives, the apprentice got a milk can

219

and a stick. The others went out to get the fourth calf. It was stubborn and heavy. Hügli swore and grabbed it by the eyelid. Krummen punched the base of its tail. Hup, you bastard! he shouted.

The man from the veterinary hospital took a step back.

Kilchenmann was ready to shoot.

The longest knife from Überländer's sheath was stuck in the throat of the first calf, and *when bleeding an animal in a hanging position, check that no urine or spittle are allowed to mix with the blood in the collecting utensil. The blood must not come into contact with either the butcher's hands or the hide of the animal,* and: paff! The fourth calf convulsed. Its limbs jerked up to its body, and it swung back. A good shot for a wriggling, overweight animal. Kilchenmann clicked his firearm open to reload. That calf won't blink, he said to the man from the veterinary hospital. Kilchenmann shoved the empty cartridge in his trouser pocket, and *an animal is insufficiently stunned if it still blinks its eyelids when the eye is touched.*

The apprentice stirred the blood of the first, already stuck calves. Überländer went up to the fourth calf, stuck it, and opened up its belly. He sliced through the hide and then, cutting from the inside to avoid damaging any of the organs, drove his blade down through the cartilaginous sternum. He opened the chest cavity as far as the base of the throat, then he felt for the heart and pulled it out between the two wings of the lungs, and *there are three circulatory systems: the major circulation (body circulation); the minor circulation (lung circulation); and portal vein circulation;* and: Here, it's still beating, said Überländer, cupping the calf's heart like a small animal in his hands for an instant, before dropping it into the open container.

The fifth calf was hanged and straightaway stuck. The blood ran into the can, the apprentice stirred and stirred, the fibrin curdled to fleecy lumps, and *the major circulation requires far more energy than the minor. Therefore, the left heart also has a much more powerful musculature than the right,* but the sixth calf put up a fight.

– Here, come out, you bastard! The calf bucked and pushed against the men. Are we going to have to carry the fucking cripple? No, the bugger's far too heavy! But we've got to get him out! Not like that! Not with your fingers under his eyelids! Don't let Dr Wyss catch you doing that! Krummen twisted the calf's tail as though trying to break it. The calf sat down, bleated and screamed, pouring out froth and gut juice over hands, aprons and boots. Krummen had got himself covered with yellow slime by pushing its behind. The calf wouldn't move.

– How did you get the bastard in here in the first place? asked Pretty Boy Hügli.

– I gave it my fingers to suck, replied the apprentice.

Pretty Boy Hügli shoved four fingers into the calf's mouth and the whining stopped, the calf stood up, stretched its neck, took a step forward, then another, and it walked out of the waiting cage.

– Ha! See that! Hügli swelled his chest and beamed. Luigi was still holding his hands out away from his body. Yellow stuff dribbled from his fingers. See what he did! The pig! he said. He wouldn't have minded having to drive the animal a bit more, shoving at it and pulling at its hide. Krummen likewise. He trotted along behind the calf in some disappointment. He would have given the bloody animal what for.

The men squatted down. The rope was fixed on the hindleg, necks stretched, hands gripped and fingers linked, and once more: Hup! and paff!

Straight after the shot, the man from the veterinary hospital said: Well, be seeing you. The container bearing the calf's beating heart was hermetically sealed. The calf on the rack swung quivering back and forth. It had three golden stripes on its back. Krummen had wiped his shit-smeared hands clean on its hide. The sheaths were strapped on again. The man from the veterinary hospital hurried off, still tiptoeing.

The diagnosis might have been simply BUTCHER'S WOUND but Jacob Haueter had his own clumsiness, even his own folly to blame when he bled to death in ten minutes on the slaughterhouse floor. Karl Brugger had stood there looking like a real killer, and *every three hours on average a working man is killed in the prosperous land. Industrial accidents are those that occur in the course of performing a task that is in the employer's interest within or without the employer's terrain.* And in the construction of the Gotthard railway tunnel, *847 men more or less were slain or maimed.* Jacob Haueter died with a knife in his belly. Karl Brugger too in a way. And the worker who was cutting a screw, and then switched the machine into reverse. A square-head bolt caught his overall which wrapped itself round the drive-shaft, and took the hapless man with it. He suffered a bruised skull, a cut stomach, and a deformed knee before his throat and chest were so tightly constricted that he suffocated. And busy fitting the wires back into the insulators on a newly replaced electricity mast, a fitter dropped into his safety harness and died, even though the cables had been switched off. Because at nightfall, a photo-electric cell automatically switches on the street-lighting which is carried on the same mast, and *there the helper falls through the unfenced hole in the floor, there the foreman falls almost 12 metres onto the scaffolding that is just being erected, there a plasterer lies crushed at the foot of a fifteen-storey block, there the painter leans against an apparently secure barrier, and tumbles down the lift shaft with it, there a man walks into space off a 35-metre-high motorway viaduct, there the floorlayer's apprentice tips off the end of a balcony with his barrow,* and here one butcher sticks his knife into the belly of another. Human beings are rarely infected by foot-and-mouth disease. Individuals with a predisposition to it develop blisters on the lips, the tongue, inside of the mouth, and more rarely on hands, feet, arms and chest. *The butcher who comes into contact with anthrax is risking his life.* Careful: disinfect every wound with iodine. Wash hands, arms, neck and throat with alcohol. Boil contaminated equipment and clothing. Immediately contact your doctor at the slightest symptoms of ill health. As well as causing a temperature, anthrax leads to the formation of coal-like carbuncles on the skin, on the neck, throat, and face, on the arms, hands, lips, and in the lungs and guts. At first a small red patch forms, which itches, then hardens and fills with a brownish liquid. The pustule then bursts, and a blackish ulcer appears. And swine fever. And glanders. And rabies. *And Bang's disease is an occupational illness among butchers, vets and farmers.* But Jacob Haueter died with a knife thrust stupidly into his belly. The symptoms of Bang's disease or brucellosis in humans are fever, tiredness, pain in the liver, kidneys and nerves, headaches, perspiration, anaemia and a stooping walk. And swine pox. And tetanus. And erysipelas. And tuberculosis. For years, Jacob Haueter wore a protective metal guard under his apron when he worked. Not even the finest blade could have got through the wire mesh. His body was safe from the dangerous butcher's cut, the fatal thrust to the groin. But boredom at work made him fool around. He played tricks. If someone came near him, he would try and give them a fright. He would pretend to slip and stick his knife into his stomach. Once he made Frau Spreussiger scream. Visitors too. And trainees. He would stand at his table, boning pieces of meat, and suddenly double up. First howling, then howling with laughter. Sometimes boy scouts came. Tidy little chaps in shorts and knee socks. They wanted hollow bones. They had little ornamented knives in leather sheaths. They wanted nice bones. To make tie rings out of. Jacob Haueter liked having the little fellows around, liked playing his tricks on them, as they stood and gawped at Haueter's knife flashing in and out among the bones. A sudden Ouch! and a yell, and the little chaps went white as sheets. Once a whole school came on a visit. Students or sixth-formers. They'd all put on white coats over their clothes, and paper hats, and labels on their chests with their names on them. They followed the abattoir director around like lambs. Every machine was explained, praised or commented on: this is where the cow goes in, and here is where the sausages come out. What really held them was the pig-scraper. In one hour, believe it or not, it scrapes the bristles of sixty pigs. It wasn't even Haueter who tried to grab the attention of the visitors with his silly trick. Jacob Haueter knew that on that day he wasn't wearing his steel armour underneath his apron. But Brugger didn't know, and he felt jealous of the machine that everyone was standing around watching, while no one noticed him, no one was paying any attention to his own skill: in just three and a half knife strokes, he would cut the heads off the pigs as they came out of the scraper. No one else can do that. After years of practice, he's like a Japanese sword artist at it, he pulls his blade round the cheekbones, along the jaws and right through the neck. And he stuck his knife in Jacob Haueter's belly. He wanted to put on an act, but this time Jacob Haueter didn't even cry out. He bled to death, pathetically. Like a badly shot pig that they go ahead and stick, and *accidents that don't occur in the course of work carried out for the employer are non-industrial accidents.*

*

Ten thirty.

This way!

Where are you off to?

Santo Cristo!

You cripple dog!

Get them, kick them, smash them. Kick their legs!

As he unto me, so I unto you.

That's the first six calves for the day.

Heavy sods.

Lifting them up!

Rest them on their own spines for shooting.

Luigi swears like crazy. So does Krummen. The animals kick and scream. Überländer shakes his arms loose afterwards, like a shotputter. The dust off their hide irritates, but calves smell fresh and dry.

I'm to stick. No, I'm to stir blood.

Buri says in Chicago they didn't have time to knock the calves unconscious first.

Or the pigs.

Oxen, yes. You'd never have been able to stick them otherwise. But the calves? A couple of guys with strong arms, and someone who wasn't asleep on the job, that was sufficient in Chicago.

They'd pulled the calves up by machine.

Not like here, where you can fuck your back up on those overfed buggers of bull calves.

We must be nuts.

And in America, the butchers wore red gear. That way, you didn't have to change every time you got a drop of blood on your clothes.

Kilchenmann keeps his blue uniform clean. He never stands too close to the animals when he shoots them.

And I stir blood.

The man from the veterinary hospital is here. Every time he puts on this show of not being amazed.

Pah, what's in a slaughterhouse!

Yes, on the outside.

Sandstone walls, fences, hedges, wire surrounds, glass bricks, frosted-glass windows. Normal factory uniform. Now and again, a distant view of a quarter of beef hanging up outside the chilling-room, or loaded onto a lorry.

It's just like in the movies.

But this.

When the blood flows, the stomachs turn and the guts void, then either they don't look, or they pretend they've seen it hundreds of times before.

But ever been right up close, rubbed your nose in it?

Never.

It has to be done. And we do it. Actually, it would be possible . . .

You'd just have to . . .

Wanted for calf killing.

For the death of . . .

I stood side on to the mirror in the locker room, and squinted at my profile.

My wanted face.

Full face and profile.

And I'm stirring blood.

How red it is. Living red and dead.

At least I don't have to be careful wth my knife. I can stand and stir and think about what I like. Those calves never saw grass in their lives. Maybe a bit of green through a crack between the boards of the loading bridge. They grew up behind a muzzle. They're not allowed to eat what they like. They're to drink milk, and nothing that contains any iron. Lack of iron keeps them anaemic and white.

And white they have to be. Veal is innocent and healthy, for children, invalids and old people. But it's not got any iron.

Even when they're obstinate, there's something gentle about calves.

Something stupid too.

What are you staring at me for?

It's Krummen who's got you by the dewlap. Luigi's got you by the tail. Pretty Boy Hügli by the ears.

Not me.

Überländer sticks the creatures.

Calves' blood is used for dyeing the outside of sausages red.

Calves don't bleed, they drip to death.

I want to clear off.

Out.

I've got to stir until the blood's no longer warm. Otherwise it congeals.

Yes, banging on the toilet walls and shouting, I'm good at that.

Or I try and wank.

Ex-press myself.

The hold between my legs.

That's how I express myself.

Who's the bigger fool? I try and steal my own energy from them. A bit of my own power for my own mill.

They want our best shot.

They want everything, from early till late.

The way we sometimes go home at night.

Collapsed, bowed, crippled, drained. A pack of beaten dogs.

Even without wanking.

Krummen's destroying himself. Anything to give the impression that we're not missing Gilgen.

He'd rather work himself to death.

When I stir, I think, and when I think, I want to leave.

Just go.

Go to Australia, New Zealand, America.

The sixth calf is bucking.

In the corner over there, there are three cardboard boxes. One's shaking. They're tied with string, and they've got airholes in the sides.

Rabbits.

Someone wanting to hang rabbits in his lunch hour.

Rötlisberger?

They can't budge the calf.

I gave him a finger to suck.

It follows Hügli's hand quite tamely and goes under the rack. Rope round its leg. Because it straddles its front legs, its rear end seems higher. Standing there, like on a chocolate ad.

In my lunch hour, I'm going to lie on my back. On the wooden slats on the floor of the locker room.

Huber and Hofer start skinning the calves.

226

My heel isn't hurting.

Nor's my back.

I stretch, and think about the veins and tendons and bones under my skin.

I think about my blood.

Reporting for duty. Triper-grenadier Rötlisberger. Thirty-two years' service on the red front. Uniform: burlap aprons and butcher's shirt. Weapons: knife and boiling water. I'll teach them! The layabouts! Pen-pushers! Trying to get me out of here, just like that! An old man I may be – but I'm not dead yet! I'm not just an empty sack with a couple of arms attached to it to scrape the shite out of cows' bellies. I've got a union background. The only man in the abattoir with one, but by God I've got it!

The words came hissing out of the left corner of his mouth; the BRISSAGO was in the right one. He stamped on the floor in his wooden clogs, and sent the water splashing through the tripery. No question! This one's going to backfire on Bössiger! You can bet on it, they won't get me. Of course that fool Buri thinks it's a good deal. And then it's always the foreigners to blame with him. Always the dagos. But I know the way the cat's jumping.

Rötlisberger stood at his triper's table. The four stomachs of a ruminant lay before him. He had cut them open. Rötlisberger's arm circled, tireless and monotonous as a machine. His hand was a claw, incessantly plunging into the inside of the second stomach, and scraping the fermenting grass from its honeycomb walls.

A greasy dough of excrement, scraps of gut, weasand and skin clogged the drain on the floor. The dirty water was already ankle deep. Safety valves hissed, in six cauldrons innards were simmering, in two others swam calves' heads and ox muzzles. *A mixture of two parts rumen and honeycomb, and one part omasum, abomasum and straight gut produces first-class tripes.* Scalded for two or three minutes at 69° C, then boiled for twelve to fourteen hours. Not in a pressure cooker, to let the odours escape. And the steam. On the walls and ceiling, thick enough to chew. It softened up the plaster and broke off plate-sized pieces, it crusted over the bare lightbulbs, and it rusted everything that wasn't chrome steel. Swathes of steam headed for the door, ducked under the cowskull hanging over the lintel and got out into the open. The cowskull dripped. The spiders' webs luxuriating from the nostrils and eye sockets, and garlanding the horns, gleamed in the damp like silver threads. Sucking noises were heard from the main drain. *Waste water from abattoirs may only be allowed to flow into open water after it has passed through a purification plant or cesspit. Where the contents of rumens and fertilizer material are not continuously removed, dungyards are to be provided with impermeable foundations, to avoid detrimental effects on the abattoir and its environs by pollution, bad smells and vermin.*

Rötlisberger banged his fist down on the wooden table, then smashed it into the honeycomb. The bastards! The BRISSAGO in the right corner of his mouth danced up and down. The bastards! He whacked a section of calf's gut. Yellow juice squirted out. The bastards! The yellow juice dribbled down the wall.

Head-gutter Buri had wheeled in the first calf's intestines. The ruffle, he had said. Fritz, you'd better take these! They're halfway to being cow's bellies again. They're no use to me. Put them with the tripes. What am I supposed to do with them? Stupid overfed bull calves!

– That's the way it goes. Cow's stomachs aren't what they used to be either, by God, Rötlisberger had replied. There was one today, Christ it must have been ancient! Take a look at what was inside it!

Rötlisberger had picked up a bundle of ironmongery off the windowsill. Screws, cable, wire, barbed wire. She must have been grazing on a building site. Look, five 10-centimetre nails! And who knows how much of it's already rusted away in her belly?

– Do they give them all one of these nowadays too? asked Buri. A magnet 1.25 centimetres thick was holding it all together.

– Yes, by God. Earlier, they just used to push probes down them. And by force. Now though. If you stand on a meadow with a compass, North is always where the cow is. See what else she had in there! That'll be aluminium. Poison. Rötlisberger had the rusty hulk of a toy car in his hand.

– The things a cow will eat, eh? Buri had stared and when he lifted the calves' stomachs out of the barrow, he had stepped up to Rötlisberger and nudged him with his elbow. The dagos! It's the dagos' doing! he had said.

Buri had a way with words, he could hang a couple of empty words up in the air and leave them for half a minute, or a whole minute, and watch them with piercing eyes, and they somehow turned into a threat. Rötlisberger, however, hadn't responded, not even after getting a second nudge in the ribs. Buri himself had had to say what he'd been hoping to hear. He had their measure, the dagos. But it was the way someone went about his work, the way he'd learned it, from the basics up, that wasn't the least important part of it, he said. Christ, he could tell Rötlisberger a few things, he'd been involved with stooges in America for a long time, and you had to watch yourself with those bastards, they would crawl to you and be friendly to you to your face, and then the moment your back was turned, your job was gone. That was quite something, when anyone, not even knowing how to hold a tool properly, could just march in and strip the butcher's shirt right off your back. For the moment it was his, Fridu's, but who could tell when some dago might not get control of the whole of offal and casings, with salting and storage and everything. Here Buri faltered, short of breath. And even if he wasn't saying anything at the moment, he, Fridu, would be ready when they came for him, and, hobbling rather more than usual, he left the tripery. Schnurri-Buri! Always the same Schnurri-Buri! Rötlisberger had said to himself.

The BOSSHARDT STEAM PRESSURE COOKER was hissing. Rötlisberger glanced at the thermostat. The pigs' bellies from yesterday. A hand rapped on the frosted glass over the triping table.

Rötlisberger didn't hear.

He could only hear the trains.

The trains thundered past on the tracks at the back of the tripery. Always punctual to the second. That was the Intercity. Rötlisberger knew them all, and took them all in. God, we're running behind today. Those cows' bellies should have been scalded long ago.

Earlier, much earlier, the young Rötlisberger had boiled tripes with the help of the railways. He hadn't had a watch of his own, and the factory clock on the wall had been little use, if any. Either it was obscured by steam, or blind with condensation. It was years since Rötlisberger had last looked at it, and its protective glass was thickly coated with grease and powdered calcium. But he'd always had the trains to go by, leaving the city or approaching it, the few that stopped at the loading ramp outside the abattoir's stock pens, a few others that stopped a little further along, outside the armaments factory.

But by now Rötlisberger had become his own timepiece. Tripes were tripes. They had to be emptied, scraped, rinsed and scalded, and you put those of the same age and thickness to cook for an equal length of time at an equal temperature. Changes to the pattern of work were extremely rare. For thirty-two years, Rötlisberger had been doing virtually the same things every day, and his heart had made good use of that time, in all those years out in the slaughterhouse behind the high fence at the edge of the beautiful city, it had learned to beat to the rhythm of the tripery. The pulse of the BOSSHARDT STEAM PRESSURE COOKER, the pulse of the ELRO BOILERS, the pulse of the whole tripery was his pulse too, and the energetic Rötlisberger had now internalized rinsing and boiling times for so long and so powerfully that he no longer knew them, but simply felt them with every fibre of his being. He had become a biological clock, a tripe alarm with built-in bell. He was set for life.

– And if that was my last cow belly, and if I never scrape another one so long as I live, I won't have anything to do with that machine! Not me! Wild horses wouldn't drag me into washing harigalds.

There was another knock on the frosted glass.

Rötlisberger didn't hear. He sloshed around in his pool, jumped up, splashed down, hopped like a child in a puddle. His hands tugged at the braces of his burlap aprons, and suddenly he doubled up with laughter. No chance! No fucking chance! The red tip of the BRISSAGO danced up and down. Rötlisberger grabbed the scraped stomachs off the table, hoisted them to his shoulder, swivelled round like a shot-putter and sent them flying through the air. They hadn't seen anything yet! The flabby green bundle splattered against the wall, stuck fast for a moment, and then, like an enormous wet rubber glove, flopped onto the lid of the BOSS-HARDT STEAM PRESSURE COOKER. Do your own fucking crap! He skipped through the tripe kitchen, spitting venom from the left corner of his mouth. Anything in his path he swung a clog at. Glass smashed, a thermostat broke, a dent appeared in the side of one of the ELRO BOILERS, a cauldron rattled across the floor, a barrow started rolling. Rötlisberger didn't mind any of them. He grabbed a ladle and started lashing out with that too. Do your own fucking crap! Do your own fucking crap! With each repetition, the words sounded more rhythmically. Do your own fucking crap! A hissed sing-along with tripe-percussion obbligato.

Something was bugging him again.

A nagging dissatisfaction, a bad feeling. He knew it well enough, but it was vague, and Rötlisberger stood there helplessly as it came and went. Sometimes it seemed to him as though the whole world was hidden behind a veil of tripe steam. Oh God, I don't know, I can't say . . . yes, the boot pinches me somewhere, but where? If only I could talk about it properly. Get it out in the open! Talk like a book. Rötlisberger would have liked to be eloquent. His angry tirades were venomous all right, but they'd always been short, and they were still shorter now. He would have liked to be able to shout abuse at Bössiger all afternoon. And Krummen and the rest of them. One item after another! Hours and hours. Not draw breath, and well and truly scrape their tripes for them! If he'd had them, he would have oiled the words with spittle, savoured them on his tongue before aiming them and firing them off. He would have told them all how immeasurably he hated gym teachers and sergeant-majors and early risers. He would have explained why the mere thought of them brought him out in a rage. I hate champion wrestlers, I hate people from personnel, I hate Social Democrats, I hate taxpayers, I hate gun-runners, I hate committee members, I hate card players and church-goers and citizens and tripers, and I hate crack shots even more than livestock-dealers, and foremen even more than television newsreaders, and Sunday hunters even more than xenophobes, and promenaders even more than PTA secretaries and butchers even more than motorists, much more in fact, and all the other foreigners, how I hate them, how I hate them! Much much worse than that I hate the President of the USA!

Rötlisberger would never have stopped, he would have gone on cursing them all for ever, and never once would he have had to say bastard, or layabout, or fool, or cretin or bonehead.

But he was all too aware of it: in the slaughterhouse a fiery way

231

of talking was no asset. If someone sounds off a bit, they'll say right away, you've got a big mouth, haven't you? Why do you talk so much? Are you a grumbler? There's no point beefing on about it the whole time! We're here to work!

But even without the fine words he so badly wanted, Rötlisberger had found himself in hot water often enough.

Fritz Rötlisberger was born on 17 March 1906 on a smallholding in Wydenau. He had two brothers and a sister. Also on the farm were a farmhand, three Freiberg horses, a herd of twenty Simmental cows and several sheds full of other smaller animals. There were hardly any machines. Everyone had to help. Fritz Rötlisberger grew up working.

In the village school there was a teacher whose favourite subjects were music and singing. She didn't want the farmers' children to grow up without beauty in their lives. Little Rötlisberger had a beautiful voice, and the teacher became especially fond of him. Your little Fritz can sing like a bird in the woods, she told his parents on the smallholding. The next time Father Rötlisberger went to market in the nearby town, he came back with a small accordion. The teacher can show you how and where to push, he said.

When Rötlisberger was fifteen, he was apprenticed to the village butcher. The butcher's shop was attached to an inn, and he wrecked his back hauling crates of beer. He was less keen on singing now, although he never missed choir practice, and still played in the village band. As well as the accordion, he had learned to play the drum.

When he was called up, he applied to join a light regiment. He wanted to be in the back-up troops. Or the mountain infantry. He finally wanted a glimpse of the mountains he'd been singing about for the whole of his young life. But instead he'd been assigned to the supply column. There was a lot of singing in the cadet school as well. 'I had a comrade' was Rötlisberger's favourite song. And finally he did get to see the mountains. He learned how to slaughter a lame horse on a mountain ledge, without a rope windlass and without a light. How to wrap the parts in the skin, how to get the individual parcels out of the gorge and to the next canteen. Less hazardous was the slaughtering of cows in the middle of a wood. There, simple pulleys could be rigged up between two trees. When, even before finishing cadet school, Rötlisberger applied to Master-butcher Hunziker, Meat & Sausages, Wholesale & Retail, he had a badge with two golden ears of corn on his uniform.

Rötlisberger was employed as an independent butcher by Master Hunziker. Every week he slaughtered four pigs and a cow on his own, and every other week a calf as well. He made cervelats, bratwursts, smoked meats, bacon, several types of sausage and ham, and soup meat, on and off the bone. His back had been strengthened by the gymnastics he'd done at cadet school, and the only time Rötlisberger felt it was after doing his rounds. Twice a week, generally on Tuesdays and Thursdays, he took Master Hunziker's army bicycle all over the highlands, going from farm to farm with a large wicker basket full of sausages strapped to his back.

Rötlisberger was paid every fourth Saturday, from the wallet that Master Hunziker somewhat cumbersomely pulled from his back pocket. The wallet was pigskin, and it was as thick as a church hymn book. Well, payday's come round again, Hunziker would say, and Rötlisberger blushed every time and stammered, Merci, Herr Hunziker, and the master said, Are you sure you don't want to check it? Then Rötlisberger would count the four notes – a fifty and three tens – from one hand into the other, and say: That's right.

Hunziker's butcher's shop was in the upper village street in Mundigen, and Mundigen had a glee-club. A male voice choir, a yodelling club and a folk group belonged to it. Rötlisberger was a member. They sang in black shoes, linen trousers, a black velvet tunic with red piping, and starched, snow-white shirts. The men of Mundigen liked to sing about glacier-white milk and red sunsets, about curds and cheese. Before they struck up, they would put their hands in their trouser pockets, bend their backs, and paw the ground. For a few seconds, their shoes shuffled back and forth, as if they really were on the side of a mountain, looking for secure footing in a slippery cowshed or out on a woodslope felling trees.

At one festival Rötlisberger met his future wife. She was the daughter of the station master at Mundigen. By then the railway had already introduced a fixed working week. Rötlisberger dreamed of a fifty-four-hour week. He liked it at Hunziker's. The work had to be done, but how it was done was left up to him. But sometimes he thought that there was so much he could do, if he had an hour to himself after work . . .

Then Rötlisberger joined the choir of the butchers' lads in the nearby town. Now he sang in his butcher's blouse and diagonally folded apron. But on occasions, when the song had been announced, and the singing was just starting, Rötlisberger would clench his right fist in his pocket. The station master had been able to get him a discount on his rail fare. He was often in town, and he saw things there that he would rather have sung about.

Once, the butchers' lads' choir sang at a meeting of workers' singing groups. They sang powerfully and well, about cows in the sunshine, and the inexhaustible quantities of butter and cream on the slopes. As ever, Rötlisberger stood in the middle of the front row. At the end of their rendition, there was tumultuous applause from the hall.

But then along came the metal-workers, and their song was about steel and sweat, and the machines in factories that didn't belong to them. It grew very quiet in the hall, and a few of the butchers' lads who were still standing at the back of the stage started rolling up their sleeves. Their rosy faces shone with desire for a patriotic punch-up. The audience applauded. Only moderately, but loudly enough to drown out the whistles from the supporters of the butchers' boys.

But Rötlisberger liked the metal-workers' song, and said so. He clinked glasses with one Max Gschwend, and that same day he became a Social Democrat. For the first time, he sang the party's version of the butchers' song, in the party choir. Rötlisberger heard from one or two more butchers' lads, who like him didn't feel they wanted to go on singing: 'We men of the mountains are emp'rors and kings, in the early morn o' the mountain!' Together they became active supporters of the idea of a butchers' association. They spoke about clearly defined tasks. About set working hours. They discussed ways of knocking out the animals that didn't put the lives of the butchers at risk. Someone mentioned accident insurance. Someone else paid holidays.

His following payday, after he had counted his four notes, Rötlisberger said: It's right – but how about, well, maybe, you see I've been with you for three years now. Master Hunziker was astounded. What? Our butcher's lad! he said. The son of a farmer! And he's a lefty! I know three dozen good butchers who'd be glad to do your job for half of what you're getting.

With a bad report in his journeyman's book, Rötlisberger had trouble finding work. Hunziker had written in black ink, in his florid hand: A good lad, but a malcontent. Rötlisberger had to postpone his wedding. His brother on the smallholding in Wydenau took him back, but unwillingly. Rötlisberger did all the work that was going, but he didn't get so much as a plate of rösti without some caustic remark about Reds, and how they were always wanting something for nothing.

At last he got a part-time job in a large slaughterhouse. He hated it there from the start. They worked in cellars that were damp and poorly lit. The chilling-rooms were so full that when Rötlisberger had to go in and get something from there, he had to crawl underneath the hanging carcasses on his hands and knees.

As a part-time worker, Rötlisberger was liable to be given all kinds of things to do. He whitewashed walls, he sprayed bark-beetle poison, he carried whole trainloads of salt into the cellar. But most of the time he spent at the sink with a scrubbing brush in his hand. He washed sausage-meat canisters, for hour upon hour. Until that time, he hadn't realized that the length of the day could be a punishment.

Once he was told to sweep the smoking chimney. He had just done a thirteen-hour day. His back had got bad again. Rötlisberger ignored his orders. The head-butcher started yelling. He was a sergeant-major in the army, and proud of it. Hadn't Rötlisberger learned to obey his superiors in the course of his own service? No, but he had been taught to defend himself, said Rötlisberger, and slapped the head butcher in the face.

After that, things became difficult for Rötlisberger. His journeyman's book was taken away from him. He could find no other satisfying work. At thirty, he was finished. Banishment to the tripery. It was the only work in his profession that was still open to him.

He had become isolated. His marriage had gone ahead, but all his other contacts fell apart. Max Gschwend and the comrades were suddenly all backing machines. You wait, soon they'll be doing all the work. In America they've got these, became some kind of refrain. And Rötlisberger watched his mates crawling into the works when the miracle machines broke down. They fancied themselves as mechanics, and they were proud of every oil stain on their butchers' blouses. Rötlisberger laughed at the machine worshippers, who were happier with a monkey-wrench in their hands than a knife. He laughed at their urge to caress all the chrome parts of meat-cutters and sausage-fillers with a duster every other day.

And as the by-product tripe came into his life, so his life became a by-product. Rötlisberger knew it. And he knew that a job as tucked away and unappealing as triping couldn't give a man the dignity he needed in life. He would have to find the dignity for it himself.

To begin with he just felt empty. He started smoking BRISSAGOS, and became introspective. His colleagues said of him: BRISSAGO right, talks left. Now and again he would get pissed. Then he realized it must be the routine. He was going about his duties slowly and unwillingly, like a slave. His days were not defined by the work he had achieved, but by the hours he had got through. The only possible solution open to him was the attempt to defeat time, and stay ahead of it. So he started his hectic regime in the tripe kitchen. Always a step ahead. Anything to avoid sagging back in his chains. Don't be dragged! Pull! Using his only available freedom, he ended up working for two.

His reign in the tripery was only interrupted once: by active duty. He spent over a thousand days with the canteen unit of a mountain brigade. There he exercised his profession to the full for the last time. There too, he sang again.

After the War, he went back to the tripery. Rötlisberger put up no resistance. Just so long as they leave me in peace. He spent summer evenings and weekends on his allotment. He managed to wangle three sections for himself. The three best ones. They were behind the armaments factory, right on the edge of the forest.

There he scratched the soil. He crawled over the beds and felt the earth under his fingernails. He rarely used tools. He worked with his bare hands whenever possible.

He stole blood from the slaughterhouse for his roses. He bred them with large thorns. The flowers hardly mattered to him. He liked it when he got snagged while cutting them, when a thorn pricked his skin, not deeply, but deeply enough for him to feel it under the callouses on his hands.

Rötlisberger also grew vegetables, lettuce, parsley, dill and tripe-weed. He made bunches of herbs. Outside the slaughterhouse, he never smoked. I'd be a fool. Sometimes he would sit in front of his garden shed with his nose in a bunch of parsley, as though it was an oxygen mask.

He kept a dog and a dozen rabbits. The dog was a mongrel dachshund called Züsu. The rabbits all had cows' names. The buck was called Bössiger. Rötlisberger sometimes had the impression that his scaled-down versions behaved like the real thing. They eat like cows, gawp like cows, they're all as stupid as cows.

He no longer sang. Least of all about the herds on the Alps. A couple of times his wife asked him, Why don't you get out your accordion again? Oh, wouldn't you rather listen to those birds singing in the woods, Rötlisberger would reply each time. But Frau Rötlisberger knew: all that soaking in hot water had made his fingers too thick and stiff to be able to play music.

– You're maltreating the machines! shouted Lukas across the tripery. He stood on tiptoe on the flooded floor and laughed. He had rolled up his jeans. Stop it! You Luddite! I'll haul you up before the Society for Prevention of Cruelty to Machines!

The chant 'Do your own fucking crap!' died down. God, it's Lukas! The colander with which Rötlisberger had been banging away on the BOSSHARDT STEAM PRESSURE COOKER splashed into a basin. But the hissing of the valves kept up, and so did the gurgling and simmering inside the cauldrons. Rötlisberger waded over to Lukas. Ha, the apprentice was saying you'd be back today. I thought, after what happened yesterday, you wouldn't . . . I'm surprised they let you in!

– They didn't. They banned me from the slaughterhouse, and *the organization of slaughterhouses, their sanitary and police supervision, their opening, closing, slaughtering and public visiting hours, etc., are all subject to licence from the local authority*, and Lukas said: The porter said I was an unauthorized person. So called. And unauthorized persons weren't allowed on the property of the city slaughterhouse.

– They slapped a ban on you? Well! Rötlisberger took the BRISSAGO out of his mouth, rubbed his chin against the collar of his butcher's blouse, wiped his hands on his inside apron, held out his right hand to Lukas and said: Welcome!

– Well, I'm persona non grata now in the slaughterhouse.

– You don't mean to say you came in over the rails, do you . . . ?

– Yes. Same way as the cows. I knocked on the window over there. But you can't have heard me.

– Now, Lukas, just watch yourself! I don't want to punish you again. Hah! He prodded Lukas in the chest. They made a right mixed grill out of you there, God, I thought they were going to turn you into chipolatas! But they didn't finish you off quite, did they?

– No, I didn't die, not quite. But I puked a whole drawerful in the vet's office. God was I sick! And he still had blood all over his hair. That stuff got incredibly sticky when it dried, he said. What about meat? He wasn't sure. Wouldn't be eating any today or tomorrow. He wrinkled his nose. Doesn't look too appetizing in here either. Is that your craft's golden foundation? he asked, pointing at the brownish-grey pool on the floor.

Rötlisberger turned a crank to get the lift going. He had loosened the spindle with his percussion work and it now wanted tightening. And the day's tripes were still only at the scalding stage. They should have been boiling long ago. Rötlisberger beckoned to Lukas, and shouted: Come nearer, you can't hear yourself think! Now what about the camera? Where had he got it? He hadn't left it behind, had he?

Lukas opened his US ARMY jacket and pointed at a bulge under his jersey. My camera's in there. Why, though? You didn't want your picture taken yesterday.

– That was yesterday! Today's different. Or not? Today's Tuesday 11 March. Get it out! Take a few snaps of me! Proper ones! Good ones! I want to see them when they're done! Got it?

– What if someone comes in?

– So what! Get going! Hup! Fire away!

The camera came out from under the jersey. Lukas photographed a Rötlisberger standing by his tripe boilers as proudly as a train-driver, holding onto his job as though he meant never to let it go. This is me, Fritz the tripes, yes, I know, I'm old, ah but if only you could get the smell into the pictures too!

Lukas clicked away. From all angles. He forgot about the pool on the floor. The film was almost finished. He still wanted Rötlisberger at the tipping lever, at the steamcock, at the salt barrel, at the scraper, over the dungpit, with knife and without. Lukas straightened up. One more shot, the last one, he said.

– Here! Rötlisberger stood right in the middle of the approach to the tripery, under the cow's skull. From the outside, he said. The cow's head! Get the cow's head up there! But mine too, mind! Look at it! Ancient thing, eh? Believe it or not, there's no bullet hole in there. We hit her on the head in the old-fashioned way, and afterwards I kept it and boiled it. She was the last one like that. He put his hand on his hips and checked that he was properly in line with the cow's head.

– There! Now you've taken your pictures, you've got your tripe-man's head. That's what you wanted, isn't it? Blood, grime and dead cows! Stuck your nose in it. Our thoughts as we kill. That's what you were after.

– That isn't what I said, but more or less, I suppose, more or less.

– And what have you learned? No need to blush. But what I wanted to say, about taking photographs, there are things a machine like that doesn't see. Still, I'm pleased you've come. There are one or two problems, so who knows how long I've still got here. Bring the pictures round to my garden some time.

– Are you thinking of quitting? So suddenly? But can you afford to, I mean don't you need the job? Can you get . . . ?

– Oh, they can stick it! I haven't scraped their cows' bellies for thirty-two years to be treated like this. As if none of us had anything but straw in our heads. And if they think it's easy standing in here, and grafting away, well, they might just have another think.

– But what about a living? Have you got enough? And your pension? They might try and get it taken away from you. I don't mean to . . . But you should at least give notice.

– What use is my pension to me, if one of their fucking machines goes and kills me? Eh? If they find me with half a mile of pig's guts, unemptied mind, wrapped round my throat. What's so funny? Sometimes it stoves your head in outright. Christ, it doesn't take much, a slip, and that's it, lights out!

– No, I don't need them any more. I live too simply. We've always looked at every fiver twice, my wife and me. Thank God. If not, I can do a day or two per week for some local butcher. I've got the allotment. And the money the rabbits bring in. And I won't be needing any more BRISSAGOS. I'll be sixty-three in a couple of days. Sixty-three! Another two years, and I'll start getting my state pension. But, here! I'll show you something else! Rötlisberger pushed open the door of the hide store.

– Here! he said. A real Blösch hide! All red. White only on the head and the tail, and on the withers. They're rare nowadays you know. That skull over the door, the cow that came from was red all over as well. A red Blösch. But this one here, she was already going grey. Like me. You can see it here, at the roots of her hair.

Hair side out, meat side in, the tied bundles lay on pallets in the hide storage room, and *wet, bloody or fouled hides from the slaughterhouse may not be salted together with clean and healthy goods*, and along the walls, on rusty hooks hung little rabbit pelts. Sheepskins lay piled up in a corner. It smelled damp and salty, and of rancid fat. There was a label on each parcel of hide, with date of slaughter, unsalted weight, and type of animal.

Rötlisberger tapped his right clog against the Blösch hide, that lay separately, on its own pallet. The rope came undone, and the bundle slipped down and opened out on the floor.

– Well? Don't you think that would have made a good hide, without the barbed-wire marks on it?

– What do I know about cowhides? replied Lukas.

Eleven fifteen.

More calves.

Another two dozen unloaded and weighed at the ramp at the front. Overweight, the lot of them.

Krummen brought them in himself.

Through the open sliding door, I could hear him shouting at them and beating them along the driving passages.

We've already got eight of them hung up. Makes fourteen in all. Schindler brought in a lorryload as well.

Busy day for him today.

There he is standing in his baggy cowherd's shirt, feeling proud of himself. Hey! See what I'm bringing in! None of your usual puny creatures!

The railwaymen on the tracks at the back, they're wearing similar things to him. Long shirts, in a thick material. Blue. But there's no dung on their boots.

Huber and Hofer like it when Schindler's around. He watches them work, and tells them where he got the animals from.

In the waiting pen calves are all over each other. They rest their heavy heads on one another's backs. Or they try and mount each other. They're clumsy creatures. Overfed, and not used to so much space. They grew up in cages. A board to the left. A board to the right. A board behind. Water and milk powder in front of them.

There's hardly anything left of the half dozen I brought in from the ramp! Luigi's loaded the heads on a barrow. Calves' heads are boiled in the tripery. Buri's gone off with the ruffles.

We hung the skinned calves up on hoists and pushed them out past the weighing machine at the entrance into the passage.

While I wait to stir more blood, I cut the seal out of these. The seal is the lungs, the liver, the spleen, the heart, the gullet and the windpipe. Everything that's in the chest cavity.

The liver sticks fast. Before I can tear the two wings of it from the peritoneum, I pull out the gall bladder. It's almost empty. The calf must have just been digesting. The gall would have been swilling round the guts.

Krummenroaring: Don't you cut a hole in the sweetbreads this time!

I won't.

That gland has to be in one piece. Money!

Huber and Hofer are skinning.

They cut the skin from the hindlegs with their knives. As soon as they've got enough to get a grip on, they punch their way along, on the inside of the skin. By the end, they're throwing their whole weight into it.

When they've finished a hide, they stick a little tin number on it. Each one has his own number.

If it later appears that a hide has been cut, whichever of them did it is held accountable.

I blow compressed air into the lungs. To make them look nicer for the cats.

I rinse the whole of the seal in a basin, and hang it up on a rack. Dr Wyss will then inspect it and give it a stamp.

Those cosseted calves are always healthy. They get oval stamps.

Pretty Boy Hügli whets his knife and comes and stands next to me.

Well? Did you get to hold them? Out in the shed?

He talks without looking at me.

Do you know where to feel them?

If you keep on practising, I'll take you along to Rösi in the canteen one day.

Or to Spreussiger.

But you've got to keep practising!

Every day.

Rösi's got something to grab hold of, you know.

Krummen.

For Chrissake! Are you keeping the apprentice from working now?

Right! Hügli! Piccolo! Überländer! Hang them!

The next lot.

I'm to stir blood again.

Stir blood and dream.

Think.

Think that I've got nothing to think about.

There they go, tugging at the calves again.

Perhaps they've never really moved before. They don't know how to walk properly.

They don't need force to push *us* around.

And tomorrow back in trade school.

An afternoon in dry clothes. No chilling-rooms. No backache. No bare forearms. Shirts buttoned down to the wrist. Like people in offices. With a satchel.

And the teacher doesn't shout out his orders.

And he doesn't call us 'du' either.

Marti! Heggenschwyler! Bühler!

The teacher likes speaking about cleanliness. The image one has of a clean butcher. Cleanliness, gentlemen! Cleanliness! Take regular showers! Don't neglect your socks! Fresh underclothes are terribly important for hygiene.

And blood?

I'm stirring blood, and thinking about cleanliness.

We have to be clean.

And then book-keeping.

I hate fucking book-keeping.

On those white pages, our hands look incredibly big, we've got callouses, plasters over infected cuts, and the lines are so incredibly narrow.

We have to write small, small and neatly.

And with no mistakes.

Well can't you even . . . ? Have you never . . . ?

Marti! What did they teach you in nine years at school?

And what if you have to write a letter?

Then they'll think.

A butcher.

And civic studies.

Then the classroom will be overheated. We're not used to warm rooms. Our eyelids will droop. Heavy as lead.

That's how they keep us meek.

Lukas is right.

God, if you suddenly believed you could talk, and you had something to say, and you could even write it down! Where would it all end!?

You should be ashamed of your handwriting.

Quiet at the back!

You should learn to keep an account of your pocket money.

Expenditure: one pencil – .25, bicycle repair 3.50.

Income: pocket money – 5.–.

The difference in the column on the right, twice underlined: 1.25.

Last night I went round to Lukas'.

He lives with some other students.

They know how to talk.

They don't apologize for every superfluous word.

And they were talking about us. Without looking at me. As though they'd all been working in the slaughterhouse for years. It was embarrassing. They knew everyone's names. The slaughterhouse director's.

And Bössiger's medical history is a clear indication . . .

And what is a slaughterhouse if not a well-kept taboo where profit-making can rampage unchecked? It's a classic example of the impotence of the working classes. Brecht already shows that the difference between proletariat and animal . . .

And Döblin, in his shambles in Berlin, is describing a kind of grey area . . .

And it's abundantly clear that seen in global terms . . .

They can build whole houses with words.

Wobbly houses.

But you don't need to know your way round them to find a hiding place.

I can take refuge in ideas.

I trust Lukas.

They chucked him in the full blood-tank.

It was Huber and Hofer who laughed loudest.

And the blood. It splattered the whole passage. Then they took his trousers down.

We would just have to work through our conditioning, Lukas said.

It was in the nature of the thing. So long as we were society's beasts of burden, we would act like it too.

We just weren't proud of our labour.

We were ashamed.

Some were conscious of it, others weren't.

And yet . . .

But we were supporting the whole thing on our backs!

It's not easy to lose yourself in a daydream at work.

Still less when there's shooting going on.

When everyone's got half an eye on everyone else.

I have to get into it.

Rhythm makes it easier.

The circus scene: the bareback rider. The sound of hooves in the sawdust. The music. The horse whinnies. A strap pulls his head down onto his chest. The neck is bent.

And round and round in a circle.

Stirring.

The horse quivers, brushes its tail across its haunches.

And the thighs of the rider.

A widening circle. Always in time. And the rider smiles. Are her thighs restraining the horse? It could fly any barrier.

And the elephants. Enormous great babies.

Round and round in a circle.

In little pinafores and baby bonnets.

Why do they grin and bear it?

I don't believe it!

Why don't elephants just get the hell out? Those enormous creatures, they could just knock over the silly ringmaster . . . run out of the tent . . . off . . . through the audience!

Jesus Christ! Goddamn the fucking idiot!

Krummen.

There's red all over my rubber apron. And my blouse. And dripping from my hands.

You call that stirring blood!

Can't you see it splashing out of the can?

Are you asleep? Or drunk?

It doesn't need any more stirring! That's not going to congeal! Right! Hup! Gut that calf!

Now they're grinning again.

You only gut a calf once it's hanging from the rack by the tendons behind its knees.

The feet have to be taken off first. The soup bones.

It's not easy to find the place in the knee where you can cut the joint. I saw around. My blade can't find the thin seam in the cartilage.

It's about time you had a feel for it.

You're always supposed to have a feel for everything.

But I don't want to . . .

I say nothing, and go on sawing. – At last: the calf's hanging.

The pizzle. Then the testicles.

Don't throw them away!

Huber's standing next to me, and grabs the two glands. They are steel-blue, and no bigger than your thumb.

Instead of a pocket in his trousers, Huber's got a plastic bag. As well as testicles, he collects marrow.

You know it helps. He nods.

Fried in butter. With salt and lots of pepper.

More bang for the buck! Right, Huber!

Hügli says he doesn't eat testicles, he's not a pig.

You don't know what's good for you.

Good for what?

Ha, go ask Gilgen.

But Gilgen isn't there. Nor Ambrosio either.

Hügli says he'd rather have a cold beer. Lugging those heavy calves around was making him sweat.

I'm not sweating.

I'm cold.

9

There it was again.

Boom! Boom! Boom! As though someone was banging the ceiling under Ambrosio's bed with a broom handle.

Ambrosio had climbed onto his bed exhausted, after a day with the hayfork on the Knuchel fields in the heat. He longed for sleep, and yet could only toss from side to side.

He lit a cigarette.

He walked over to the window. The night was humid, and the moon shone down on the hills of the highlands.

Ambrosio swore. All day his body had absorbed the heat. Now his senses were sharpened. Every square millimetre of skin on his body glowed.

'Hijo de puta! Maldito sea!'

Ambrosio rubbed his fists along the wooden panelling. He went from one corner of the room to another. The wood felt warm and rough.

He stopped in front of one of the framed reproductions on the wall.

He had noticed by now how popular they were up in the village, these scenes from farming life. They were everywhere, the blonde-pigtailed girls, and hushed children.

Ambrosio whispered the name of his wife.

He gripped his mattress, curled up, then flung his arms and legs wide again. He had an erection. He rumpled the bedding, cursed the Knuchel farm, the whole of the highlands, the moon, whose cheesy light had driven him to take refuge in the bottom end of the bed. Lying in shadow, he wrapped his pillow round his ears. He wanted to escape the banging and the sound of cow bells.

He banged his head against the board at the foot of the bed: boom, boom, boom, and relished the pain on his bald pate. He gave a start. Like a response to his own banging, the banging below

247

had started up again. Immediately below him. Pitiless: Boom! Boom! Boom!

Goddamned bloody Knuchel noise! Ambrosio buried his face in his hands. Had he really produced those crashing and grunting sounds? Knuchel German words from his own mouth?

After his face, Ambrosio felt the muscles on his shoulders and upper arms. The itching in his neck hadn't gone away yet. Ambrosio felt his tiredness with his own hands, smelled the cowshed, the milking fat and the STEINFELS soap on his skin, which was tanned and dry as leather.

Ambrosio rubbed aftershave on his face, his shoulders, his chest and belly, his arms and legs, his penis.

And Ambrosio saw the farmer's wife.

All day he had worked by her side, smelling her nearness. White soft skin with tiny wrinkles in her armpits, sweat-soaked material clinging to her back.

How did they make love, she and the farmer?

Such broad, full hips. Hips to burrow in and hide.

And the bicycle woman?

Ambrosio heard panting. He watched her pedalling past, followed the levers of her tremendous thighs. And he had only to reach out an arm, to touch her head gently, for the knot of her hair to come undone, and long chestnut strands would fall about her shoulders, a mane tossing in the breeze.

Blösch's horns tipped back. Knuchel's lead cow pressed her occipital bone against her neck, crumpled the skin behind her ears and bared her larynx. The bridge of her nose making a horizontal extension of her back, withers and neck, she raised her head, dropped her jaw and sent out a moo that started way back in her belly. It was her very best booming: cantankerous and obstinate.

Mirror and Gertrude voiced their impatience in like manner. Up in the pasture, the Knuchel herd was waiting for their morning milking. Those cows that weren't mooing were standing stubbornly by the fence, or, like Baby, Stine and Spot, lying crookedly in the grass. Their swollen udders made a more comfortable position impossible.

On the farmyard, Ambrosio dipped his face in the water, rubbed his eyes, splashed himself, let water trickle over his chest and arms. He ignored the mooing. Once more, with open eyes, he dipped his face in the well.

As Ambrosio walked through the farm to the pasture, the sun was just rising. The trunks of the apple trees shone like silver, the hoar-frost glittered on the grass and in the flat dawn light the shapes of the cows loomed in contrasting darkness.

'Ho! Ho!' and, 'Gum sessy!' Ambrosio called out to them as he opened the gate. Blösch was the first to start moving. The others followed, with their milk-weighted udders they hesitated a little with every step.

Knuchel entered the cowshed in a freshly washed tunic, and he held out another one to Ambrosio. 'Here, get into this! We're slaughtering today!' he said. There were sticking-plasters on his chin and throat, he had shaved first thing.

The farmer was extremely liberal with the formula feed, and was keen to get on to milking after only the bare minimum of cleaning.

'Does a cowshed always have to look like a parlour? Come on, Ambrosio, let's get started!' And he reached for the milking-fat tin.

Even before breakfast a large trestle and a wooden trough as big as a bathtub had been taken through to the threshing floor. The potato steamer was filled brimful with water. 'For scalding,' said Knuchel.

When Ruedi returned from the cheese dairy after breakfast, and untethered Prince from the milk-cart, he asked: 'Does the sow get another meal?'

'No, no! Just one more bucket of milk and apples, so she doesn't scream like a stuck pig before we've even begun,' replied Knuchel, emerging from the cellar with a couple of bottles of white wine under his arm.

'But –'

'No buts! Unload the swill! Then go and ask your mother for some knives. I don't know what she thinks she's waiting for. No towels or aprons in there either. Not even any basins.'

'Well, it's still a nonsense,' said Ruedi under his breath as he went to pick up the churns from the dog-cart. 'The Boden farmer's cutting his rowan, and what are we doing? Slaughtering! In the middle of summer!'

'You can stop your muttering!' Knuchel told him. 'Just do as you're told. Fritz Überländer will be here any minute, and we won't be ready.'

'Well, he's not here yet, your butcher,' the farmer's wife reported from the kitchen door. 'And when he is, then you'll have your towels. Don't worry about that! And as for knives, I hope your dear Herr Überländer will have remembered to bring some himself.'

Grandma, climbing the outside staircase up to the veranda, concurred with a wag of her head: 'Whatever next! Providing knives for the butcher!'

'What on earth's the matter with you all?' Knuchel irritably picked up the hosepipe to wash the pig down first. 'All that talk about just one little sow!'

By the time Grandma called down from the balcony: 'He's coming! He's coming,' and Custom-butcher Überländer rattled into the Knuchel farmyard, the labels had long ago come off the bottles that had been put out to cool in the well.

'About time too,' muttered the farmer, and his wife said, 'Has he got a noisy motorbike?'

'It's a JAVA,' said Ruedi.

No sooner was Fritz Überländer standing on Knuchel soil by the side of his bike, unbuttoning his heavy leather coat with one hand, than he asked: 'Well, have you got the sow ready? Can we start?'

'Yes, Fritz, we're ready.' The farmer took some liqueur glasses off the kitchen windowsill, filled them with kirsch, handed them round and said: 'Here's to the sow!' They drank together. 'The sow!'

'Do you want this in the kitchen? Or where do you want us to make the sausages?' asked Fritz Überländer, who, as well as his box of equipment, was taking a sausage-filling kit off the back of his motorbike.

'Yes, I thought we'd slaughter outside, sausages inside,' said Knuchel.

'Right then!' Fritz Überländer hauled the box onto the threshing floor, unlocked it, laid a gun across the trestles, slipped into a butcher's smock, tied on his apron and said: 'There. Now we can start as far as I'm concerned. What about you? Shall we take her?'

The light went on. The door of the shed squeaked. The bolt on the pigsty slid back. From the far corner, there was sniffing at shoes, aprons, then a grunting, there were hands pushing, a noose, there was delay, hesitation, some words of doubt from the door of the shed, short legs were dug in on the concrete yard, and there was squealing, pulling and kicking for dear life.

'Ooh, you bugger! Not much wool and a lot of noise!' Butcher Überländer exerted himself. The rope tightened round foot and snout, and cut into the pig's flesh. Prince slipped out of his kennel and crept down towards the farmyard, Grandma took herself off to her hens. The children silently peeled away from the wall, stepped a little nearer. The pig's throat rattled as it was pressed to the ground, and after the shot, Thérèse asked: 'Is she dead now?'

'Sshh! Otherwise you'll hurt her even more!' The travelling butcher drilled the sticking-knife into the sow's throat.

The farmer's wife held a frying pan under the pale red fountain that flowed from the keeled-over pig. Ruedi and Ambrosio pumped the legs, and the farmer knelt on her belly. Fritz Überländer wiped his upper lip with the back of his hand, and sharpened his dripping knife.

'Who would have guessed the little pig would have so much blood in her?' said the farmer's wife as she carried the brimful pan back to the kitchen.

'Right, now let's scald her!' The butcher put his knife away. Hot water by the bucketful was carried from the potato steamer to the threshing room to be poured over the pig's bristles as it lay in the trough.

'All right!' said Knuchel. He scraped across the pig's skin with a scalder. Beads of sweat formed on his brow. 'All right!' he said again.

Scalding water splashed across the barn. Butcher Überländer gave instructions. Ruedi and Ambrosio scraped away at the hams. After the bristly skin had been scalded off, the pig's body was laid on the trestles. It seemed to be getting whiter all the time.

And when Fritz Überländer took up a long-handled razor to take off the last few hairs himself, he told of the local slaughterhouse: how on a single afternoon they slaughtered well over a hundred hogs, and how the whole thing went like clockwork.

And they were just about to expand their capacity still further. A larger scalding tub and a new scraping machine would be added shortly.

'Over a hundred pigs? In an afternoon?' asked Ruedi.

'That's right,' said Fritz Überländer, taking a step away from the trestle. Knuchel had brought in one of the bottles, poured out a couple of glasses and said another 'All right!'

'Whew! What about this weather! Pigging hot!' said the butcher after the first taste.

'Yes, but the scalding's always the worst of it,' said Knuchel.

'And we've done that.' In a single draught, Fritz Überländer emptied his glass.

'Yes, we've done that,' Knuchel repeated.

'And your wife? What's she doing?' asked Fritz Überländer.

'My wife?' Knuchel refilled the glasses. 'My wife can help make the sausages later. Butchering's not women's work.'

'Oh? You don't think so?'

'No.'

'And why?'

'Well, Fritz, butchering is men's work. Just like milking is.'

'You mean they turn the cows' heads in the cowsheds, and then they cry into the milk later till it sours?' said Fritz Überländer laughing.

'Yes, the way they'd cut themselves if they were butchers,' said Knuchel, laughing too.

'Yes, that's what my old man used to say,' the butcher carried on laughingly. 'It's all right for a woman to bathe in it, that makes her beautiful, but actual milking's something for a man to do.'

'That's it,' Knuchel pursed his lips, put the empty bottle away, scratched his neck and said: 'Well, shall we get back on the job?'

The pig was hung up on the wall head down, and was slit open from top to bottom. The innards tumbled out, grey-brown-green. Überländer worked swiftly, and the men stood and watched open-mouthed as he pulled out intestines, womb, lungs, liver, heart and kidneys, and laid them all out in separate bowls and dishes.

Ambrosio was sent to the well with the straight intestine. That had to be washed first, so they could get started on the black pudding, said the butcher. 'Lavare bene! Girare subito,' he said to Ambrosio.

'Black pudding! In the middle of summer!' muttered Ruedi, who was blowing up the pig's bladder with a bicycle pump, and Knuchel said thoughtfully: 'So you know Spanish.'

'No, just a few words of Italian,' said Fritz Überländer, as he got ready for the first blow to the backbone of the gutted animal. The farmer stood behind him, watching attentively as one vertebra after another split, and he complained about the cheeser and the mayor, about how they were all kicking up a fuss over his Spaniard, and how he had been looking in vain for a solution to the problem.

When the last vertebra had been split, Überländer straightened up again, felt the bacon on the two split pig halves, wrinkled his nose and said: 'Hans, that's just silly. Send us your Spaniard. Anyone's allowed to work at the slaughterhouse. There's no fuss there. He can start next week, if you like.'

'Are you sure?'

'Of course. I'm telling you, aren't I?'

'Well, maybe there's not such a great hurry as all that.' Knuchel rubbed his right wrist, and first looked round the farm and then down at the meadow. 'Let's see, first there's the rowan coming up, and the wheat we could use him for. Then it's already nearly time for the potatoes, and all the fruit has to be boxed. And the beets. Who's going to dig them? No, it's not as urgent as all that. And milking goes on all the time of course.'

'Whatever you say, Hans. When the time comes, send him to me. I'll take him up to the office. They'll find him a room too.'

'A room too? Yes, in town, I suppose.' Knuchel took the left half of the pig, slung it across his shoulder, and said: 'Right, shall we, er, take this pig in and put it on the kitchen table then?'

The farmer's wife was standing outside the threshing room. She looked first at the empty bottle, and then, as though to ask him: 'Well? Does he drink?' at the farmer. But she actually asked: 'Are you already finished with the butchering?' Without waiting for an answer, she leaned forward, sucked in her stomach, looked down her front and said: 'You know, that pig made a right mess of my apron.'

'Well, you did go and wear a white one, didn't you? It's not Sunday,' said Knuchel from under his half carcass.

'You put on clean things too. And you shaved early.'

'But that wasn't on account of the sow, though,' Knuchel replied and went on into the kitchen. The pig's neck wobbled and smacked against his back.

'Why else?' asked the farmer's wife quietly, and picking up a bit of gristle from the ground, tossed it in front of the kennel to which Prince had again retreated.

Ambrosio knew this road. He knew it well. It led along the hills across the highlands, a winding grey asphalt ribbon through woods and meadows, from village to village. When Ambrosio had driven into town, alone or with Luigi, he had sat on the post bus and looked out at the landscape, always a little sceptically. Those people, those villages, those hills and woods and mountains, were they all quite real?

Ambrosio still had his doubts. He was sitting on the tractor, behind Livestock-dealer Schindler. They were going slowly; the engine was straining, it could only manage a crawl up the steeper slopes, but Schindler wasn't impatient, he was towing a considerable prize: in the trailer at the back stood Pestalozzi.

'Wh-hey, won't those cattle-dealers be quaking in their boots when we roll up with that great bull-trailer and come out with him!' Schindler chuckled and jerked his thumb over his shoulder at Pestalozzi.

The livestock-transporter that Schindler had hired was an open wooden box the size of a small house. It had three axles, as many hand-brakes, and a double floor. Since its centre of gravity was actually below the surface of the road, no raging bull could upset it. The side walls were reinforced with iron, and so high that Pestalozzi's back only just cleared them. Chained by his nose-ring, his curly head held down by ropes tied round his horns, there wasn't much an earth-bound spectator could see of the massive body of the ex-village bull of Innerwald.

But from up on the tractor, Ambrosio could see the mighty curved back, and the froth at the bull's nostrils, and he could also

254

see the pink neck of the livestock-dealer, which seemed to be glowing with satisfaction over his purchase.

Once more, Ambrosio saw the saturated green of the grass and the heavy dark brown of the earth in the ploughed fields either side of the road. The woods were bright, suspiciously bright, and suspiciously beautiful.

Demonstratively slowly, men and women went about their labour in the fields with horses and machines. Low and broad, they stooped down over potatoes and beets. They moved as though they were doing it for their own enjoyment, like actors convinced of the importance of their gestures.

Ambrosio took out a cigarette, lit it from his tinder lighter, which proved its worth in the breeze on the open tractor, and inhaled deeply. No, if everyone and everything here, the ploughing men and the flower-watering women, and the bright trees and tall fences and great-uddered cattle, if they were all props in a gigantic theatrical production put on for the sole purpose of misleading him, then the enterprise had failed. He, Ambrosio, wasn't deceived.

How those farms were bragging again, with their dungheaps on show by the roadside. But Ambrosio no longer respected this world, he had managed to find out a thing or two about it, he had helped spread the dung on the fields himself, and even the day before, his last full day on the Knuchel farm, he had seen past the geraniums into the rooms of the Innerwalders.

Talk of his departure had gone on for weeks. The farmer had brought in Luigi as an interpreter, they had telephoned, and it seemed Fritz Überländer was right. The wages he might expect to earn in town were considerable. Ambrosio had agreed, and written home to say that he would soon be earning more as a 'carnicero'. The mayor had returned his papers, and up on the Galgenhubel, they had toasted the new job. If Ambrosio liked it there, Luigi would pack his bags and follow him, for the moment he wasn't quite sure. But for Fritz Mäder, the field-mouser who had worked on the Knuchel farm for much of the harvest as a day-labourer, there was no doubt: 'Go! Go to the city! Why lose your sweat on foreign soil!' he had counselled.

And yesterday after the evening milking, when the herd was

already bedded down in the straw and contentedly ruminating on chopped beets, then Knuchel had rubbed his wrists in the alley behind Blösch and said: 'Schindler's coming tomorrow, you know. He's collecting the tired bull up in the village. He could give you a lift into the city. You want? Then come on, if it's got to be. Let's go and sit in the parlour and do our sums!'

'Como no,' Ambrosio had replied, and followed the farmer out of the cowshed. But there it was again: Boom! boom! boom! Not muffled, the way it sounded up in his attic, but louder and harder. Ambrosio had paused in the kitchen doorway, but as he entered the parlour he had flinched. The Knuchel children! There on the sofa right in front of him, Stini on the left, Thérèse on the right, little Hans in the middle, and all three of them rocking backwards and forwards, beating the backs of their heads against the parlour wall. As hard as they could. Boom! boom! boom!

'Those kids, eh?' the farmer had said with a sidelong glance at Ambrosio. 'They like doing that, it quietens them down they say. But look, here's the money!'

Absent-mindedly Ambrosio had picked up the notes the farmer paid out, and even when Knuchel had poured schnapps into a couple of glasses and said: 'Cheers! It's some of our own. I'll give you a bottle to take with you when you go. Anyway, here's to you!' even then he was still feeling shaken by the rhythmic banging of the children's heads against the wall.

Knuchel had then explained that he was thinking of distilling some more schnapps in the autumn. Twelve bottles as usual, that was his entitlement, one bottle per head of cattle, that was the custom and the tradition, because you sometimes needed it to treat the cows with. And Knuchel had had one more go at the village farmers: 'They can go to hell as far as I'm concerned, and take their milking machines with them!' But Ambrosio had already emptied his glass, and was backing away towards the door, twisting his beret in his hands. 'Buenas noches,' he had said.

Then, pursued by the knocking, he had walked up and down the cowshed, listened to the Knuchel cows chewing, and recited their names to himself: Baby, Patch, Check, Snail, Bossy, May, Flora, Tiger, Stine, Gertrude, Mirror and Blösch, but still he hadn't managed to escape the Boom! boom! boom! that resounded through the whole house.

Later that evening, Ambrosio had packed his little wooden case, laid his suit across the back of the chair in readiness, and counted his money. It was more than he had expected. Farmer Knuchel had thrown in the whole of an extra month's wages.

Sitting on the tractor, Ambrosio felt for the money in his waistcoat pocket. He took his eyes off the fences and barns, the model farms, and looked at Schindler's head. Those contours! That neck! There was meat there, and fat. But didn't that skull look surprisingly flat at the back? Was the back of that head anything more than the vertical extension of the neck?

Ambrosio's thoughts were rudely interrupted. With all his strength, Schindler pressed both boots down on the brake pedal. 'Now what does he want?' he said.

A highway policeman in a black uniform waved the vehicle over to the side of the road. With his hand on the brim of his cap he stepped up to the tractor: 'What's that you're carrying in the back?'

Schindler looked down into the trailer, as though he first had to check to be sure what it was himself, then he turned off the engine and said: 'A bull.'

'Will you unload him, please! Vehicle inspection!'

Schindler went bright red. He slid about on his seat, gulped, turned the steering wheel and first said, very quietly: 'You great fart!' and then very loudly: 'Oh, that's Pestalozzi we've got in there, from the Breeders' Syndicate in Innerwald. He's the best-behaved bull for miles, I can't just . . . anyone would think he had foot-and-mouth disease or something!'

'Is he temperamental?'

'No, quite the opposite, but he is incredibly big and wide. The time it would take to get him unchained.'

The policeman climbed onto one of the trailer wheels and peered over the side. 'Ah yes, I see. Well, he must have a bladder like an elephant,' he said, and pointed back down the road: 'You see that dark streak, going back all the way to the corner? You see how wet that is?'

'Oh now, you know if he drinks he piddles!' Schindler scratched his belly through his smock.

'But not on our roads!' the policeman snapped. 'What if everyone just started fouling the roads like that! Now you open up the back, if you won't unchain him.'

Schindler climbed down off the tractor and let the back of the trailer down.

'Right,' the policeman reached for his leather wallet. 'As I thought. No container provided for urine or excrement. I'll have to take your name!'

'Oh officer, please. This is the first bull I've ever taken. I'm a calf-trader by profession. This trailer doesn't even belong to me!'

But the fine was meted out. Red with rage, Schindler took the slip of paper and folded it, and went on folding it until he couldn't fold it any smaller, only crush it, and the policeman had long since disappeared in his white VOLKSWAGEN.

'That bastard! For a bit of bull's piss!' muttered Schindler. Before he closed the back of the trailer again, he rearranged the handful of straw under the bull's hindquarters, and said: 'Now mind you piss on the straw, you fool!'

At the outskirts of the city, there was a sign announcing a diversion for livestock traffic. 'That's what we want,' Schindler turned to Ambrosio. 'First we'll flog off Pestalozzi to some foreigner, then we'll take you round to the slaughterhouse.'

Ambrosio nodded.

The bull market was held on common land that was also used for military exercises, sporting events and as a children's playground. There were hundreds of bulls standing in rows or being led, snorting and heavy-headed, by rings, poles and chains. The drumming of their hooves, as they were led down steep ramps from trailers and lorries, sounded like salvoes of gunfire.

From the approaching tractor, Ambrosio could see a red-and-white sea of massive necks and backs, and the acrid sexual smell of bulls filled his nostrils.

A pent-up restraint emanated from the powerful animals. They were chained according to age groups, with up to fifty bulls standing side by side, but positions were still being changed as the judges in their long white coats worked to produce an order of merit based on appearance and performance.

Their decisions were not uncontroversial. Dealers and farmers stood in groups, expressed laconic opinions, behaved formally, shook hands with newly arrived acquaintances – long and hard they shook hands – then went back to gripping their own cowherd's smocks, the lapels of their tunics, digging their thumbs under their collars as they looked over the judges' shoulders, and, depending on what they saw there, either nodding in agreement or muttering in dissent.

Buyers were apprehensive about rising prices. They were convinced that the bull they were interested in couldn't possibly deserve such a high ranking.

Owners, on the other hand, found that their own bulls had been unfairly treated. Wasn't he the most splendid bull in the whole park? Standing there on his pillars of legs, on hooves the size of soup plates! And how good the leather harness with its little embroidered flowers and crosses looked on his head! What other bull had been so lovingly curry-combed, even under the tail?

They frowned in dissatisfaction, got down to peer under the bulls' bellies themselves and examined the high-ranked animals with an especially critical eye. 'He flatters to deceive,' was said of this bull or that one. Whoever doubted the measurements would stand next to the animal, take a step back and say: 'That's about right,' or again: 'The bugger's short! Hardly reached up to my armpit!'

The toughest judgements were passed by those farmers and dealers who were neither buying nor selling. According to them, the one bull was too upright, the other too low slung, a third had uneven horns, the ankles of a fourth were too thick, on the fifth someone pointed to hooves that hadn't been greased, and said: 'They didn't even bother to put polish on his shoes!' the sixth had forequarters too large, with the seventh it was the hindquarters, the eighth didn't have enough flesh on his scrotum, the ninth was suspected of having a shot of cross-bred blood in his veins, and the tenth was either bandy-legged or stiff-legged, and thus according to the observer, his hindquarters had either collapsed, or they were too elevated.

Miming disappointment, these unpartisan critics turned their backs on the bulls and gave vent to their poor opinion of the whole: 'That's what you get with artificial insemination, an elite but no class!' and they looked out for acquaintances among the other visitors. An old farmer in a linen-mixture suit said: 'Yes, before my boy took over the farm, I always used to go up to Knollenfing. Those were real bulls there, ooh, yes!' Another, even older farmer, rammed his stick into the ground and said: 'Yes, Knollenfing. But on foot, eh!' and after a pause: 'Hey, Fritz, let's have a talk and a bottle of wine in the pub. We never used to have the time, now we do.'

The arrival of Schindler with Pestalozzi created the biggest stir of the day. Even as they were unloading, people milled round the great bull-transporter, craned their necks and said: 'Yes, there's one, that's what I call a bull!' And someone squinted at Ambrosio and laughed: 'And a tiny wee bugger of a farmhand!'

When Schindler led Pestalozzi across the market terrain, he was greeted on all sides, conversations were interrupted, and heads turned to watch the dealer with the Innerwald bull.

At the assembly point for five-year-olds, Schindler smacked his forehead. 'Hah, made a mistake,' he called out, and led Pestalozzi right the way back across the market to the four-year-olds, where a judge came towards him, unbuttoned his white coat, pulled out a red handkerchief, buried his face in it, blew his nose long and loud, then folded his handkerchief up again and asked: 'Who's that you've got there?'

'That's Pestalozzi,' said Schindler.

'Ah, yes. Thought so. With those curls. The son of, er, what's his name?'

'Son of Jean-Jacques.'

'That's right.' The judge took a walk round Pestalozzi and asked: 'Do you just want to get him a prize, or is he up for sale?'

'Well . . .' Schindler hesitated. 'If someone could lay the money on the table, why not?'

'Then chain him up right at the front,' instructed the judge.

'Come on then!' Schindler pulled lightly on the bar. Pestalozzi, frothing from the nostrils, lowered his head and mooed. When the bull was finally standing in the sawdust, tethered round the horns and chained in first place in the four-year-olds category, a young farmer in green overclothes came away from one group and went up to Schindler. He nudged the calf-dealer with his elbow, jerked his chin in the direction of Pestalozzi and asked: 'Why don't they want him any more up in Innerwald?'

Schindler cleared his throat, raised his hand, his nails were already poised to scratch his neck, but then he dropped his hand again. 'Well, you know! It's the mountain air! Some do well on it, others don't. And then besides, they've still got Gotthelf up there too.'

'Isn't he getting on a bit?'

'Who?'

'Well, Gotthelf.'

'Hm. Hardly.' Schindler rubbed Pestalozzi's curly head.

'He'd be too expensive for us in the Oberland anyway,' said the young farmer. 'We still breed our own. But round here, they say everything's going to be beefed again.'

'Well, if they're not wanted any more, or only the very best of them.'

'But there are supposed to be some gentlemen from abroad here too. They say they're buying everything over 1000 kilos for their insemination stations back in Holland and Austria. Oh, they'll pay something for him, I'm sure.'

'Oh, but he's worth it,' said Schindler.

'Yes, that Pestalozzi,' replied the young farmer, jabbed Schindler in the ribs again, and laughed.

Ambrosio, who had watched the whole thing and interpreted it as a coming to terms, went into the festival tent, sat down at a wooden table and ordered a beer. 'A spezial,' he said, half in Knuchel German, half in Spanish.

: 10 :

And all over the slaughterhouse behind the high fence at the edge of the beautiful city, things were happening with a vengeance. With all the driving and shooting and sticking and bleeding, the men were swearing and spitting till their throats were dry. Their shoulders ached, and their hips, and their backs. They had visions of a cigarette, or a cool beer. They suppressed sighs.

Ernest Gilgen – still in his street clothes – strode along the rows of half cows hanging in storage in the cattle-freezing-room. No, I'm not changing today. Not today. My rags are staying in my locker. With every step he punched one of the cows. The carcasses shook on their spreaders. Gilgen smashed the congealed-fat layer of well-fleshed animals.

– Hugentobler! Hugentobler! You deaf bastard! he yelled. Where are you? Where are you keeping your great wooden blockhead? Nom de Dieu, show yourself! The shouting wouldn't quite come. However Gilgen exerted himself, his words didn't acquire the resonance that he liked to feel filling his own ears, and that was the fault of the roaring of the mighty air-coolers in the ceiling, and *a cooling-plant works to lower the temperature in an enclosed space, or that of objects, especially highly perishable goods; generally a heat-insulated room in which the temperature is lowered by a refrigerator plant*, and in the face of their massive assault on the undesirable livelihood of microbes, even the great Gilgen was forced to silence.

He bent down and looked under the dangling cows for Hugentobler's legs, but he saw only a thicket of stiff fraying necks. Nom de Dieu! Where's he go to? When you need him . . .

Hugentobler was pushing yesterday's pigs out of the second freeze room. Their split carcasses were hung up on hoists. Hugentobler leaned his shoulders against the sides of bacon. Gilgen had to roar to get his attention.

– Hey, Hugentobler, how cold is it now in the blast-freeze tunnel?

– What's that? Hugentobler fumbled with his fur cap and brought out an ear.

Gilgen repeated his question.

– That's the thermometer over there. The gloved hand was slowly raised. It pointed to the entrance of the ante-chamber to the blast-freezing plant.

– Don't be so ratty, how cold is it there?

– Cold.

– How cold?

– Didn't you hear me? I said it was cold. Hugentobler's face barely moved as he spoke: he sounded unclear, slurred, like a man with a hare-lip.

– Arsehole. A man who doesn't know which way he's looking. Forget it then. You won't stop me, though, you can bet your life on it.

A row of heavy, matted army coats hung on the wall, next to the entrance to the freezers. Gilgen threw one across his shoulders, and pressed down the lever to open the insulating door. The layers of ice around it cracked apart. Gilgen lowered his head. It was a low door. Flakes of man-made snow caught in his hair and splintered onto his coat. A wave of cold air washed over his shoes, and bit into his feet and legs. Merde, ce n'est pas drôle. Next to the doors to the various deep-freeze rooms, the walls were covered with switches and little control lights which bathed the ante-camber in a matt reddish fog. Where was the overhead light switch? Which of the doors led to the freezing-tunnel? Crusts of ice gleamed like red glass. The empty ante-chamber trembled with machine noise. Everywhere ice-covered pipes, white rods and tubes. Gilgen turned round. The light had come on. Hugentobler was standing behind him.

– Why didn't you shut the door behind you?

The two men faced each other silently. Stretched tight in the dangerous stillness, leaning forward as though to land a blow or an insult, instinctive and alone, like hostile animals.

With his heavy legs and bad Bang's back, Hugentobler couldn't stand there as insolently and provocatively as Gilgen. But his shoulders were mightily inflated by the refrigerating-room gear he was wearing, and the army coat thrown over them made him an imposing sight as well.

Away from the cooling-plants at the slaughterhouse, Hugentobler was always extremely quiet. As soon as he left his place of work, he saw the world as shyly as a child. As if the city, the streets, the shops, the public buildings and institutions only existed for other people, people in other professions, other classes, people of a different appearance.

And now this shy man stood challengingly in front of Gilgen. Here I stand. Immovable. As if he had built all the deep-freeze rooms with his own hands, and could dispose of every gram of what was stored in them as he saw fit. This is mine. For once, his eyes looked straight out of his angular face. He didn't make the slightest attempt to justify his risky attitude. He mentioned neither the weight of responsibility for the unnumbered tonnes of meat that were in his charge, nor the scale of work he did here. He didn't have to say I have, I do, if it wasn't for me, if I hadn't. He didn't brag about the two thousand sides of bacon that he had stacked in the third deep-freeze room, under arctic conditons, to save precious space elsewhere. He had no figures or formulae to hand. He didn't even think of trying to demonstrate the value of what he did. The housewife, unthinkingly reaching for her plastic-wrapped roast, never crossed his mind. Whether there was someone outside, on the other side of the slaughterhouse walls, the other side of the high fence, whether there was someone who thought highly of his labour, and who was selling it to whom, and at what price, all these questions were far removed from him. Once again, here was a case of someone remaining silent, using all the words he didn't know, and under 'freeze' it says: *to solidify a liquid, for purposes of preservation, by cooling it to below its freezing point: with organic substances, especially food, also cell-tissue, the freezing point of water;* and he didn't say either that he, Christian Hugentobler, had never been to prison, and that was something not everyone at the abattoir could say of themselves. And if the fact had occurred to him that he'd never missed a day's work in his life, then that wouldn't have struck him as being in any way remarkable either.

Still, Ernest Gilgen understood. He wasn't just in any cold, any ante-chamber, any refrigerator installation. This particular biting cold, the whole of this ante-chamber where he found himself confronted with such resolution and hostility, the cooler-rooms this side of it, and the freezer-rooms beyond, they belonged, with all their contents, to Hugentobler. And Gilgen stepped back. As he cautiously withdrew the challenge from his posture and his expression, until he stood there with his tail between his legs, like a dog who has strayed deep into the clearly marked territory of another, so too Hugentobler's gaze lost its menacing sharpness. The eye muscles tensed again, the pupils flickered and quivered towards the nose, and the sight axes crossed again.

Gilgen looked for a conciliatory tone:

– You see – it's just about this – I wanted to, oh, surely it's all right to ask. I wanted the key. The key to the freezer-tunnel. I need it, and you've got to help me. Don't you understand anything? Tell me how cold it is now, or aren't I even allowed to know that? It's true, isn't it?

Hugentobler went on staring at Gilgen in silence, then he raised one foot, and started to move, stiff and angular as ever, and keeping Gilgen in view. What's Big G doing coming on like a shy secretary? What's he up to? Instead of getting changed, as though there was no meat left to dress. Hugentobler turned several knobs, and pulled a key from his coat pocket. It was tied to a bone, a hollow grey marrow-bone. The door grated, as if it was made of glass, and *a freezer-tunnel is a long chamber where storage goods are exposed to forced-air circulation, and thereby rapidly cooled.*

– A blast-freezer, said Hugentobler proudly.

– Whorish cold, said Ernest Gilgen.

– Wait, that's nothing. The machine isn't even on. Hugentobler pressed a button. A hellish din started up, and a tornado of cold air whisked the few ice particles out of the tunnel.

– Nom de Dieu! Regarde ça!

– Minus 36. Goes down to minus 44.

– Hey, a man would cool down pretty quickly in there, wouldn't he?

– If he stays in there, he'll be dead within two hours.

Hugentobler locked the door again. That showed him. He seemed to think it was a toy or something. As though the machines were there to show off with, but that's how they are, no idea what a plant like that can do, now he's looking like a monkey bit him, and he's cold. That's shock-freezing, and you've got to understand it, otherwise something'll go wrong, and *the cell structures of plant and*

*animal tissue have their cellular fluid torn by freezing, and as a result,
frozen good when they're thawed, make a soft, 'floppy' impression
which is not the result of any process of chemical decay,* and Hugentobler, who also attracted attention outside the cooling-plant by
seeming to be unable to adjust the loudness of his voice to other
conditions, now screamed at Gilgen, entirely suitably. Despite the
roaring and thundering of the cooling equipment, every word was
clearly audible:

– If there's something you want, Gilgen, the key or whatever,
then you know where to find me.

– Can that door be opened from the inside too?

– No, only from the outside.

– And if someone's really feeling a bit hot, how long would it
take to cool him down, and still leave him able to walk out?

– That depends if he's really boiling or not. Ten minutes might
not do him any harm.

– Ha, you see!

Together the two men left the ante-chamber and took off their
heavy army coats. The second cooling-room, where Gilgen had
interrupted Hugentobler as he was pushing out pigs, seemed
warm by comparison, and *low temperatures destroy certain parasites
in meat, e.g. tapeworm larvae, by freezing.*

Time was when the ox and the lamb were slaughtered out of doors,
in the open air. *And they shall take a heifer which has never been
worked and which has not pulled in the yoke. And they shall bring the
heifer down to a valley with running water, which is neither ploughed
nor sown, and shall break the heifer's neck there in the valley.* Later on,
more sheltered places came to be in demand. They swung the axe
in the shadow of an oak tree, preferably near a stream. Then in a
back courtyard in the town. At the front was the shop, on the street,
and while the butcher and guild member waited over a bled
carcass for customers, he began stuffing this and that part into the
inverted gut. The sausage lay down with the roast. But because of
the stench that rose from the town stream, the bloody craft was
moved out to a slaughterhouse. Every butcher was allotted an
individual slaughtering booth under a common roof. From that
time forth *it was forbidden Master-Butchers and their Apprentices to*

slaughter secretly great or small beasts in private dwellings. On payn of
a fyne of ten shillings, and the impounding of said Meat.

It was in that same corporate or block system that the regional slaughterhouse behind the high fence at the edge of the beautiful city had been built almost a century ago. Abattoir abutted abattoir, the first for cattle, the second for sheep and calves, the third for pigs. All in one building. The machine room, the offices, the canteen, the cooling-plant, the freezer-rooms were all situated in blocks under one roof. And all routes went through the main connecting passage, which led for 200 metres right through the whole slaughterhouse.

This passage was always white and always clean. Three factory clocks hung from the overhead rail supports, under the glass-brick roof. The tracks from all the halls met here, everything had to come through here. The beer and the empty bottles passed each other here. The tank full of cows' blood came here, and the plasma in clean milk churns from the machine room came here again, on its way to the loading ramp. Buri wheeled the intestines in here, and rolled the barrel with them, salted, back out again here. In the main passageway, steps slowed, breaths were drawn more deeply, an eye looked up at the clock, and a man veered off to the toilet. Here curious spectators spoke to the butchers, here Dr Wyss encountered the smoking Rötlisberger, and here Bössiger circled one of the freshly slaughtered calves.

The calf hung from a hoist on its own.

– Oh, come, come! The farmers! Who do we do business with? Is it you or is it the farmers? Bössiger gesticulated. In one hand he held his black notebook, in the other his spectacles. Behind his ear, pointing straight at Livestock-dealer Schindler was a red pencil. That's a fox! An out and out fox! How can I help it if farmers nowadays don't know how to produce a proper vealer any more?

Slaughterhouse-Marshal Bössiger had got Schindler worried. The dealer would have liked to go right up to Bössiger, belly to belly, he would have liked to talk to Bössiger the same way he talked to the farmers. Three-minute handshake, the steady gaze into the other's eyes: Eh, Hans, yes Fritz, look here and look there, and then the pressure, gradually strengthening as the men reached an agreement. Instead of which, Bössiger only saw the calf, saw its reddish meat and its yellowish fat. He opened his black notebook and put his glasses on. Here! Yesterday. Numbers 6, 13 and 19! Red, the lot of them! Useless! Foxes! You dumped four foxes on us. Do you think we can pay you the market price for vealers for them to be made into sausages? What colour is this? Veal is meant to be white! White! White, Goddamn it!

– But ... I really don't understand it. Schindler tried to meet Bössiger's eye. He held out his hand. Bössiger ignored it. In desperation, Schindler turned to the disputed calf. He pulled open the ribcage, and stuck his head into its chest. He rubbed its back and its shoulders, as though to massage a little warmth back into its already cooling flesh.

– But it can't be as red as all that, he said after his inspection. I don't know. I'll swear the eyes were white as snow, and there was nothing under the tail either. I mean, I buy my calves with the muzzles practically still on them. Where's one of them going to get hold of something to eat?

– Oh come now! Yesterday we did a check on the stomach of one of them. Exactly! It had real nodes in it. That hasn't just been fed on milk.

– Nodes? In its stomach? Schindler buried his head in the chest of the calf again. I expect it was hair, he said. Hair! That's right. They've got to try and crop something. That's what the vets say too. These aren't little three-week-old bobs, these've got proper bellies on them. And those bellies want to work, want to digest something. And so, if they have to, they suck the hair off their hides, through the little holes in the muzzle.

– But what we want is white meat. We get enough frozen stuff from America to make bratwursts with. You'd better watch your farmers. They know a few tricks. They give them pepper to make them thirsty, or they'll open a vein on them. All that's no good.

– Well, I've never come across that before. Schindler looked at the dangling carcass again from all sides. You know, this calf here comes from Knuchel's farm in Innerwald. And if that isn't a healthy animal! God knows what city people would rather eat instead. So much fat on it! It's only ever drunk full-cream milk. Those kidneys! They must be worth money. No butcher ever lost money on a Knuchel calf from Innerwald. That young Ruedi Knuchel, he knows how to fatten up an animal. But all right, I'll take it back, that 'eating' calf. It won't be down to me. Schindler lifted up his baggy dealer's overall and dug out a notepad from his trouser pocket. There, I've crossed it off. So, that's settled. All right? Schindler held out his hand to Bössiger.

– If you say so. Bössiger shook hands quickly and went off. Without another word, he strode past the wooden chest at the entrance to the cattle hall, and away down the long passage.

– There are some who'd be pleased if I even offered them a Knuchel calf, muttered Schindler as he stuffed the notepad into his back pocket. But there you are, Bössiger can tell the price of petrol by looking at a cow's arse. That man's as thick as an ox. Everyone must know what the truth of it is. The water on Knuchel's farm is far too good. It's real Christian Scientist water. If anyone doesn't want veal like that, that's their look-out. It's been that way for years. Of course it has. With a last look back, Schindler too set off down the long passage, but he was headed for the canteen.

Squealing could be heard from the pig-loading ramp. A sharp and plaintive screaming, swelling and falling. Then grunting and squeaking, then more panic-stricken screaming.

'Silly bugger!' muttered Livestock-dealer Schindler, and he went into the little bar and said to Frau Bangerter, the barmaid: 'Oh Rösi, make me a coffee will you?' dropped onto a chair, and straightaway began recounting how exhausting it all was, how he sometimes felt he'd had it up to here, and how he was constantly getting it from both sides, with no room to move.

He wrapped his hands round his neck, rubbed his throat with both thumbs and sighed.

He'd been on the road since four this morning with his livestock-transporter, picking up calves and a young cow, driving over rough roads to farms that were so remote it would scare you. It had been cold as well, and even though he was rushed, he'd gone into the cowsheds of more than one farmer to see what they'd wanted to show him. And he'd listened to complaints about the rising cost of feed, the new machines, that tacky stuff, bunch of rusty tubes. He'd had to listen to every little goat farmer sounding off, and each time he'd tried to open his mouth, they'd say, ooh you, don't come that with me, what have you got to moan about, with your enormous new truck and your bulk purchasers, you've got us over a barrel. As if it was viable, driving round with that vast transporter empty half of the time, because those farming misers thought he was made of money, and were demanding fantasy sums for their goods. Wasn't he allowed a livelihood? Didn't he have a right to that? It was true. And then they'd got him chasing up the highlands. Just because there was one little cow who had a knot in her gut, and would neither dump nor ruminate, the farmer had wanted to hang himself on his own telephone wire. You got the impression his whole farm and everything was crashing down around his ears. And it was only because one of those modern vets had rumoured something about the meat getting infected. The fear of being a fiver down in his budget was enough to make one of those farmers shit himself. The little cow had to be flogged off on the spot, to be sure she still made the beef price.

– And who is it they decided to phone up? Eh? If they want someone in a hurry? Who'll do in that kind of situation? Livestock-dealer Schindler asked the barmaid.

– Why, they phone me! Yes, Rösi, it seems that I'm all right again, and of course like an idiot I go along, even though I know darned well there's nothing in it for me. But what am I supposed to do? I'm so pleased about every single bloody tail that the big boys leave me. Even if I don't earn much here, I still have to look to my volume of trade, because otherwise I don't get cut into any of the import distribution. Everyone's trying to make more, it's only my margins that are going backwards. Am I supposed to get up even earlier and drive even further, across to Swabia or God knows where, just to bring those guys things that don't exist? Why don't the miserly fools go and butcher moon-calves? Maybe they'll have whiter meat than Knuchel's. So there you go, driving across country with your back hurting you so badly you can't even stand up straight, and you remember to make a fuss of every farmer's freshening cow, and you have a good word for their wives, and sixpence for the kids, but do you think one of them's ever satisfied?

Schindler was haranguing Frau Bangerter as though she was the local council. He tore at his hair, rubbed at his neck, which was so swollen it looked like a hog's neck. With shaking hands, he picked up his glass of coffee. His eyes were watery and inflamed. He had been coughing and wheezing as he spoke. Every successive torrent of words had cost him more effort. His whole body was heaving; once the last bit of air had been pressed from his lungs, Schindler collapsed, shrivelled, his chest looked narrow, and from the folds of his trader's blue smock, came the smell of animals and barns and sweat.

And then weren't those miseries of farmers trying to sell him an ox for a cow the whole time too? he asked. Didn't it keep him as busy as Dung-Hans at his wedding, avoiding all the trips and traps and ruses they set him? And if he ever once dared look in the mouth of one of their so-called cattle in their presence, then wouldn't those farmers make a face like an offended liver-sausage? And then they wanted to be paid in cash for their goods, preferably on the spot, and preferably in spanking new notes! Yes, she was right to stare, but that was the way it was. The number of times one of those whingeing large-scale farmers was practically about to hang himself from the nearest apple tree, and just because he hadn't been willing to pay the going rate for new rope for the frayed and shitty thing round his cow's neck. And earlier, when they'd still calculated on the basis of live weight, by God they'd tried everything, but everything to put one over on him. No, no, this cow has got nothing inside of her, hasn't eaten for days, and the grass is sticking out of her mouth in bunches. Or an animal had 30 or 40 litres of water sloshing about inside her, and he was expected to pay for that. It could make you weep. He couldn't have every cow X-rayed after all.

– You know, Rösi, said Schindler quietly, I'm sure it's happened sometimes that I've shaken hands on something, and there I was holding his hand and shaking it, and I knew damned well that I'd been tricked, and there was something wrong with the calf. But then, how can you go on dealing, if you can't trust anyone any more? I can't go around thinking he's lying the whole time. Livestock-dealing would be finished if it got like that. I can swing around with the prices till I get quite giddy, but whatever I do, I can't do any more than bankrupt myself. I'm always too cheap for the farmers, and too dear for the butchers anyway. They're never satisfied, and if they were, then Fritz Schindler's the last man who'd ever get to hear about it. I know what they're like!

271

– But the worst of the lot are the big, he began, and stopped in a fit of coughing. Those new firms, those distributors and contractors from the feed mills. They send these agents and reps round the country with their prospectuses and plans. They're troubadours, they are! You can't drop in on a farm any more without coming across one, with his briefcase full of the *Farmer's Paradise*. The kitchen table's not good enough for the bloody farmers then, come into the parlour won't you, and then the lying starts, Christ. Can they ever lie! You know, if telling lies gave you the runs, you could send those fellows out on the fields with muck-spreaders strapped to their bums! Right! And when the farmer's wife goes out to see why the dog's barking, you should see how softly she closes the parlour door behind her. You'd think they were discussing world issues. But what is it they put their signatures to? Contracts! Contracts in such fine print that you can't read a sausage. And that's where the promises are set out. They promise you the earth and not the trace of a blush. They carry on as though their own fine words were the secret of successful farming. Bloody stupid nonsense!

Schindler coughed again. He wheezed and sipped at his second glass of coffee, spilt a little on the table, wiped it off with his sleeve, and still addressing Frau Bangerter who had perched on the edge of a chair and was nodding in vigorous agreement, he resumed:

– So, they pay well the first few months, sometimes it's so much money the richest farmers get trembling fingers when they count up all the hundreds. But why? Only because they overdo it. They have to push, they can't afford to miss out on a single standing heat, and they chase after the cows till their bellies are creaking. And what sperm do you think they order up for some sawn-off little cow, for her very first time? Eh, which one? Well, it has to be the very biggest bull's, doesn't it. I saw the results myself, at Fritz Marti's in Holperswil, or Hungerbühler's in Moos. Ah, it's horrible when a cow's carrying a calf that's far too big for her, and by God they have to use a winch to pull it out. And after that they all say they need to build, extend, add on. If it kills them! Build an extension to the barn, another storey under the roof, every little bakehouse will make an extra byre. They park the tractor under the overhanging roof, and use the tractor shed to house three more oxen. But they're feeding their animals about three times as much as they can grow on their land. And that can't go well. You don't get rich on bought feed. I've never heard of it anyway. Then, later on, when they've got so many animals that the calves whine at you from the wash-house and the hayloft, and they've stuck a beef steer at the side of every pile of firewood, that's when the reps wing in again with their briefcases, and they start squeezing the farmer. I've seen it happen more than once, I know how it is. I always told my brother, be careful Max, no trees grew right into Heaven yet. Because suddenly there are no more payments, only the unlimited purchase guarantee, but no mention of any price. That's how the big firms operate. When they've got you by the tail, they start twisting it. And then there's another contract for the feed. It's a nasty business, and the worst thing about it is that all of a sudden they think of old Fritz Schindler once again. When they can't earn any more money from their pumped-up goods, and when they don't enjoy going into their cowsheds any more because they can't tell whether their animals are healthy or sick because they have to inject them the whole time anyway, then they suddenly feel like doing business with me again. Why don't you look in on us, eh, if you're in the area? I've got something you might like to take a look at. That's what they tell me down the telephone, and suddenly my smock is more acceptable than the flashy suits of those other characters. But what am I meant to do with their water-driven battery calves? A1 vealers are what I need. I don't make anything on artificially reared produce, there's only deductions there, and by the end half of them wind up with triangular stamps anyway. Or the liver's bad and the kidneys aren't worth anything, and what's left of a calf for you without the liver and kidneys? That's where the butcher earns his money. No, Rösi, I'd rather drive up into the Oberland, wipe my feet on some farmer's doorstep in the back of beyond. But it's terrible, because even then some Bössiger comes along and rubbishes my best goods. Now the fool's gone and complained about the Knuchel calves again. He's done it for years and they're the best calves there are. He must be out of his mind with greed. They just don't want to pay anything any more. Why don't they try getting their quality veal where they get their factory stuff from for the sausages? Ha, but they don't show you that, they could use a whole flowerbed of parsley for garnish and it still wouldn't look any healthier on a butcher's display. Thin, watery, piss-awful stuff. And then there's Krummen, such a toiler, he thinks he's someone just because he's in charge of a couple of part-timers that don't know how to wipe their bottoms. He doesn't have to start swearing at me, just because I'm taking in one more cow that's lost her appetite. They hadn't even finished dressing their beef, it didn't matter a bit, and along comes this fool and lectures me like he was God Almighty. Do I have to take all that too?

The sweat glistened on Schindler's neck. He mopped his brow and coughed.

Frau Bangerter kept on nodding at him. She was in complete agreement. She got to hear about this and that, the ways things were going at the slaughterhouse, you might think nothing would ever happen, and you knew the people and you knew what sort they were, but then suddenly it was as though they were completely different, as though you'd never seen them before in your life.

She had stood up, held out a newspaper to Schindler, pointed to a picture of a calf in it, and said:

– Read what it says in the article!

And Livestock-dealer Schindler, sweating, tired from talking, pulled out his unbreakable spectacle case from under his smock, pushed his empty coffee glass to one side, moved his chair slightly, and got ready to read. He smoothed the paper one last time, then, holding it by the corners, and moving his lips, he began reading the story of the calf.

It had been hit by a car on a mountain road, the poor calf, and its owner had demanded compensation. The driver had paid up, but had then insisted on being allowed to keep the animal. He had had its broken leg set in splints at a vet's, and had arrived at home with a new playmate for his children in the boot of the car. Bloody stupid, muttered Schindler. A calf's a calf! But the children, it said in the newspaper, had been thrilled. The good calf had grown, which didn't surprise Schindler. It had eaten roughly three times as much as the dog, in particular porridge, milk powder and lawn grass, and all the children in the neighbourhood had been invited along to ride on its back, and many of them had fallen off, some fairly frequently, but all of them had still so, so loved the little calf.

But the calf had gone on growing. They had bought hay from a farmer, and all of them had looked after it. But then, when it had become a young cow, and they had begun to think of having it slaughtered, they had felt unable to go ahead, on account of the children. What were the children to think of life? They couldn't just murder their friend just like that, brutally in a slaughterhouse and Schindler couldn't believe his eyes, he took off his spectacles, put them on again. A committee had been founded. Their slogan was : Our Lisi must not die. Then they had set up a charity to save the cow. Schindler coughed. Save the cow! He wheezed and spluttered. A charity to save the cow! His face shone, each pore swelled up singly, his mouth and nose were covered by a net of blue-green and whitish veins, and tears squeezed from his screwed-up eyes. He coughed violently. Save the cow! His body shook, his dung-encrusted boots slithered about under the chair. Save the cow! His voice scratched and wheezed, and from outside the screaming of the waiting pigs penetrated the little canteen, and grew louder.

– Oh my goodness! Frau Bangerter pressed her hands to her mouth. Oh my goodness!

Schindler gaped at the paper again through crooked glasses. The charity for the cow had succeeded in finding a place for her in a zoo, and saved her from the abattoir. Schindler read about how happy and relieved all the children felt. There had been a party. Schindler fought for breath. The first cow in a zoo. He got up, and stood there, wheezing and rocking. A charity for the cow! A Simmental cow in a zoo! His chest rose and fell like a bellows, the wheezing and scraping grew louder. Schindler gripped the edge of the table, and leaned forward as though to vomit. Reddish froth dripped from his mouth. Frau Bangerter thumped him on his broad back, tried to pull him down onto his chair, but the chair tipped over and fell, the table slid aside, crashed against the wall, the coffee glass smashed, and the pigs' screaming grew louder.

– Oh my goodness! wailed Frau Bangerter, her hands clutching her hair. Stop it! She tugged at Schindler's smock. Sit down! But the dealer stood up and gasping for breath, ripped at the blue cloth across his chest. He stuck his tongue out, his breath whistled, his glasses slipped down in front of his mouth. When his legs slid away from him, Frau Bangerter caught him, for a second he was in her arms, then he slipped further, onto the shards on the floor. He rattled very quietly. Trembling and pale, Frau Bangerter stood beside the massive body.

Ernest Gilgen stood in the doorway of the canteen.

– Oh my goodness! sobbed Frau Bangerter.

– It's the blood, said Gilgen.

Eleven forty-five.

Standing.

Standing still.

Leaning over the table, while time stands still.

Will you stop stirring at that damned blood. Go to offal! Right now!

Krummen can only yell.

I trim pancreases: snip away veins and fat and membranes from the valuable tissue.

Fifteen minutes to go.

Till I can take my boots off.

Lie down. Stretch out.

I'm not hungry.

Can't see a clock from here.

That's where the new gut-cleaning machine is going to go. They were just breaking open the chest in the corridor a while ago.

The monotony here at this table has been a hundred times worse in the past.

Thoughts.

Everything in my head gets smashed straightaway. Like in a mincing machine.

Mustn't cut myself.

All day, alone with a knife.

And the students yesterday, they had a printing-press hidden away. It was just like in the pictures, in a basement room, through a door that was concealed by a bookshelf. At the bottom of a creaky flight of stairs.

That's where they printed their pamphlets.

And they had a dark-room as well.

But so much light in the apartment itself. Big windows everywhere. Newspapers lying around. Masses of them. And open books, and books with strips of paper in them, marking the place. On the walls, posters of Karl Marx and Engels and Lenin and Ho Chi Minh.

A bottle of Chianti on the kitchen table.

I wanted to tell them about monotony.

Monotony is the worst part of it.

I couldn't make them understand it.

Why else would they be racing each other again in the calf hall, if not to escape the monotony?

But that doesn't interest the students.

Someone should try and take a picture of that!

It's in your throat. Your gut. A void that swallows up everything. Nothing hangs together any more. You don't know anything. Don't know what you're doing, don't know what you want, nothing.

Trapped.

It hurts.

In your throat. All over.

Your head feels muzzy, but the time is so clear.

So dead.

It's impossible to describe it properly, I said. You couldn't keep listening to the same thing over and over again all day long. You couldn't keep listening to the same thing over and over again all day long. You couldn't keep listening to the same thing over and over again all day long. You couldn't keep listening to the same thing over and over again all day long. You couldn't keep listening to the same thing over and over again all day long. You couldn't keep listening to the same thing over and over again all day long. You couldn't keep listening . . .

They don't get it.

For them, alienation is something different.

There goes Buri.

The way he limps.

Have you got the time?

He wipes his hands on his trousers and pulls his watch out of his trouser pocket.

He holds it up to my face. It's a fine OMEGA.

277

A special present from the company.

Gold.

Because I've been here twenty-five years.

It's nearly twelve.

Buri puts his watch away again.

If you listen to those friends of Lukas'.

They make us out to be heroes, us here in the slaughterhouse.

Maybe we should all eat testicles.

And bone marrow.

Fried in butter.

A man should be able to face his fellows without having to turn his cap in his hands obsequiously.

And there's no point in withdrawing to a private underground.

My world: cows, guts and glands.

And in my head, movie images.

And the second hand wriggles down the right-hand side, takes the bottom curve, turns into the final straight, and click! Hour hand and minute hand are both vertical, and it's twelve o'clock, noon, lunch hour! Don't shout, we're only halfway there, and after hours of cows, hands dip into buckets and human hide is washed, and out of slaughterhalls and workrooms come the slaughtermen, the tripers and gutters and foreign workers, it's gone quiet, the compressors are silent, only the ventilators continue to hum, the hush of noon, listen, can you hear the doves cooing up on the glass roof? Well? You, standing in the doorway like a great ox, let me by! Well? How does the shit get on the roof? The cow, she dumps it in a pail, and flicks it up there with her tail. God Almighty! That was some morning, someone ought to write it all down, write it in blood, but I'm hungry, shove over Piccolo, let me in, I always sit here, and you keep your regular place, even in the dining hall, and Rötlisberger's in a hurry, he wants to dress his rabbits in his lunch hour, and Huber and Hofer open their mess-tins hot out of the warming oven: potatoes, noodles, sauerkraut and what have you got with it? Escaped the axe, beset anew, tied, thrown in water, hangèd too – what suffers all the tortures of the damned, yet still finds itself much in demand? And what are you eating today? Steam rises from opened canteens, beer next to them, all the bottles replenished, thirst, thirst, thirst in butchers' throats, haven't we sweated? Cattle are a battle, lift arms, cheers! aim, fire, ah, that's better, and foam dribbles down chins, lips smack, backs of hands wipe, a cow would envy your capacity, erps, belching competition, and now go, holes open, greed, forks, spoons digging, bread broken, fingers tamp, stuff bulging cheeks, gulping throats, Adam's apples yoyo, shoulders aid swallowing motions, and what have you got over there? Pork chops, want a bit? Not on your life! No pork, the doctor told Schindler, it's very bad for you! Oh, but who was ever killed by a pork chop! Haven't you heard, Schindler suffered a stroke? What? Where? In the canteen, with Rösi . . . You see, it's schnapps! Fritz Schindler? Yes, collapsed, apparently, and where is he now? In the meat-inspection office, with Dr Wyss. They've called an ambulance. Well, what can you expect if someone drinks spirits first thing in the morning! Must do something for your health, he always said. Take a glass of potato brandy with your rösti in the morning, it'll warm you up and help the digestion, now he's got his comeuppance. What did Bössiger tear him off a strip for? They don't need him any more, the two or three calves he brings in, and Foreman Krummen through a throatful of dough: Eat! If you don't eat . . . he gulps, swallows . . . you won't be able to work, and it tickles, shut up Krummen, you slave-driver! Only one of them thinks it, and how the calf hair itches your neck! Some scratch, others don't, insensitive skin, beer swills everything down, but if you always tank up like a cow . . . Überländer wipes his face with his sleeve, he's got dark sweat stains under the arms of his butcher's blouse: Now leave the lad alone! But that little pussy-cat of a cow knocked him off his feet! He needs to eat more! Do you have to start too? Oh leave him, the cows that low the most give the least milk, and that's filled the hole for the moment anyway, and a few words are heard among the chomping and swilling, heads are lifted, and moomoomoo calls the cow, we give her lots of fodder, she gives us milk and budder, and silky-smooth Hügli lights up a MARLBORO: Who really knows what he did to that cow? Say, where did you grab her to get her so excited? But oh, I have oh-nly myself to blame, said the cow, when she had to cart her own dung out into the fields. Buri's plate is scraped, Hofer's army spoon licked clean, hand on tum and: gerps! So the spindly thing threw him? Yes, one of those, all veins and hamstrings, nothing up top, no meat on her rump, bone for thighs! A skinny thing like Spreussiger, and if you plough with young oxen, you'll drive a crooked furrow, ergh, please! Goddamn it! Krummenmutter: I had to catch her myself, that cow, if the lad won't eat anything, thecowrantillshefelloveronherear! Till-she-found-cow-clover! Ah, Spreussiger, Huber laughs, Hofer laughs. And for every workplace a soupplace, smokeplace, swearplace, fartplace, and behind the eatplace the drinkplace, the cardplace, the shitplace, the changingplace, and even for the pigs screaming through their baconfat throats a waitingplace, but Frau Spreussiger, she's one that got away, eh Hügli? What she needs is a real sperm technician, ha apprentice? And an old cow's rather apt to forget, she isn't still a young calf yet, yes, a sperm technician, one of those who goes from farm to farm, or a bull, what she needs is a bull! And beware the front of the bull, the rear of a horse, and the milker on every side! You'd better start eating testicles too, Hügli! Eh! Eat bollocks! And Buri stretches his back and groans: The blacks, the blacks in Chicago, they always used to eat testicles. Never raw though! What a bastard! Eating raw testicles. And where's Hugentobler? Didn't anyone call him? A Franggesta eatta inna goolroom. I told you to call him for Christ's sake! Huber laughs: And bring Spreussiger along too, for Hügli, and Hofer chips in: But she's just being serviced in the pen at the back. Off you go now, lad! See how it's done. Oh, stop it! He's a big Neubau . . . a big boy now! Did you know that where Spreussiger comes from, cows are a protected species? No, why's that? Because they can't tell them from the women. And did you know why the farmers over there have got such long arms? It's so they can kiss their cows while milking, but you know I'll bet Spreussiger rattles in bed! Like a ghost, a skeleton! But why does the farmer hang a bell round the cow's neck? Hugentobler's deaf, he's got the hearing of an artillery man. Fetch him, for Christ's sake! Now . . . And what's the matter with you? The lad's not hungry, and another laugh between mouthfuls of beer, the farmer made his cows so happy, gave them all a little tranny, and Piccolo keeps missing the fly on the wall, rats, missed it again! Luigi? Fernando? Game of cards? Ambrosio's missing, and I saw him at the fair on Sunday, eh Luigi? We had a beer together. Has he got a woman! Not one of those cadaver cows, she's got a bit of veal on her. And what are those dagos doing at the fair? Eh, Buri? The place was swarming with Eyeties, half the beer tent was speaking Italian. Ha well, if they all get to bring their wives over! And a dozen kids apiece! Soon it won't be any fun putting on your Sunday best any more. You go out for a walk, and it's wall to wall foreigners! Effing dagos! But they've got the biggest cows, that's true: near Milan, Chianina, they're called! Well, just goes to show, the stupidest farmers grow the biggest spuds, and it's the littlest runts who have the biggest cows! What have you got against Eyeties? But it's true! Huber sniggers, Hofer sniggers, of course he's got a good-looking wife, he was buying her elder week after week from the cheap-meat department, but it didn't do much for her measurements, you should eat a few more brains yourself, you mutton-head, and bollocks and pizzle, but he's right, it's getting to be as bad as it was with the blacks in Chicago, those Negro bastards, you know they employed one of those chimney-sweeps here once. What? Here? That was an Arab! He looked black enough, and in Chicago when the butchers went out on strike, then they started taking on blacks at s w i f t & c o., but in the bacon room, where everything was white, the walls, the lighting, the tables, where they show the visitors around, they didn't let any niggers in there, no black hands on their white fat! And they washed the hands of the black women every hour with detergent, and checked their fingernails before every shift. And Rötlisberger holds out his empty water bottle: Hey, Luigi, will you fill this up with blood for me, you know, for my garden? And have you heard this one? The farmer's son is out walking with his sweetheart in his father's meadow, and just at that moment the bull mounts a cow. Oh, he says, that's what I feel like doing now, and she, quite unabashed: Well, what's keeping you, they're all your cows aren't they? Ah, that's like the woman at the agricultural show. They had a fine bull there, and the woman asked the lad who was minding him, how often he would, you know, in a week. Every day, the boy said, and then she looks her husband up and down, you know, like that, and then the lad says: But with a different cow every day! And the neighbour's wife? Rötlisberger snaps his army knife shut. The neighbour's wife comes along complaining, and says, your boy, your boy, he just called me a cow! Now, says his mother, the little rascal, and I'm always telling him not to judge people by their appearance, and mouths grin round cigarettes, and little Hansli? Yes, little Hansli's late for school one day, and the teacher's cross with him, and Hansli says: I'm sorry, miss, I had to lead the bull to the cow, and the teacher says: But couldn't your father have done that? Yes, I suppose he could, says Hansli, but not half as well as the bull! See! Till he gets to feel like the bull in Cuba, oh you mean the bull that came in from the cold? Yes, tell us about him. Oh, they'd imported this expensive bull, enormous great creature. But as soon as he got here, couldn't do it. Didn't seem to fancy any of their cows, just stood there and did nothing. Well? And did they have to send him back? Not at all! One Cuban had the bright idea of installing an air-conditioner in his stall, and as soon as it had got a bit cooler, he was all over the lot of them! Have you heard the one about the two cows? It's true, that one about the bull, isn't it? And you? Haven't you? Come on, tell it, what are you waiting for! Well, these two cows meet up again at the end of the summer, and one of them's contented, and the other isn't, and who are these men in unbuttoned butchers' tunics, behind layers of sweat and apron? Who will count the wounds and tell the scars of those that crudely clashed here? Get your milker's mitts off my beer! Ee, what's that? Coffee, want some? Faugh! Is it medicinal? External use only? It's just like a cat crapped in it! Oh shut it! Would I fancy going to a funeral today, eh? To whose? To yours, but do you know how many of them it takes, where Spreussiger hails from? How many to milk, you mean? Oh, that one's ancient! That's right, twenty-four! One on each teat, and twenty to lift the cow up and down! Hey Buri, why have so many of the pigs got wooden legs over there? Come on, Buri! And Buri turns scarlet, and the room falls silent. Go on, Buri! Come on, leave him alone! Because they didn't want to slaughter a whole pig each time they ate trotters, and heads lean forward and peer at Buri, eh Buri! Hofer hoots, Huber laughs, Hügli sprays coffee out of his mouth, and here's one for you Überländer! What does the cow say when she gets artificial insemination for the first time? Well, it won't be a whole hell of a lot, because cows don't talk, they moo . . . that's what you think, up in Simmental, in the wilds, they had talking cows! Rötlisberger takes the BRISSAGO out of his mouth, Huber gets up: yeah, probably the same shit as you talk, only not quite so much! Now listen! The farmer didn't believe it either, so he went and hid himself up in the hayloft on top of the cowshed, this was on Christmas Eve, and he's lying up there, and then suddenly this one cow says to the other, she'd have to be yoked up in three days because she'd be taking the farmer down to the churchyard, feet first. When he heard that, our old Oberland chappie was out of the loft like a streak of lightning, ran straight out into the night, and fell over the edge of a precipice! And by God, three days later, there was that cow taking him down to the churchyard feet first! Huber gets up, Hofer's away: load of twaddle. Krummen turns over a sports page. Garbage. And popular prose blossoms forth: female mortality no fatality, cows' doom spells instant ruin! And three butchers went out hunting together, and two of them tell the third one to stay down at the bottom, and drive the game up towards them at the top, but he comes up himself, and bang! he cops one. In the hospital the doctor says, that bullet in his brain, we can remove that and repair the damage, but why did you have to take out his heart, lungs and stomach? Oh you're crazy, so are you! Well, look at the cow, she's got a long face, she gets to see a bull once a year, and you just laugh! Yes old Fritz Rötlisberger still believes in ghosts, and tell me, why has a milking stool only got one leg? And why oh why do cows wear bells? Poor cows! It's to keep the lonesome cowherd from mounting them! Yes, and don't they love their cows! The poor things, get given green grass to eat, and still have to make white milk out of it, you stop helping yourself to my beer! That bottle's mine! But in Ireland there was a cow who gave as much milk as you wanted, she filled every pail! Till this old witch came along, and shoved a sieve under her. And at that the cow ran off, to somewhere where they hadn't heard about her, and they went and slaughtered her! You know, Fritz, there's a whole miracle race of them in Holland: only one teat gives full cream milk, but the others are low fat, milky coffee, and cream! They milk into four separate pails over there! And if you twist her tail, I suppose the cream comes out whipped, eh? Like the cows in America, they get gelatine and strawberry flavouring with their grass, and, bingo, you get a pailful of ice cream! Hey Buri! America! Chicago! Why's he turned as red as a blood pudding again? He sowed his wild oats in America, that's why! Eh, Buri, the cows were so big, you had to milk them into lakes, and the cheesers rowed around them in little boats, skimming off the cream! Ah Chicago! That was the real thing, eh! Hey, Überländer, isn't that where they have the cows with such long horns, you blow into them at Easter and they don't sound till Whitsun? Well, who was it who went there? Was it you or me? Of course you went there, you worked in Frau Baumann's jam-mine, didn't you! And he smelted straw hats in the Wild West, eh Buri! Chicago! God what a bunch of idiots you are! How can you have any idea of what it is to think generously, on a real American scale! To guard against fire, he went around the fat-boiler at SWIFT & CO. in a submarine, and Buri stares at the wall, raises an arm, puts out his hand, speaks: As far as the eye can see, as far as the horizon, oxen, nothing but oxen, back by back, one ox next to another, a whole sea of oxen. The way the smell goes up your nostrils, and the bellowing, and the drovers are bellowing too, and they've got spurs on their boots, and whips, and Hügli laughs: You must get plenty of dung from a sea of oxen, eh Buri! And Buri's eyes narrow, his outstretched hand trembles. And the roads, straight as an arrow, all of them straight as an arrow, unending, mile on mile, and if you . . . oh, what a lot of arseholes you are, and Buri gets up, tears on his cheeks, and cows sitting around in milk bars, doesn't do the farmer much good, and over here we don't slaughter any more than we can salt, and Buri goes, and hey what's happening today, are we going to get brought up to strength? Seeing as Gilgen, and Ambrosio . . . Does each one always have to do the work of two? Hügli smooths his hair, it's not as though we were paid for it, and now that Fernando's going to the tripery, and it isn't till a cow's lost her tail that she realizes what it was worth to her, and where's it all going to end? At the door of the eating room, Krummen turns round: It's nothing to do with me! And one knife whets the other, and we can ask, though, can't we? Just do your own work properly! Not so much standing around, chewing the fat, not so many fag-breaks in the bog! Oh don't start that! You graft away, and then . . . come on, let's go to the canteen! They'll send in some more Italians. Trainees. Stooges. Oh, shut up! Who's got more to do than before? That's putting the cart before the horse, that is. They bring them in from all kinds of places, and what we need are trained butchers, professionals, and Überländer goes. That Rötlisberger is cutting his nose to spite his face. But why do the Italians come? We're just lucky enough to live in a wealthy country, yes by God, and why wouldn't a country be wealthy on the work we do, hang on, I'll come too, what about you? Do you want to slaughter rabbits? And why oh why does the farmer hang bells? And one goes, and another, and the apprentice goes, and the calf follows the coo, and the coo goes . . .

Twelve twenty-five.

And out again, through the driving passages.

A rat and its terrain.

I've got itchy feet.

I feel like kicking something. A football. A hundred thousand times. Till my leg drops off. Or punching a sack of salt down in the storeroom, blindly, with both fists. Or half a cow in the chilling-room.

Fucking abattoir.

Now my hands and forearms are dry. I can feel them in my trouser pockets.

A train on the tracks.

Expresses. Intercities. And always passengers who haven't sat down yet, or who have already got to their feet. The trains are long. Longer than the pens, the tripery, the ramp and the weighing house put together.

I wasn't hungry again.

Didn't feel like lying down either.

I couldn't have slept properly anyway. But it still does me good, shutting my eyes, taking the strain off my back. On the wooden slatted floor in front of the lockers in the changing room.

Not today.

In the changing room Luigi, Piccolo and Fernando will be rapping their cards down on the bench now. Without Ambrosio. They laugh and shout over their lunchtime card games. Sometimes they quarrel, then they look upset.

At the rear of the abattoir, where small livestock come in, the

pigs are huddled together, grunting and squealing. They're pushing against the bars.

Just you wait.

At least they're squealing.

Here, it's only the animals you hear. And the rattling and
humming of machines, the shots, the trains. You never hear the
people.

Yes, you do in the break.

And at lunch, when the beer starts to flow.

Everyone gets their marrow tapped here.

Their most precious, innermost resources.

Till they all slink around, with their tails between their legs.

Who do you think you are?

Why even try and hold your head high?

Something special, ha!

Every bit of self-confidence is scraped away.

Systematically.

They throw us a nice bone now and again.

Arf – arf!

Blood!

Somebody went crazy here.

The outside wall of the cattle slaughterhall is covered with blood.
It's a bull!

Someone has drawn the outline of an enormous bull. The legs
galloping; the head lowered to charge; the horns like antlers. The
furious bulge of the neck. The swinging balls.

I don't believe my eyes.

There'll be hell to pay for this.

On the lawn in front of the administration building is a syca-
more. I lean against the roots, close my eyes, open them again.

The bull's still there.

I shut my eyes again, and lay my head against the tree-trunk. I
can see so many things that way. Whole heavens. I press the backs
of my forefingers against my closed lids. Stars flare and fall.
Squares, like a chessboard, whirling circles: There's a kaleidoscope
in me. If I push harder, it all turns red. Luminous figures. A
reservoir of shapes.

The ground is wet.

On.

It's a good bull.

Krummen mentioned something about an emergency slaughtering. Someone must have phoned.

Will it be another one for me?

Hey, lad!

There's another sick cow in the pen outside. I'll bring it in, and you can slaughter it.

And you can slaughter it.

Can I? May I?

Should I say thank you?

The honour. I am to slaughter the sick cow.

Such confidence they have in me.

Then again, no one else is allowed to go. They need everyone they can get for the pig slaughtering line in the afternoon.

I go past the pen. I don't even want to see what's in store for me. Big or small, horned or polled, black and white, red and white, brown, blue, black, green, half dead or otherwise, I don't care.

So long as it isn't another one of those half-gassed accident cows that they needed seven winches to tow out of their cesspit.

Why don't the farmers cover over their shitholes, or at least keep a better watch over their animals.

I don't want to see their stinking filth.

But you'll do as you're told.

Not much longer.

And you can slaughter it.

Yes, and I can slaughter it.

A scream. The scream of an animal in terror.

In the calf slaughterhall, old Rötlisberger is pulling a rabbit out of a cardboard box. He holds it by the scruff of its neck, hits it just in front of the ears with a sawn-off piece of broom handle, loops a noose round its rear feet, and hangs it up on the rack. The rabbit wriggles. It swings back and forth like the calves did before. Only harder.

Rötlisberger grins at me.

Yes, I'm a rabbit farmer.

In the box, a jumble of little bundles of fur: Belgian Giants, Pied and Black.

The sound of loud laughter comes from the canteen.

They're drinking again.

Rötlisberger shakes his head.

Who?

Gilgen, Hugentobler – a whole bunch of them.

Is Gilgen back then?

And Ambrosio?

It must have been them who painted the bull on the wall.

On the outside wall of the great cattle hall, someone's drawn the most enormous bull. In blood.

Really?

I saw it. It covered half the wall.

Well.

Rötlisberger shakes his head and smokes.

He's in a bad mood.

Go up to people: Tell me about yourself! Tell me everything you know! I'd like to quiz Rötlisberger. Listen to him. Cow stories. Jokes.

Talking is hard.

The way those rabbits squeak!

Not for much longer.

I pull a black-and-white dappled one out of the box, and hold it out to Rötlisberger.

Hey! Not by the ears!

But you're just about to . . .

Doesn't matter. Not by the ears.

I pick up the rabbit by its scruff. It wriggles.

What shall I say?

Is there going to be roast rabbit at the Rötlisbergers' tomorrow?

Oh no. We don't eat them all ourselves; I'm selling these to the Italians.

He's a fast worker.

Some of them when he hits them relax their paws, others pull them in convulsively. The slit throats bleed. Feebly. They don't overflow, the way pigs do. A dozen rabbits are hanging on the rack, wriggling.

Rötlisberger sharpens a knife.

There, now let's pull the wool over their eyes.

Why do you leave a rabbit's back paws on?

Why?

So you can tell it isn't a cat. A cat's got a different-shaped skull, less pointed, but when the head's taken off, and you buy a bunny without paws, you're buying a cat in a sack.

Now he's grinning.

But surely not any more. Who slaughters cats nowadays?

Ha, if you knew. Be careful. His face is quite lopsided from talking with a BRISSAGO in his mouth.

You can hear the pigs the other side of the sliding door.

Ah, yes. If it weren't for meat inspection, there would be some nasty goings-on. As there were in the War. How old are you now?

Eighteen.

You're young. Cheer up! In the War, by God there were a few people around who couldn't tell the difference between a rabbit and a cat. Or a calf and a dog.

I don't believe it.

It's true. Especially those big St Bernards, they were used in sausages a lot. You've got no idea how people used to tuck into dogs. Well, and in the War, even an old donkey on its last legs suddenly got turned into a little horse in the slaughterhouse.

The rabbits look cold without their fur.

How quickly their squeaking stopped. But the pigs, they're still at it.

If you ask me, there's not that much wrong with it: meat is meat.

Yes, meat is meat.

And it doesn't grow on trees, not yet anyway. While hunger, real hunger, nothing at all to eat, no bones, you know, nothing, absolutely nothing. That exists too, doesn't it?

Suppose so.

Well. It's true then.

Think of what dogs get to eat.

And cats.

Nothing but the best. Not just lungs any more. Liver. Nice cutlets. Lean mince.

Rötlisberger scrapes fat off the inside of a skin.

Yes, those bucks, they're healthy. Plump. Get lots of parsley when they're young. It's good for them. Gives them strong bones. Vitamins.

He pulls the scraped skin over a hide-stretcher.

I think of the pig slaughter. What position will I be chosen for?

Everyone laughs at Rötlisberger. The way he sits on his VELO-SOLEX in his leather jacket, his crash-helmet and his goggles. He needs protection. Wraps up against stone and asphalt.

They laugh at Hugentobler too.

Everyone laughs at everyone else.

Should I ask?

What is . . . Is it true that . . . ? I mean . . . Is it true that . . . ?

Rötlisberger stops. He looks up from his rabbits and looks at me.

I . . .

I can tell you, and who knows how long I'll be staying here, but Buri talks a lot of baloney. If anyone listened to him, it might get quite ugly. Chicago this, Chicago that, at SWIFT & CO. we . . . He's so much hot air.

Hasn't he ever really been to America then?

Buri? And how! His left foot's still there. Ha, you didn't know that, did you? But that's how it is. It was amputated. Exactly.

Buri?

A wooden leg.

So that's why he limps.

No, he never talks about it. And he only changes when there's no one else around. First in in the morning, last to go at night. Schnurri-Buri.

Rötlisberger slits the rabbits open.

Just think about it, God! He hates the foreigners. He used to be one.

They took everything off him in America. Everything.

Yes. I've seen a few go there. Like Buri. Before the oil crisis. Each of them a Columbus in his left foot, and another Rockefeller in his right.

Listen to me, lad. He missed once, when he was splitting oxen. Imagine: splitting oxen for days on end.

And the foot went.

And what did it teach him? Not this much. Not this much. Rötlisberger clenches his fist furiously.

Not this much.

The fool.

And now he brags. Prating on about SWIFT & CO.

There were a few others around, and they saw Chicago differently. Maybe it didn't go to their heads quite so much. Progress, Christ! Progress! Straight into the jaws of death.

When our little association here used to be something like a trade union, there was this book. I remember it. It was green. Green as a cow's stomach. It was called *The Jungle*. That told you what it was really like in Chicago. It was obscene. The biggest obscenity on earth. It wasn't just oxen and swine that were slaughtered and broken up. The odd butcher finished up filling a can. Exactly.

Rötlisberger plucks the innards out of the rabbits' bellies. Liver and heart are left in. He chucks the little grey-green sacs in the waste.

Buri's got a wooden leg.

Time to start again soon.

His leg.

Just went.

Like Ambrosio's finger?

Yes, it's time to get back.

I wash my hands.

Rötlisberger sluices away the traces of his rabbit slaughter with a hose.

There, that's that done. Maybe just time for a half at Rösi's.

Rötlisberger dries his hands on his sacking apron.

Here, if you want a towel.

How did Buri take it?

Buri in Chicago.

And Ambrosio?

: 11 :

After Livestock-dealer Schindler had taken him to the slaughterhouse behind the high fence at the edge of the beautiful city, how did Ambrosio's engagement there proceed?

Smoothly and without complications. Bössiger inquired as to Ambrosio's marital status, then said, yes, they preferred married men, because they worked harder, and would always agree to do overtime. Part-time Custom-butcher Überländer was paid an agency fee. The terms of the residence permit were quickly altered. Ah well, as it was the slaughterhouse, it would be possible to make an exception and turn a blind eye, said the official on the telephone.

What were Ambrosio's first and enduring impressions of his new workplace?

The clattering of the bone-saws, the humming of the ventilators and coolers, the noise as a whole. Then the pervasive smell of blood. Also the posture of the workers as they went home at the end of the day, as bowed and stooped as if they had been on the losing side in a war.

Where was Ambrosio housed?

He and three colleagues shared a converted attic in an old tenement belonging to the company.

How was the tenement off for sanitary facilities?

They were inadequate. There was neither bath nor shower. Every Saturday, Ambrosio would go to the municipal swimming-baths for a thorough wash and scrub. He liked standing under the hot shower and letting the water patter down on his scalp. Soon he developed an insatiable urge to lather and scrub himself. To the amusement of his fellows, he was exceptionally painstaking in the way he styled his few wisps of hair, training them right across the top of his head with the help of pomade. The weekly visit to the baths became an indispensable ritual for him.

What were Ambrosio's earnings like?

Compared to Coruña, very good. Other comparisons were at first not available to Ambrosio at all, and later not in sufficient measure.

In what form was Ambrosio paid?

In cash. The banknotes, together with a counterfoil for social security payments, came in a window envelope. The envelopes were handed out by Foreman Krummen. Payday was every other Friday. After work, the men stood in line, bumping and barging each other playfully, trying to look over each other's shoulders, making jokes, barely able to wait for their turn to come.

What particularly attracted Ambrosio's attention?

The fact that the majority of the men thanked Krummen as they picked up their envelopes.

What chiefly characterized the work in the city, as against that on Knuchel's farm?

Principally its monotony, the result of the extreme division of labour practised in the slaughterhouse. However, the fact that Ambrosio now found himself among people who spoke the same language as he did was an inestimable compensation for this.

But did Ambrosio makes no efforts to learn the language of the country?

Yes he did. Great efforts. He wanted to get away from the speechlessness that had made his positon in Innerwald so difficult. However, the language courses of the various adult education institutes began very early in the evening. Tired and without having eaten, Ambrosio still forced himself to attend one for some weeks. Finally he gave up. When he then discussed another possibility with colleagues, and proposed to the slaughterhouse management that the company itself might usefully organize courses for its foreign employees, this was dismissed as unnecessary.

What was the result of Ambrosio's fruitless endeavours?

He acquired a few phrases of abattoir German, but otherwise shared the indifference, prevalent among his foreign colleagues, towards the affairs of a society of which they did not feel themselves a part.

What were the names of Ambrosio's friends and acquaintances?

Giovanni, Mario, Diego, José, Pasquale, Domenico, Fernando,

Juan, Vincenzo, Nicanor, Manuel, Félix, Ernesto, Marcial, Domingo, Luigi, Enrique, Ignacio, Luis, Manuel García, Chicuelo, Vicente, Mauro, Fabrizio, Roberto.

How did the numerous inhabitants of the beautiful city refer to workers of foreign origin?

Salami-Turks, knife-stickers, hod-carriers, skirt-chasers, video gamesters, dagos, no-guest-in-my-house workers, Spaghetti-Chinese, smelly feet, Fiat-stallions, gypsies, money-senders, fornicators, exploiters, pimps, Chestnut-Fritzes.

Why did Ambrosio never go to the bar in his own street?

Because guest-workers were not allowed in there. There was a sign on the door to that effect.

Was Ambrosio himself ever the object of xenophobia?

Oh yes.

For instance?

At the Kursaal on Saturday nights, a biggish dance orchestra would sometimes play lively southern tunes. Ambrosio was a good dancer. He saw a woman who reminded him of Coruña. She was wearing a white blouse, red shoes, and black skirt. 'Le gusta bailar, sí sí por favor!' he said, going up to her. But she turned to her friend and asked: 'What do you think he wants, Sophie?' Her friend replied that he probably had a screw loose somewhere. 'Sí, sí, bailamos!' insisted Ambrosio, and twirled round his own raised arm, making the little table shake. She of the black skirt and white blouse hid behind her friend's back, and said: 'Nix dance with Italianos!'

Could such an episode be described as an unfortunate exception?

No, quite the opposite. Once, an acquaintance of Ambrosio's was almost arrested for singing an Italian song on the street. Someone took such exception to this that he called the police.

Where did Ambrosio's friends often spend their days off?

At the station.

What would Ambrosio do before leaning against the railing outside the station, for an hour's smoking and chatting and laughing?

He would wipe the dirt off the railing with his handkerchief.

Which sentences of German did Ambrosio soon come to master?

1. 'Attention, please! The express train is due in on Platform . . .'

2. 'All passengers please board the train and shut the doors behind you.'

3. 'The buffet car is at the rear of the train.'

4. 'The doors on this train will close automatically.'

Why these?

Because Ambrosio liked to walk along the platform.

To what class of person did Ambrosio feel himself strongly drawn?

To waitresses. Behind their professional friendliness, their trained public front, he suspected they had a degree of self-confidence most people lacked. He admired the ease with which these women could defuse potentially unpleasant confrontations. The way they stood, looking for the right change under their white frilly aprons, or at the cash desk, one knee bent and slightly in front of the other, making out a bill, as though oblivious of all the looks hovering at the back of their necks.

Why, on the other hand, did Ambrosio feel pity and sympathy for foreign waiters, feelings that prompted him to leave generous tips?

Because foreign waiters seemed to him like driven animals, because most of the clientele would constantly poke fun at their imperfect or accented speech, because all foreign waiters seemed to have flat feet, because he read terrible sorrows in their faces, because Ambrosio thought that even abattoir work was more humane than being hustled from table to table, spurred on by dissatisfied faces, unfriendliness, complaints of all kinds, and always in a white jacket, always in a tie, and never allowed to have an opinion of their own.

When Ambrosio once expressed himself to this effect, what conversation could be heard in the changing room of the municipal slaughterhouse?

– That he himself had worked in the hotel industry before coming there.

– Really? As what?

– As waiter and room service.

– Where?

– In a cow hotel.

What were Ambrosio's relations with his colleagues like?

Very good. Ambrosio was popular. He was cheerful, made many jokes, and was able to infect the whole of the workforce with his good humour, and make the work easier for all of them.

What was Ambrosio's style of humour?

Ambrosio was something of a clown. He would pretend to be smaller or stupider than he really was. For instance, with his rubber apron as a red cloth and a cow for the bull, he staged a bull-fight in the pens at the back, to loud calls of Olé. Or he would scratch his head under his beret with a bloodied finger, and when he dropped the beret on the floor, there would be a red cross on his scalp.

With which of the butchers did Ambrosio hit it off from the start?

With Ernest Gilgen, who was about three heads taller than himself.

What was it about Ambrosio that first attracted the attention of his colleagues?

His tinderbox. They laughed because it seemed old fashioned and cumbersome. Also because Ambrosio swore that as soon as the ball of tinder was used up, he would go to Spain.

Did he keep his word?

Yes, after three years he went for the first time. He wanted to bring his wife and children back with him, but only returned with a new ball of tinder rope. The government had foiled his hopes by making an agreement with Spain, that wives and young children should not be allowed to follow their working menfolk to the small country.

What were the adverse consequences of this visit?

Profound apathy, loneliness, and depression. Free time in the no-man's-land between slaughterhouse, bed, baths, supermarket and station, became a torment for him. Some Saturdays he was already looking forward to Monday morning. He sometimes tried to sleep right through Sunday. He would try to convince himself that he was still asleep, that he was dreaming, even though he had been lying awake for hours.

How often did Ambrosio visit Innerwald?

Once only. To visit Luigi on the Boden farm, to tell him about conditions in town.

Was it then that Luigi decided to work at the slaughterhouse?

Yes.

How was Ambrosio received on the Knuchel farm? Did they remember him?

Ambrosio went walking on the Galgenhubel with Luigi. He sat

on the side of the road, below the little wood, and looked down on the Knuchel pastures. He counted the cows, and tried to recognize them from a distance. A milking machine had been installed on the farm. Otherwise nothing seemed to have changed. He did not want to go down there himself.

Did Ambrosio bear Farmer Knuchel a grudge?

No. He often spoke about Innerwald and the Knuchel farm as something dream-like, unreal.

Was it perhaps the news that Fritz Mäder, the field-mouser of Innerwald, had hanged himself from a fir tree near the shooting range that deterred Ambrosio from making further visits to the highlands?

Possibly.

What was the greatest material acquisition that Ambrosio made?

A bicycle (make of TIGRA).

What amused Ambrosio about the others, only for him to do the same himself?

The widespread enthusiasm for gloves among slaughterhouse employees. Many could imagine nothing more elegant on a woman, and they would often talk about that. If talk was of presents, someone would usually make the suggestion: 'Buy her a pair of gloves, that's always useful and beautiful too.' Ambrosio took his wife a pair of fine kid gloves. The children were given woollen ones.

How long had Ambrosio been employed at the slaughterhouse?

Seven years.

What was the work he hated most?

Feeding meat into the mincing machine, which he had to do for weeks once to the exclusion of all other tasks. Every morning at six o'clock, he would go off into the machine room, to feed tonne after tonne of partly thawed frozen meat into the funnel of the mincing machine. Since the meat was like ice, the circulation of Ambrosio's hands suffered. He was troubled by the conviction that he had only insentient stumps at the end of his arms.

How does a mincing machine work?

'In a casing with screw threads, a worm-conveyor pushes meat against cutting tools: perforated steel sheets, between or in front of which are revolving blades.' (Brockhaus)

Why did Ambrosio often wake up in the middle of the night?

There was a rock-hard vibration in the inside of the mincing machine, comparable to the gurgling from a bottomless gorge, and this vibration had slowly transmitted itself from the shaking machine casing to Ambrosio's body. It was particularly bad when pieces of bone or cartilage got into the cutters. Whenever Ambrosio heard that happen, he would swear at the machine, Krummen, the slaughterhouse, and the whole country where everything seemed to be turning incessantly as on the worm-conveyor in the mincing machine. And if he dreamed of the noise, Ambrosio would wake up sweating.

How did Ambrosio try to avenge himself on the machine?

He pummelled its iron plating with his numb fists. He tried to break it by over-feeding it. He pressed as much meat as he possbily could into the gullet of the machine at one go. But it kept turning and grinding and spitting out everything he crammed into it, without losing its composure.

What happened when Bössiger caught Ambrosio kicking the machine?

Krummen brought Ambrosio orders that the frozen meat needed to be passed through the machine twice. At the same time, he was able to report that there would soon be more fresh meat on the market, and that, therefore, Ambrosio's unpleasant task would no longer be necessary.

What did Ambrosio do when shortly afterwards his right hand emerged from a pile of meat above the machine's gorge missing the middle finger?

Holding the hand out before him, he went to the office of the vet, Dr Wyss, and in complete bewilderment rested it on a pile of letters, forms and meat-inspection reports.

Did he cry?

Yes.

What did Bössiger then successfully look for in the mincing machine?

Ambrosio's pulped finger. To avoid the sausage-meat having to be impounded.

How did Bössiger say he was able to recognize it?

By the colour. He had seen a lighter coloured patch.

Was that Ambrosio's worst experience in the slaughterhouse?

One of the worst.

:12:

Hands stroked callouses, stroked wounds, smoothed over strained wrists and finger joints. Where was the scab that had been there this morning . . . ?

Hands probed at nails torn loose, they massaged wrists, skin rubbing skin, the hands turned, faced each other, palm against palm, and for an instant were folded as in prayer, and hands with the strength to grip knives, to work and graft away, to move mountains of flesh and bone, these hands now lay on the tables of the little slaughterhouse canteen: rosy bunches of sausage fingers, trembly flesh, exhausted animals.

They lay next to glasses, or they were holding playing cards. The forearms too were dry, and the bodies of the abattoir workers relaxed in their unbuttoned working clothes. Grateful lungs sucked in smoke from cigarettes and cigars, and *during working hours employees are strictly forbidden to indulge in alcoholic drinks and tobacco*, and under the table, feet were resting in boots: It was still the lunch hour.

– Oh, this is so terrible! The landlady spilt coffee, served warm beer, took it back again. Heavens above! You can't imagine how awful I felt. What was I to do? He was clinging onto me, as though he never meant to let go. Such a heavy man! Without fingering the coins, without counting them, Frau Bangerter just slipped the money she took into her apron pocket. And when he was lying on the floor, just there, and not moving a muscle, God, I thought for a moment that's it, he's dead.

– Oh, it'll take more than a tongue-lashing from Bössiger about a poxy fox calf to kill Schindler, said Pretty Boy Hügli. Fritz Überländer straightaway concurred:

– Just because Bössiger shows his teeth a bit? That'd make a horse laugh! It would take one hell of a row to finish Schindler.

– And one hell of a thunderbolt to crack his thick belly, said Huber and arranged the cards in his hand.

– Well, but if he goes on drinking schnapps, then I'm not so sure, said Überländer.

– It's nothing to do with schnapps, Gilgen butted in. He spoke loudly to make himself heard above the squealing of the pigs.

– What is it then? What else, if not schnapps?

The three card players turned their heads and Gilgen got to his feet. It's his blood. Schindler's got too much blood in him!

Frau Bangerter plucked at her hair, covered her ears with her hands, and said: 'What's the matter today? Those pigs! The way they're grunting! All day they've been going like that!'

– Here, sit down, have a cup of coffee. Buri pulled Frau Bangerter down onto a chair. You mustn't take Gilgen so seriously, the stuff he comes out with. God knows what they did to him at the Red Cross.

– Did you even go? asked Pretty Boy Hügli. Or was donating blood just another one of your jokes?

– You should try going yourself! Gilgen sat down again.

– Oh, he's much too sensible to let those fools have all his worldly bloods. Rötlisberger walked into the canteen, stood behind Gilgen, drew on a BRISSAGO, and kept one hand tucked under the bib of his apron. Giving blood! What an idea! It takes you to come up with something like that. But you were just taking the day off, eh? But you're right enough, Ernest, right enough.

– Nom de Dieu, Fritz, you should have seen it! Gilgen put his arm round Rötlisberger's shoulder. Those little nurses in their little white uniforms! Feast your eyes on them! Not even one little stain on their aprons. And blondes, the lot of them blondes. So you lie on one of these beds, with a tube stuck in your arm, and there's guys either side of you, and they're being tapped too, and the place is as quiet as anything, and these nurses are twinkling back and forth, and you can practically see their legs through their white skirts, and not a drop of blood anywhere. None at all, Fritz! No blood. Just in the plastic bag, and it's so dark, darker than an old sausage-cow's blood, nom de Dieu, Fritz! It's a clean, well-ordered business, donating blood, and they could teach us a thing or two, they don't splash it all over the walls. And I said to one of the nurses: You should come and see us do it some time, over at the slaughterhouse. And then afterwards, everyone gets a sandwich and coffee with a little red cross on the cup, and there's these little red crosses all over the shop, the nurses even have them on their udders. And you know, Fritz, when they take the needle out of your arm here, do you think they make a mess? They don't lose a drop of it! Nom de Dieu, if only Schindler had gone there . . .

– What, you mean instead of making black pudding out of it at home, eh, giggled Rötlisberger, and Buri growled:

– If only Aschi Gilgen would work nineteen to the dozen too!

– So long as they don't try passing it on to me, said Pretty Boy Hügli. And Huber and Hofer wondered why he hadn't just stayed there at the Red Cross if he'd liked it so much. He should show them just how gifted he was at drawing blood. But Gilgen overheard their remarks. He stood up and glared at Hügli.

– Hey, say that again!

– Didn't you hear me?

– Say it again!

Bloodshot eyes avoided each other, jaws worked, lower lips trembled, hands reached nervously for beer and cigarettes.

– I said I didn't want to be the one to get your blood! said Hügli.

– It's enough to give anyone the creeps, said Huber, and Hofer said:

– Sooner die than run around with Château Gilgen in your veins!

The muscles lifted on Gilgen's arm, and his fist smashed down on the table. Glasses shook, coffee spoons rattled in saucers. Gilgen went back to his chair. Arseholes!

– Why don't you stop bullocking around? Buri laid a hand on his shoulder. Not now. When you can see they're holding a knife to our throats. We're drowning in work, with all the animals they say they're having to shoot, and first you leave us in the lurch, and now when you come back you talk garbage. Get your gear on! Hey! Where's your butcher's blouse? Your boots! Give us a hand! Listen to those sows! They've unloaded over three hundred of the cunts.

– Forget it! Hügli waved his hand dismissively. We don't need him. If he thinks he's too good for us. What do we have to go to him on bended knee for?

301

– He's just here for Spreussiger anyway, the randy sod, said Hofer.

– Well, if it's that, let him at least screw her good and proper. Hügli gathered the cards together. So she leaves the rest of us in peace.

Rötlisberger laughed. See what you've done now? Hey, Aschi . . . God Almighty, Ambrosio! What's up with you?

– Here, Gilgen, flowers! Ambrosio stood in the doorway with a bunch of gladioli.

– Him too. And what do you want? asked Buri.

Ambrosio had stripped off his blood-drenched clothes in the changing room. The sodden material had stuck to his arms and legs. He had stood under the shower for a long time, sniffing at himself, and cursing the sweet bloodsmell. Then, without getting annoyed about the placement of the mirror, which was far too high for him, he had combed his strands of hair. And he had emptied out his locker. Number 164, going, going. He had torn up his card and watched the pieces flutter to the ground. His rubber boots would be going to Piccolo, everyone else would get a knife each.

Ambrosio had stood in front of the dustbin. He had taken a deep breath and smelled the blood on his work clothes: fresh blood, dried blood, decomposed blood. And only then had he thrown his clothes away.

He had gone out into the main passage of the abattoir, for the first time without lifting his head to look at the clock, and *after a trial period, notice during the first year of employment is two weeks. It must be given at the latest on Saturday for the Saturday but one following, and should take the form of a registered letter,* and then for the last time he had got up on tiptoe and posted his card once and for all into the clocking-in machine at the entrance of the slaughterhouse, and then he had gone on to the kiosk, the kiosk at the main gate of the armaments factory. Big Gilgen had told him to buy flowers. Lots of fresh flowers, he had said, don't forget the flowers, Ambrosio! and *for certain overriding reasons, both employee and employer may terminate their contract with immediate effect,* and now the little Spaniard stood in the canteen doorway, and saw the bottles, the glasses, the landlady, the smoke and all the faces. He saw the way they were looking at him, some in disbelief, others in outrage, and once more the thought crossed his mind that they must have colossal quantities of snow under their skin. Un montón de nieve. But the little fellow had stopped playing the foreign worker! How about a little respect? Why is he standing there like that? A bit of chat, some incomprehensible witticism, OK, but this dumb insolence! What's wrong, what's the matter, what do you want? Did he know it wasn't quite the thing for Italians just to wander off in the middle of slaughtering, until now things had been run in a fairly orderly way, so it was appropriate to say something now, and what the hell was he up to, what was he thinking of, what was he playing at, and what if everyone, and what if the regular butchers among them didn't, and then he popped up in the bar in his Sunday clothes just as if nothing had happened, flaming cheek, yes, that's right, cheeky little bugger, and it wasn't as though he was the only one who something had ever happened to, accidents did happen, and worse ones than just his finger too, and he should stop playing the innocent, and really he was just laughing at them the whole time because it was them who were doing the brunt of the work, and Ambrosio's head tilted further and further over to the side. So many serious words, so many mouths moving at once, and all on his account, and the whole thing somehow underlined by the screaming of the pigs, but he handed Gilgen the flowers, bracing the yellow petals with one hand, and he moved up a chair and sat down where no Italian, no Spaniard, no Turk and no Yugoslav had ever sat before: Ambrosio sat down at a table in the slaughterhouse canteen, and *for certain overriding reasons, both employee and employer may terminate their contract at any time. Overriding reasons are taken to refer to circumstances in which either party, for reasons of morality, or otherwise in good faith, finds the continuation of their relationship impossible*, and Ambrosio rubbed his hands, ordered a beer, birra, cerveza, and said not a word besides.

– Until now, you've always drunk your Chianti in the changing room. Intestine-man Hans-Peter Buri choked and coughed. Why do you have to come in here, and inflict your Italian on us in the only place we've got left?

– Anyone would think the Spaniard had done something to offend you personally.

– You stay out of it, Fritz! You especially! You're off your head anyway. Whose job is it they're taking now, eh? Whose? It's yours, not mine!

– Well, Christ, what's that to do with Ambrosio?

– And what if all the foreigners show up here? Pretty Boy Hügli had stood up. If you can't play a quiet game of cards in here, because they're monkeying around, the way they do in the changing room now, then where are you going to go then?

– Then it'll be too late! Buri too got up. Then we'll have been had again! And Hofer said:

– Quite right!

Huber too pushed his chair back, agreed with Hofer, waved his wallet at Frau Bangerter, and said, as he put the coins on the table, that Ambrosio was just running away from hard work, and that was the doing of those two gentlemen, their influence. Left to himself, he hadn't been a bad lot.

But they would see, said Hofer, it wasn't all over yet by any means.

One o'clock.

Drops of rain on the glass roof.

On with the show.

We start in the killing bay.

Piccolo, Luigi, Fernando, Pasquale, Eusebio and me.

In the pig-killing bay.

Get rid of those bloody ciggies!

Krummen.

Sí, sí. Bene, bene!

The killing bay is at the back of the pig slaughterhall. It looks like a stage covered with tiles. A white, walled-in platform. When it's clean and empty, it looks harmless enough. Menacing in its sterility. There's something about it, this bay.

– Get the first lot in!

They're screaming. The other side of the sliding door.

There are drains all over the floor. I'm standing on the middle of a huge kerbstone. If you turn on the tap, the pigs will start to flow.

This is where the slaughtering line begins. On the left is the scalding-tub, behind that the dehairing machine. Then chutes of iron tubing. Work surfaces. Hydraulic hanging gear. The empty spreaders like great coathangers on the overhead rail.

Krummen prowls.

Luigi and Pasquale and Piccolo are in the first waiting pen.

High-pitched squealing, interspersed with grunts.

Where are the rest of them? Huber? Hofer? Hügli? Buri? Überländer?

The sliding door opens.

The first of the pigs.

They stop, sniffing. They are a refined country breed, with long ears above their eyes. Their pink snouts tremble over the ground. Examining every square millimetre.

They don't like it.

Too late.

Others are coming after.

The shouts of the drovers: hey hup! Yah fucka sow! Porca miseria!

Piccolo and Pasquale are armed with lengths of rubber hose, Luigi with an electric goad. It's a kind of staff, like a battery torch, with two electrodes at the end. On contact, the pig gets a slight shock, squeals, and jumps in the air. With any luck, in the direction you want it to go in.

Pasquale! Pasquale! Attenzione!

The herd is trying to do a U-turn.

Porca miseria! Pasquale lashes out. With rubber boots and rubber hosepipe. They leave red streaks.

Hans Locher is the man responsible for knocking them out. He's a company man. Supervisor. He stands waiting in a corner of the killing bay, checks his firearm, and picks shells out of a box. Little copper cartridges that he slips into his right trouser pocket.

We catch the pigs.

By the hindlegs.

Cemented into the walls of the killing bay, at 3-metre intervals, about half a metre off the floor, are a set of hooks.

A rope round the ham, the iron ring at the other end onto the nearest hook, and you've tied your hog.

You rarely succeed first time round.

The trick is to loop the rope just in front of the pig's hooves, get it to take another step, and then not to let go.

If there's no hook to hand, we have to drag the struggling creatures across the floor. For metres. And they fight for their lives. You hurt your hands.

Luigi is the expert here.

He can lay two loops at once, and catch a pig with each hand. They set off in opposite directions. Luigi stands in the middle and laughs.

Or he plays the torero.

Hey! Hey!

Locher yells at Fernando, who's lamming into a screaming pig with his rubber piping.

Not like that! Maybe they do that where you come from. These sows here, you just catch. I'll silence them. And no kicking. Got it?

Alwess you gomplain!

And suddenly I'm in the middle of it.

Yah, get those sows on the hooks!

I'm a stoker on the ship of Death. Only, instead of coals, I lug struggling pigs.

Krummen's standing by the scalding-tub, checking the temperature of the water. He looks up: What about the frigging butchers? Where've they got to?

He holds the thermometer in his left hand, his right is digging into his trousers.

Someone's to go to the canteen.

If the gentlemen require personal invitations.

And get Hugentobler out of the chilling-room!

The tied pigs are all higgledy-piggledy. They try to pull free. Hindlegs kick air like machine parts, tighten the ropes around the trotters.

The smell!

Grunting and shrieking, in all kinds of different pitches. Those animals that are trapped underneath others sound weak and miserable. Hoarse. Slobber froths over their jaws. Many of them piss and shit over each other and themselves.

I'm on the trail of the last pig.

It dodges the noose, runs off, at a canter, drops back into its wobbly trot. Turns its fat, low-slung rump to me.

Sometimes pigs walk like prostitutes: High-heeled, dainty-footed, hip-swinging.

Missed again.

Bastard.

I can see the pigskin through the bristles. Dry, light pink, floury.

I give it one with the rope across its back.

The pig's got a damaged ear. Docked, as a distinguishing mark.

A pig that escapes castration by not dropping them both into its scrotum gets given a mark in the cartilage of its ear. Its flesh can stink, can be as inedible as a ram's.

The last pig's been tied.

Now here comes Locher.

He clears a way through the grunting pigs' heads, and gets into position to shoot. He stands in the middle of a bunch of them radiating out from a hook.

Squealing.

Those screaming snouts between stretched-out trotters.

Locher puts the muzzle down on its neck, and the pig flattens itself to the ground, then Locher climbs the ridge of fat behind its ears, his hand is steady, the steel moves on the flat skull, carries on, to just above the eyes, there Locher adjusts the angle, and the black bolt-hole is bang in the middle of the head. Alas, poor pig!

Who will remember it with affection and gratitude?

The funeral will not take place. Not even family and a few close friends.

I'm coming.

I pull my apron back, and put a basin down beside the throat of the keeled-over pig to collect its blood.

It's stiff.

My left knee is on the pig's neck, with my right boot I block its snout, with my left hand I pull its upper foreleg back.

I stick it.

I push the knife in flat, aim it towards the tail, and give the point a quick turn.

The blood spurts up in a red arc.

The pig is held as in a vice.

I am the vice.

I move the vessel to catch the blood. The flow will let up after fifteen seconds.

Locher has carried on shooting. I move on to the next sow.

The others have been busy too. Little red fountains bubble up out of the pigs.

And Krummen's shouting again.

I kneel on my third pig.

What's going on in the canteen?

After just three, four pigs we are covered in blood.

The air is red.

– That's just it, Pretty Boy Hügli interrupted Huber and Hofer in the little canteen. Ever since that Tyrolean began swaggering around as if the whole slaughterhouse belonged to him, ever since then there's been a devil of a mess here. Just look at him! Half drunk at this time of day. But big as you are, said Hügli, getting up on tiptoe, big as you are, you'll be out on your ear!

– I'm not drunk.

– Tell that to Hugentobler, not me.

– Je ne suis pas soûl.

– Why talk like a drunk then?

– J'ai dit que je ne suis pas soûl. Gilgen spoke quietly. And as for being thrown out of here, Hügli, I tell you something else will happen before that.

Huber pushed Hügli away from Gilgen, and *the employee is under contractual obligation to observe scrupulously the prescribed working hours*, and the big bodies of the butchers bulked in the doorway, the higher pitched squealing of the pigs indicated that work had begun in the killing bay.

– We ought to, said Fritz Überländer. Go on Gilgen, Ambrosio, get changed. Come on! For Chrissake! What are you shaking your heads for? Then at least you come, Fritz, don't you start too!

– Give Krummen my regards, replied Rötlisberger and swivelled right round on his stool, smoking. Huber and Hofer, Hügli and Buri were still all standing in the doorway. Well off you go then! Chop chop! Or are you planning on spending the night there? Knocking Ambrosio's one thing.

– I've just about had enough of you, you old fool. Pretty Boy Hügli took a step back inside the canteen, and called Rötlisberger a stupid, ancient, veal calf. A calf that thought itself smarter than a cow. What a sheep's prong! In fact, the old triper was as thick as a

308

bull's pizzle. The biggest pizzle in the world, said Hügli, and Buri wheezed, joined in, he was a right fool, and why wasn't he glad to be able to work at the new machine, what was he being so pig-headed about? He didn't have any right to talk such tripe. And where had he been yesterday when they were dunking the student in the blood-tank? Buri asked old Rötlisberger. Eh, where? Why, he'd been hiding behind a salt barrel, giggling like a little girl. That was Rötlisberger for you. A two-faced bastard. Exactly! said Hofer, there was Bössiger already running down the passage towards them, and old pork-belly here was still shouting: grab his willy. And now that little idiot of a student had been seen around again, and apparently he was taking photographs.

– Well, now all the scum's risen to the surface, hasn't it? Rötlisberger laid his BRISSAGO in the ashtray, hooked his thumbs in the bib of his apron, and spat at Hügli's feet. Why, your face is still green, you slime-shitter! Rötlisberger stood up, Hügli retreated. Have you any idea how long I've been working here for? That should give a man the right to open his mouth, eh? Now get out of here. Huber and Hofer withdrew, Hügli and Buri followed.

– You're yellow, and you're green, like double-slimed pig's guts! Rötlisberger shouted after them. Take a look at your snot-rags some time. You think that's just your snot in them. Well, I can tell you the last of your calves' brains have just been blown out between your fingers! Yeah, God! Snot-brains! And you've got terminal hair loss. Who was it held your potato heads with pincers and boiled them in nitric acid? Eh? Any calf's head's got more jelly between its ears than you have between the lot of you! Stupid jackasses! While Rötlisberger roared after them, he stood stiffly upright in his wooden clogs, rowing in the air with his arms, as though he had trouble keeping his balance.

– Gah! Go crawl back up his arse, you stacked-up lymph nodes! What do you know about breeding animals, you bunch of mercenaries! You wipe your pustular spleen-tongues round your dribble-noses, and you imagine you've spoken! You couldn't stand as godfathers to an erysipeletic pig, in fact you'd better look out in case they take you for pigs, so watch out for the man with the gun-gun! But then again you're so stuffed with cotton wool anyway, they could smash you on the head with a forehammer, and you wouldn't blink! But you just wait, he slaughters best who slaughters last!

Shaking their heads, and stabbing at their temples with their fingers, the men had tied on their aprons. They joined the bloody welter of the killing bay late.

Rötlisberger giggled. He tucked his head in, swung a fist to and fro in front of his body, stamped a clog on the floor, and sloshed back through a puddle.

– There, that's settled their hash! That did me good, he said, as he sat down on his chair in the canteen. But what's with you two?

Gilgen was bending over a bag on the floor between his feet, a red-and-green-checked sports bag. Ambrosio was blowing smoke rings.

– Did I say an untruth? asked Rötlisberger. I had enough. And now I feel like a beer.

Ernest Gilgen sat up, looked at the old triper, took the wrapped flowers off the table, sniffed them and said:

– Tell me, Fritz. Are there any goods left?

– Anything left in the pens? Yes, they unloaded an emergency. Why?

– What is it?

– A cow, said Rötlisberger. What else would it be?

– What kind? A Simmental?

– No, it's a little black thing of an Eringer. But what the devil's going on now?

– An Eringer in the pen! Gilgen had leaped to his feet. Fritz! An Eringer! That's just what we need! Nom de Dieu! We'll drink to her! What was it you said out there a moment ago? He slaughters best who slaughters last.

On your workplaces, get set, go!

Krummen strode along the slaughter line, and circled the newly installed intestine-washing machine. His rubber apron smacked against his boots. He looked at the waiting containers, and kicked at the empty trough.

– I want pigs hanging here! Why aren't there any pigs up yet? Those bastards! I'll show them! We start at one o'clock here, sharp! This isn't fucking Butlin's! We're butchers! Krummen went to the back of the scraping machine. The first pig carcass was turning in its drum. Krummen pushed the speed setting to maximum. You gentlemen seem to think this here is a drinking club! The machine's roar intensified, and inside, the pig's feet drummed against the metal walls as it was hurled around, and the men straightened up, listened, scratched their necks. Buri and Überländer exchanged looks, Pretty Boy Hügli squinted at Krummen, said nothing, but his nostrils trembled and dilated, as though to smell their fill of gunpowder, because *pigs are stunned by: the 'poleaxe' or 'knocking-hammer', the 'bolt-axe' (an axe with a gouge-fitted bolt), the 'slaughter mask' (also with bolt), the 'captive bolt-gun' in which a bolt is fired into the brain by a small quantity of explosive, and the 'electric clamp' which quickly knocks any animal unconscious by means of an electric charge to the temple,* and only Pasquale, Eusebio and the apprentice were left in the killing bay. Holding onto ropes and knives, they stood in a blood bath. Time and again they were vigorously baptized red, till they looked like Roman legionnaires standing in the pit of a taurobolium, where once men refreshed themselves with the blood of a bull killed and stuck in seven places on a metal grating over their pit, but Eusebio and Pasquale and the apprentice could draw little strength from the pigs' blood which stuck and crusted on their fingers, itched on their faces, and *'Zap' high-pressure cleaner: the logical way to achieve the outstanding sanitary standards demanded in today's meat trade. Utensils, tables, walls and floors are speedily and effortlessly cleansed of all traces of fat, flesh and blood. In the case of especially unyielding deposits of dirt tucked away in corners, we recommend highly effective 'Zap' cleaning agent,* and the first scalded pigs were about to arrive at the bottom. Thereafter, at intervals of forty-five seconds.

Behind the scraping machine, Huber and Hofer straightened their aprons. They had buckled on their sheaths, wearing the belts on their hips. Hofer spread and clenched his fingers, bit his lip. Huger too was doing finger exercises.

The first bald pig dropped onto the metal frame next to the scraper.

– Here we go, said Huber, and both set to. They gripped the pig's wet legs. With their longest blades they passed over the skin, shaving off any remaining bristles, then, changing the angle of their knives, Huber cut slits in the leg between bone and tendon by which to hang the pig, while Hofer cut through the cheek meat.

Piccolo was waiting.

– Una testa, subito una testa! he yelled.

Hofer slipped his blade along the occipital bone, felt the weak spot in the neck, and nicked the tendon there, pushed away with his left hand, and suddenly the whole of the head tipped back showing a gaping wound behind the ears. Hofer didn't turn round. He let the pig's head fall to the floor.

– La prima testa, porco Dio! Piccolo picked it up by the ears and, holding it high above his head, he jigged from foot to foot. Una testa! he cheered. Water, blood and spittle dribbled onto his shoulders and hair. Una testa!

Then Piccolo took up his knife. He worked on a chopping block. His blades were short and sharp. He set the pig's head down in front of him, with the trunk-like snout facing him. First he stuck out the left eye, then the right, he removed the brows, then cut away the left and right ears: that was it, the first of three hundred heads.

In the meantime, Huber had pushed the body onto the cradle of the hydraulic hanging equipment, and hooked it onto a hoist. Piccolo hung the skull by the lower jaw on the hoist and sent the whole thing on to Hügli.

Pretty Boy Hügli whetted his knife and made an incision from between the hindlegs down to the sternum. He removed the rod and foreskin; a bluey-white serpent on the granite floor.

Hügli had to be careful not to prick the bladder or the intestines. Meat and bacon were not to become contaminated. He cut apprehensively, delicately, feeling for resistance. He wanted to work. His left arm disappeared up to the shoulder into the pig's belly, and came out with a load of steaming entrails which he clasped to his belly and then dropped into a waiting trough.

Soon the second pig was dangling upside down from a hoist. Pig after pig rolled up, at a pitiless pace, and while right from the start they had to get stuck in as never before, the butchers still managed a quick look left and right, each reading the gestures of the others. Hügli studied the expressions of Huber and Hofer, and Huber didn't need to understand the words Luigi's lips were forming, to know that there was someone else cursing the hectic work rate.

And Hugentobler! Without even giving him a couple of minutes to get changed, Krummen had pulled him straight out of the cooler-room and given him a position on the line. Standing behind Hügli in his three pairs of long johns and all his arctic clothing, he was sweating as though he himself was being scalded alive.

Hugentobler had to take the lungs, liver and heart out of the pigs' chests.

The butchers barely had time to sharpen dulling blades on a whetstone. Their faces smeared and sweated, but today none of them was fighting his own battle, they were together converting these pigs, which were pressing into the killing bay at the top in fantail packs, but down at the bottom were in an orderly sequence rolling along the overhead track from station to station in Indian file, and *it took capitalism decades to train a compliant workforce. Even between the wars there was a factory slogan which ran: 'Whoever works and doesn't shirk must be berserk.' The turning point probably came with the beginning of consensus politics in 1937, which pushed socialism and the trade unions into taking an affirmative view of wage labour. Factory discipline increasingly became subsumed into the work-force's own perception of itself, and today it exists in the form of completely internalized self-discipline, as 'the work ethic'*, and keeping his eyes on the pelvic bone of the first gutted pig, Überländer spat on his hands, picked up the cleaver and let it whistle through the air once or twice for practice. He felt his shoulder muscles under his butcher's shirt whose rolled-up sleeves cleared the humps of his biceps. No hold-up would occur on his part of the line! Überländer wound himself up for the first swing of the axe.

The tempo of the slaughter line could not be sustained with this level of undermanning. If one man didn't finish his task on time, the one behind had to do extra, and then risked falling behind in turn.

It was Hugentobler who fared the worst. Hügli watched as the freezer-room worker fell further and further behind. He was three pigs in arrears. His sweaty face had a sickly gleam, like white-glossed wood. He's about to croak, thought Pretty Boy Hügli, and hissed:

– For Christ's sake say something! Get Krummen to help you! Or at least he can slow the fucking scraper down!

Hugentobler didn't say a word, and Foreman Krummen went on his rounds, kept an eye on the machines, made sure that the carcasses that rolled onto Kilchenmann's weighing machine at the hall entrance were all in impeccable condition. Here there was a hair left on a ham, there a drop too much blood on the inside of the ribs, and on one pig, not all of the bone marrow had been scraped out of the split backbone.

– And shave them! Eh! Tidy up a bit there! And you Luigi! Niente dormire! Lavare bene, or else there'll be trouble! E poi niente dimenticare the marrow!

Krummen noticed that Pretty Boy Hügli had already half filled one of the wheeled troughs with entrails. Suddenly very calm, he stood in front of the new intestine-washing machine, rested his hands on his hips, and gazed at the switchboard, the hose connections for water and pressurized air. He looked at every single dial, lever and tap. He stared at the pediment and the chrome-steel veneer, and, as if to wipe away a speck of dust, he brushed his palm over the aluminium table at the front of the machine that served as a work surface. He pulled a lever and pressed a button. The motor hummed, wheels and rollers began to turn, as in a printing-press. Krummen pulled another lever. Water sprayed against the casing from inside and splashed out from underneath. Krummen got down, put his head in the drizzle, and looked up inside the machine. Then he got up, looked around, and, catching sight of Buri over by a water trough, he shouted:

– Buri, come here! You can treat the guts later. I want you to start to get the hang of this machine! I'll show you how it works. Bring that entrail trough over here!

Buri, Hans-Peter, casings specialist, born on 30 October 1909 in a mortar-grey tenement on the edge of the beautiful city. First of seven children. Father, shift-worker in the city gasworks. Occasional hardship. Mother (tubercular) collects firewood, grows cabbages and potatoes on a rented plot.

The bread bin is often empty. Early on, little Hans-Peter suffers from the thought that bread is something that isn't available in unlimited quantities. (When he ate bread, he ate it quickly,

gulping it down, gripping the crust with both hands, and afterwards resting his left hand on his stomach.)

It's the time of the first automobiles, the time of long dresses.

He is a quiet, chubby, sturdy fellow. Little interest in playing.
Throws wooden toys out of the window. He slits open the belly of a
teddy with the bread knife and picks out the stuffing. He might
make a doctor, says his father, who punishes him for performing
the stomach surgery. Or a butcher! What kind of boy would
slaughter his teddy? says his mother, stooping to pick up the bread
knife.

At school he has trouble with authority figures. Violent teachers:
one foams at the mouth when he uses a stick.

Also fear of the janitor, the school doctor, the louse lady. On his
way to school, Hans-Peter throws stones at cats. Then his first toy:
a catapult.

The resources of the Buri family are stretched by the mother's
illness, they owe for the rent. Master-Butcher Affolter, owner of the
tenement, accepts errand-boy and other work from the oldest child
(Hans-Peter, ten) in lieu. The boy gets up with his father. Sleep and
school suffer.

On Saturdays and holidays, Hans-Peter works for Affolter. The
butcher's journeymen often put a knife in his hand. Hans-Peter
picks things up quickly, keeps his eyes and ears open. The
journeymen speak coarsely about love, reverently about the greatest meat-packing plants in the world. The corned-beef mills in
Chicago, they're all whorish big places!

Why does little Peterli talk like that? complains mother. Father
hits him. Hans-Peter hits back, is unrepentant: that's just a
whorish pile of shit! He is bigger and stronger than everyone else
in his class.

When he finishes, all are agreed: Hans-Peter should stay with
Affolter, and serve his apprenticeship there. It's a good place for
him, says the teacher. He'll get his board and lodging, say his
parents. He can do quite a bit already, thinks the master-butcher.

Buri shows off his muscles, and gets his teeth into the work. He
apes the journeymen. Coarse is good, and so is loud and stubborn.

In his apprenticeship, Hans-Peter is mostly called upon to clean
and do bicycle deliveries. The more he enjoys it when he gets a

chance to hold a knife or a cleaver. He boasts, makes a bet. He says he can split a pig with seven blows. The best butchers need twelve to fifteen. Buri loses and can't pay up. He agrees to leave the small window over the shop door open. At night, his friends use a walking-stick to hook up several sides of bacon from Affolter's rack.

The resulting investigation is inconclusive. But an unspoken suspicion rests on Buri. He is called upon to work still harder, and he gets his teeth into that still more rabidly. That apprentice does the work of two men, say many. And Hans-Peter Buri becomes a mighty colossus of a man, given to kicking, spitting on the street and swearing: when he looks up from work, everything's a pile of whores' shit. The sausage-kitchen, the attic at Affolter's, the flat in the tenement, they're all whorish tight and whorish small. Something is decaying inside him. He could smash half the world in pieces. Already he's splitting hogs better, faster, in fewer strokes, than the very best. He's ambitious. What to do with it?

At the end of his apprenticeship, he is advised to specialize. Train to become a sausage-maker! – Bah, what's that! – It's difficult. – Use as little as possible of the good stuff, and as much as possible of the cheap rubbish you've got in stock, then add a bathful of water. – That might make you a good sausage-maker, but they're bad sausages. – Then you add spices, and colour and smoke and polish them up afterwards with an oily rag. That's a pile of whores' shit! Stuff sausage-making! Buri dreams of Chicago.

At cadet school, he gets wind of a government programme to encourage emigration to Canada. And several of them are agreed: Everything here's just a pile of whores' shit!

Buri has his work clothes, wooden-soled boots, knives and tools soldered into an oil barrel, and rolls it from the station at Calais onto the emigration vessel *Klondike* on 11 May 1929.

When the anchors are raised, Buri is standing up on the promenade deck, with the expression of a man going to the butchers' Olympics.

In return for the money for the crossing, Buri has to undertake to work for two years on the railways in the west of Canada. There he chops down trees, piles up ballast, lays track, and swings the pointed sledgehammer. What he likes best is working with an axe.

316

It reminds him of a meat-cleaver, and of his own profession. He learns a few tricks from the lumberjacks.

He experiences the brunt of the Canadian winter, and the scourge of insects in the summer. But he likes the raw human climate, the roughness and directness of the people. He likes sitting in bars where women aren't allowed. Here, when he smashes his fist down on the table, people don't point at him and whisper: He's a butcher, a rough meat-hacker who doesn't know any better.

He spits as frequently and as forthrightly as his workmates.

The men work from sunup to sundown. Mounted foremen shout commands. Drivers keep the work rate high. When Buri lies down on his cot at night, in his tent, he only bothers to pull his boots off. And there's talk about the 'old country'. What it was you did before you came. Yes, says Buri, as a butcher, you always had a piece of bread and a sausage in your hand.

But here they don't eat sausage. Meat is left in its original form, raw and red, with bones and tendons, and great slabs of it lie on Buri's tin plate on the canteen table. Meat and bread. The men work, eat and drink, they have neither time nor energy for anything else. At twenty-one, Buri is a giant. He likes the way that on the official forms, straight after your surname, they ask for your height and weight. They worked it out for him in the new units at the Consulate. Buri writes: 6 feet 3 inches, 207 pounds.

The two-year spell on the railways comes to an end. Buri works for a German-born butcher in Winnipeg. Contact with Poles, Ukrainians, Irish. All speak of Chicago. The slaughterhouse in Winnipeg, one of the world's biggest, has nothing to compare with the 'stockyards', the abattoirs of Chicago, where half the world's lard is produced.

Buri joins the subsidiary of an American meat-packing company. He learns to walk tall, he enters beer-joints with inflated lungs. He is as strong as an ox. He spits at people's feet in the streets.

To entertain the immigrants, unemployed lumberjacks stage tree-felling contests. Buri joins in. He swings his axe, hears the polyglot murmurs of admiration, hears the applause.

And Chicago beckons.

Buri hears that the big firms are hiring strike-breakers. Well, if they don't want to work! He travels to Chicago on a freight train. 'SWIFT & CO.' give him a job as a 'knocker and sticker'. All day, he hits oxen on the head, and jabs a knife in their throats. Buri works to save his life, earns little, casts sidelong glances at the 'splitters', who work with cleavers and earn the most money.

Some of the strike-breakers are Negroes. Freddie Lewis, the slaughterman, and his brother the trimmer, are the first blacks in the red trade of Chicago. Gangsters are hired. Former distillers and smugglers left high and dry by the end of Prohibition. The men work in felt hats, under ceilings that drip blood, with a barrel of water in the corner and a stoup. Buri puts the inadequate sanitation down to a more generous way of thinking. In the changing rooms, the men find mice in their clothes. Buri is entitled to a holiday. One week every five years.

In 1932, Buri is one of 27,869 employees working for twenty-four companies at the corner of Ashland Avenue and Madison Street, near the Bull's Head Market, the meat-centre of the world. Buri is proud. That you must see. For Buri the sea of oxen roaring in wooden pens behind the slaughterhouse is a guarantee of a job for life.

In the slaughtering and dressing of an ox, 157 men perform 78 precisely defined operations. The extreme division of labour makes the staggering productivity rate possible. 1050 head of cattle in a ten-hour day.

Sickness and accidents are grounds for dismissal.

Machines are brought in. An acquaintance of Buri's, an Austrian named Karl Theny, works on one of the first skinning machines, cutting the rinds off hams. One day his own skin winds up under the knife. Hooks on a turning roller catch his thumb as well as pigskin, and skin his arm past the elbow.

Buri slowly moves up through the wage scales. There are thirty-four in all. Right at the top are the 'splitters'.

An alert observer might visit Chicago and not realize that there were gigantic slaughterhouses there. Only when the wind is in a certain quarter does the smell carry into the residential areas, the business streets. The smell is of rancid fat, carrion, and dung, and when it's there, it's everywhere.

Bread is piled high in the shop windows of Chicago. Everything is piled high, in windows, on shelves, in the cooler-rooms at SWIFT & CO. But the people in the street look pale. Queues of unemployed, striking, sacked men and women stand outside locked factory gates.

At first Buri hires a filthy mattress in a dormitory, later he sublets a tiny room. His best shirt disappears off the clothesline, bottles of milk vanish from the doorstep. Buri cooks for himself to save money. He opens tins, and puts them on his small stove. He cooks in the tin, eats out of the tin. Sometimes Buri goes to the horse-races. There are the funnies in the paper. He can't understand baseball. Why isn't there any action? Chasing after a ball!

One Monday morning he ties on a heavy apron of ox-leather, and picks up a cleaver. He's made it. Buri is a 'splitter'. When he walks into the changing room, people make way for him. His position commands respect.

Buri splits the backbones of sixteen oxen in an hour. Buri splits for years. His work demands strength and concentration.

Soon he starts seeing everything, people, animals, the whole world in terms of splitting. Everything can be split down the middle in two equal parts. He sees acquaintances, and imagines them stuck, split, chopped up. He wonders what they would look like split, who would offer him a challenge. Sometimes he holds his head. Something is wrong. And he feels himself growing tired. His eyes are burning.

Buri only misses once in his life. A blow, executed with full force, smashes his foot. He is operated on, later amputated below the knee.

His savings are gone. He is grateful to SWIFT & CO. for taking him back. Even so. New start in the casings department, on a low pay scale. He works in damp cellars. With a wooden leg.

Soon Buri's health is completely ruined. The authorities get involved. The man has been unfortunate. What to do with him? Just before the outbreak of the War, the Consulate pays the crossing home. As part of the campaign 'Your Country Calls'.

Back at home, Buri disguises his condition as best he can. He talks about America and the slaughterhouse there. Incessantly. The journeymen and butchers made fun of him. When everyone at the bar table was asked in turn: Where do you work? In the slaughterhouse! You? In procurement! You? In the tripery! And Buri? In pomposity! They all shouted as one.

At thirty-five Buri seemed older. He put his faith in age. They'll come to me for advice, they'll show a bit of respect to an old man at any rate. Who's been to America? Who's seen the slaughterhouses there with his own eyes? Whom did they call 'John the Splitter'?

When he was taken on at the slaughterhouse behind the high fence at the edge of the beautiful city, he still wrote after his name: 6 foot 3 inches, 207 pounds.

That was the last time Buri ever climbed on any scales.

Thick as fog was the steam that rose from the scalding-tank of the dehairing machine, that condensed under the ceiling of the hall, that dripped down from steel beams and glass-brick roof, and mingled with the sweat and the blood on the men's skin, and *the acceleration of production processes will bring up the noise level in a plant*: Krummen had to explain the new intestine-washing machine to Buri by bellowing in his ear. Buri kept nodding and saying: Yes, right, ah, that's how it works. But his words were lost in the squealing of the pigs and the clattering of the hoist on the overhead rails. Everywhere iron met steel, or steel met screaming flesh.

Casings specialist Buri looked attentive and seemed impressed. His name was not Rötlisberger. He would manage to win the necessary prestige for the new machine. Such an expensive piece of equipment. A key job. My responsibility for a major new investment. After all, he'd been a witness to the ballyhoo with which the machine had been brought into the pig slaughterhall before lunch!

When Works-engineer Forestier plied his crowbar between the boards of the fir trunk, Krummen had turned his back on the calf slaughtering, and even Bössiger had come out of his office into the long passage. Buri had noticed how excitedly they had all capered about and got in each other's way. Krummen had loaded the machine on the fork-lift, and in his excitement carried it so high that it had collided with one of the clocks and damaged it. Bössiger and Forestier had both shouted, 'Watch it!', but already there was a tinkle of glass. Now it'll have a dent! How worried Bössiger had been then, and how careful Krummen was when unloading it in the pig slaughterhall, as gingerly as a crate of china.

In the gut-washery, Rötlisberger had nudged Buri and said:

They're setting up their stupid machine bang in the middle of the hall. It'll get in the way of everyone! You'd think it was a new colour telly and they were sticking it in the middle of the room so that everyone could see how wonderful it was!

But Buri was having none of it. They'll know best where to put that new intestine-washing machine. It's them that laid the wiring and the pipes, not you! he had said.

The only thing that had Buri worried was the chance that the new job might go to a foreigner, and now that he himself had been chosen for the honour he was pleased. In his delight, he was even able to forgo informing Krummen that such a machine was by no means a novelty to him, and that some thirty years previous he'd worked with similar ones over at SWIFT & CO. in Chicago. Instead, he showed curiosity, turning his head this way and that like a schoolboy, nodding till his neck hurt, and staring as though he, the intestine expert, had never in all his life seen a pig's ruffle.

– Right! You pick the stuff up and put it on the table, you tear the small intestine away here, maybe this much of it, and then pack it into this slit until the rollers catch hold of it, and then it takes it away! yelled Krummen, and *the intestines of healthy animals are shiny and smooth, pale yellow to yellow-grey, and they always contain excrements*, and the rollers gripped, pulled in the intestine, metre by metre was pulled away from the surrounding ruffle fat at lightning speed, Krummen just had to hold on to it, and no sooner had the last few metres of it been swallowed up than the gut started to come out at the back, crushed to a white rope, de-fatted, de-slimed, then ran over a roller and landed in a metal container, still wet but ready to be salted, while all it contained – acid, water, dirt and gall – was sprayed out from under the chrome guard at the front. Buri withdrew smartly, but Krummen shut his eyes hard and shouted: You see, that's how it's done!

Buri wiped his brow, first with the back of his hand, then with a dry bit of his right sleeve. There was slimy-brown shit on his face.

– Get yourself a hat, shouted Krummen, and impervious to the shower coming out of the bottom of the machine, he pulled up the next set of guts. Rectum, great intestine, fat, pancreas, everything that was left over from the first one, was left to drop into a barrow. We'll see to that later. Have to adjust the machine first. Different calibre! More water for rinsing!

– God! That's some machine! Buri nodded, squeezed his eyes shut, stuck out his tongue, and lifted the third set onto the table himself.

Krummen folded his arms and watched the experienced gutter's hands going to work. Straightaway he realized those hands knew what they were about. Krummen turned away. And there I am shouting at the old fox, telling him what to do! I bet he's stood in front of something similar before. But he never says anything does he, Buri.

Krummen marched along the slaughter line. He avoided reproachful glances. He didn't want a discussion, he knew who he was looking for.

When he reached the queue of pigs in front of Hugentobler, Krummen stopped and stood still. His hand twitched. Those fucking bastards! He punched a pig's back so hard that the whole row of them swayed on the rail. They'll catch it! he yelled and left the hall by the back exit.

From up in the killing bay, from the scalding-tank, from the shaving-table, from everywhere, they stared after him until the swing door closed and Foreman Krummen went out in the rain, swearing, with his wrestler's gait.

One forty-five.
  The level of pigs' blood is rising in the tank.
  Shit!
  Fucking shit!
  Why didn't you squeal to death!
  And they're supposed to be intelligent animals.
  Locher shoots in a frenzy.
  I stick.
Pasquale and Eusebio drag the bled pigs to the trapdoor. Piccolo's standing by the scalding-tub. As soon as the skin's soaked soft, he shoves them into the scraper. He looks up. His face is brown from the splashing water. The shit also boils. Hair, bristles, nails, bubbles scum at the top.

The others are in their places on the slaughtering line.

I go over to the water-hose and hold my face in it. The murder at my feet. Greedily I lap at the water.

On!

Oi! Niente dormire!

And this is where Lukas wanted to take pictures.

They got him.

No pictures!

But . . .

We said no pictures!

They grabbed him by the seat of the pants, and Lukas went on clicking.

Locher puts a rubber boot on a pig's belly.

Here, you missed one. This sow's not been stuck. Wake up.

I come.

I with my knife.

I step over a pig and feel the oil-slick layer of blood and water and shite underfoot.

Mustn't slip with a knife in my hand.

And don't miss a sow.

There was already one pig came out of the scraper that hadn't been stuck. Shaved white, but no hole in the throat. Krummen swore at me.

At the meat inspection Dr Wyss will only give the ham an oval stamp if he can see a hole: meat that hasn't been bled isn't saleable.

Krummen stuck his knife in its throat, but it was too late. Not a drop would come.

Porco Dio!

Pasquale's yelling at me.

What have I done to you?

Everyone's got their personal scapegoat.

The director's has got Bössiger, Bössiger's got Krummen, Krummen's got Huber, Huber's got Hofer, Hofer's got Buri, Buri's got Luigi, Luigi's got Pasquale.

And me?

I give the stubborn pig in front of me a kick.

And Pasquale's got nothing to complain about. The bled bodies

323

slide easily across the ground. Blood, slime and shit are good lubricants. Pasquale doesn't have to exert himself.

Pasquale and Eusebio go swish, swish, swish, and there are three pigs lying in front of the iron plate of the trapdoor. A wooden gag jammed in the snout, to prevent water running down the throat, and the pigs are ready to be scalded.

And I've got to stick. And not forget a single sow.

Locher's banging away like crazy.

How they stiffen, stand there for a second, then topple over and start to wriggle. How they offer me their throats. How they bubble over my hands.

A sow that's still at large climbs up on top of a dead one, tries to get her front feet onto the wall on the open side of the killing bay.

The sow looks down the slaughtering line.

Steam everywhere.

They go sailing past down at the bottom. Split in two, hung by the rear feet.

In winter the scalding basin produces so much steam you can't see a metre in front of your face.

A bull got out once, and found his way into the pig slaughterhall in the fog. They were only able to hear him. The hooves on granite. Occasionally a shadow. He went around skewering pigs, upsetting tubs of guts. Several butchers were hurt.

And I'm carrying one basinful of blood after another to the collecting-tank.

The handle of my knife is slippery.

This rush the whole time.

I'd like to hold my face and hands under the water jet. Blow my nose. Smoke half a cigarette in the corridor outside.

Even the dentist lets you rinse in between.

Just half a cigarette.

When Pasquale and Eusebio drive the pigs in, they light up on the sly outside.

My knife, Jesus. I should whet it. Can't get anything out of the throat under my knee again.

But it's pouring out of the sow's nostrils instead. Like a nose-bleed. I must have punctured the windpipe.

Here, watch it.

324

Internal bleeding, eh?

Now Locher's come over to put his oar in.

You like me to jump up and down on her? Or lift her tail? That might be good for a teacupful.

He can laugh at his own stupid fucking jokes.

Sticking is one of those things. Everyone thinks they can do it better. Those are the two art forms. Sticking and splitting. The butcher's touchstones. Shit. Whoever pumps the most blood from a dead sow rules OK.

And Locher.

You've had so many shots at sticking, why do you always get the blood flowing back to the lungs, or out of the mouth? Why don't you get it right?

Wish he'd leave me in peace.

Hurl my knife down into the pig hall below. Empty the basin of blood over Locher. Take off my apron and boots. Climb up the side wall, like the pig tried to do just now. Roar.

And in again with the blade, push my red-encrusted hand against the bristles at the throat. And this time, alleluia, it spurts out in a high arc. A whole metre it goes.

See, see! So you can do it. You just have to make an effort. You're a dreamer.

The way he's standing over me. Why doesn't he push off? Back to shooting.

And I kneel on a bleeding sow.

Out of this place.

And the snot in my nose?

I'd like to open out a white handkerchief, spread it out over a hand that's clean and dry. I'd like to feel the material cool on my cheek, bury my face in it.

Instead, slime to slime.

Thumb on it, pressure, left side a couple of drops, right a claggy string.

Red thumbprints on my nostrils.

Have I stuck all the unconscious pigs?

Don't forget any.

I look around. Pasquale and Eusebio are grinning at each other. They pretend they enjoy cavorting around in the dirt, carting dead pigs around. When it's hot, they take their shirts off. With bare chests, only apron bibs, they cover each other with slime and blood.

Spaghetti gladiators.

Locher's getting new shells from his right trouser pocket. The used cartridges go in the left one.

There's more squealing. This batch isn't finished yet.

I think I can feel a couple of dry places on my forearms, just below the elbows. As I change from one pig to another, I brush them over my lips and feel cool skin, the skin on my eyelids. My tongue licks salt.

There are over two hundred pigs waiting outside.

We always save the dams till last. They go into salami production. They lie in the killing bay like mountains of meat and fat. It takes four of us to get them down to the scalding-tub. They have heads like runkled boulders.

The dams are unbelievably fat.

Once a sow suckled eleven piglets under a thick layer of snow for a whole month without food. After a storm, they had put her down as lost, but then the farmer had seen steam rising from a snow-drift not far from the farmyard. Only two of the piglets had been frozen.

The fat in the bacon was a reserve, said Überländer.

Like a camel's humps.

But Christ! Hell!

Pile of whores' shit!

And another one's throat cut.

Keep it up.

Hup! Hup!

Learn to work.

I'd just like . . . not to think anything. Just forget everything. Not know where I am.

And another with my knife in its throat.

Whenever I empty my basin into the blood-tank, I'm sure there are a couple of drops of my own blood there too. I can feel it.

Stuck.

Drained.

I feel DRAINED!

Poor pig.

Dear dead animal.

Why pigs don't revolt.

Don't revolt?

But they do. They all scream like stuck pigs.

But they are stuck pigs.

Any resistance will be beaten down at once.

By me? By us?

There's the death penalty for being a pig.

Out of here!

This whore-damned shit killing bay!

And into the throat with the knife.

I stab down viciously.

The way this sow bleeds! Wriggles! It's squirting out like anything. Jet propelled. Light coloured.

Goddamn it! Now what have you done! Locher yelling at me. That sow wasn't even unconscious! You watch what you're fucking doing, or else . . .

I feel dizzy. Nauseous. Like sitting down. On the belly of the nearest pig.

Or else?

I want to puke.

Or else I'll get the vet. No one needs to stick here before I've shot. Understand? What a botch-up. Get a grip on yourself, boy! You wait, and I'll get onto Krummen.

He even wags his finger at me.

Pasquale and Eusebio are grinning.

Let him shout.

And when someone remembers the incident, over a beer, the boastful tone goes out of his voice, and he talks quietly, yes, he was there:

A bull got loose, snapped the chain, bent aside the iron bars, ran out of the driving passage, galloped snorting through the night, get out of my road I need to breathe, out of the slaughterhouse terrain, up the approach road, then he turns into a residential street, charges a tree, rams his head against the trunk, lights go on in the windows around, a gigantic shadow over the whole width of the street, an enormous animal, and a VOLKSWAGEN comes sweeping

327

along, the hooves rattle over the asphalt, the bull attacks the car, puts all its weight into his loins, smashes into it head on, one horn buries itself in the right headlight, he withdraws, spiked fender on his head, he shakes himself, attacks the car again, knocks it over on its side, metal crashes, the broken bumper clatters, air hisses out of a tyre, glass tinkles, and the bull goes on horning through paint and metal, a shot, then another one, then silence, the terrified driver pukes by the side of the road, a streetlamp sways in the breeze, the policeman fired with his hands out in front of him, the bullets went through the bull's chest and pierced his heart, the neck and head are flat on the ground, next to the damage, the bulge of muscle flat and dead, and the tip of the tongue out in front of the foaming mouth, the local people come out of their houses, coats thrown over shoulders, cover their eyes with their hands: a bull! a bull! a circle forms round those 1000 kilos of meat, so dead and empty and collapsed, the scrotum like a ninepin, and the police clueless, and another siren sounds, an ambulance races up to the scene, flashing lights throwing shadows round the walls, what's happened here, the ambulancemen run up carrying a stretcher, they clear a path through the crowd, who called them? and what are we doing here? you must be out of your minds! A bull! An animal? How priceless! Must be a joke, in the middle of the night, you need a winch, and a cadaver-transporter, and unbled like that he's only good for feeding the fishes . . .

. . . and an injured bull they hadn't yet stunned breaks loose in the slaughterhall, his red-and-white flanks pump, the hair on his neck bristles like a dog's, his bellowing curdles the blood, he pushes over carcasses that were being dressed, gallops on his short legs from tiled wall to tiled wall, his head down low, his tail flying behind, the tip of his rod pink in the tuft of his belly, then he tosses his head up high, bellows louder, makes firewood of wooden containers, upsets water troughs and canisters, the blood-covered floor turns slippery, the men keep back, such a whorish big fucking bull! The doors are bolted, protective barriers come down, and the bull attacks, the black look from his red-and-white skull, he puts them all to flight, we need a gun! Who's got a gun? The bull chips fist-sized lumps out of the wall with his horns, and the over-eager young butcher who thinks he's exhausted himself, he has the gun knocked out of his hand, gets a horn in the groin, he falls to the floor, the bull tramples over him, then hurls himself against the slaughterhall door, bangs into it like a ton of bricks, a battering ram, the barriers creak, next he rams the door of the little weighing office, the unreinforced wood splinters, the bull is trapped in the doorway, the forehooves smash table, chair, weighing machine, kicking out again and again like a couple of forehammers, a carbine-butt breaks the glass of the little peep-window behind the weighing machine, take your time, Hans! Aim carefully! The front flank is ripped open, a black hole, gunpowder smoke, good shot! And the hooves don't reach quite as far, the head droops, the eyes roll, the bull's throat rattles as he plunges into a pool of blood on the floor, and the wounded butcher is unconscious, his apron is torn open, his guts are showing, quick, get him to hospital! And all the arms in the slaughterhouse aren't enough to get the bull out of the doorway, so half in the weighing office, half in the slaughterhall, the hide is cut, the meat chopped . . .

And in the little slaughterhouse caff, Rötlisberger grinned, took the BRISSAGO out of his mouth, rested it in the ashtray, rubbed his palms over the pimpled rubber mat used for playing cards on, and said: Aschi, that's exactly what happened to me. God! No sooner had the little bugger bitten than I went weak at the knees. I felt like hurling my new rod miles away. I didn't even dare to touch the little fishy. It went back into the lake, hook and all.

– You see, that's how it is. Gilgen and Ambrosio laughed loudly. Rötlisberger laughed too, but his laughter soon turned into a giggle, then a wheeze. His eyes became smaller and the lids grew puffy. A coughing fit shook the old triper. In order to get the better of the spasms in his chest, Rötlisberger slid his chair back, leaned his arms against the edge of the table, and bent down. His wooden soles scraped on the floor. The cap fell off his head. His face went from red to blue under the grey stubble. The inflated cheeks were white. Bloody saliva ran down his chin and dropped onto the burlap apron between his knees.

– Nom de Dieu! What's the matter? Gilgen smacked Rötlisberger between the shoulder blades. Rösi, a schnapps, quick! Fritz swallowed something the wrong way. And a couple for us too! No? What do you say?

– Sí, sí, uno más, said Ambrosio.

Frau Bangerter, who had gone on wiping at a beer glass that was well dry already, frowned and sucked in her cheeks. She gulped.

– Another schnapps? What if it takes him like Schindler? she asked.

– Here come on, get on with it!

– Well, if you say so, but I don't know. She pushed the wrapped flowers that Ambrosio had brought to one side, wiped all round the rubber mat, and put three little glasses down in front of the men. There, cheers! she said.

– This'll do you good, Fritz. Gilgen nudged Rötlisberger with his elbow. Have a sip, it'll stop you coughing.

Rötlisberger was wheezing. His face had swollen up. He tipped his schnapps down his throat, shuddered, and pointed with his empty glass at Ambrosio's tinder lighter.

– You know, that I can well understand. You've used up your tinder and now you want to go home, and you'd be a fool not to. But just one thing: when you're down there, don't drag us all through the dirt! You understand? Spain'll be the same as here, there are people like that, and there are the others, and then there are the workhorses. But we don't even talk about them, eh Aschi!

– You're a gut mann, said Ambrosio, as Rötlisberger was laid low by another fit of coughing. Ambrosio drank to the old triper. But if he had had the words, Ambrosio would have done more than listen and laugh, and more than chip in a wonky sentence or two. Instead of pulling faces, he would have liked to tell them about how he had arrived in their country. And Rötlisberger and big Gilgen would have got the point about the red cow too. If he'd had the words, these two would have listened and understood. He knew that, he felt it. Gilgen and Rötlisberger would have laughed with him about the crazy Innerwalders, the midwife, the field-mouser, Farmer Knuchel, his cows and their dung. These two wouldn't have gone straight onto the defensive if Ambrosio had told them about the Knuchel children, who would be grown up by now and proud of their flat-backed heads. And he could have told them about leaky Bossy, hairy May, stupid Baby, and Check's map of a hide. And Blösch.

330

No, he hadn't gone soft. Blösch was just a cow. Perhaps it was coincidence that she turned up here, but no one, not even Ambrosio, could be surprised that she would end in a slaughterhouse.

But caramba! The emaciated body that had been dragged out of the cattle-truck onto the ramp, that had mooed so pathetically into the morning mist, that body was also Ambrosio's body. Blösch's wounds were his own wounds, the lost lustre of her hide was his loss, the deep furrows between her ribs, the hat-sized hollows round her hips, they were dug into his flesh, what had been taken from the cow had been taken from himself. Blösch's limping and dragging and hesitating, that was him, Ambrosio himself on a halter. Yes, he had laughed at Knuchel's cows for their passivity and meekness, but the display of unconditional obedience, of obsequiousness and motiveless mooing that he had witnessed on the ramp, he had also witnessed them in himself, to his own disgust. In Blösch on that Tuesday morning, Ambrosio had recognized himself.

He would have liked to warn Gilgen and Rötlisberger in particular, but he had no idea how, not even in Spanish.

For Ambrosio there was no going back. Something inside him had pulled away and upset the scales. There were bound to be administrative problems at the office, and financial penalties, *the party responsible for the immediate termination of the employment contract will be held accountable. In the case of the employee, his surety and outstanding holiday claims will be forfeited. He will in addition lose his current fortnight's wage, and in some cases will be asked to make up for any losses accruing to the employer as a result,* and that had previously deterred Ambrosio. After the loss of the finger he had gone back to work rather against his will, but then he hadn't been willing to act so irresponsibly as to jeopardize his guest-worker status either.

Now, though, he didn't see any insuperable obstacles, he would make up his lost pay somehow, in fact it was all extremely straightforward. The only thing that mattered was the good feeling he'd had for the last couple of hours, to which the alcohol now contributed.

– Olé! he said, and reached for his glass. Olé! He stood up and shook his limbs. Rötlisberger and Gilgen thought the little man was about to demonstrate to them for the third time by how much his children in Coruña had outgrown him, but this time Ambrosio didn't stick his hand up in the air. He grabbed the sports bag under the table, unzipped it, and by a leather band colourfully embroidered with flowers and little bears and crosses, he pulled out a cow bell.

– B . . . b . . . but . . . stammered Frau Bangerter behind the bar. Rötlisberger stopped coughing. Gilgen lit a cigarette and laughed. He had won the bell some years previously, as a prize in a wrestling competition. Tailor-made for you, Arlecchino, he said as Ambrosio looped the band over his neck, tried out the clapper once or twice, and then stood on his chair, ringing it loudly and mooing at the top of his voice.

– Just like a young cow in front of an empty water trough, eh? Rötlisberger and Gilgen laughed. Hey, Arlecchino on heat, ha!

– I can just see him going up the mountain in spring, can't you? asked Gilgen.

But Rötlisberger didn't reply. Foreman Krummen was standing in the canteen doorway. He was soaked and out of breath, his chest heaving. The livid expression of his face was accentuated by the wet hair on his forehead. He cleared his throat to speak. His right arm swung out, the fingers were already spread to pince and grab. But after a faint hesitation, his hand didn't bury itself in the seat of his pants as usual, it thrust forward and an accusing finger pointed at Gilgen and Rötlisberger and Ambrosio, who was still standing on his chair, with the cow bell round his neck. Only slowly, choking and swallowing, did Krummen find his voice:

– So there you are, you bastards! Sitting here drinking and arsing around! I can't stand it! We're left to drown in work! But we're not having it! You can't just turn up when you feel like it. Now I want you to wash that blood off the wall, yes don't look blank, you know what I mean! Now get out of here, I want the three of you up in Bössiger's office right away. Or else there'll be so much fucking trouble you won't believe it! I've had all I can take! This is the last time! He turned and stomped off. The muscles in his neck were twitching.

– Well, he knows all the tricks, doesn't he! Rötlisberger picked

332

up his BRISSAGO. You see how wet he was? By God, I think he must have been looking for us out in the rain.

– That Grummen allbays loco, said Ambrosio, taking the bell off and climbing down off his chair.

– Nom de Dieu, he's going to catch it! said Ernest Gilgen.

Two thirty-three.

How time creeps.

That bastard Locher.

He's hassling me the whole time. Keeps looking over my shoulder.

Always fighting.

Knife-fighting.

With pigs.

The minute hand has been there for hours.

The longest day.

Nothing but blood and sweat.

Locher shoots a pig, then stands there and expects me to stick it.

My knees are weak, I can feel every one of my vertebrae. My fingers are twitching.

Locher talks and talks. He smells.

Haven't you got any eyes in your head? Come along here to catch up on your sleep, do you? Who goes and sticks a sow I haven't shot yet? I could understand it if it was one of them Eyeties, but you!

But me?

I slipped a couple of times. Damaged the point. And there's a blunt place where the blade curves.

I have to use strength to pierce the thick pigskin.

But the Lord is the shadow over thy right hand.

Watch it!

I jump to my feet.

A pig's gone apeshit.

Some blood splashes up out of my basin.

Fucking hell, watch out!

Pasquale and Eusebio piss themselves laughing. I've drenched Locher. All down his apron. He's standing there bellowing, with outstretched arms, and the gun in his right hand.

I carry on.

333

Backbreaking.

While the pig's actually bleeding, I don't have to bother about anything.

A pig pukes. Green spew down its chin. Some of them were fed grass to keep them quiet on the way here.

They get tranquillizers too.

I feel lumps in my throat and gut. And the twitching. In all my muscles. Watch the knife.

Where is the shadow over my right hand?

If only I was allowed to whet my knife.

No time. Locher gets the cartridges up out of his right pocket with such speed. Bang. The eyes close. The pig furrows his brow in thought.

Now they're all puking.

The animals are supposed to be delivered here with empty stomachs.

Instead of going on shooting, Locher might take the hose and swill away some of that gravy.

In a corner of the killing bay, the last group out of this batch are huddled together.

One pig mounts another.

Is it trying to copulate?

Your bristly hide is just about to be singed off.

And my bristles?

A butcher has to have a bare neck. Part of professional hygiene.

But it's my head and my hair.

On Saturday I hid my face behind a magazine at the gents' hairdressers.

A tidy butcher has a tidy neck.

To have to spend my free time in a place like that.

The men who came in after me all got onto the chair first. The way they moved into position. As though it wasn't a torture.

All of them knew the rules. The poise and practice with which they moved. The right expressions on their faces.

I was always horrified by the razors and scissors waiting for me. The blades on my neck. I distrust the cutting hands. Sitting there in neat rows. Like pigs out of the scraping machine.

Shaved, razored, scraped.

Bald.

In amongst them, the done-up cosmeticians. Smiling at the men with paint-patched faces, trimming their claws. Like china, their red red lips.

A tidy butcher has a tidy neck.

Get a haircut, will you.

I should have shouted: Stop! No entry! Private estate!

What business of Krummen's is my neck?

In the corner, the castrated pig's still trying. Grunting and foaming away, anyhow.

Why should I quarrel with Krummen over a haircut?

Over my haircut.

How randy pigs can get.

Here.

Like bulls.

The bulls caught in the act in the breeders' journal.

I walked into the canteen, and saw everyone's heads huddled together. Poring over a couple of colour photographs. Gawping.

Look at his.

What a pole.

And the way she's taking it, woar!

I thought they must have got hold of a porn mag again. But no one tried to keep me away. I was allowed to see. They were pictures of bulls and cows. Stud bulls and prize cows, fucking al fresco.

Make sure you bleed that sow properly, or else Locher'll be onto you again.

Shit.

After school we sometimes went to the piglet market. There was a lot going on in all the different squares. What interested us most were the animals, waiting in wooden cages for a buyer.

Rabbits. Hens. Doves. From time to time a calf, and in flat crates, under wooden slatted lids, pink piglets in straw.

Little piggies.

We would eye the dealers. When they were busy talking to farmers, and had their hands buried especially deep in their trouser pockets, then we would take the lid off one of the crates, and help one or two of the piglets to get away.

How the dealers in their blue smocks used to caper about,

chasing them. Their huge hands kept clutching empty air. The squealing pink piglets proved elusive.

We ran off too. Slateboards rattling in our satchels.

And now here I am, killing them.

Fucking shitting killing bay.

Now another of those stupid sows is going crazy. Wriggling in rigor mortis.

And at the back, on the loading-apron, Weighmaster Krähenbühl leaned his rake in a corner, left the weighing office and locked the door, and trudged down the driving passage to the cattle slaughterhall. A train went by on the track outside. It was only raining a little. The sawdust on Krähenbühl's boots stayed dry.

The lorry from the glue factory was due some time after four to pick up the week's load of hooves, horns and bones. Krähenbühl had to be there for that. And then some culling cows had been announced. A whole goods-train full. More than forty head, he had been told on the telephone. In order to be able to accommodate these animals overnight, Krähenbühl had shovelled fresh sawdust into the pens, mucked out and cleaned up. Of today's consignment, there's only that one little Eringer left in pen two, thought Krähenbühl, an emergency slaughtering. As soon as they're through with the pigs, they'll come for her. She'd been weighed already, and the live weight registered in the control books long ago.

So Weighmaster Krähenbühl had a few minutes to go through the slaughterhalls and check that there wasn't the odd forgotten bone-bin knocking around somewhere.

Immediately next to the guillotine at the entrance to the cattle hall, he found an iron container full to the top with hooves and horns. That would have to be taken to the collecting point next to the tripery at the back. Krähenbühl looked around for one of the trolleys that were used to move the containers. He couldn't see one. He stepped out into the main passage, and a boy in glasses went up to him.

– I wondered . . . The boy stopped, looked down at Krähenbühl's boots. I wondered, you see it's for school, and are there any horns? The boy was sheepish. He peered up at the white pig halves which Luigi had pushed further out into the passage.

336

– Are there any horns? Weighmaster Krähenbühl asked in puzzlement.

– Yes, because we're making masks in art. Big ones out of cardboard.

– Ah, you're making masks. Of the devil and that?

– Yes, and ghosts and bulls and all sorts.

– Come along then, and we'll see if we've got something for you. Krähenbühl went back into the cattle hall, and with wrinkled nose, started scrabbling about in the bone-bin. The boy followed, encouraged.

– Hm, not much worth having here. That machine there breaks it all. Krähenbühl nudged the bone-guillotine with his elbow.

– What about that one? The boy had stood up on tiptoe and pointed at a grey-black horn tip that poked out among dungy hooves in an unsightly mess of hacked-up cow parts.

– You mean this one? Krähenbühl pulled one of Blösch's double-curved but emaciated horns out of the bone-bin, first gazed at it sceptically, and then handed it to the boy. That must come from a very old cow. It's nicely curved, though. Well, if you like it, we'll look for the other one. Ah, there it is. You're in luck, said Krähenbühl and pulled out the second of Blösch's horns.

– Merci. Oh thanks tons, said the boy, and ran out of the hall with the horns under his arm.

– You'll get your pullover dirty, Krähenbühl shouted after him down the passage.

Two forty-nine.
Blood.
Off to get first aid.
My blood.
I cut myself.
It's deep.
There's all hell let loose out there.
A wriggling pig. One of its hooves kicked the point of my knife. The slimy grip slipped through my hand. I found myself gripping the blade.
For the Lord is the shadow over your right hand.
There are delays on the slaughter line.

337

Not enough manpower anywhere.

Index and middle fingers will definitely need stitches.

Accident.

Unfit for work.

No blood, no backbreaking.

Hugentobler was shouting.

Why Krummen wouldn't take it down a bit.

Give us a break.

It'll be hard playing pinball like this.

Just coming.

Hall-supervisor Kilchenmann is weighing pigs. He leans over the sliding-weight, gives it a little nudge, blinks. He pulls the blocking lever, and writes down the weight.

Dead weight.

I can feel it dripping from my fingers onto the floor.

Rage.

Krummen, you silent cripple.

It's burning, I'm sweating. Tears. Sweat.

Rage and joy.

Do you want a sedative? You're pale.

That look of Kilchenmann's.

A pleasant feeling of weakness comes over me. I felt the pain earlier, when it happened, now I don't feel any. I lean back on my chair, put my head against the wall and look up at the ceiling.

I'm not knife-proof. A slip, and this machine's out of commission.

Kilchenmann's washing his hands.

Just coming.

That look again, over the rim of his glasses.

Locher's look. He spits on everything, looks down on everything. Now he can find someone else.

As I climbed out of the killing bay holding my hand out in front of me, Pasquale and Eusebio stopped dragging out pigs for a moment. They laughed at me.

They're just jealous.

Kilchenmann dries his hands on a red-and-white cloth. City property. He opens the white wooden box with the red cross on its lid.

He dabs my wound with cotton wool.

I turn away.

Deep, not too bad, but deep.

I know.

Does it hurt?

No, I didn't feel much earlier either.

Yes, the body reacts quickly. It puts the place to sleep, stuns it. It's only later that the pain comes.

Kilchenmann is a good Samaritan. He doesn't ask questions. He must have dabbed at worse things. Butcher's stab wounds in the groin. Accidents with machines. Ambrosio's hand. He stays in practice. He knows how to stop the blood. He's there to prevent bleeding. Here of all places. He knows how to dose iodine. He bandages neatly. And thickly.

You cut yourself before, didn't you?

You don't say.

You'll have to go to the doctor with this anyway.

I know what'll happen.

The warmth in the factory doctor's waiting room.will put me to sleep. I'll sit there, perfunctorily washed. The magazines won't interest me.

How will I get my bloody rags off?

With one hand.

The nurse will give me an injection.

She's always encouraging.

You must be used to pain.

Then the doctor will take his needle to my finger. A concerned look at my index card will tell him that this is the third time I've cut myself.

He'll tell me some trace of it will always remain.

Even a tiny cut destroys nerves. You can never restore anything to exactly what it was before.

No, doctor.

You should really be very careful.

Yes, doctor.

I'm not allowing you to work. The finger must be kept dry. Take these tablets three times a day after meals.

I'll go to see every film on in town. Every one. The lousiest spaghetti Western.

This butcher won't be whetting his knife for a while.

Come back in a week.

Yes, doctor.

Very well, doctor.

Kilchenmann says you should be especially careful with pig-sticking. Because of the dung you can get very bad blood-poisoning. Terrible infections.

But the scars will always remain, the doctor will say as I'm leaving.

The scars of freedom.

The nurse will smile.

Well?

All right?

My hand feels for the doorpost.

Yup.

Just felt a bit faint.

Look after yourself now! See a doctor right away!

Kilchenmann has gone back to weighing pigs. They swing past on the overhead rail. Their eyeless heads stare at me.

Calm!

What time is it?

Take it easy. Shit! My knees are like jelly.

Now they're shouting again.

Hugentobler! Where's he going? His stiff, clumping walk. Frankenstein. Back to the cooler-room. Krummenroar. Time I wasn't here!

The devil's cow is still hanging up in front of the meat-inspection office. But it wasn't just me she got the better of. Krummen too.

She's disfigured. Her flanks chopped to buggery. The flesh black and slack. The triangular cheap meat stamps are barely visible. Not a gram of fat on her.

Are they still doing tests on her in the lab?

Perhaps she won't even be fit to be sold.

My knives!

I go back. I must get my sheath.

I want to sit down.

Take a deep breath, come on!

I grit my teeth.

This hand won't make a fist easily.

But I stick my chin out.

Fucking pigshit abattoir!

– Yes, it's been pouring down. Rötlisberger took his cap off and looked up at the sky. Ah, that's good. It's rained like a cow pissing on cobblestones from both barrels.

– Comme vache qui pisse, said Ernest Gilgen.

– But look, it's clearing up! Won't be long now, and the sun will come out. Rötlisberger put his cap back on, and sucked a BRISSAGO. He stood in the enclosure in front of the pens, and held the Eringer cow, the late arrival, by her rope. She was a brown-black cow, with short, sharp horns. Her muzzle was wet like a dog's nose, and her eyes were lively and sighted. She wasn't much bigger than a small Simmental, but broader, and low slung on short, sturdy legs. Her healthy udder had four almost black teats. Her body was still, only the tail moved, and *an emergency slaughtering is the slaughtering of sick or seriously injured animals, whose life appears to be in danger, and which must be slaughtered to prevent the meat losing most of its value*, but Gilgen and Ambrosio took such pains over the cow's appearance, it was as though she was shortly to be shown to a thousand know-ledgeable eyes at an agricultural exhibition: they curry-combed her hide, cleaned her hooves with a brush, polished her horns with one of Rötlisberger's hessian aprons, buckled Gilgen's cow bell round her neck, and wove the gladioli in a wreath and placed it on her head.

– That yellow really shows off her dark hide, said Rötlisberger. She's a good-looking cow. I can't for the life of me understand why she's down as an emergency slaughtering. She looks the picture of health!

– Well, let's go then! Come on! Let's take a walk! said Gilgen who had also been admiring the tricked-out cow.

– Vámonos! said Ambrosio, and the three men set off with the willing cow.

Rötlisberger opened the gates between the driving passages, Gilgen led the cow on a loose lead right through the whole slaughterhouse yard, but, finding the cattle entrance to the slaughterhall barred, he turned and said:

– Right, then we'll just go in the front way. With such a well-turned-out cow, I don't see why we shouldn't. Come on! We're going through the pig hall! He tugged a little at the rope, the cow's neck bent, and her bell sounded. Gilgen pushed open the swing door and walked into the steam-filled pig room, followed by Ambrosio and old Rötlisberger.

– Now, I don't believe it! God Almighty! gasped Überländer as a cow appeared amid the din of pig slaughtering. What the hell! He rested his cleaver on its end, and scratched his neck.

Pretty Boy Hügli gaped. He forgot to throw the intestines that were on his arm into the trough, and stood there, hugging them and staring at the wreathed cow following Gilgen among the half pigs and machinery.

At first Huber and Hofer merely shook their heads. Jesus Christ! Then Hofer's eyes shone, and he took a few paces away from the razing-table and stared after them, still holding his long blade while Huber picked up the whetsteel absent-mindedly to sharpen his own.

Up on the killing-bay floor Locher forgot to pull the trigger, even though he already had the barrel down on a pig's forehead; and Pasquale put his bloody fingers in his mouth and whistled piercingly.

The whistle was louder than the noise of machinery and cow bell, like an explosion its sound went right through the hall, and even Buri looked up from his labour at the intestine-washing machine. Covered in shit from head to foot, Buri just caught sight of the cow disappearing past the weighing machine into the long passage. He turned round. His face was brown and caked, like a mask. He looked for some explanation, and watched the others through the steam. How were they taking it? What did their gestures mean? Mouths gaped in sweating, blood-soiled faces. They stood and gasped. Gilgen! That jailbird! They've flipped! An Eringer cow with flowers round her horns! And that bell! Jesus Christ! And that little spic Ambrosio's in on it too! Those buggers, they want! Instead of working, those idiots! But they haven't seen the last of it! Won't they just catch it! And with the image of the

342

garlanded cow deep in their brains, the men furiously went back to work. They set about their tasks as though chained to them. But the rhythm had gone: the lines of pigs lengthened in front of each of them, every one of the butchers fell behind, swore, raged with his knife.

But Ernest Gilgen walked quietly and proudly down the passage with the cow. He didn't need to look round, she obeyed the slightest pressure on the rope. The sound of the bell didn't carry, but it was bright and clear.

– That gave them a bit of a welcome distraction, said Rötlisberger.

– Yes, did you see the way they were sweating? replied Gilgen.

The little procession filed past the meat inspectors' offices, past the carcass of Blösch hanging from the overhead rail, and reached the cattle hall where Gilgen led the cow to the first slaughtering bay. Whoah! Easy! The cow wanted to go on. You hold her, I'll get my tools. Gilgen held out the rope to Rötlisberger.

– No you won't! roared Foreman Krummen from the entrance to the hall. You'll take that cow straight back to the pen! Immediately! I'm not giving you another chance!

The veins stood out on Krummen's forearms. He bulked tall, blew up his lungs and clenched his fists, he thrust his chin forward, covered his mouth with the thin line of his lower lip, but his face looked flabby, his eyes were barely visible, and the ranting and raving that had become a habit with him no longer impressed the men, and *if an emergency slaughter requires to be performed according to paras 1 and 3, then this must occur at a time and place, or at least a place, different from normal slaughtering,* and Krummen tried desperately to look fiercer, he lowered his head and stepped closer. Only the smack of his rubber apron on his rubber boots could be heard. Take that cow back!

– And I say she stays here! Gilgen stepped out in front of Rötlisberger and Ambrosio.

– Then I'll take her back!

– Just you try!

Aiming an elbow at Rötlisberger, Krummen grabbed at the cow's halter, but Gilgen's long arm shot forward and snatched it just below the cow's ear, while with his other arm he pushed Krummen away. Krummen rocked back, but immediately he leaped back at Gilgen. You big bastard! You Tyrolean arsehole! I'll teach you!

Gilgen had gone into a wrestling crouch, and fought off the attack, then he grabbed Krummen by the belt through the rubber apron, and *as the President of the Military Department, I am especially heartened by the valuable contribution made by our wrestlers to the state of our military preparedness. 'Schwingen' wrestling is one of the oldest forms of unarmed combat. It demands not only toughness, courage, discipline and endurance, but physical and mental agility. Also the 'Schwingen' wrestler is taught from the outset that he must fight fairly, and despise dirty tricks and unfair tactics,* and as Gilgen and Krummen stood locked together, each with his chin boring into the other's back, Rötlisberger untied the knot on the cow's halter, and Ambrosio held the animal by the bell-band, and *after an uneventful and indecisive early phase, Champion-wrestler Krummen almost won the bout several times, in spite of brave opposition, by means of repeated head-holds and left swings.*

Veteran wrestler Ernest Gilgen had beads of sweat on his forehead as thick as cod-liver oil, but he didn't accept defeat, and *at the decisive moment came the lightning counter-attack. An immensely powerful, sweet and well-aimed move of incredible strength that almost inevitably secures victory.*

Krummen propped himself up on an elbow, and slowly got to his feet.

– Ha! you amateur! You Sunday wrestler! Gilgen dodged behind the cow. He had pulled Krummen up by the belt, and thrown him onto his back, and *the trouser-lift, so this year's wrestling president tells us, is gaining in popularity at the present time,* and Krummen was pale, he rubbed his back and groaned. I'll teach you! Jesus Christ! I'll teach you! I'll . . . I'll oh what? It's always me, I always have to see to everything myself! Slowly Krummen stepped back. He stood stooped, had one hand rubbing his kidneys. You can't . . . why doesn't someone else come and run the show? His neck quivered. He looked at the ornamented cow that Ambrosio was now leading in a circle round him, bell ringing. His face darkened again. He turned to leave the hall, but saw the twin doors were barred. In front of the bar stood Cooler-man Hugentobler.

Krummen straightened his apron, and pulled his torn shirt

together. He stared down at Hugentobler's stiff, dangling arms, and then up at his eyes. Hugentobler wasn't squinting.

Over his shoulder, Krummen caught sight of Gilgen coming at him again. Have you taken leave of your senses . . . ? Hugentobler grabbed him. With a grip of iron. Krummen measured his length a second time on the granite floor. Gilgen took him by the boots. Stop it! Stop! You great idiots! Krummen no longer tried to resist.

Rötlisberger tossed Gilgen the cow-halter. Ernest Gilgen and Christian Hugentobler took Foreman Krummen, tied hand and foot, and carried him out of the hall on their shoulders, like a quarter of beef.

– Got the keys on you? asked Gilgen in the first cooler-room on the other side of the passage.

Hugentobler, who had pulled his fur cap down over Krummen's face, nodded, and *tolerance of cold is the genetically conditioned capacity of organisms, graduated by genus and species, to withstand cold to a certain limit without detriment (q.v.: resistance to cold).*

Is that two fifteen or ten past three?

Who cares?

Krummen smashed the clock. When he had the machine on the fork-lift.

The long passage.

I picked up my sheath.

I hung the belt over my right shoulder. The blades clink as I walk, in time with my steps. But we'll lock them away for the next fortnight or so.

I'm clearing off now.

I shoulder open the door of the changing room.

Dr Wyss is standing with Frau Spreussiger up there by the devil cow. He's telling her about something. Maybe . . .

Who cares?

My locker is at the back.

The mirror!

My face.

Head on.

In profile.

Those stupid bloody mirrors on those filthy walls.

To get us to stare at ourselves, in case we go out into the world with red noses.

So we don't look like what we are!

That grinding.

Is the grinding of my own teeth.

You damn . . .

I rip the sheath off my shoulder, and hurl it . . .

Crash!

The mirror shatters. The glass falls onto the wooden slatted floor. The knives are halfway out of the sheath. I hurled it at the mirror as hard as I could.

Damn!

My hand is hurting again.

There's a pale square on the wall where the mirror was.

Seven years of bad luck!

Ha!

Now out of this place!

With one hand I peel off my wet rags.

Getting the rubber boots off is hardest.

The big wash basin.

This is where Gilgen grabbed us all yesterday and called us cows. Because we let Bössiger lecture us.

I keep my bandaged hand out of the way, and try and wash. I need a shower really.

There's blood in my hair.

When I lift my bandaged hand, it hurts less than when I let it hang down. Then I can feel the blood throbbing in the wound.

Towel dry, brush my left hand over my hair, shut my locker.

I'd like to throw the key somewhere far away.

The broken glass. Someone'll have something to shout about.

Who broke the changing-room mirror?

Step forward!

It was me, Abattoir Commander Sir!

Once more down the long passage.

I'll have to leave my LAMBRETTA here. Can't ride it one-handed.

The devil cow. Away from that drooping flesh. Those chopped bones. Away from it all.

The calf slaughterhall is squeaky clean.

The cattle hall is barred.
Emergency slaughter?
Who cares?
I'm off.
I . . .
Stamp.
Small, tidy and red: 15.19.
In the box to the left of the clock-in, only three cards.
Ambrosio, Gilgen, Rötlisberger.
And now mine.
I'd like to tear it up.
This is where I start to count.
This is my hand!
The asphalt in the yard is wet, the sky is blue.
This is my hand! I want to shout.
My hand!
Shout!
This is my hand!
And again!

I know what goes on out here behind this fence! This is where we are, where I am, where the rest of us are, and nothing else!

As of now I'll piss when I please, as of now I'll determine the rhythm of my day. As of now I demand freedom and independence and not to be judged by others!

I stand panting by the fence.
I've been running.
The bandage on my hand is red.
There.

That attack! That lowered head! Those horns, that neck, that force. The bull on the wall. The giant bull. Smeared with blood on the abattoir wall.

This is my hand!

And even if no one notices it for a thousand years to come, I declare myself here and now to be a free sovereign territory!

No entry for unauthorized persons!
I'm not a fucking colony!
I appeal to the Geneva Convention!
No power on earth has the right to encroach on this territory and

347

wreak devastation on it to suit its own ends! Not any more! Today
is my Independence Day. Flags! Music! A speech: The consciousness of my class lies bleeding in the slaughterhouse of my soul.

Red drops on the pavement.

Kilchenmann didn't bandage me up thickly enough after all.

The bus.

I run across the road.

Climb in at the back please!

I come away from the slaughter defeated. I'm a wounded and
sentimental fucker of a cheerleader.

I sit down in the corner right at the back of the bus.

Now the doctor, quickly, and then the cinema.

Entrail-man Hans-Peter Buri left the machine working unattended.
He forgot to wash with the pressure-hose. Slime ran down his
apron, gut-slime and excrement. His face was encrusted with shit,
and his eyes were red and inflamed. He hobbled quickly down the
main passage like a startled moorhen, stopped briefly in front of
the cattle slaughterhall, shook his head disbelievingly, and hurried
on. His boots smacked on the tiles like webbed feet.

Buri burst into the abattoir office, didn't knock, just stood there
on the carpet in his filthy boots and dripping apron and didn't
know where to begin. He wheezed and choked, and pointed
through the open door back down the passage.

– About, er, I thought, over there, er . . . there's . . .

– What's the matter? Bössiger came out from behind his desk as
though to say, Why isn't that Buri at his job, and what's he doing
coming in here and behaving like a choking calf?

– It's about, well, it's Krummen!

Buri stared so penetratingly at Frau Spreussiger sitting at her
typewriter that she typed his words as though he'd just dictated
them to her, and at the same time she stared, wide-eyed, at his
encrusted face. Er, it's Krummen! They've locked him up in the
freezer-tunnel. You should come and look! And there's all hell let
loose in the pig hall too. The scraper is throwing the sows right
over the razing-table onto the floor, and everything's clogged up
and all over the place. And I don't know where to turn this machine
off. Buri scratched his neck under the butcher's blouse. It's the cow,

you see. They walked out, Hugentobler led them. Yes, they brought in a cow, with a bell on her! You should have a look, it's very bad! he said, already half turning to go.

– I'll be back in a minute, Bössiger told Frau Spreussiger, who only then relaxed her pelvis, and sat back in her chair. She looked at the pigshit-fouled carpet and automatically reached for her mirror: Frau Spreussiger was very pale.

In the cattle hall, Hugentobler, Gilgen, Ambrosio and Rötlisberger stood around the garlanded head of the Eringer cow, whom they had tethered to one of the iron rings in the floor.

Rötlisberger puffed at his BRISSAGO. His hands were in his pockets. Gilgen was in his shirt-sleeves, and had put on a rubber apron. The cow molar, with its tridentine root, hung from the silver chain against the white apron-bib. Ambrosio was stroking the cow's neck, and saying softly: Sí, sí, ya estamos, no te preocupes. He had a ladle from the tripery under his arm.

All three of them were watching Hugentobler.

He had taken off his fur cap, and was sharpening a knife on an oiled whetstone he held in his hand. He checked the sharpness of the medium blade with his thumb, whetted it some more, and brushed it over his left forearm. When he had shaved a white streak in the dark hair, he looked up, his eyes straight. He pulled down one of the hoses that hung from the ceiling over every slaughter bay, rinsed the knife, and held it out to Gilgen. Here's one that cuts! he said.

Gilgen was on the point of crossing himself with the freshly whetted knife when Bössiger walked up to him. Who told you to slaughter this cow in the middle of the afternoon? Where's Krummen? What's going on here? And you, Rötlisberger! You're smoking! And so's that Italian too!

– Well, this little cow here has to be slaughtered some time, drawled Rötlisberger, cigar in mouth, and Ambrosio shrugged his shoulders as if to say, well, what can you do, that's the way it is.

– What? Bössiger looked from one face to another. What? None of the men flinched or lowered his glance. Bössiger scratched briskly at his ear, and stamped on the floor like an angry child. What's going on here? Will someone tell me what's going on?

– Well, if you want to find out, you'd better hang around and watch. One of the electric lifts came down behind Bössiger's back, humming quietly. Rötlisberger had his thumb on the red button. Look, something's just arrived for you! Gilgen swiftly put his knife down on the floor and grabbed Bössiger round both shoulders. A hook, quick! Hugentobler took one of the iron hooks for half carcasses off the rack, pulled up Bössiger's white apron, worked the hook under his belt, and hung the other end on the hoist. Rötlisberger pressed the green button. The lift hummed again, it hitched up Bössiger's trousers, the belt rode up to his chest, and then, kicking and struggling, it lifted him off the floor altogether. Police! Frau Spreussiger, call the police! he shouted, and not until he was hanging directly under the overhead rail, with hands and feet dangling helplessly, did Rötlisberger take his thumb off the green button and say: There, I think we can start now.

Without looking at Bössiger or the little group of his fellow-butchers that was assembling at the hall entrance, Gilgen again crossed himself with the whetted knife, took it to the throat of the garlanded cow, and drove it home.

The little Eringer's head darted back but only a little. She stood there steadfastly, and so still, the bell only sounded once.

But the gleaming black skin on her forehead was thrown into confusion, she mooed feebly, and her eyes lightened as they looked at the men standing in front of her. The cow stood and bled, and it was as though she knew the long history of her kind, as though she knew that she was one of those mothers cheated of their rich white milk, who had offered their teats for thousands of years, and for thousands of years been devoured in recompense. It was as though she knew that her kind had always had to beat their hooves sore on the stoniest of fields, that for her kind there was no escaping the leather harness of the plough that kept this world alive. It was as though this cow knew about her ancestors, understood that she herself could only be a pale reflection of the mighty aurochs, who with his curved, arm-length horns had established a dominion that stretched from the bright woods and rich parkland of central Europe as far as the distant heart of China, an empire on which the sun seldom set, and that neither the treacherous Asian yak nor the sullen gaur had been able to take away from him. It was as though this little cow understood the scorn and contempt that had been

350

levelled at her subjugated species since that time, but as though she could still just hear, from the very back of her skull, from where the extended marrow began, and the cerebellum, a vague rushing, a softened roar that filled her head as the sound of the sea fills the dry shell, and that could be none other than the echo of her ancestors' hoofbeats as they thundered across the steppes, like storm clouds, in their great herds, and it was as though this rushing and roaring showed itself unmistakably in the humility in the eyes of the little cow. As if she were without horns and without strength, as if she were beyond body and beyond pain, and rid of the imperative of self-defence, so did she stand there and bleed, and *in the transport of animals to be slaughtered, in the slaughtering itself and in the preparations for it, all forms of cruelty are to be avoided. The slaughtering and bleeding of animals that are still conscious is forbidden under Article 25 of the Federal Constitution,* and Ernest Gilgen, the giant butcher at the slaughterhouse at first just stood still, with his hand on the knife in the cow's throat, aproned, and muscular and bold. The blood flowed over his hand and arm, and then he pulled the blade away, and threw it right across the slaughterhall at one of the arched windows. The steel crashed against the frosted glass and jangled on the granite floor.

With the ladle, Ambrosio caught the stream of blood as it poured out past the bell, from the throat of the still almost motionless cow. The blood foamed and swirled in the utensil, and filled it to the brim almost immediately. Ambrosio held it out to Rötlisberger. The old triper threw his BRISSAGO away, and took a deep draught. He drank reverently, and *if an animal loses a great deal of blood, and is unable to replace it quickly enough, its life may be saved if it is injected with the blood of another animal. A donor has to be found whose blood is compatible with that of the recipient,* and then Hugentobler took the ladle, and, no longer squinting, he set it to his lips, and then it went on to Ambrosio, and to Gilgen.

Gilgen poured the last of the blood so avidly down his throat that some of it ran down his face and body and stained his shirt. As soon as the ladle was empty he held it under the already failing flow.

The cow's front legs now gave way, she swayed, her bell rang leadenly and the garland of gladioli fell from her horns as her brown-black body rolled over on its side. Her head still moved and her clouded, tired gaze lit up once more as though shocked by all the blood, then went out.

Gilgen held out the ladle in front of him, and with Ambrosio, Hugentobler and Rötlisberger took a step away from the dying cow. Above them on the lift, Bössiger had stopped shouting, and Überländer now approached them from the entrance. Come on! Give me a sup! he said. And behind him was Pretty Boy Hügli, and behind him were Fernando and Luigi, Huber and Hofer, Piccolo, Pasquale and Eusebio, and the ladle went from mouth to mouth.

Only Buri stayed away. He stood by the double door of the slaughterhall. In front of him, Frau Spreussiger was leaning against the wall, vomiting in sobbing spasms. Buri moved his head, as though talking to himself. He was about to leave the hall.

– Hey, Buri! Wait! Ambrosio went up to Buri with the ladle, cupping it in both hands, with the handle out to one side.

Buri looked at Ambrosio's face, his hands, and the gap where the middle finger should have been. What nonsense! he said, and took the ladle, and drank.

– What about Fritz Krummen? asked Rötlisberger. Isn't he going to get any?

– Wait, I'll go and get him. Leaning forward as always, arms swinging, Hugentobler set off.

When he came back with the foreman, Krummen went round them all saying: JesusChristAllfuckingmighty. Then he wiped his hands on the seat of his pants, took the ladle and drank.

Krummen was quaking.

And in the slaughterhouse behind the high fence at the edge of the beautiful city the trailer-lorry from the glue factory had driven up and stopped between the tripery and the waiting enclosure. The loading crane hummed over the driver's cab. A crateful of bones hovered over the trailer. The planks of the crate were greasy and stained brown with dried blood. Flies swarmed around the jumble of hooves and horns and bones.

The lorry driver released the hook from the crate, and swung the crane back round. Well, that's it for today then, he said to Krähenbühl who had helped him loading

– Yes, that's it, Weighmaster Krähenbühl replied.   And now? Got a lot further to go today? he asked

– Oh no, look! Got a full load.

– But you'll have to unload it today, won't you?

– That's true. What you load you have to unload, eh?

– That's right, said Krähenbühl.

And, climbing onto the running board of the lorry cab, the glue factory driver asked: What about you? You knocking off as well?

– No, not me, said Weighmaster Krähenbühl. We're still expecting a whole trainload of sausage-cows. I'll have to weigh them. And then I have to go to the incinerator. Dr Wyss has been really strict lately. All the condemned material has to be destroyed right away.

– Ah well, said the driver, shutting the door. He turned the ignition and then stuck his head out of the window again. Hey! What are the police doing over there? he asked, and nodded in the direction of the administration building, where a police car had just driven up.

– Search me, said Krähenbühl. There's always some bother with Italians not having documents, that kind of thing.

– Or maybe someone killed a calf, ha! said the driver, laughed, waved and drove off. Krähenbühl waved back and went off to pick up the cow which, having failed its lab test, had been stamped over and over in large blue letters INEDIBLE, and *animals and parts that are found to be unfit for human consumption are to be buried in the knackery at a depth of no less than 1.25 metres, having been covered with quicklime (CaO). However, their destruction is achieved more quickly and reliably by incineration at 1000°C,* and the cow with poisoned flesh that Krähenbühl pushed along the overhead rail and out of the back of the abattoir was Blösch.

About the Author

Beat Sterchi was born in Berne, Switzerland, in 1949. In 1970 he went to Canada to study English. He lived on the American continent for the next twelve years, traveling widely, teaching, and working. *Cow*, his first novel, was originally published in Switzerland in 1983. He now lives in a village in a remote part of Spain.

About the Translator

Michael Hofmann was born in Freiburg, West Germany, in 1957. He has published two books of poems in Great Britain, *Nights in the Iron Hotel* (1983) and *Acrimony* (1986).

Cow is a magnificent first novel, masterfully translated by Michael Hofmann, which happens to be about cows and dairy workers, but which transcends its immediate theme to become a powerful and moving piece of fiction about man, his work, and his food at the end of the twentieth century.

Not since Herman Melville has an author so powerfully and intricately explored the life-and-death cycle of an animal preyed upon by man. From pasture to dairy to abattoir, Sterchi follows Blösch, the lead cow of farmer Knuchel's herd, describing in exquisite prose each detail—glorious and stomach-turning—of bovine existence.

At the same time Sterchi creates a modern-day Ahab named Ambrosio—a dark-skinned Spanish guest-worker in milk-white Switzerland, who is not pristine enough, according to the Swiss, to handle live cows, and who is thus relegated to cutting up dead ones.

Starting with these two unlikely characters, Sterchi creates a monumental and important work of fiction about beasts and men, about how they prey upon each other and upon themselves.